Praise for *Rock Angel*

Debut novelist Bogino clearly has a passion and great understanding of Nineties-era rock culture. Shan is a complex and well-written character whose struggles have the reader rooting for her.

—*Library Journal*

Bogino portrays an authentic landscape of what it's like to be a rock band in the early '90s. Shan and Quinn both read as fully realized, flawed characters.

—*Kirkus Reviews*

In a show-business tale filled with ego clashes, sexual tension, drug addiction, dreams of success and nightmares of stardom, the rarefied world of ambitious musicians is rendered with a relentlessly keen eye and ear.

—*Music Connection Magazine*

I applaud Ms. Bogino's brave portrayal of the music industry circa 1990 and anxiously await the next book. *Rock Angel* is a page turner that will cause you to suffer at least one book hangover—guaranteed!

—**Sandra Bunino, author of** *The Colors of Us*

rock angel

rock angel

A Novel

Jeanne Bogino

Prashanti Press

spark
press

Prashanti Press, LLC
PO Box 83
Pound Ridge, New York 10576, USA
www.prashantipress.com

SparkPress, a BookSparks imprint,
A division of SparkPoint Studio, LLC
Tempe, Arizona 85281, USA
www.sparkpointstudio.com

Editorial production by Marrathon Production Services. www.marrathon.net

Book design by Jane Raese
Set in 12-point Adobe Garamond

Cover design © Julie Metz, Ltd./metzdesign.com
Cover image © Getty Images

ISBN 978-0-9852313-6-1 (paperback)
ISBN 978-0-9852313-5-4 (e-book)

Printed in the United States of America

FIRST EDITION, SEPTEMBER 2014

For Gram, who always knew I could.

And for Frank, of course.

part one
1990

Music is a beautiful opiate,
if you don't take it too seriously.

—Henry Miller

chapter 1

Time was running out. The audition was that night and there were only a couple of hours left to prepare. Normally Shan could get by with a fraction of that, but the clinkers she was hitting today were glaring enough to set her teeth on edge.

She took a deep breath and hoisted Joanie into her lap, touching the guitar's ebony fingerboard for reassurance. She could do this. She'd played the song a hundred times. She'd written it herself. Shan started again, fingers forming the opening chords with new resolve.

Another clam, this one even more strident than the last. She ignored the mistake and kept going, but had to stop in the middle of the next phrase when a fit of shivering seized her. The pick slipped from her fingers and dropped to the floor.

Shan set Joanie aside, then sank to her knees beside the futon she used as a bed. She laid her hands against the worn Mexican blanket, fingers spread, and stared down at them. She had small but capable hands, nails unpolished and filed sensibly short. They were guitar player hands, sturdy and limber, the pads of the fingertips on the left one layered with thick, neat calluses. They didn't often fail her, but today they shook so hard she couldn't hold on to the pick.

Well, this day of all days, her hands had to function. They, and she, had to be at their very best because she had a chance at landing the kind of gig she'd always wanted, in a band she'd normally get close to only after the price of admission.

It was a pure fluke that she'd scored the audition in the first place. She was a popular act at small venues, but acoustic folk at a coffee house was a long stretch from playing lead guitar in an up-and-coming rock band. The guys in the band were pros and she was a kid only just starting out, so she'd been shocked when she'd gotten the call from the band's drummer the night before. Still, Shan was a quick study and that was what they needed, so she had a shot. A long shot, maybe, but a shot just the same.

She resolutely took up Joanie. She'd do this. She'd *make* herself do it. She began again, this time playing "Street Ballad," one of her favorite originals. It always had a tonic effect on her.

Except today, apparently. Halfway through the opening riff, her gut began to roil. She gritted her teeth and tried to play through it, but her stomach heaved and she tasted bile at the back of her throat. She set the guitar down with a dissonant jangle and dashed for the bathroom.

Ten minutes later, Shan staggered back to her room and collapsed on the bed. Pulling the blanket over her head, she closed her eyes and tried to will away the tremors that quaked her limbs.

After a time, she reached for the phone, her hands still shaking.

Later that night, she was still shivering. Even her heavy sweatshirt couldn't keep out the cold, because it wasn't coming from the warm air of late May. It emanated from inside, a rank chill that made her limbs feel as icy and dead as frozen poultry parts. *Maybe that's why they call it cold turkey.*

She checked her watch. Almost nine. If she didn't hurry she'd miss it, the audition she hoped would take her to a new place. Instead she was here at the old place: Jorge's crack house in Spanish Harlem, a boarded-up derelict of a building as bleak and forlorn as the crackheads and junkies it housed.

She'd thought she was going to make it this time. She'd gone four days without a fix. Four endless, miserable, heroin-free days punctuated by bouts of shakes, cramps, and nausea. Diarrhea, too. Sometimes all four at once, but she'd forced herself to tough it out, at least until it became clear that she couldn't pull off a performance in her present condition.

She could still make it. Shan took hold of her guitar and grasped the iron railing to pull herself to her feet, but another spasm shot through her abdomen. She doubled over until it passed.

Who was she kidding? She wasn't going anywhere. Maybe she'd come because of the audition, but now she wasn't leaving until she got what she came for—the big H.

She blinked, momentarily blinded by the headlights of a passing police car. She shrank back against the building and shut her eyes against the sudden glare that shot laser-sharp pinpoints into her brain. Then, in the cruiser's wake, she heard footsteps crunching on the sidewalk.

Shan opened her eyes. A blurry silhouette materialized, gradually coalescing into the tall figure of a man. "Jorge?"

The figure stopped. "Hey, Shan," he said, swaying. "Am I late?"

"Two hours." She jumped to her feet, grabbing the railing again as her knees quavered. "You told me to come at seven, remember?"

"I guess." He scratched his head. His black hair was limp and greasy. "You need something?"

"Why else would I call?"

He grinned and she saw he was minus a few teeth now. "I thought you missed me."

Shan was seized with a fit of coughing, her slight shoulders hitching in time with her hacking. "Can I get something?" she asked, when she was able to speak. "I'm dope sick."

He started up the stairs. Shan let go of the railing and followed him up the four flights to his apartment, Joanie clutched against her chest.

Once they were inside Jorge switched on the light. The harsh glow from the bare bulb assaulted Shan's eyes and she ducked her head as he vanished into another room. She blinked, then moved toward a sagging couch of indeterminate color.

She set down her guitar case and sank onto the couch, the only piece of real furniture. There was a wooden crate that passed for a coffee table, its top littered with razor blades and rolling papers. Shan watched a cockroach nose its way across the scarred surface, long feelers quivering as it encountered a pizza crust amid the debris.

Jorge emerged from the other room with an enormous brown rock in his hands. In the bright light Shan could see that he looked far worse than the last time she'd seen him, just two weeks before. Since then his thinness had turned skeletal and his skin, always bad, had taken on a yellowish cast.

All signs of a long-term junkie. She'd seen it before. Someone could use for years then, seemingly overnight, a relatively normal-looking person turned into a walking corpse.

He smiled and again she noticed the missing teeth. "I was wondering when you'd come around," he said as he sat down beside her. "I figured you must be running low."

Shan nodded, running her tongue over her own teeth to make sure none of them felt loose. There were the two on the side that had been missing for a couple of years, otherwise they were all intact. "I was trying to get clean," she said. Her knee jittered up and down in a nervous staccato.

"Again?" Jorge sniggered. "When you gonna learn?" He set the rock on the table and picked up a razor blade to chop off a small chunk. The cockroach appeared interested. Shan grimaced as it scurried toward her.

Jorge's lips stretched into an impassive grin as he reached out, drawing his index finger back against his thumb. With a flick, the cockroach was airborne, sailing across the room and disappearing into a stack of cushions. Jorge settled back, resting his arm along the back of the couch behind Shan.

"How much?" Shan asked, shifting away from his touch.

He didn't respond, but his grin widened.

"How much?" she repeated. "I'm in a hurry. I have to be someplace."

"Where?"

Like she'd tell him. "Just someplace."

"One of them music things?"

"Yes. Now how much?" When he didn't reply, she reached into her pocket and tossed some folded bills onto the table. "Just give me fifty, then. Can I use your bathroom?"

He nodded and she could feel his eyes on her as she stood up. "How about I talk you into skipping the music thing?"

She paused by the bathroom door. "Why?"

"I just got a special delivery." He pointed to the rock. "We could ride this horse all the way to Belmont."

"No thanks." She shut the door and her stomach flipped over again as she switched on the light. The toilet was filthy and she could see more roaches scurrying for cover in the bathtub drain.

Breathing through her mouth, she surveyed her reflection in the cracked mirror over the sink. She looked like hell, face flushed deep red and shiny with perspiration, eyes clouded and teary. Her pupils were so dilated that they almost obscured the green of her eyes. Her dark hair clung to her forehead and cheeks in long, snakelike strands and she saw one lock was twisted around her silver nose stud.

She untwisted it, turned on the faucet and splashed cool water over her face, then used a sliver of soap she found to scrub it, as if she could wash away the febrile redness. When the door opened behind her, she didn't hear it.

Then she felt a hand. She jerked upright, startled.

Jorge was right behind her, grinning his gap-toothed smile. "All nice and clean?"

She shrugged away from his touch. "Get your hands off me."

"Why? They been on you before."

He moved closer. Shan sidestepped, but he caught her wrist.

"Oh, come on," he whined. "It'll be just like old times."

"I already paid you. In *cash,* remember?"

"Well, how about a discount?" He caught her wrist again. "It's always nice doing business with you. Besides, I miss you, *querida.*"

She swatted his hand away and tried to push past him, but he when kicked the door shut Shan was momentarily disconcerted. "Will you get out of the way?"

He caught her by the waist. The glare from the uncovered bulb highlighted the yellow tinge in his complexion. His dark eyes were narrowed, predatory, and for the first time she felt a cold shock of fear. "Jorge, stop it. You need to let go of me. *Now.*"

"There's only one thing I need, *querida*," he informed her. When he pulled her close, she felt his erection against her stomach.

She pulled away but he held fast and kissed her, forcing his tongue into her mouth. His breath was sour and she felt a surge of revulsion, then a sharp burst of anger. She brought her teeth together, hard, and tasted the warmth of blood in her mouth.

He jerked his head back and his amiable, stoned grin vanished. "You little cunt!"

She kicked him, eliciting a yelp when her foot connected with his shin. He caught her by the neck, gripping hard, and she made a small sound of pain, then clawed savagely at his face.

His expression twisted into a mask of fury and he slapped her hard enough to knock her off her feet. Then he was on top of her, ripping at her clothes. Through a daze, she felt his hands fumbling at her crotch. He gave a hard yank to the zipper on the front of her jeans and it broke.

When she felt him groping between her legs, it jolted the fuzziness from her brain. Her nails connected with his eyes, wresting a snarl of pain from him, and he slugged her, slamming her head against the base of the toilet. She lay dazed as he pulled back to tear open his pants.

The sight of his penis jarred her back to full consciousness. Her leg jackknifed.

His howl of pain assured her that her knee had found its mark. She heaved him off her, then watched as he rolled heavily against the door, where he lay twitching and clutching himself.

His body was blocking the only way out. She was trapped.

Her eyes shot to the tiny window over the toilet. She scrambled to her feet and pried it open, then poked her head out, praying for a fire escape or even a ledge.

Instead she saw a sheer drop to the street four stories below.

She heard a moan and whirled. Jorge was pushing himself up off the floor, pausing when he made it to his knees. "You," he growled, "are going to be very sorry you did that."

"Oh no I won't!" Her fingers curled around the edge of the top of the toilet tank and, summoning every bit of her strength, she heaved it through the air and brought it down squarely on his head, knocking him flat. He didn't move again.

Shan crept a little closer, eyeing him suspiciously, and prodded him with her foot. His head fell to one side and his lips parted, emitting a wheezing sound, like air escaping from a balloon.

She tugged at him, managing to slide his body far enough to inch the door open, then she slipped through the crack and ran for the front door.

She stopped dead with her hand on the knob. *Joanie!* She reversed direction and snatched up her guitar from where she'd left it next to the sofa. Then her eye fell on the big rock of heroin.

What about her stuff? She'd paid for it. She stared at the rock. Her fingers tightened, digging into Joanie's case as the craving dug at her insides.

She jumped when she heard a throaty moan emanate from the bathroom, followed by a dragging sound, then a thud.

She paused only long enough to jam the whole rock into Joanie's case, then got the hell out of there. *Nice doing business with you, asshole.*

chapter 2

Quinn strode down Bleecker Street, raindrops striking the top of his head and the shoulders of his leather bomber jacket. His eyes went from storefront to storefront as he made his way along the crowded, narrow sidewalk. *Where in hell is this place?*

Out of the corner of his eye, he spied two women coming up a set of stairs and checked them out as a matter of course. One was a chubby redhead, not to his taste, but the other was his favorite flavor: tall and blond, with an impressive set.

The blonde returned his gaze, but when she moved into the raw light of a neon sign he immediately lost interest. She had bad skin and her attempt to conceal it with a thick layer of foundation offended his finicky sense of cleanliness.

He started to turn away and glimpsed, over her shoulder, a sign announcing the name of the establishment from which she had emerged: THE GROTTO. He pivoted.

The blonde's face lit up at his approach but fell when he squeezed past. "Evening," he said with a polite nod, passing her and not looking back.

As he went inside, he heard the blonde arguing with her red-haired friend. "Let's go back in for one more drink," she was saying, and her friend was holding out for someplace called Gatsby's. He hoped Red won.

Inside the club was murky, like an underwater cave. Even the neon signs that canopied the bar were hazy, obscured by layers of cigarette smoke. A wooden stage dominated the room, where a folksy brunette with a guitar was singing a Judy Collins song in a faulty soprano. Quinn grimaced.

As his eyes adjusted to the dim light, he spotted a familiar mop of sandy hair at one of the small tables near the stage. "Danny boy!" Quinn's face lit up in a big grin.

Dan Reynolds turned, revealing a wide nose, sloped chin, and friendly brown eyes. He was husky and broad, almost too big for the café-style chair he sat in, and he held a drippy double burger in his enormous fists. "Dude! Where've you been?"

"Trying to find this hole. Next time give me some landmarks." He slid into a chair and signaled the bartender, a statuesque black woman with dreads.

"Man, *everyone* knows this place," Dan laughed. "It's famous!"

"Really?" Quinn glanced around doubtfully. It looked like a dump to him, although the clientele resembled industry wannabes. He saw men with pony nubs and women dressed to emulate various musical flavors of the month, even one shaved bald like Sinead O'Connor.

"Definitely," Dan said, taking a bite of his burger. "Dylan was discovered here, you know."

Quinn smirked. "There are a dozen places that make the same claim." He turned to inspect an approaching waitress, another busty blonde but with better skin than the last one. "How are you tonight, darlin'?"

"Fine," she said pleasantly. "What can I get for you?"

"Tanqueray and tonic, please." He watched her as she returned to the bar.

When the waitress looked back at him, Quinn drummed his fingers on the table and idly engaged in a little visual foreplay. He was used to the power he had over women; all it usually took was a smile and they responded. He knew that part of it was the way he looked. He was tall, with broad shoulders and narrow hips. His face was angular with a razor-sharp jaw, his nose thin and pronounced, his lips firm with their constant half smile. He had fair, shaggy hair that just brushed his shoulders and a small diamond chip that glittered in his left earlobe. But it was his eyes that ultimately got them, bright blue and intense, deeply set under his well-defined brow.

The intense eyes seemed to be holding the waitress captive. She returned his gaze steadily, then leaned back against the bar and crossed her ankles, slowly rubbing one over the other. *This one's in the bag.*

Dan cleared his throat and Quinn pulled his attention back to the table. Dan was grinning. "Sorry to interfere with target practice, but we have stuff to go over. Where's Ty?"

"He said he'd meet us here. He's probably cruising up and down Bleecker Street like I was, trying to decipher your crummy directions."

Dan rolled his eyes. "Anyone in New York could tell you how to find the Grotto."

"Maybe, but I'm not from New York, remember? I'm just visiting from the cold, crappy town of Boston."

"You're not from there, either," Dan said, between bites. "You're a California dude, like me."

"And I can't wait to go back there," Quinn said. "I miss it, don't you?"

Dan shrugged. "There's things I like about the East."

"Not me. I have dreams about being back in Cali, riding my Harley on the PCH. The minute I finish school, we're gone. Remember that, Danny. Thanks, darlin'." He shifted his focus back to the waitress as she delivered his drink.

"Do you need anything else?" she asked.

"Not right at the moment, but be sure to check back later, okay?"

Dan laughed as she walked away, wiggling her ass. "I see you haven't changed a bit!"

"Well, *you* have, judging from the way your apartment looks."

Dan looked sheepish. "So you found the key all right?"

"Yup. You did some redecorating," Quinn said. "I like the curtains. The Tampax in the bathroom is a nice touch, too. There's Ty." He raised his hand to hail a tall, black man just coming down the steps from the street.

Dan popped the final morsel of his burger into his mouth as Tyrone Cowan joined them. He was lean and bearded, with close-cropped hair, chestnut-brown skin, and tiny gold hoops in both ears. "Dan, my man, 'sup? Thanks for putting us up. I was sick of listening to the Q-man bitch about staying at a hotel."

Quinn looked affronted. "Like I have money to burn? Besides, most hotels aren't furnished as tastefully as Dan's place. That feminine touch, you know?"

Ty regarded Quinn with amusement as Dan seemed to shrink into his chair. "At least the dishes are washed. That's new."

"There's an upside to everything," Quinn agreed. "Also, it was good to see your refrigerator without any science projects growing in it."

"Look, I have a steady girl," Dan said. "Why should that bother you?"

Quinn shrugged. "It doesn't. I'm just wondering when the wedding plans will start."

"No wedding anytime soon. I *have* been thinking about moving in with her," Dan said, after a pause, "but she's got roommates. It's tricky."

"Good, because she'd really have a leash around your balls then," Quinn said. "Wait'll she starts yanking it. She'll have you heeling in no time."

"Denise isn't like that," Dan said.

"They never are in the beginning. Just you wait," Quinn said. "That one has *marriage* spelled out across her forehead in neon letters."

"Would you lay off? I've been with her a couple of years now and I like having her around. What's it to you?"

"We've been working on getting this band established for more than a couple of years," Quinn said. "What's gonna happen if Denise decides she wants something bigger than your little studio and starts making noises about how unreliable a musician's salary is? You gonna cut your hair and start working for IBM?"

Dan shook his head, his long hair swinging from side to side. "Dude, there's nothing wrong with having *one* girlfriend. It's called monogamy."

"No," Quinn sneered, "it's called pussy whipped.

"Enough," Ty interjected. "I'm freaking bored with this conversation. This meeting is about the band, not Dan's love life. Where are we at?"

"Our first gig is here and it's next Saturday," Dan replied, "working for the door. If the crowd likes us, they'll book us regular for the summer. We get free beer, too."

"I'm not playing for the door all summer," Quinn said. "The door is shit. You can't count on the door."

"If you didn't suck so much, the door wouldn't *be* shit, Q," Ty snapped, just to shut him up. The truth was that Quinn didn't suck at all. The man had an ear like a bat and his technical skill was extraordinary.

"Excuse me?" Quinn regarded Ty with mock indignity. "I don't suck. *You* suck. You handle that bass as if you were whacking off a three-foot dick. That's why you never get laid. It scares all the chicks away."

"Maybe it scares *your* chicks away," Ty said. "You oughta borrow one of Dan's drumsticks. At least it'll stay hard."

"He doesn't need my stick," Dan said. "He can just keep diddling himself on his keyboard. He plays better when the keys stick." Ty gave Dan a high five, snickering.

"Very funny," Quinn said. "The door is okay for this first time but when they hire us, we renegotiate. This time let me do it," he told Dan. "You're too soft."

"That's not what my girlfriend says," Dan said.

"Let's get back to the gig," Ty prompted. "Do they have a house sound system?"

"Yes," Dan nodded, "but we have to bring our own man. I hired Bruce. He's willing to do us all summer, same as last year. He's upped his price, though."

"That's okay. He's the only one who ever gets our sound right." Quinn drained the last of the gin and tonic. "Tell me about the system," he said to Dan. "What's the monitor situation?"

"Should be fine. They've got a bunch of JBL fifteens."

"Sounds like we're good to go then, gentlemen. Let's drink on it. Another round, darlin'," Quinn called to the waitress with a wink, "and add a seven and seven."

The waitress leapt to attention, hips undulating as she walked to the bar. Quinn watched for a moment, then turned back to his bandmates. "Too bad Jason couldn't make it tonight," he remarked. "What did he have going on?"

Dan's smile faded. "I was going to mention that next. There's one more thing we need," he said. "Another guitar player."

"What do you mean?" Quinn asked. "We've always had only one."

"I know. But now we've got none."

"Come again?" Ty stared at Dan. "Where's Jason?"

"Rehab."

"*Again?* Christ," Quinn spat. "I'm so sick of this bullshit with him!"

"Poor guy." Ty shook his head. "He just can't seem to get off the crystal."

"'Poor guy' my ass," Quinn growled. "That fucking basehead is way more trouble than he's worth. I wanted to get rid of him last time. This time I will."

"I think so, too," Dan said eagerly. "We ought to find somebody right away. In fact—"

"Not right away," Quinn said. "There's no time. We're stuck with him for the summer, at least after he gets out. When's that?"

"Uh, it's more complicated than last time."

Ty frowned. "Why?"

"Meth lab," Dan replied, avoiding Quinn's suddenly intense gaze, "in his kitchen. After he gets out of rehab, he has to do some jail time."

"Shit," Ty gasped. "When's he getting out?"

"Not for a couple of years. At least," Dan added.

"Fucked!" Quinn exploded, slamming both fists down on the table. Dan's beer bottle fell over. It rolled off the edge and shattered on the floor, the shards tinkling musically. "We are *fucked!* How long have you known about this?"

"The sentencing was Friday," Dan said, "but I have a plan. This isn't a catastrophe."

"It *is* a catastrophe," Quinn corrected him angrily. "Jason does not just play guitar. He sings twelve of the fucking songs. Why didn't you say something sooner?"

"Because I wanted to break it to you gently. I knew you'd freak, and I was afraid you'd stay in Boston and take that session shit if you knew. Besides, we are not fucked," Dan reiterated. "I found another guitar player."

Quinn continued to glare, but Ty leaned forward. "You have a replacement in mind?"

"Yes. She was supposed to be here tonight, but—"

"*She?*" Quinn's eyes were huge again. "A girl?"

"Yeah," Dan nodded, "and this girl is a major talent. Seriously, you've never heard anything like her."

Tyrone looked thoughtful. "What kind of music does she play?"

"Folk, mostly," Dan said and Quinn groaned out loud, burying his head in his arms. "But she rocks, too," Dan added hurriedly, "and, man, can she sing!"

"Didn't you say she was supposed to be here tonight?" Quinn interrupted, raising his head. Dan nodded. "Then where the fuck is she?"

"I don't know." Dan frowned. "Something must have happened. She's reliable, usually. And she learns superfast. I've played with her before."

The waitress brought their round and knelt to pick up the pieces of broken bottle, affording Quinn an ample view of her cleavage. Normally he would have jumped to assist, but now he had other things on his mind.

"Is she a babe," Quinn asked after the waitress walked away, her ass now twitching with indignation, "or is she one of those nasty girl-musician-dyke types?"

"What does that matter? You're gonna play music with her, not fuck her."

"I don't want some ugly rug muncher fronting our band, that's all."

"Nobody said anything about her fronting. She's just gonna play guitar."

Quinn held up three fingers on his right hand. "Three guys." He raised his left hand, index finger extended. "One girl. And you said she sings. Who do you think everybody's gonna watch?"

Dan was silent.

"Does she have the right look, is all I'm asking."

"Enough arguing," Ty said. "When can we meet her?"

Dan sighed. "I'll set something up for tomorrow. We need to move fast on this."

"Can you get ahold of her?" said Ty.

"Yeah, no problem. She's Denise's roommate." Quinn let out a snort and Dan reciprocated with a dirty look. "Q, you are really beginning to bug me, bro. Why don't you stop with the negativity and give her a chance?"

"I can't wait." Quinn said. "I mean, seriously. How many decent female rock guitarists do you know of? Bonnie Raitt. Maybe Nancy Wilson. What are the chances that one just *happens* to be living with your girlfriend?"

chapter 3

Shan's knees were shakier than ever as she made her way out of Jorge's building. She hurried a few blocks down to 112th, then cut over Lexington to Desperado's, a cantina she occasionally played. She recognized the bartender, a tall Latino she knew only as T-Bone. He was a regular at Jorge's so she avoided him, heading straight for the restroom with her face averted.

Shan squeezed into a stall with Joanie and opened the guitar case. With shaky hands, she pulled out the rock of heroin, a piece of foil, a lighter, and a short plastic straw. Pinching a bit off the rock, she put it on the foil, sparked the lighter, and applied the flame to the bottom of the foil.

The heroin sizzled, its vinegary aroma filling the air. Shan used the tooter to inhale the smoke, savoring its chemical tang. She took one hit, then another. As the first effects began to filter through her brain, she felt the nausea melting away, the shakiness evaporating, and the wonderful lightness stealing over her. She slid to the floor and closed her eyes as she took another hit.

A sudden hammering made her eyes fly open. "There's a line!" said an angry voice.

But the restroom was empty and she'd only been there a moment. She checked her watch.

It was after eleven. She'd nodded out, for over an hour. *Oh no.*

Shan crammed her stuff back in Joanie's case and stumbled out of the stall, avoiding the hostile glares of the women in line. She left Desperado's and hurried down the street to the subway station. She missed the eleven-twenty train and was afraid to linger in Spanish Harlem, so she trekked downtown to the next stop. By the time she finally caught the train to Bleecker, it was after midnight. She gave up and rode to her usual stop in SoHo.

Shan wearily climbed the steps to her building and let herself into her apartment. She fastened all the locks, leaned back against the door, and heaved a sigh.

Just as well. That band was out of her league and she knew it. She went into the dark living room, shrieking when she walked smack into one of her roommates. "*Denise!* You scared me!"

Denise Jennison recoiled. She was a tall, slim girl of twenty-five, with spiky red hair and round blue eyes. "I was waiting up for you. Dan called. I was worried." She flicked on the light and her eyes widened. "My God, what happened?"

Shan looked down at herself. Her clothes were disheveled and the zipper on her jeans was broken. Her neck hurt, too, and she wondered if she had bruises. She shook her head to clear the H-induced fogginess. "I got mugged," she improvised, "on the subway."

Denise gasped. "Are you all right?"

Shan nodded, heading for her bedroom, but Denise dogged her. "Did you call the police?"

"No," Shan said. "What's the point?" When Denise erupted into a chorus of protests, Shan interrupted her. "Is Dan furious?"

"No, but—"

"Do you think he'd give me another chance?"

"Definitely," Denise said. "He wants you to call him first thing tomorrow."

Shan felt a glimmer of hope. "Good. I'm glad he's not too angry."

"For God's sake, don't be silly! Just tell him what happened."

Shan went into her bedroom without replying. She set down Joanie and surveyed her reflection in the mirror. She *did* look awful. The torn clothes and shadowy bruises were the least of it. It was her expression that was most telling. She looked haunted, shell-shocked.

Denise was hovering in the door. "Are you sure you're okay?"

"I told you I'm fine," Shan snapped, then experienced a stab of remorse at the hurt on Denise's face. "Look, I'm sorry. It's just been a lousy night and I'd like to be alone."

"Do you want me to make you some tea? There's chamomile."

"No thanks. I'm going to take a bath." She moved past Denise, pausing when she reached the bathroom. "If you talk to Dan before I do, would you tell him I'd still like to audition? I'm gigging at the Grotto tomorrow night. Maybe they could come."

"Why don't you invite them over for dinner before you play?" Denise said. "A free meal is always a perk for starving musicians, especially when they're male."

"That's a great idea. I'll do that. Good night." Shan closed the bathroom door. She ran a bath as hot as she could stand it and stripped off her ruined clothes, searching for a place to put them. The bathroom was big and cavelike, with heavy black fabric over the window and a countertop cluttered with equipment and vats of chemicals. Denise was a photographer and used the bathroom as a darkroom, so space was tight. Shan closed the lid of the toilet, set her things on top of it, and climbed into the big claw-foot tub.

She wished she could afford to live alone. Both her roommates were fine, nice people really, but she just couldn't get the hang of the female bonding thing they were so into. Both Denise and Oda Solomon, their third roommate, seemed to view their living arrangement as some sort of substitute family, but Shan had worked too hard to escape her own family to surrender herself into the clutches of another one.

She leaned her head back, rubbing a cake of sandalwood soap between her hands. She closed her eyes, inhaling the bright, woodsy fragrance that rose through the steam. It reminded her of her mother, like it always did. That was why she used it.

Abby O'Hara, who always smelled of sandalwood, had died when Shan was twelve. At the time it had seemed sudden, but now she understood that her mother had been sick for a long time.

The illness didn't make her mother didn't look any different, not at first. She was slim and pretty, with the same dark curls and big green eyes as her daughter. She still went to work every day at North Adams State, the western Massachusetts college where she taught piano and voice.

Abby sang like a nightingale, played the guitar as well as the piano, and loved music more than anything in the world. Shan's earliest memories were like a mixed tape of the music her mother made on her petite Takamine guitar and the records she played on their battered stereo.

Shan loved to sing, too, and from an early age she hummed and crooned almost constantly. As she grew, she trilled rock songs like

"Rave On" and "All You Need Is Love" the way other children chanted "The Wheels on the Bus." She used her toy tambourine to tap out reggae rhythms like the ones she heard on her mother's Bob Marley records. She listened to rock, bluegrass, gospel, and jazz, but mostly the folk music that was her mother's passion, especially her idols, Joan Baez and Joni Mitchell. Abby loved them so much she named her Takamine after them. She had a couple of other guitars, a basic no-name classical and a beautiful Fullerton twelve-string, but always preferred the smaller, sweeter-sounding Joanie.

Abby began teaching Shan to play the piano when she was just five years old. She took to it so quickly that she surprised even her mother, who was used to teaching the musically inclined. By the time she was eight, Shan was playing Mozart from memory and making up her own songs.

At ten, she taught herself to play the guitar. She still remembered the look of amazement on her mother's face the day she found her with the classical, playing "Blackbird."

That night after she went to bed, Shan could hear her parents arguing.

"Gary, do you know how difficult that song is?" her mother asked. "I've never even given her a guitar lesson. And her voice," she added, "her pitch—it's unbelievable."

"Forget it, Abby," her father said. "You know we don't have that kind of money."

"But she's gifted," her mother persisted. "She can hit notes that even I can't sing. LeBarron is the best music school in Berkshire County. That's where she belongs."

"That school costs a fortune," her father said. "Can't you teach her to sing?"

"Not yet. She's too young to study voice, but she still needs training. We owe it to her."

"We *owe* her food, and clothes, and a roof over her head," her father said, his voice rising. "*That's* what we're spending our money on, not lessons at some hoity-toity music school!"

When her father started to yell, Shan stopped listening, putting her head under the covers so she wouldn't hear. Her father scared her when he yelled. He had a nasty temper, especially when he drank, which he did a lot. Shan was very young when she learned to give him a wide berth at those times, and even more on the mornings after. That was when he was most irritable and if Shan did something to make him mad, he would spank her, spankings that hurt for days.

Sometimes Shan noticed her mother moving slowly, like it hurt, and she thought maybe he spanked her, too. Whenever that happened, her father acted all loving toward Abby and things would go back to normal—at least until the next time.

Her father never did agree about the music lessons, but by the time she was eleven Shan was attending the LeBarron Academy in Williamstown. She flourished there, although she didn't do quite as well in her regular classes. She was always dreaming up new songs instead of listening to her teachers, writing down lyrics instead of taking notes.

One night after Shan had been attending LeBarron for about a year, her mother fainted during dinner. At the hospital, a doctor came and talked to them, using scary words like *cancer*, *chemo*, and *late stage*. It wasn't long after that Abby began to change. Her body, always slender, became gaunt. Her skin took on an odd translucency and her curly hair vanished overnight. She sang less, saying that it hurt her throat, so Shan sang while Abby played Joanie.

Eventually Abby had trouble holding on to the pick, so Shan played and sang. She took Joanie and sat at the foot of her mother's bed for hours, performing her entire repertoire over and over, especially the folk songs her mother loved. Her father cut back his hours at the paper mill to spend more time at home. He cooked for his wife, bathed her, even helped her to the toilet. The family revolved around Abby, although Shan and her father never said much to each other. He'd never said all that much to his daughter to begin with, but Shan could remember when her singing could make him smile. Those days he never smiled.

Shan wasn't smiling, either. She was too scared to smile. Her mother was slipping away, right in front of her eyes. Each day there seemed to be a little less of her.

Not just physically, although Abby had shrunk to a bare seventy pounds. Her spirit seemed to be departing, too, her essence wasting away. She rarely opened her eyes and hardly ever spoke. The only thing that roused her was the music. Shan played longer, sang louder, trying to drown out the death knell that haunted their house.

One night Abby woke up and couldn't breathe. Another trip to the emergency room, more scary words, and the next day she was gone.

Even now Shan couldn't remember much about the first days after her mother's death. The funeral was like a dream, fuzzy and surreal as a heroin buzz. Afterward, her father dropped Shan off at home, then went down the street to the tavern.

Shan thought she would go crazy, that first night. Her mother was dead—she had no mother. Those two facts reverberated through her head in a sonorous, 3/4 rhythm. She couldn't understand how the world could have changed so much in just a few days.

She cried for hours. Each time she thought she was finished, the 3/4 rhythm would begin anew and her eyes would fill again. She'd never known she could cry so much. Her eyes hurt, her nose stung, even her chest ached from the force of her sobs.

Sometime around midnight, she heard the front door open, then her father's heavy footsteps climbing the stairs. Shan was still crying, but the footsteps continued down the hall to the bedroom he shared with her mother. Just his, now.

Shan's eyes were swollen nearly shut and she'd cried herself into a bloody nose, but she still couldn't stop. Then she thought of something she thought might help her sleep.

Shan slipped out of bed and crept down the hall. When she opened the door to her father's bedroom, she saw Joanie leaning against the wall. Quietly, she crossed the room and reached for it.

"Leave it."

Shan jumped and turned. Her father's eyes were wide open and staring at her.

Shan backtracked to the door and ran down the hall, jumping back into her own bed, shaking. A moment later her father appeared in the doorway. For a few minutes he stood there, eyes red and bloodshot, a cigarette now hanging from the corner of his mouth.

Then he said, "Your mother is dead."

It was like hearing it for the first time. Shan's face broke and she was crying again.

"She was sick for a long time," he said. "Longer than you knew. Longer than *I* knew. She hid it from me. You know why?" He took a couple of steps toward her. "Because of your fucking music school. She didn't go to the doctor because there wasn't enough money to pay him and still get you your goddamned piano lessons." Now he was standing right over her bed, staring down at her. "It's your fault," he said tonelessly. "You killed your mother, Shan."

Shan remembered when she'd first started her classes at LeBarron, how her mother had said she would do anything, just anything to get her into that school. She began to cry harder.

"You'd better shut up," he said, "before I give you something more to fucking cry about."

With a tiny, mewling sound Shan lowered her face, trying to control her sobs.

Suddenly, blinding pain against her leg. She screamed, jerked her head up—

And saw the bright ember of her father's cigarette coming toward her again.

Shan sat up in the tub, wide awake. She flexed her legs, her knees emerging from the tepid bathwater to expose the round, white blemish that was a permanent inscription from that night. It was the first of many scars she would receive at the hands of her father.

He never got over his wife's death and he never stopped blaming his daughter for it, either. For weeks he'd barely speak to her then, out of the blue, he'd fly into a rage over some small infraction. Once he threw her into a wall for setting the beer she'd fetched on top of his newspaper.

Shan's life developed a routine. She tried to stay out of her father's way, which wasn't hard, since he was rarely at home. After school she hung out with a few other kids like herself, losers whose parents didn't care what they did. Sometimes one of them had pot or beer purloined from a parent or older sibling, so they'd hole up at somebody's house, get buzzed, and listen to music until it was time to go home for dinner.

At home, keeping the house clean and doing the laundry had become Shan's responsibility. She did the chores, fixed herself a can of soup or Chef Boyardee for supper, then played guitar and sang, working on her music until it was time to go to bed.

And so she got by, for a long time. For more than two years, in fact.

Then one afternoon she came home and fell asleep on the couch instead of doing the laundry. Her father was working the night shift then and when he got dressed, he found he had no clean socks and hit her so hard he knocked out two of her teeth. Shan waited until he went to work and within half an hour she was gone, taking only a backpack and her mother's guitars. She could only carry two, so she took Joanie and the twelve-string. She'd long since graduated to steel strings so she never played the classical anymore, but to leave it behind still wrenched.

Shan lived on the streets for over a year, eventually hitchhiking to New York, where she met Jorge. He was only one of many street people she encountered there, but he offered his couch one night when the temperature dipped below freezing. She took to coming by on subzero nights. He never seemed to mind and there were always people there, since he was a dealer.

It was only natural to partake of whatever drug was being passed around. Shan sampled them all, enjoyed the different highs, but she was especially captivated by the brown rock Jorge referred to as the big H. She loved the way it made her feel, how all the sorrow and tension she carried inside her simply dissolved, just floated off. She hadn't even realized how sad she was, how scared and confused and lonely, until the H took the feelings away.

She couldn't wait to do it again, but she was vaguely uneasy. "Doesn't this make us junkies?" she asked Jorge.

"Hell no," he said as he chased the black, smoldering blob of heroin around the foil with a tin cylinder. "Junkies are those sorry scags who shoot it."

What he said made sense. The antidrug propaganda at her North Adams high school had depicted an emaciated wreck with a needle in his arm. There was no needle so she was okay, or so she thought, until the night she found Jorge's place deserted and curled up inside the vestibule to wait for him.

When he finally showed up almost twenty-four hours later, she was a sweating, retching mess. He took one look at her and shook his head, but let her follow him inside.

"I can't keep feeding you dope," he said, loading up the foil. "This ain't a charity ward."

His words made little impression. Her eyes were glued to the foil. When he applied the flame she reached for it, but he held it away. "What are ya, deaf? No more freebies, I said."

"But you know I don't have any money," she said, with an edge of desperation.

When she tore her gaze from the foil, she found him watching her with a predatory gleam. "I think we can work something out," he whispered.

It wasn't terrible, and it wasn't as if it was her first time. There'd been a few guys since she left home, starting with Greg, the fellow runaway who'd taken her virginity one night when they were both sleeping under the same bridge. She'd hung out with him for a few days, then never saw him again.

And Jorge was gentle with her. Afterward he held her and told her he would take care of her. Then he did, by giving her the heavenly release that came from the slim trail of smoke.

It was the first of many nights she'd spend in his bed. He wasn't a bad guy, really, and before long she was living there. At times he seemed to really care about her, stroking her hair and calling her *querida*, then piling up the H on the foil and holding the flame for her.

Shan endured the arrangement for about six months, until the night she found herself in bed with not only Jorge but another participant, a hollow-eyed girl named Chloe with a bad case of the shakes and blue-black road maps up both arms.

She'd gotten through it, gotten her fix, and gotten the hell out. She'd been trying to get clean ever since. This was her third unsuccessful attempt at turkeying, but she knew it wouldn't be her last. Even through a heroin fog, she knew she had to find another way, before she turned into Chloe. She'd seen what was waiting at the bottom of the abyss.

Shan climbed out of the tub and toweled off, then put on sweats. It was nearly two-thirty, but she was still too keyed up to sleep. She remembered Denise's suggestion of chamomile tea and went into the kitchen, stopping when she found it occupied. She suppressed a sigh. "Hi."

"You're up late," Oda Solomon said. She was a meaty woman in her late twenties with dreads, coffee-colored skin, and eyes that seemed to see everything. She tended bar at the Grotto, which was how Shan had met her.

"I'm on my way to bed," Shan said, "but I thought I'd fix myself a cup of tea first."

"I was just brewing some." Minutes later, Shan accepted a cup and went to her bedroom. Oda followed and sat down on the futon, mindless of the unfriendly look Shan shot at her.

"You had Dan wondering about you tonight," Oda remarked.

"I ran into some trouble."

"Mmm-hmm." Unlike Denise, Oda never asked. She saw. She had a way of looking at Shan that made her feel as transparent as a pane of glass.

"I'm supposed to call him and reschedule," Shan said, "but it's probably pointless."

"So why bother?" Oda's eyes were fixed on her, deep brown and clear as rain.

"Well, they need someone now and I'm a quick study. I don't think they'd want me permanently, but I could fill in until they find a replacement."

"I don't know. You should have heard Dan. He was raving you up to the other two guys."

"So you met them?" Oda nodded. "What did you think of them?"

"I thought Dan's friend Ty was a stone fox," she admitted, wresting a laugh from Shan, "and he's very nice. Struck me as straight shooter."

"How about the other one? Quinn?" Dan swore he was a genius, but Denise couldn't stand him. She'd confided to Shan that Quinn demonstrated every repulsive characteristic of the male persuasion. He was arrogant, she said, overbearing, and much too full of himself.

"Hard to say." Oda looked thoughtful. "He's a charmer. Good talker. Cute, too. Nice smile, but there's something a little bit chilly about him. He keeps blinding you with that smile, though, so you don't notice right away."

"Dan says he's brilliant. He thinks he's the most talented musician he's ever met."

"If he is, then he's sure to snap you right up. The Grotto's jammed every time you play, Shan, and that says a lot about you."

After Oda went to bed, Shan twisted her hair into a braid and thought about Oda's words. The Grotto was known as an industry showcase and not without justification. The owner, Mike Shapiro, had a reputation as a music visionary. He was selective about who graced his historic stage, but he'd selected her and the prestige of the place helped her land other gigs. Now she was earning enough to support herself. She liked her roommates well enough, the apartment was comfortable, and she had enough money to live on. Her needs were simple; she could get by as long as she could afford guitar strings and food and the drugs that were a necessity, despite her repeated attempts to get clean.

Even with the tea Shan couldn't sleep, so she reached for Joanie. She left the apartment quietly and climbed the stairs to the roof. It was a clear night and the stars winked down on her as she took a seat in the folding metal chair she kept up there.

She looked out over the SoHo rooftops as she began to play. The air was chilly and she recalled what it was like to live on these streets. She'd moved from neighborhood to neighborhood, sleeping on benches and in subway tunnels, foraging through supermarket Dumpsters for food, and begging for nickels and dimes. She'd never forget that first January on her own, huddling inside doorways with nothing but a denim jacket between her and the cold of the New York winter.

She shivered and began to sing. It was a song that didn't have a name, really, just a song that she sang when she was on the roof, the verses changing according to her moods.

I'm in a place where I'm allowed
To let the things that hurt
Drift on up among the clouds
They don't bother me
And I don't care
'Cause I'm on the roof and dreaming

She played for a long time, gazing up at the sky as her melodies wafted down over the sleeping city.

chapter 4

Quinn stirred as voices infiltrated his sleep. He burrowed his head into the pillow to muffle the noise, but a burst of laughter jarred him further awake. Annoyed, he yanked the pillow over his head and his forehead hit the arm of the couch with a solid thwack.

Tossing the pillow aside, he sat up and scowled at Dan and Ty. They were at the kitchen table, drinking coffee and smoking a joint. Ty lifted his cup. "Wake and bake!"

"No thanks." Quinn hoisted himself off the couch and headed for the bathroom clad only in his boxer briefs. He slammed the door behind him and positioned himself in front of the john, the seat of which was conveniently upright. That'll change soon enough, he reflected, eyeing the pile of mascara, lip gloss, and other cosmetics on the shelf behind the toilet.

He came back and scrounged for his jeans at the foot of the couch, then fished through his duffel bag for a T-shirt. He found one and pulled it over his head. BERKLEE COLLEGE OF MUSIC curved lyrically across his chest.

Quinn poured a cup of coffee then sat down at the table. "That couch is the most uncomfortable thing I've ever slept on," he told Dan. "Where'd you find it, an S&M shop?"

"Considering some of the places I've seen you wake up, that's saying a lot." Dan fitted the joint into an ornate roach clip. "If you'd come in at a decent hour you could have fought Ty for the other side of the bed, but you'd rather stay out all night fucking some frequent flyer."

"Why not? It's preferable to sleeping next to your hairy ass."

"You could have stayed with the waitress," Ty said, taking the joint from Dan.

"Uh-uh. One of the golden rules. You wake up with a chick, next thing you know she wants you to meet her mother. Pass." Quinn's eyes were on the joint. "We have a lot of ground to cover today. It's a little early for that, don't you think?"

Ty rolled his eyes and changed the subject. "Are we going to hit the Bitter End?"

"We should." Quinn took the roach clip from Ty and flicked the joint into an ashtray. "They liked our demo. Let's go over there tonight and sweet-talk them."

"It'll have to be late," Dan said, "because our new guitar player called. We're meeting her at six."

"Did you find out what happened last night?"

"She just said she ran into some trouble," Dan replied. "She offered to feed us to make up for it, though."

"Cool!" Ty exclaimed, but Quinn shook his head.

"The last thing we want is to hook up with someone unreliable."

"She's not, usually," Dan said. "I've never known her to miss a gig."

"You also never answered when I asked you what she looked like," Quinn reminded him.

Dan radiated a heavy sigh. "She's cute, okay? Just give her a chance, dude."

"Look, we can get by without a guitar. I can do those parts on keyboard. I can sing all the fucking songs, too, if I have to," Quinn said. "I'd rather do that than play with some second-rater."

"I'm looking to do more than get by," Ty broke in. "The whole point of coming here for another summer was to make some money. How are we going to do that with only half a band?"

"She's not second rate," Dan insisted at the same time. "You think I'd hook us up with an amateur?"

"But when you introduce a new element into an established band, it changes the dynamic," Quinn said. "We've got a good formula, Danny. I don't want to fuck with it."

"I hear you," Dan said, "but I have a good feeling about this. Trust me, will ya?"

Quinn looked up at the funky metal building, a type he'd only ever seen in SoHo. "Denise is still living in that loft, huh?"

"Yeah." Dan nodded, his long hair stirring in the breeze.

"You should move in here, then, if you're really serious about living with her," Quinn said. "This would be a great place to practice. I bet the acoustics are good," he added as they climbed the three flights to the apartment.

Dan rapped on the door. They heard the clicking of multiple locks and the door opened. "Hi, sweet stuff," he cooed as Denise's round blue eyes peered through the crack.

They went into the apartment, redolent with the smell of marinara. Quinn recognized Oda Solomon, the bartender from the Grotto, who was at the stove stirring the vat of sauce.

Denise was smiling at Ty, reaching out with both hands. Her red hair stood up like a rooster's comb. "Ty, it's good to see you again."

"And you remember Quinn, of course," Dan prompted as Ty squeezed her hands.

"Yes." Denise's smile lost some of its warmth. "Hi, Quinn."

"Denise—always a pleasure," Quinn replied, his tone polite but guarded.

Denise led Dan and Ty into the other room, but Quinn lingered in the kitchen with Oda, who was now mixing tomato juice and Worcestershire in a glass pitcher. "Need any help?" he asked. "My Bloody Marys are famous."

Oda laughed, a deep sound that seemed to emanate from the bottom of her belly. "I'll put mine up against yours any day. I'm a bartender, remember?"

"Me, too," he said. "At least when school is in session. I guess I'll have to have a couple to see if your Marys taste as good as your cooking smells."

Oda poured the tomato mix into tall glasses, adding a healthy splash of vodka to each. "I'm not the cook," she confessed, handing him a drink. "Your guitar player is."

Quinn experienced a surge of annoyance as Oda went into the other room with the tray of drinks. Everyone seemed to think this was a done deal, but he wasn't going to accept a musician just because it was convenient. He wanted only the best in his band.

He followed her into the living room, which was big and open, furnished with a couple of Papasan chairs, a low table, and a big ottoman. The sparse room was bathed in a soft glow by the late-afternoon sunlight filtering through the wide windows. The walls were covered with matted photographs, city shots, mostly, although there were a few pictures of Dan. Naturally, since Denise was the photographer, a student at the New York Institute of Photography.

One of the chairs was occupied by Ty. In the other was a girl. When Quinn saw her, he paused with his drink halfway to his lips.

She was sitting with one leg curled underneath her, a beat-up acoustic guitar in her lap, her fingers twisting a string around one of its tuning pegs. Her hair was shiny black, hanging to her waist in a riot of corkscrew curls. Her face was a stunner, with high cheekbones and eyes that were almost too big, wide set and soulful, their color a striking light green. Her mouth was full, her lips a soft, clear pink.

When she looked up at Quinn, he caught the full voltage of her laser eyes. "I guess you're Quinn, the keyboard player?" she said shyly.

"And I guess you're Shan, the guitar player." She bobbed her head, the black curls dancing around her slim shoulders, and turned her attention back to Ty.

Great. Quinn took a big gulp. *Now she'll think I consider it a done deal, too.* It was rare that he was at a loss for words, but this girl had caught him off guard. She was a babe, all right. A serious knockout, in fact. He turned to Dan.

"Nice fake. You did that on purpose," he accused, whispering so Shan wouldn't hear.

Dan smirked. "You're the one who decided she'd be a shaved whale in a flannel shirt. I told you she was cute."

"Yeah, you said *cute*. You didn't mention that she was a fucking *goddess*."

"I don't think she's your type," Dan said, "but wait'll you play with her."

"I plan to play with her, all right. And we can skip the audition!"

"We're looking for a guitar player," Dan reminded him, frowning. "Behave yourself."

A timer went off and Shan set her guitar aside, unfolding herself from the deep chair. Quinn moved out of her way as she headed for the kitchen. She was slim and very slight, he saw as she paused to look up at him. The top of her head barely reached his chin. "I'm sorry about last night," she said to him. "Thanks for letting me feed you to make up for it."

"No problem," he said, zapping her with one of his high-caliber smiles as Dan and Ty exchanged knowing looks. "It gave us a chance to check out the Grotto. You're a regular?"

Shan nodded. "It's a nice gig, and the money's great."

As she moved past, Quinn met Dan's eyes, grinned wolfishly, and did a quick about-face, following her into the kitchen.

Shan was peering through the glass pane on the front of the oven. He gave her another once-over. She was dressed in that hippie bohemian look he hated: faded jeans ripped at the knees, an Indian shirt with little mirrors all over it, and a silver ankle bracelet that tinkled as she walked. She had a tiny silver stud attached to her nose, too. Starving artist style.

Not his usual type at all, but for this girl he'd make an exception. "Can I help?" he asked.

"No thanks. Linguine is my one specialty," she said, beginning to grate a block of Parmesan. "So you go to Berklee." She glanced at his T-shirt.

"Yup," he replied. He could tell she was intimidated. Berklee was a prestigious music school, one of the best in the country. The place was highly competitive and admitted only the best students from all over the world.

"What's your major?" she asked.

"BA in composition and a dual master's in professional music and contemporary performance."

"Wow." She looked impressed. "Your parents must be really proud of you."

Quinn grimaced. "Not so much. How about you? Are you studying?"

"I'm not in school."

"Do you plan to be?" Quinn asked and Shan shook her head. "Have you had any formal training?" he persisted, his mind turning to business. He was big on education, especially when it came to guitar players. So many of them had no formal background at all. "Can you sight-read?"

"Yes," she said, with a sideways glance at him. "I took piano for years."

He cocked his head to the side and grinned, his light hair falling across one eye. "Me, too."

"I can tell. I've heard your demo. Great chops."

"Glad you like it," he said, pleased. "What made you switch to guitar?"

"It's tough to bring a piano to a gig, don't you think?" she asked him.

"Not if it's electric. Mine's pretty transportable."

"I'm guessing it's a Kurzweil?"

"How'd you know?" he laughed.

"If you can afford Berklee, you can probably afford the best."

Quinn shrugged. "I suppose. What's that axe you had in there?"

"Well, Joanie's a Takamine—"

He tilted his head quizzically. "Joanie?"

"My guitar, I mean," she said, looking embarrassed. "I have a Peavey electric, too, and a Fullerton twelve-string. Nothing fancy. Someday, I'll get a Martin acoustic and a Gibson ES. Those are *my* dream machines." She was perspiring, suddenly, and Quinn saw her hands tremble as she took out a metal strainer. She looked flushed, too.

"You okay?"

"Oh, yes," she said. "It's just hot in here."

It wasn't, really, but Quinn took the strainer from her. "Here, let me get that."

"Would you excuse me? I just want to splash some water on my face."

"Sure," he said, and Shan disappeared into the living room.

Obviously he made her nervous. Well, a lot of girls became flustered around him. Still, he'd expect more poise from someone used to an audience. He was frowning as he strained the linguine, but a few minutes later she reappeared looking cool and composed. "Everything's ready," she pronounced. "Can you put it on that on the table while I call the others?"

"Sure." Quinn picked up the bowl of pasta, looking around. "Where's the table, exactly?"

Shan pointed at a doorway behind him. Approaching to investigate, he discovered another room, furnished with a rectangular table set with six places. "This place is huge," he marveled.

"I know. I'm so lucky. Oda just happened to mention that she and Denise were looking for another roommate. It's rent controlled, so I could actually afford it."

"Choice location, too."

She nodded. "And it's a great place to practice," she added. "Good acoustics."

He shot her a keen look as she turned back toward the kitchen. "Can I do anything else for you?" he asked, with a little smile.

Shan paused. "Sure. You can open the wine." She disappeared. Quinn gazed after her for a moment, still wearing the inscrutable smile.

Ty pushed his plate away. "Shan, that was great. The only time I get a home-cooked meal is when I go home to Detroit for Christmas."

Shan topped off his wine. "Don't you like to cook?"

Ty chuckled. "No way. I'd starve if it wasn't for the microwave. Quinn's a pretty fair chef when he gets the urge. Unfortunately that's not too often."

Denise gaped at Quinn. "I'd expect you to think cooking was beneath you. Women's work and all that."

Quinn gave her a sour look. "I don't mind cooking," he replied, thinking that Denise Jennison was as much of a rag as ever. Charming women was usually effortless for him, but she clearly detested him and had from the moment she'd met him more than two years before.

For the life of him he couldn't understand why Dan was so hung up on her. She was attractive, leggy, and hot in a punky New York way, with her spiky red hair and kohl-lined eyes, but she'd probably turn into a skinny shrew as she got older. By then, she'd have squeezed out a couple of puppies so Dan would be stuck with her forever. He suppressed a shudder.

"Why don't you do it more often, then?" Shan broke in. She and Dan had been deflecting Denise's verbal attacks on Quinn all through dinner. Every comment Quinn directed at Denise was tinged with sarcasm, too.

"No time," Quinn said. "I'm in class all day and either gigging, working, or in the studio every night."

Shan regarded him thoughtfully. "You take your music pretty seriously, don't you?"

"I take it *very* seriously," Quinn agreed.

"It's a shaky career choice to invest all that time and money in. I mean," she said as he frowned, "it's not a sure thing. If you have an engineering degree, you get a job as an engineer. When your degree is in music, there's no guarantee. You must have a lot of faith in yourself."

"I do." His dark look cleared. "I've spent too much time listening to second-raters complain how they never got a break, and that's why they never made it. If you have enough confidence in yourself, I think you can make your own breaks happen. It just takes dedication. And talent," he added. "You can't learn that, no matter how hard you try."

"Remember, I warned you about this guy," Dan interrupted, looking at Shan. "He's a frigging slave driver. If things pan out, you'd better be prepared."

Shan smiled, but Ty chimed in. "Listen to the man, now. He's not kidding. It ain't always a party in this band, not with the Q-man cracking the whip. He'll be all over your ass until you're playing the way he wants you to. And he never lets up, ever."

"Somebody has to take the lead," Quinn said. "Are you sure you want to get mixed up with a tyrant like me?" he asked Shan. "I've been told I fall slightly to the right of Attila the Hun."

"I'm tough," Shan said, "and I don't think you're *too* scary. I know it'll be a stretch to be ready by Saturday, but I've already started learning the songs."

"Good," Quinn said. "We'll see what happens once we check out your chops."

Shan nodded, then rose from the table. "Anyone for dessert?"

"Dessert!" Ty's face lit up. "Shan, you just scored my vote!"

She beamed at him. "Terrific! Now I just have to convince Quinntila."

They all laughed and Quinn shot her another killer smile as he jumped up to help clear the table. "No convincing's required. Just show me what you can do."

They carried the plates and utensils into the kitchen where Shan opened the refrigerator and took out a glass bowl filled with whipped cream and chocolate. "I'm looking forward to hearing you play," Quinn said. "I have a hunch I'm in for something special."

"I hope I don't disappoint you." She turned her eyes to him and Quinn again admired their unusual color, noting that the green was speckled with flecks of gold. "I really want this to happen. I think I could learn a lot from you."

He smiled. "Well, maybe you will," he said, a trifle loftily. "Just don't be nervous."

When Shan reached up to retrieve a jar of chopped nuts from a high shelf, Quinn surreptitiously checked out her chest. Nice set. Not huge, but perky.

She scattered the nuts on top of the dessert, then picked up the bowl. As she did, he noticed an angry bruise just below the curve of her jaw. "What happened here?" he asked, touching it.

She flinched. "Nothing."

He slid his hand to her shoulder. Her scent was intoxicating; some kind of musky, woodsy blend. "Looks sore," he said, his gaze traveling to her mouth.

Shan didn't reply. He began fingering the soft hair at the nape of her neck. Their faces were only a few inches apart and he moved closer, his eyed riveted to her lips.

Abruptly she thrust the bowl into his stomach, wresting a pained *oof* out of him. He grabbed the bowl and shot her a look of confused indignation.

"Why don't you take that in the other room before it starts to melt?" She snatched up the dessert plates and stalked into the dining room.

Dan hurried into the kitchen as Quinn shifted the bowl to one hand and touched his stomach with a grimace. "What'd you *do?*" he whispered.

"Nothing much." Quinn glowered.

"I told you to behave." Dan frowned. "I thought you never mixed business with pleasure."

"I could in this case. Might take some persuading, though." He rubbed his gut gingerly.

Dan placed a restraining hand on his shoulder. "I'm serious, man. You don't want to mix it up with this one."

"Why? Is she gay?" He watched Shan head back toward the kitchen, emanating outrage.

"No," Dan hissed. "She's only sixteen. Isn't that another one of your golden rules? Never overnight, never unprotected, and never underage?"

Quinn's jaw dropped.

chapter 5

The Grotto turned down most of the lights on coffeehouse night, relying on candles and the neon glow from the bar for illumination. Only the performer onstage was bright, incandescent under a stark-white spotlight. It was reminiscent of the beatnik joints from the sixties which, Dan guessed, was what they were going for.

He risked a glance across the table at Quinn, who was staring into his drink sullenly, and mentally kicked himself for not mentioning the age thing sooner. He'd worried that Quinn would nix the girl up front if he knew. Even Ty might not have been willing to overlook that particular detail, although he was more open-minded than the Q-man.

The potential problems with an underage band member were multitudinous, the very least being that some of the clubs might not let her in. More seriously, if the kid got caught drinking or drugging, the adult members of the band were right in the line of fire for a "contributing to" charge.

Then there was the sex thing. Three adult males traveling with an underage female were at high risk anywhere, anytime, for any number of unsavory situations.

He'd planned for them to meet the girl and hear her play, then he'd casually mention her age after they got excited about her. The trouble was that Quinn had gotten a little too excited a little sooner than Dan anticipated.

He should have foreseen that wrinkle. Expecting Quinn not to hit on a hot babe was like asking the sun to stop shining, but Shan didn't fit his usual specifications. Quinn invariably went for long-legged blondes with big tits, and Shan was totally at the opposite end of the hotness spectrum. She was smoking, though, in her cute little hippie chick way. He'd expected the guys to appreciate her looks but he hadn't anticipated Quinn snapping at her like a trout at a worm, especially since his typical MO with women was to play it cool while transmitting subtle encouragement. Quinn liked the chicks to come to him and they usually did, captivated by his good looks and facile charm, but tonight he'd followed Shan around with his tongue practically hanging out.

Now he was sulking, joining the conversation only when asked a direct question and even then giving monosyllabic responses.

Man, what an ego. One turndown and you'd think the world was ending.

Quinn was annoyed. He didn't see the point of this audition. The girl was too goddamned young, so it didn't matter if she was any good. Even if she sang like Whitney Houston it wouldn't make any difference, so she was wasting his time.

He glowered at her. "I play folk," she was telling Ty, "because that's what people want from a solo acoustic. I'd really prefer to experiment with different kinds of music."

"What are your desert isle picks?" Ty asked.

"I like the Grateful Dead," she said and Ty nodded his approval. "B.B. King. Joni Mitchell."

So far Quinn had been quiet. Now he spoke up. "How about from this century?"

"Van Halen," Shan replied, lifting her chin. "Bonnie Raitt. The Chili Peppers. Valentine. Guns N' Roses. Cyndi Lauper. And Madonna, of course," she added.

Quinn gave a derisive snort. "Now there's a shining example of musical prowess."

"Maybe she's not the strongest singer, but she's got terrific style and she's a great performer. I think an artist has an obligation to put on a good show."

"I agree," Ty nodded again. Quinn thought he looked like one of those dogs people put in their rear car windows, the ones that bobbed their heads in sync with the potholes. "Look at Michael Jackson. Good singer, kick-ass performer. You'll have to excuse Quinn," he added. "He's a bit of an artistic snob."

Quinn noticed that Ty was gazing at Shan like a lovesick puppy. Christ, what was it about this chick? "I'm not a snob. I just believe that talent counts more than glam. There are too many musicians who spend more time on their stage act than on their skill."

"I think there's something to be said for both," Dan said. Quinn gave a contemptuous roll of his eyes and drained his glass.

"What are your favorite bands?" Shan asked Quinn.

"Rush," he replied. "Steve Winwood. Faith No More. Pink Floyd." Shan grimaced and Quinn raised his eyebrows. "You have a problem with that?"

"They're just not my taste. I like music that makes people move, but when was the last time you saw anybody dance to Pink Floyd? I put them in the same class as Yes. Dull."

Rick Wakeman, the legendary keyboard player for Yes, was Quinn's all-time hero. He saw Dan wince.

Quinn sneered in what he knew was a condescending manner. "That would be consistent with someone who's more concerned with image than talent. Maybe you can pick up a pair of metal cone tits, like Madonna. Then nobody will notice what you sound like. They'll be too busy checking out your set."

Color rushed to Shan's face. "Are you always this obnoxious?" she asked. "Or are you just threatened when someone expresses an opinion that's different from yours?"

Quinn had a stinging response on the tip of his tongue when a fresh drink appeared in front of him. His eyes traveled up the arm that delivered it and he discovered the blond waitress from the night before. She was smiling expectantly at him.

"Hi . . . uh . . ." He paused and a faint line appeared between his eyebrows. The smile faded from the waitress's face as he stared at her blankly.

"Jessica," she said. "I'd think you'd remember me after last night."

"How could I forget *you*, darlin'?" he improvised, summoning up his lady-killer smile. It was forced, though, and the words sounded phony even to him.

The waitress looked affronted. "That's on the house," she said, indicating the drink. "Consider it payment for services rendered. That's about what it was worth." Quinn's expression changed to one of indignation as she stormed off.

"Losing your touch?" Ty inquired. Quinn shot him an annoyed look and Ty's face split in a delighted grin. "Dude, are you *blushing?*"

Shan snickered. She'd been observing the exchange with a faint smile. "Sorry to have to step away at such a dramatic moment," she said, standing, "but it's time for me to go on."

"Go right ahead," Quinn snapped. "Sedate the place with a little folk Muzak."

Her face stiffened and she turned toward the stage without answering.

"That was rude," Ty observed as she moved away. "Why *are* you being so obnoxious?"

"I can understand why you're pissed off at me, but you don't have to take it out on her," Dan chimed in.

Quinn turned on Dan. "I can't believe you have the balls to even open your mouth, after putting us in this position. You don't tell anyone when we lose a crucial band member, then you hook us up with a player who turns out to be jail bait. Now, because of you, we're wasting another night waiting on Marcia fucking Brady instead of putting together some viable alternative like we ought to be doing. Where's your brain, you stupid fuck?" Dan started to answer, his chin quivering defensively. "Do me a favor, okay? Shut up."

Dan closed his mouth and mutely shifted his attention to the stage. The spotlight was on, bathing Shan in stark-white light. Her black hair glimmered under the lights, almost as much as the tiny mirrors sewn into her shirtwaist, and she sparkled all over as she climbed onto the tall stool. She adjusted the microphone and smiled at the audience.

"Welcome to coffeehouse night at the Grotto, ladies and gentlemen."

The audience gave her a hearty hand. A ripple of anticipation seemed to pass through the room as she began the opening chords from "Diamonds and Rust."

Quinn sipped his drink, noting that her playing was tight and polished, her changes smooth. He knew Dan was waiting for a reaction and kept his face impassive, but he approved of her tasteful style. Technically she was quite good. It wasn't a particularly easy piece and her fingers moved over the frets with skill. She had none of the hesitancy about her movements that was the first indication of an amateur.

Quinn's approval grew when she broke into the opening verse. She had a solid voice: sweet, clear, and confident. Her breathing was even and measured, her diction clean, and she held the notes with strength and purpose.

Dan was watching him openly now. Quinn was determined not to give him the satisfaction of any kind of response, so he picked up his drink and downed it, his face arranged in an elaborate expression of bored tolerance.

Shan moved into a difficult part of the song. Her vocals took off, swelling with conviction and filling the room, and the audience burst into a spontaneous wave of applause.

"Jesus Christ," Ty croaked. Quinn ignored him, leaning forward to listen intently. He forgot to worry about feigning indifference for Dan's benefit, focusing instead on the powerful things that were happening to his hypersensitive auditory canals.

Dan was right; he'd never heard anything like her. Her pitch was perfect and her range amazing, slipping from dusky lows to shimmering highs with flawless ease. She sang with a profound intensity that he could feel himself react to on a visceral level. And he wasn't the only one, he realized, sneaking a glance at the rest of the audience. She had charisma, enough to match her astonishing vocal chops, and she had the crowd on the edge of their seats.

Angelic was the word that came to mind. *She sounds like a fucking angel.*

Quinn experienced a chill. He looked down at his arms and saw his flesh rising up into small, tight pinpricks. He watched for a moment, as the sensation spread across his chest, then met Dan's eye across the table. An unwilling smile crossed his lips as he held up his fist to display the back of his forearm.

Dan grinned from ear to ear. He knew what the goose bumps meant. And the goose bumps were never wrong.

Forty-five minutes later, Shan finished her first set. She'd performed the best of her covers, "Sugaree," "Big Yellow Taxi," and "Blackbird" among them, tossed in some originals, and finished with a modified Bob Marley tune. She went to the bar for a club soda, took a deep breath, and swiveled to face the table.

They were all watching her. Even Quinn.

Her mouth went dry and she could feel her stomach gyrate. She went to the table, suddenly wishing she'd never agreed to this at all. She'd die, absolutely die, if she had to watch that contemptuous look fall over Quinn's face again, this time in response to her music.

She sat down. The three of them continued to watch her, so she fidgeted and played with a strand of her hair. For a moment, they all just stared at each other across the table.

She couldn't stand it anymore. "*Well?*"

Quinn was the first one to respond. He brought his elbows up on the table, laced his fingers together, and rested his chin on his hands. Finally, he smiled.

"Angel," he said, "welcome to Quinntessence."

chapter 6

Shan was up early the next morning, awakened by a painful cramp. She clenched until it passed, then struggled out of bed. Her eyes were watering and her nose running, the usual symptoms of a morning jones, but her mood was already high as she replayed the events of the previous night in her mind.

They liked her! Dan had beamed with self-congratulation as Ty gushed superlatives and even Quinn, whom she sensed was not effusive with his praise, made a few positive comments.

"You have a strong voice," he'd said, "and your playing is solid. I can tell you work at it, but you're going to have to work a lot harder now. It's a big jump from folk to hard rock and there's not much time to prepare. Are you up for it?"

"Yes!" Shan insisted. "Absolutely! I like playing folk, but I really want to rock!"

"Well, now's your chance," he assured her.

When he went to the bar, Shan had turned to the others. "Did he *really* like me?"

"Honey," Dan chortled, "you blew him away."

She looked at Ty. "Really? He's hard to read."

"*Really*," Ty said. "He was transfixed. Don't expect him to shower you with compliments, though. That's not the Q-man's style."

Well, he didn't have to. He liked her enough to let her in his band and that was enough for her. Besides, she'd have plenty more opportunities to show him what she could do.

Starting today, at their first practice session.

She reached in her dresser for the bag containing the brown rock and a piece of foil. She chopped off a bit, dropped it onto the foil, then sat down cross-legged on her bed. She lit the candle she kept on her nightstand, held the foil over it, and waited for the heroin to boil. When it did, she pulled out her tooter, then hesitated.

She wanted so badly to quit. She'd come close last time, and she didn't care about the high. Her new band would be a high all on its own.

She thought about the craving that would dig at her with white-hot pincers. The nausea and the diarrhea and the tremors. The insomnia that would keep her awake for days. Then she thought about trying to play while in that condition.

She lifted the tooter to her mouth and inhaled the smoke.

At precisely eleven o'clock there was a knock at the front door. When she opened it, Shan was greeted by an enormous pile of equipment seeming to sprout arms and legs. "Wow! What can I help with?"

"Just stay out of the way, angel." Quinn squeezed past with his keyboard, a coil of electrical cables over his shoulder and a crate of microphones under his arm. Dan and Tyrone staggered by next with the drum kit and amplifiers.

"You can grab the rest," Dan tossed back. Shan retrieved the bass and mic stands from the hallway, then followed them into the living room where they were stacking the gear into an empty corner.

She set down the equipment and watched the pile grow. Quinn untangled the cables from his shoulder, dropped them onto the snare drum, and flung himself into a chair. He was dressed in jeans, sneakers, and a Yes T-shirt. "Danny, next time you hire us a guitar player, make sure she lives on the ground floor."

Dan collapsed onto the floor pillows, his hair fanning out around him. "It's a prerequisite."

"There's a service elevator at the end of the hall," Shan said.

"Why didn't you say something?" Ty demanded amid a chorus of groans. Beads of perspiration dotted his forehead, standing out in sharp relief against his chestnut skin.

"I would have, but I didn't know you'd be bringing so much stuff."

"Well, it's good. It'll be easier to load in and out," Quinn said. "We brought all the stuff," he told Shan, "because I thought it should live here. I'd like to make this the official practice pad."

"There's only me here, though," Shan said. "All three of you are at Dan's."

"Not for long. I found a sublet. I move in on the first, if I can make it that long. Another week on Dan's couch and I may be permanently disabled."

"What about you?" Shan asked Ty.

"I'm staying with Dan. I get enough of Quinn during the school year and it'll almost be like living alone, since Dan's over here half the time."

Quinn shot Dan a contemptuous look. *Pussy whipped*, he mouthed.

Dan ignored him. "Did you get a chance to look over the schedule?" he asked Shan.

She nodded. "I can't believe you're already booked three nights a week."

"We are right now," Quinn said, "but by next month it'll be more."

Shan was skeptical. She'd never been able to get work more than two or three nights a week on a consistent basis, no matter how much she lobbied. "What makes you so sure?"

"There's a lot more work for a band than there is for a solo," Quinn pointed out. "Don't even question it—it'll happen. You don't have other commitments, do you?"

"A few. I play the Jubilee every other Thursday, and there's the Wonder Café."

"Cancel them," he said.

"All of them?" She was rattled. "What about the Grotto? I'm booked every Sunday."

"Cancel. You don't have a day job, do you?" She shook her head.

"Good." Quinn's eyes narrowed. "I want to make sure you understand that this is a full-time commitment. It'll be to your advantage. You'll probably make more money over the next three months than you usually do in a year."

"How do you manage to get so much work?"

"We've had quite a bit of radio play," Tyrone explained. "Most of the places we played last year jumped to get us again. Quinn does most of the booking. He's a good negotiator."

"How long have you all been together?" Shan asked.

"Q and I have known each other since we were kids," Dan said. "We went to the same music school, then we played in bands together right through high school."

"Right," Quinn said, "until Dan absconded."

"I didn't abscond," Dan said and rolled his eyes. "I went away to college."

"Whatever," Quinn said. "Eventually I wound up at Berklee, which is where I met Ty, and that's how Quinntessence was formed. There have been a couple of other guys that came and went for various reasons, but the three of us have been together for almost four years now."

"But you only play together during the summers?" Shan said. "You must hate that."

"I do. That's Dan, too," Quinn said, shooting him an annoyed look. "We tried to talk him into moving to Boston when he graduated, but he wouldn't."

"No, and I still won't," Dan said. "Denise can't go anywhere until she finishes school next year and I'm not moving three and a half hours away from her. Not even for you, dude."

"Whatever," Quinn said again and Shan could tell this was a sore subject. "This is a good time to go over the ground rules. They're simple. We never turn down a reasonable gig. We practice three days a week for three to four hours a day. It's cool with your roommates to do it here?"

"It's fine," Shan said, "and there won't be any problems with the neighbors, either. There are four other musicians in the building. One of them plays the trombone," she added, wrinkling her nose.

"Great." Quinn nodded. "There's just one more thing. You." He pointed at Shan. "No drinking on a gig. No drugging on a gig. Ever. And I mean *never*. Understood?"

Shan froze. She stared silently at Quinn for a moment, then found her voice. "So what if I drink or do drugs? I mean, what's it to you?"

"Nothing." Quinn shrugged. "I don't give a fuck what you do on your own time. It's none of my business. But when we're gigging, you're on *our* time. And you," he pointed at her again, "are underage. You get caught partying when you're with us, *we* get it in the neck."

"But I'm sure you drink when you play . . ." she began.

"That's different. Ty is twenty-six. Dan and I are twenty-five. We're legal but even so, none of us ever gets fucked up while we're gigging. That's another ground rule. It's unprofessional. And definitely no drugs. I've had enough of that bullshit in this band."

"But—"

"This isn't open for negotiation," he informed her. "It's a condition. Take it or leave it."

She hesitated for a moment, then nodded.

"Good," Quinn said curtly. "You remember that. Because if one of us catches you partying at a gig, you're fired."

Her temper flared. "Don't talk down to me. I don't need to worry about Big Brother watching my every move. I can take care of myself."

Quinn shrugged. "I'm not questioning that. You seem pretty together for a sixteen-year-old. We wouldn't take you on otherwise."

"Almost seventeen," she corrected him, slightly mollified. He turned away, but not before she saw his grin. She flushed and turned to Ty.

"I'm surprised you're not all living together," she remarked, just to change the subject. "It'd be a lot cheaper."

Quinn turned back. "I told you we're going to be rolling in dough. Don't you believe me?" She nodded, but still looked doubtful. "We get top dollar for a bar band. Now you, you're used to gigging solo and getting the door. The cover's three or four bucks and you pull maybe a hundred and fifty on a good night?"

"A *really* good night," she said ruefully.

Quinn's smile was openly patronizing. "Well, the cover is seven to ten bucks for Quinntessence, depending on what night of the week it is, and we play a lot bigger venues. A good Friday or Saturday for us is around fifteen hundred. Minus the sound man and split four ways, you're talking about three or four hundred bucks. *Each*," he emphasized, as Shan's jaw dropped.

"Yeah, but the door is shit, Quinn, remember?" Ty jeered.

"I'd still rather have a set fee going in, then get anything over a predetermined door take as a bonus. You can get screwed." Quinn looked back at Shan. "Cat got your tongue, angel?"

"I wasn't expecting that much money," she said, shaken. "Do I get a full share?"

They all stared at her in astonishment. "Of course," Dan said. "Did you think it was slave labor, since we have a resident slave driver?" Quinn gave him the finger, lips twisting sardonically.

"But I'm new," she said, "and I don't have as much experience as the rest of you."

"Better start catching up, then." Quinn snatched up the coil of cables and tossed it to her. "Time to learn how a big-time rock band sets up."

Forty-five minutes later he surveyed the loft. Cables crisscrossed the floor and Dan's drums filled an entire corner. His keyboard had a choice spot in front of the window. "Excellent spot for the Kur," he said.

Dan grinned. "Better than my kitchen table, hey?"

"You bet," he agreed and turned to Shan. "This place doesn't seem so big now, does it?"

Shan pushed an errant curl out of her eyes. Her hands, covered with grime from the cables, left a smear of black across her face. "We do this every time?"

"Yep." Quinn grimaced. "Then we have to break it all down again at the end of the night. My most immediate career goal is to be able to afford roadies so we won't have to do it ourselves."

"I'm used to hauling just a guitar and an amp." When she gathered her hair into her hands and lifted it, Quinn again noticed the bruise under her jaw. Now it was a mottled purple-black. Then he saw two more marks on the back of her neck. They looked like fingerprints.

When Shan caught him staring at her, she dropped her hair. "Shouldn't we get started?"

"Yup." Quinn looked away as she went into the bathroom to wash the grime off her hands. Maybe she had a boyfriend who was into bondage, although it didn't seem likely. She was a little too young and wide-eyed to be the whips-and-chains type.

Too young to be on her own, too. He wondered briefly what her story was, then pushed the thought away as Shan came back into the room. It was none of his business.

She took up her guitar. "What'll we start with?"

Dan settled behind his drums, rapping a ska beat on the ride cymbal. "Let's do something you feel comfortable with," he said to Shan. "You're the new kid."

"Not for long," Quinn said pointedly, "but we can start with a Dead tune. I assume you know 'Friend of the Devil'?"

"Doesn't everyone?" she laughed, picking out the opening guitar riff.

"Okay. I'll sing lead. You and Ty shoot for three-part harmony on the chorus. I want to hear how you do with it."

Shan went into the opening chords. When Quinn began to sing, his voice was strong and mellifluous. He used it like an instrument, easy and flowing. Shan paid close attention and joined in on the chorus, struggling to blend her voice with Ty's deep baritone.

"Stop," Quinn directed after a minute, holding up his hand. The music jangled to a halt. "You haven't sung much with other people," he said to Shan. It wasn't a question.

She shook her head.

"Okay. Be quiet on the next verse. Danny, take the third vocal. I want her to hear how it's supposed to sound." They did another chorus, Dan's voice merging easily with Quinn's and Ty's.

"Wow," she breathed when they finished, "you guys sound fantastic!"

Quinn shrugged. "We've been doing it for a long time. And it's harder to blend male and female voices in a harmony. They have different qualities. When it works, though, it's powerful. And we're going to make it work. Try it again."

They went back into the same piece and she tried harder, emulating what she'd heard Dan do with his voice. After a few minutes, Quinn held up his hand again. "Better, but you still haven't got it. You sing lead and I'll harmonize. Listen to the difference."

They went through it again and Quinn joined her on the chorus. He danced around her main melody, not competing with her voice, but enhancing it. She was shaking with excitement by the time they finished.

She wasn't the only one. "Hot damn!" Ty yelled gleefully. "What a fucking sound! We'd better add some duets to the old repertoire."

Quinn nodded. He wasn't altogether displeased himself. They were good together, as he'd suspected they would be. "Right now she has to learn the playlist. You need a lot of work," he said bluntly and Shan's face fell. "You're going to pick up most of the lead vocals, but there's a few I'll have to keep. They're guy songs," he added, "and Dan and Ty can handle the harmonies temporarily. Not long term, though, because it's hard for Danny to sing and play drums."

"But I don't want to take the lead away," she said. "You're such a good singer."

He nodded. "I am. I'm a good singer. A very good singer. But *you*," he reached out and tapped her lip lightly, "can be a great singer. And you will be, because I'm going to coach you."

Dan rolled his eyes and Ty chuckled. "Here comes Quinntila the Hun," Dan said, sending Shan a sympathetic look. "Better make sure you have your armor on."

Four hours later, Quinn flipped the cover over his keyboard. "We can break for today."

Dan stood and stretched, checking the clock. "Hey, my girl oughta be home soon."

Ty grinned. "I have a date myself tonight. Man, I *love* New York!"

Shan placed Joanie in her case. She couldn't believe they were talking about doing anything at all after the grueling afternoon they'd had. Her shoulder hurt, her back ached, and her fingers felt like she'd held them on a grindstone. Her legs were starting to cramp, too, and her eyes to water, signals that it was time for a fix.

Since none of the guys showed any signs of leaving, Shan excused herself and went into the bathroom. She pulled out the small stash she'd hidden inside her cosmetic bag, pushed aside the heavy black curtain to open the window, and sat down on the toilet, lighting the strawberry-scented candle that resided on the tank. In her bedroom, she used incense to camouflage the fumes.

She discovered that she'd left her tooter there, so she pulled the last few sheets off the toilet paper spindle and used the cardboard tube. Just a couple of hits were enough to quell the jones. Another hit and she'd be feeling fine, but instead she blew out the candle. She returned the stash to her cosmetic bag, spraying air freshener to further disguise the smell.

When she came back to the living room, Ty was gone and Dan had vanished into Denise's bedroom. Quinn was waiting for her. "You're not gigging tonight, are you?"

"No, thank God," she groaned. Her eyes felt fuzzy and she blinked hard to clear them. "I'm exhausted. And starving," she added, realizing she hadn't eaten anything since that morning.

"You want to split a pizza?"

She felt a rush of dismay. She didn't want to go anywhere with *him*. As Dan had predicted, he'd been all over her ass all day. After he finished criticizing her voice, he'd started in on her playing. He had a problem with one of her solos. Too rough, he'd said. Too wild, not enough structure. He'd made her play it over and over till her fingertips felt like chunks of raw hamburger.

"Not tonight. Maybe some other time."

"I'm not asking you for a *date*," Quinn sneered. "You and I aren't finished yet. You need coaching on your vocals and, if you're not gigging, then we're starting tonight."

"But I thought you liked my voice. Why would you want to mess with it?"

"I'm polishing it, not messing with it. You oughta be thanking me, angel. When I coach people at school, I get forty bucks an hour. Now, what do you like on your pizza?"

"Mushrooms and pepperoni," she said meekly. She went for the phone, suppressing a sigh. It was going to be a long night. In fact, she was starting to think it was going to be a long summer.

chapter 7

For the next week, Shan spent four to five hours a day practicing with the band and another two being coached by Quinn each night. Every minute she wasn't practicing, she was scrambling to memorize the twenty-six songs she had to know for the Saturday night playlist. She'd never worked so hard in her life.

Her head had to be clear so she dosed on small amounts of heroin, but had to do it often to keep stable. She developed a routine of dosing when she first got up, again during midafternoon, once more before they started their evening coaching session, and at bedtime, to take her through the night. She knew it was the least she could get away with, because she could feel the jones setting in just before she dosed.

When she thought about it, which she tried not to do, she acknowledged that the H was the dominant force in her life. She had to arrange everything around it—her time, her work, even her sleep—and she hated being such a slave to it. She fantasized about getting clean, being able to live like a normal person, but she knew it wouldn't happen anytime soon. Turkeying was definitely not compatible with the nonstop work required by her new band.

At least she had plenty of H. The rock she'd taken from Jorge was huge, enough to keep her supplied for a long time, and so far she'd seen no sign of its owner. She'd always been careful to conceal her address from him and she'd cancelled all her solo gigs, so it would be hard for him to track her down that way. Still, she experienced a twinge of unease every time she scraped a chunk off the rock.

When she wasn't dosing, she didn't think about Jorge much because she was so focused on learning the new music. She loved playing with her talented bandmates, although Quinn's coaching sessions were less enjoyable. They consisted of a grueling, repetitive series of voice exercises that went on and on. He worked with her in her bedroom, which was tiny. Quinn usually sprawled across her futon with a beer in his hand while Shan stood. Sometimes he made her sing with her hand over her abdomen to feel her breathing. Occasionally he had her play guitar while she sang. She had to practice the scales endlessly and it was torturous. Her throat was killing her by the end of every session.

When she complained, his face took on the condescending sneer she was growing to hate. "It hurts because you're singing in your throat. If you don't learn to control that, you won't have a voice left in a couple of years. You'll burn it out. Now do it again, and pull it down into your chest this time." And so it went, on and on.

Band practice was much more pleasant most of the time. Quinn was still a tyrant, but at least there were three of them in his line of fire. She was the usual target for his abuse, but he jumped all over Dan and Ty, too, if he disapproved of something they did.

At first she wondered why they tolerated it. Dan was an incredibly adept drummer and Ty's intricate bass playing approached the level of a virtuoso. Why did they put up with him?

Because he was invariably right, she discovered. No matter what musical debate erupted, he had an answer and could always back it up. Also, while the rest of them occasionally went flat or hit a wrong note, Quinn never did. He was always on pitch, on key, on time. It was uncanny.

Once she asked Dan why no one ever challenged his decisions. There were four of them in the band, after all, but Quinn was unquestionably the leader. He always had the final word.

"Well, it's his band, technically," Dan told her. "He formed it, named it, then handpicked the rest of us. And, musically speaking, Quinn is a genius. He plays keyboards, piano, and bass expertly, and drums and guitar well. You already know he's a great singer, and you ought to hear him on hand percussion. He's an awesome composer, too. He wrote all our originals."

She'd figured that out already, because she'd been barked at for suggesting minor changes to the arrangements on a couple of them. "I know he's brilliant," Shan said, "but he's not willing to listen to anybody else and I can't believe how mean he can be."

An unpleasant incident had occurred at practice that day. She'd been searching for a particular high note and she'd scooped, her voice wavering uncertainly. Scooping was one of Quinn's pet peeves and he'd swooped on her.

"You sound like a reamed-out sow squealing an orgasm," he'd snarled. "If I wanted a hack, I'd have at least gotten one old enough to get in the clubs without a hassle. You're supposed to be a professional. You'd better start sounding like one," he'd concluded in a threatening tone.

She'd gone white-faced as both Ty and Dan turned on Quinn in a chorus of indignation. He'd backed off sullenly, but she'd been shaken and sang badly for the rest of the day, quaking every time he looked in her direction. "It was so humiliating," she moaned to Dan later. "And what if he decides he wants me out? I'll be screwed. I gave up all my other gigs, and you and Ty always go along with whatever he says."

Dan was quick to reassure her. "That won't happen. First of all, we don't *always* let him have the last word and, secondly, he's really impressed with you. He told me so himself."

Shan was still dubious. During their session that night she continued to sing badly, her voice uncertain and lacking her usual self-assurance. When she scooped again during a standard voice exercise, she cringed visibly and stared at Quinn, awaiting a verbal blitzkrieg.

He sighed, then sat up and patted the futon beside him. "C'mere."

She hesitated.

"Come on," he said. "I won't bite you."

She perched on the edge of the futon and eyed him with mistrust. *Here it comes,* she told herself. *You're not going to work out, he'll say. Sorry, but that's rock 'n' roll.*

"I owe you an apology," he said instead. "I had no right to lambaste you like I did today, especially not in front of the others, and I can see that it's really upset you. I acted like a dick," he concluded, not without difficulty, "and I'm sorry."

"You mean I'm not fired?"

"Fired?" His eyes widened. "Why would you think you were fired?"

She pulled her legs in against her chest. "It seems like you're not happy with anything about me. I've been just waiting for the axe to fall."

"Just because I critique you doesn't mean I'm not happy with you. You're a superb musician," he said. "One of the best I've come across."

She eyed him doubtfully. "Well, why are you so mean, then? Don't get me wrong, I appreciate all the time you spend with me," she added when he frowned. "I'm learning a lot, but you get so frustrated with me . . ."

"The main thing that's frustrating me is your fucking lack of self-confidence. You're a great singer, or rather, you *could* be a great singer, and you've got the potential to be an ace guitarist, but you never will be until you start believing in yourself."

All of a sudden she'd had enough of him. "I *do* believe in myself, in my music, but this is intimidating. *You're* intimidating," she clarified, "and I'm sick of you yelling at me all the time. I told you up front that I wasn't at the same level as the rest of you. I'm trying as hard as I can."

"I know you are," he said, "and it won't be long before you're completely up to speed. All you need is training, which is what I'm trying to give you. You already have the talent. Come on," he urged as her green eyes narrowed. "Haven't you spent enough time around me to know I wouldn't say that if I didn't mean it?"

"Yes, I guess I have." She smiled a little. "You're not big on compliments."

"No, I'm not, but I don't mind giving credit where it's due. I can't believe how far you've come in just the last few days. You should be excited about it. I am."

A warmth started building in her chest that tingled as it spread all the way down to her toes. "I can't tell you how much it means to hear you say that, Quinn, because I respect your opinion more than anyone else I know. About music, at least," she added with a little laugh.

"Well, I'll take that as a compliment. And I'm glad to hear that you believe in your music, because sometimes you act as if you're just figuring out that you have talent. People pay to listen to you every time you gig, though. What did you think they were paying for?"

"I know that a lot of people like my stuff," she said, "and it's a good thing, because it's all I really know how to do. It really was a revelation when I realized I could use it as a way of supporting myself."

"How did it come about?" he asked curiously.

She cast her eyes down at the futon. "I used to play in the subway stations," she said, after a moment. "At first it was just a warm place to work on my tunes, but then people started dropping money into my guitar case."

"Sounds rough, if the subway was the only place you had to get out of the cold."

Shan looked up and examined his face for derision. There wasn't a trace of it. "It was, I guess, but it turned out to be the best thing that ever happened to me. I made okay money for a busker, but it wasn't really enough to live on. There was one guy who I'd see in the Washington Square station, though. He always listened, then dropped me a twenty. One night he asked me if I wanted to audition for his club, the Grotto." She grinned. "It was Mike Shapiro."

Quinn chuckled. "Not bad, for your first gig."

"I know. It still blows my mind that people like my music enough to pay for it. It's a great feeling." She beamed at him. "Almost as great as hearing you say I'm as talented as all of you."

Her smile seemed to hit him right between the eyes. He turned his face away. "Okay, let's get back to the scales. And don't scoop them this time."

The next day at practice Quinn was his usual bossy self, but Shan felt better equipped to handle his criticism. He didn't seem quite so scary now and when the band was rehearsing one of his originals, a blues-rocking tune called "Wanderlust," she improvised a little on the guitar solo.

"This tune should be tight as a drum," Quinn growled. "Why can't you get this right?"

"I think I do have it right," she said, quaking inside.

Quinn cocked his head, the beginnings of his customary sneer moving across his face. "Come again? I don't recall a ragged, nonintegrated guitar riff being part of the arrangement. And I think I'd probably remember, since I wrote the goddamn song."

"I think the way we do this song is dull," Shan said. "It has no groove to it."

Dan winced and glanced at Ty, who shook his head. Quinn was staring at her as if he couldn't believe his ears.

"*You're* telling *me* that you think my music is boring? Give me a break. Don't start thinking you're a composer just because a few people tossed quarters at you in the subway."

She drew back, stung. "I'm sorry I ever told you about that, you insensitive jerk! I should have known you wouldn't understand. You don't know anything about emoting or moving people with your music. Yours is as mechanical as a metronome."

"You a music critic, all of a sudden?" he inquired, his brow descending.

"No, I'm not," she shot back, screwing up her face and scowling right back at him, "but how come everything we play has to be *your* style? There are four of us in this band, you know. It's not just the Quinn Marshall show."

His face reddened and he glared at her silently for a few moments. Then, in a quick reversal, he nodded. "All right," he said. "We can try it."

Her mouth fell open. "We can?"

"Sure." He shrugged. "I said I wanted you to develop more confidence. If this is what it takes, let's give it a try. Even though I happen to think you're dead wrong."

He let her do it her way, adding a new, looser interpretation to the guitar riff around the tight rhythm line and, when they finished, Dan looked thoughtful. "We might be on to something here," he said, keeping a wary eye on Quinn. "What do you think?"

Quinn didn't answer. He was too busy staring at his forearms, watching the goose bumps rise up in tight little knots.

During their session that night Quinn was moody and noncommunicative, but Shan was feeling playful, high on the triumph of the afternoon. She ran through her usual series of voice exercises without eliciting a single comment from him. After she deliberately sang flat without getting a reaction, she took a thin paperback from her bookcase.

The book bounced off his head. "Ow!" he yelled, rubbing his injured cranium.

She grinned. "When I sing flat without you letting out a single swear, I know something's wrong with you. What's up?"

"Nothing," he said testily. "I'm just tired."

"An admission of a human failing? That's not like you, either, Quinn."

"Well, there *is* something I want to talk to you about." He waited until she flopped down beside him. "I think we ought to try some composing. Together, I mean."

"Really?" She knew he didn't like to collaborate. He preferred doing it on his own and invited input only after he'd completed a piece to his own satisfaction.

"Yeah. My compositions tend to be very structured and methodical. Your stuff is looser, a little more off-beat. I wonder what would happen if we combined those two elements. I'm thinking we might produce some pretty cool stuff, if you're into it."

"Are you kidding? I'd love it!" He didn't return her smile, just continued to eye her morosely. "Why do you look like you're sorry I said yes?"

"I just don't know if I'm up for all the angst. We'll probably argue all the time."

"So what? We do that anyway."

His gloomy expression dissolved as he laughed. "Okay, we'll give it a try." He got up and pulled her to her feet. "Let's drink on it."

Shan followed him to the kitchen, the beatific smile still lighting up her face. They were alone in the loft, since Oda was working and Denise was out somewhere with Dan. She boosted herself up onto the counter as he took a couple of beers from the fridge. He had great hands, she noticed as he passed her one. Firm and capable looking, with golden hairs growing up the backs of his forearms.

"I'm allowed to drink tonight," she observed, accepting the frosty bottle.

"We're not gigging. Different rules apply at home, angel."

"Why do you always call me that?" she asked. "Is it one of your generic girl names, like 'darlin' is?"

He took a long slug of his beer and thought about it. "No," he concluded. "I've never called anyone that before. It's because, the first time I heard you sing, that was what I thought you sounded like." He rested his arms on the counter and gazed up at her, a lock of blond hair slipping down his forehead and over his eyes. "An angel. Sweet and pure and beautiful."

Shan felt the warmth spread through her again. Impulsively, she reached out to smooth away the lock of hair.

It was the first time she'd touched him. The contact was electric. His eyes shot up to meet hers and she stared at him with a spellbound expression, a startled awareness dawning on her face.

He drew back. "Break's over," he said, pushing her off the counter. She headed toward the bedroom, but he hesitated. "Let's work in the living room," he said, a trifle uneasily. "Better acoustics."

At the end of Friday's practice, Quinn announced they could take the next day off. "We don't want to sound stale tomorrow night."

"Right," Dan said. "We need to make a good first impression." Ty nodded in agreement, setting aside his bass.

Shan rubbed her eyes, which were starting to water. The practice had run longer than usual and her jones was beginning to kick in. She saw Quinn watching her and suppressed a sigh. No day off for you, he'd say. Had to work on her voice, or her solos, or her rhythm. Needed more work, more practice, more polish.

"What are you going to wear tomorrow night?" he asked instead.

She was flabbergasted. It seemed an outlandish question, coming from him. She could show up stark naked and he'd be too busy watching her picking to even notice.

Well. He *might* notice. "Uh, I don't know. I haven't really thought about it."

"You're not planning to dress like that, are you?" He pointedly looked her up and down.

She was wearing jeans and a T-shirt, her hair pulled back in a ponytail. Perfectly acceptable attire for band practice.

She started a slow burn. Her voice and her playing weren't enough? He had to start in on her clothes? "No, I'm not. I know how to dress for a gig."

"I've never seen you in anything but jeans," he said. "Do you own a dress?"

She didn't, actually. She'd never needed one for anything. Also, she didn't like to show her legs. Too many scars. "No, I don't."

"You ought to pick one up tomorrow. You're a cute chick," he said off-handedly, "but you downplay your looks. Maybe you could get something a little more on the feminine side. It'll give the people something to look at."

Her cheeks burned. "Great. I'll pick up my metal cone tits from the dry cleaners."

Ty whooped, Dan gave her a high five, and she was gratified to see even Quinn break into a smile. And he had a nice smile, she noted. Really nice. When he smiled, the irritation with which he normally regarded her dissolved and he looked endearingly boyish.

He'd called her cute, too. Just why that pleased her so much she wasn't sure.

"Okay." He chuckled. "I'm not a wardrobe consultant. I'll leave it up to you."

So the next day she went shopping, a pastime she'd rarely indulged in. As she wandered down West Broadway, a flash of dusky green caught her eye. She went closer to examine a spill of silk in the window of an artsy boutique.

She went into the store, emerging half an hour later with a satisfied expression and a shopping bag. She'd spent way more than she could afford but, for once, she'd shut Quinn up.

Maybe.

chapter 8

Shan had just finished dosing when she heard a knock at the front door, then a chorus of male voices. She went into the living room, where she found her bandmates and Denise. The guys were stacking the gear in preparation for the gig and she lingered in the doorway, hoping to make an impact with her entrance.

Ty was the first to notice her. He whistled. "*Damn,* honey! You're looking fine tonight." He did, too, in khakis and a red silk shirt that shimmered against his dark skin.

All eyes turned Shan's way. Quinn was kneeling beside the keyboard, winding up the power cable. He was dressed in black jeans with a braided leather belt and a black button-front shirt.

Shan was wearing the jade-green sarong she'd admired in the boutique. It was wrapped and knotted around her slender hips, falling to a midcalf length. With it, she wore a black strappy top of raw silk, with shiny beads adorning the scoop neckline. She'd replaced her silver nose stud with a rhinestone one, then rubbed glitter gel on her shoulders and arms. She sparkled when she moved.

"Fabulous!" Denise pronounced.

"Hot," Dan agreed. "You look awesome, princess." He was dressed up too, for Dan. He'd foregone his usual worn, faded jeans for a more intact pair and a bright-yellow wife beater.

"Thanks," Shan said. "I ought to, for what I spent. I hope you were right about what we'd pull in tonight, because I just blew my rent money," she told Quinn.

"Don't worry. I am." He looked ultra hot, she decided. His blond fairness against his black clothing made a sensual contrast, all darkness and light. "Okay," he said, rising. "Let's go."

Shan concealed a rush of disappointment. He hadn't even noticed her transformation.

But as she hoisted an amplifier, Quinn grabbed her arm. "Don't do that," he said. "I don't want you to tear anything. You look too perfect." She glowed as he took the amp from her.

The guys hauled the equipment to the service elevator, but Shan and Denise took the stairs and lingered next to the van. Shan was smiling to herself as she carefully smoothed her new skirt.

"Are you sleeping with Quinn?" Denise asked abruptly.

Shan's smile froze, then she gaped at her. "Why would you think that?"

Denise was watching her closely. "Well, he was all over you that night they came for dinner. He's obviously hot for you. Besides, he's always in your room lately."

Shan was still openmouthed. "No! I mean, of course I'm not sleeping with Quinn. That's the craziest thing I've ever heard." Although it was all she'd been thinking about since the night he'd asked if she wanted to compose with him. "We're bandmates, that's all," she said, flushing.

"Good." Denise nodded.

Shan eyed her quizzically. "Why would you care?"

"Because he's bad news for anyone who's not one-night-stand material," Denise replied. "He's a real slut, you know. He sleeps with a different girl every night. They think he's a nice guy because he turns on the charm, but he's done with them once he has them. He doesn't even give them a courtesy call, just disappears. It's disgusting and you shouldn't get mixed up with him," she added, the color rising in her cheeks, "because I know you aren't casual about your involvements. I mean, in all the time we've been living together I haven't seen you go out on a single date."

A chill had settled around Shan's heart. "Are you sure? He doesn't seem that cold to me." Although, she reflected uneasily, it would explain that scene with the waitress at the Grotto.

"He's cold, all right." Denise's face hardened and she lowered her voice as the subject of their conversation came out of the building, followed by Dan and Ty. "Just ask him about his 'golden rules.'"

Shan took her guitar and climbed into the van while the guys loaded the equipment. When they finished Quinn slid in beside her, although she noticed there was a lot more room next to Ty. Joanie was taking up half her seat, so Quinn was practically in her lap.

"You nervous?" he asked her.

"A little," Shan said. "I hope I don't blow any lyrics."

He put his arm around her. "Don't stress over it. Just relax."

She tittered, pulling away a bit. "You'll get glitter all over your shirt."

"So I'll sparkle. I'm not worried." He drew her back into the crook of his arm and inspected her face. "You're wearing makeup. You don't usually, do you?"

"No." She was very conscious of his hand resting on her shoulder, the pressure of his fingertips against her skin. "Only when I'm gigging. The lights make me look washed out."

His eyes seemed to caress her face. "You don't have to worry about that tonight, angel. You look stunning." The passing streetlights reflected off his blond hair, giving it a silvery glow.

"Thanks," she said, flustered. "I wanted to wear my hair up, but I couldn't get it to stay. I have too much hair. It's always such a mess." She knew she was babbling and bit her lip. His physical proximity was making her jittery, almost like a jones. She could feel his long, muscular thigh pressing against hers and, as she breathed in the citrusy scent of his aftershave, she knew she'd never in her life been so drawn to a man.

Quinn was having a similar revelation as he slipped his hand through her long, springy curls, lifting up a fistful and rubbing it against his cheek in a completely natural, unpremeditated gesture. "It's not a mess," he said. "It's beautiful." It was, he thought. Soft as a cloud and scented with that tantalizing woodsy fragrance. He'd wanted to bury his face in this hair from the minute he'd first laid eyes on her. He wondered what it would be like to hold her on top of him and have that hair surrounding him, like a curtain blocking out the world. He'd sure like to find out and he was beginning to think he was going to have to sooner or later, jail bait or not.

He once again noticed her lips. Soft and full and bubble-gum pink. The urge to kiss them was overwhelming. He let go of her hair and fit his hand back over her shoulder, feeling her velvety flesh under his palm. She wasn't pulling away this time.

"Quinn?" she whispered. Her green eyes were smoky, reflecting the passion in his gaze.

"Mmm?" He raised his hand to play with a soft curl dangling in front of her ear.

"What are your golden rules?"

He blinked. "What?"

"Your golden rules." She was watching him closely. "What are they?"

Quinn's eyes shot toward the front seat, where Denise was scolding Dan about something. When he looked back at Shan her face was clouded, revealing something close to disappointment.

The overhead light flashed and he blinked, then realized the van had stopped. Shan twisted out of his grasp. "We're here," she said, suddenly cool as ice cream.

He got out and turned to help her, but she jumped down without his assistance, holding her long skirt up in one hand and passing him without a backward glance as she proceeded toward the back of the van. He scratched his head and followed her.

Ty and Dan were stacking the gear on the sidewalk. Shan reached for a couple of guitar cases and headed for the service entrance to the Grotto. Quinn grasped a pile of equipment and followed her. She was at the bar talking to Oda, so he continued to the stage and knelt, setting down the gear. In a moment Shan came up behind him, put down the guitars, and moved away without a word.

"Hey," he called after her. She stopped, looking back over her shoulder. He crooked his finger and she retraced her steps. Still kneeling, he watched her approach, her face expressionless.

"I can usually tell when I say or do something to piss you off," he said, "but I can't think of anything during the last five minutes. Am I missing something?"

"No," she said, folding her arms across her chest. "I'm not pissed off."

"Bullshit, angel. *You*," he pointed at her forcefully, "are pissed off at me about something or other. I'd like you to tell me what it is. We have to be onstage in an hour. I don't need this kind of crap right now."

"But I'm not pissed off," she repeated. "I haven't said a word."

"I know. That's my point exactly. Why the silent treatment?"

Her face changed, just a touch, and he thought he saw a hint of regret in her emerald eyes. "Let's just say I gave you a test and you didn't pass." She turned and went back outside to the van.

Forty-five minutes later, Quinn snagged an empty pitcher off the amplifier. "I'm going for more beer before we start. You want another Coke?" Shan shook her head as he headed for the bar.

They'd struck a tacit truce, each recognizing that any tensions between them had to be put aside, at least until after the gig. It was hard to fight with someone and play with them at the same time. Another good reason not to mix it up with her, Quinn decided. Nothing good could come of it, no matter how hot they were for each other, and it wasn't like he was in the market for a girlfriend. As a rule, he only saw women whom he felt could appreciate a good bone dance without getting syrupy on him.

He misread them occasionally and wound up in the uncomfortable position of having to extricate himself from the clutches of some smitten female. He always backed off fast in such situations, his powerful aversion to attachment causing whatever desire he felt for the lady in question to evaporate. He had one focus in his life—music—and the last thing he needed was a lovesick chick demanding his time and energy.

He felt a light touch at his elbow. Turning, he found himself face to face with the object of his uneasy reflections. "We're finished with sound check," she reported. "Are you ready?"

"Yup. Are *you*?" She nodded and he followed her back to the stage, gave a high sign to Bruce at the sound board and the lights dimmed as they swung into their opening number, a hot Santana cover that usually got people moving.

Quinn brought his mouth close to the microphone. "Hi there, ladies and gents. We're Quinntessence. Here's a little fire to light up your dancing feet." He launched into the opening vocal, his hands flashing over the keys with lightning-like precision, although the rest of his body didn't move much. Some musicians were big on emoting physically, but he wasn't one of them. At most, when a tune really rocked him, he'd sway a little on the balls of his feet.

Not like Shan, who played with her whole body. When they switched to a classic Beatles medley, the intensity of her voice was mirrored by her lithe, fluid movements as she waltzed around the stage with her guitar. It was a synchronicity of sight and sound, musician nearly indistinguishable from instrument in the perfection of their union, and

Quinn congratulated himself again on his decision to put her out in front. By the end of the song the whole place was singing along with her.

They shifted to one of his tunes next, which was his usual formula. Two covers to grab the crowd's attention, then an original. This one was a forceful rock ballad called "Voluntary Exile."

Fire lines the road I walked, consuming me with shame
Burning all that once was good can only bring me pain
For simple peace of mind I turn to total isolation
It may be weakness but I find a sort of strange salvation

It was one of his favorites. The lyrics were deeply personal and hearing them sung so powerfully by such a tiny, fragile-looking girl made them even more compelling. The song wound to a close with a hearty round of applause.

By their first break, they had the crowd grooving. Shan turned to Quinn as he emerged from behind his keyboard. "How do you think it's going?"

"Okay," he said with a nod, "but watch the edges. Tight, remember?"

"*I remember.*" He watched her stomp off toward the bar, wishing he'd said something a little nicer.

When Quinntessence returned to the stage for the second set, they were charged up and ready to rock. They started off with a Faith No More cover, then upshifted to Queen's "Somebody to Love." Shan adored Queen and worshipped Brian May, but she privately felt that the Quinntessence playlist relied a little too heavily on this type of music: artsy, prog rock–inspired stuff that was complicated and interesting, but not particularly fun or danceable. She hoped that down the road the band would be willing to add a few more sprightly tunes, some Madonna or Cyndi. Throw in some Springsteen, maybe, or Guns N' Roses. She'd love to try her hand at "Welcome to the Jungle" with such a talented group.

Of course, *this* particular Queen song was a classic, so people were up and moving. When they switched to "Wanderlust," the crowd was ready to rock, just as Quinn had said they would be.

A lifetime of time before me
The open road is what I see
The wanderlust is beckoning
It's the thing that keeps me free

And, when they finished the bluesy tune, the response of the crowd was so enthusiastic that the intro to the next song was barely audible over the applause.

It really was annoying, the way Quinn was always right.

At the end of the night, Quinntessence was called back for three encores. When they were finally allowed off the stage, they concentrated on celebrating. Shan hung out at the bar with Oda, feeling distinctly out of place. Dan and Denise were huddled in a cozy, private conversation and Ty had hooked up with a cute hostess who liked bass players. She didn't know where Quinn was.

Onstage, he'd slipped back into the role of lofty instructor, signaling with a frown when she made a mistake and giving her barely perceptible nods of approval when she pulled off a difficult piece. During the breaks, he'd mostly ignored her.

By two A.M., Shan wasn't even sure he was still there. Her legs had begun to cramp, so she slipped outside for a quick fix. When she came back, she spotted him at a remote corner of the bar. He wasn't alone. There was a woman beside him. She had long, straight blond hair and long, tanned legs; everything about her looked long and slim and tight except her breasts, which were huge, straining the tiny tank she wore. Shan could see down her cleavage from halfway across the room. She could also see Quinn's hand on her leg. His thumb was massaging her inner thigh.

She joined Denise, who gestured at Quinn. "See? There's his 'frequent flyer' for tonight. That's what he calls them." She wrinkled her nose.

Shan didn't answer. She couldn't have even if she wanted to, since the pain blossoming in her chest seemed to have lodged in her throat.

Dan was chuckling as he rose. "Ready to call it a night, ladies?" Denise followed him outside while Ty went to check in with Quinn. Shan paused, then trailed after Ty.

Quinn looked up as Ty gestured toward the door. "We're splitting. You coming?"

"No. I think the road ends here tonight. Right, Jillian?" he said, fixing the blonde with a questioning smile. She giggled and simpered, clutching his arm.

"Okay. See you tomorrow." Ty headed for the door and Shan followed, keeping her face impassive.

Quinn watched Shan turn away and wished with all his might that he was going with her. It wasn't even that he wanted to fuck her right now—he just wanted to hold her. His breath caught as he realized that he'd never had a thought like that about anyone in his entire life.

"Hey, angel?" He waited until she looked back. "You made me proud."

She stared at him for a moment. Then she took a step toward him, and another, and suddenly her arms were around him in a spontaneous hug. He froze, startled, then held her slender body close for just a moment. When she moved away, he gave her waist a regretful little squeeze.

"Good night," she said wistfully and then he watched her walk away.

The "good night" had sounded like "good-bye" and he supposed it was, in a way. Good-bye to something that wasn't going to happen. Nothing had been said directly, nor did anything need to be said. Through the odd connection they'd forged, they seemed able to communicate perfectly well without words.

He summoned up a smile and turned back to the leggy blonde.

chapter 9

"There's no point in pretending we're composing together if I'm going to wind up doing it all myself," Quinn said. He was in Shan's bedroom where he'd spent the better part of two days. They'd been experimenting with a melody he'd come up with, but he had yet to wrest a single constructive comment from her.

"You're my mentor," Shan said. "It's hard to think of myself as an equal."

"You know, during band practice you're on my case constantly. Why are you sitting there like a mute now, when I'm actually inviting your input?"

"No, I am *not* on your case constantly during practice," she told him heatedly. "You just can't stand it when anybody disagrees with you."

"Well, all you're doing now is wasting my time. I didn't ask you to do this for the pleasure of your company. I don't need a goddamn fan hanging around."

That pissed her off, as he'd expected it would. "Fine. I think the hook on this tune sucks."

He suppressed a spurt of annoyance. This was what he'd asked for, after all. "All right. What's wrong with it?"

"It's completely predictable, so it's dull," she said. "Why not do some kind of a fake out on the bridge? Let the music rev up as if you're going into the chorus, then shift into the second verse instead."

She had his attention now. "Like how?"

"Like *this*," she said, picking up her guitar.

The change Shan suggested added an appealing groove to the tune, especially after she produced a set of lyrics, a storytelling song about hope and thwarted expectations that she'd been working on for quite some time. "I conceived of it as a folk rock song," she told him, "but I think it could work as hard rock."

Quinn thought so, too. He liked the lyrics, enough to modify the lines to fit his hard-hitting tune, and within a few days they had a rollicking, balls-to-the-wall piece they christened "The Only Perfect One."

Dancing last night at the ball, I bumped into a pretty girl
She had just one slipper on and a mile-high pile of curls
She said "Have you seen my shoe made out of glass?
If my stepsister took it I will kick her ass"
Oh, the only really perfect one
is the one that got away

"This song is what kicks ass!" Ty declared when he heard it. Dan nodded so vigorously he almost fell off his drum throne.

Quinn grinned and Shan could tell he thought so, too. They had their first collaborative song.

A week later, the whole band was working on their second one. As they practiced, the morning rain struck a staccato rhythm against the cast-iron exterior of Shan's building. It was loud, but seemed only a backbeat to the music pounding inside the loft.

You've got to be tough, you learn to be mean
If you're making your home in the big city streets
You give up your spirit but live on your dreams
When you have to survive in the big city heat

When Quinn raised his hand, the metal tempo ground to a halt. "Not bad," he said over the rain. "It's coming together pretty well."

Shan tapped her fingers on the neck of her Peavey. "The arrangement is fine, but those lyrics need work."

"You wrote most of them," he reminded her, an edge creeping into his tone.

"I know. Now I'm thinking the song should end with a more positive message."

"The lyrics are fine. In a metal tune, the music is what matters anyway."

"The lyrics are just as important," Shan insisted, "and I think they're too dark."

Quinn snorted as Ty heaved a deep sigh. "I didn't realize we were going for social commentary here. Who are you, Joni fucking Mitchell, like you call your guitar?"

"Don't knock Joni," Shan said, as Dan rose from the drum kit and collapsed onto the pile of floor pillows. "She brings social issues into a public arena, unlike *your* heroes who are all form and no content."

"Like who?" he challenged.

"Like Rick *fucking* Wakeman," she shot back.

Dan sat up and flung a pillow through the air, whacking Quinn squarely in the face before he could respond. "Will the two of you please *shut the hell up*?" he roared.

It was such an uncharacteristic outburst from mellow Dan that both Shan and Quinn were startled into laughter. Dan wrapped another pillow around his head with a groan.

Ty set his Fender Jazz aside and cleared his throat. "It's time we set some new ground rules."

Quinn regarded him dubiously. "What do you mean *new* rules?"

"You're spending too much time debating every fucking thing. We're supposed to be *practicing*. That's why we call it *band practice*."

"*We're* the ones coming up with the tunes you're so excited about," Quinn said.

"Q's right," Shan chimed in. "*We're* doing the work. All you have to do is learn the songs."

Dan sighed. "You know, I've noticed that it seems to be just fine for the two of you to insult each other, but if me or Ty state a different opinion, then one of you immediately jumps in to defend the other one. How is that fair?" Quinn shrugged and Shan thrust her chin out, frowning.

Ty tried again. "Look, we're not saying anything negative about the music. It's the balls—we're all in agreement there. It's your method that needs to change."

"Ty's exactly right," Dan said. "When we're together, we should be concentrating on learning the new material. There's *four* of us, remember? It isn't just the O'Hara-Marshall show."

Shan's eyes went huge with guilty realization. "I'm sorry. I never thought of it that way."

"I'm not sorry," Quinn said disagreeably. "The music we're turning out benefits all of us, and you two"—he pointed at Dan and Ty—"are blocking."

"Can't we just go back to the way we handled your writing before? He always had it finished before he played it for us," Ty told Shan.

"But we're bringing it to you as we go along so you can be part of the process," Shan said. "This way, the whole band is contributing."

"They contribute plenty after the songs are written," Quinn said, "and that's how it should be. You were the one who insisted on a group love fest, which I knew would turn into a cluster fuck."

"But don't you think it's better if we all work together?" Shan persisted, ignoring Quinn. "It's a more organic way of writing and then the songs belong to all of us, not just me and Quinn."

"You two are having enough trouble collaborating just with each other," Dan said. "If all four of us are involved, we won't get anything done at all."

"Right," Ty said, "so let's drink on it. All composing takes place *outside* of band practice. Agreed?"

"Agreed," Quinn said immediately. Shan nodded reluctantly and, as a clink of bottles carried the motion, she swiped a hand across her eyes. They were a little watery and she was perspiring, too. "Excuse me for a minute."

Dan waited until she left the room, then leaned forward to fix Quinn with an evil grin. "Hey, Mr. Footloose," he whispered, "who's pussy whipped *now*?"

Quinn's face turned to granite. "Certainly not me."

"Bullshit," Dan jeered as Ty chuckled. "I can't believe the shit that little girl gives you. And you're not even fucking her!"

Quinn scowled. He didn't have a good comeback, because he definitely did put up with more shit from Shan than he'd ever put up with from anyone else, male or female. Dan's barbs were right on, which made them supremely irritating.

Not that he was whipped, he assured himself as Shan came back, now dry-eyed and composed. Pussy struck, maybe, but not pussy whipped. There was a difference. A big one.

She settled down on the pillows next to Quinn. "They're right," she said to him, "and I feel terrible. I never meant to act that way."

"You're hanging out too much with Quinntila here," Dan said, "and you're picking up his bad habits."

"Not much chance of that," she assured him, "unless I acquire a taste for inflatable blondes."

Quinn raised an eyebrow. "I never said I was opposed to an occasional brunette."

He loved her curly hair and was always ruffling the shiny locks playfully. There was one little curl in particular that fascinated him. It dangled down her forehead just over her right eyebrow. Even when she pulled the rest of her hair into a braid, that one curl escaped defiantly.

He grabbed that little curl now and gave it a tug, but she tossed her head to yank it out of his grasp. "I'm not your type," she said. "You're just as rigid with your women as you are with your music."

"I'm all for equal opportunity, though."

"I'll bet you are," Ty chortled, "especially when you're rigid."

Quinn rose and flipped the cover over his keyboard.

"Are we stopping?" Ty asked.

"Might as well. You've completely destroyed my concentration." Quinn dropped to his haunches to wind up the power cable to his Kurzweil. His T-shirt slipped out of the back of his jeans, exposing the bare skin of his lower back. Shan stared, transfixed.

"Give it a break," Dan said. "We've been at it three and a half hours already. Don't want to get stale, right?"

Quinn laughed. "Right." He stood back up, and turned to check the clock. "What do you want to do about dinner?" He looked at Shan.

She quickly pulled her eyes up to his face. "You read my mind."

"Why, you cooking?" he asked hopefully.

"Nope. I'm not a den mother. How about Chinese?"

"You'll never make a good wife," he told her. "You rely too much on take-out."

"So do you. I've never eaten so much pizza in my life."

"Yeah, but I don't want to be a wife," he said with conviction. "Or get one, either."

"Neither do I," she said. "Why should I have to cook some guy's food?"

"I like the Chinese idea," Dan said. "But I'd rather go out. How about if I call Denise and tell her to meet us at Big Wong?"

"Speaking of wives," Quinn snorted. "Works for me, as long as you keep the missus at the other end of the table."

Shan rolled her eyes. "Yes, call her," she told Dan, ignoring Quinn.

Later that night, they came back to the loft for a coaching session. Quinn assumed his customary position on the futon while Shan stood in front of a mic stand with her hand on her diaphragm. He watched her mouth formation as she began the scales.

As her lips shifted position with each note, he noticed again how lush and sensual they were. Watching them positioned against the cylindrical mic led him to idly wonder how they'd feel pressed against another cylindrical piece of equipment.

His erection was instantaneous. And obvious, he realized with dismay. If she happened to glance up, she couldn't help but see that he was standing at full attention.

Abruptly, he rolled over on his stomach and tore his gaze away from her mouth. Instead he concentrated on her breathing. It was a hot night and she was dressed in a cropped white tank that stopped just above her navel. Her hand was resting over her diaphragm and, with each breath, the thin material tightened over her chest.

She wasn't wearing a bra.

Suddenly his jeans felt two sizes too small. He had to get out of that stifling little room before he grabbed her and let her have it, right there on the convenient futon.

Shan broke off in the middle of a *ti* note. "Are you all right?" she asked, with some concern. He'd broken out in a sweat and his face was flushed.

"Fine." He rolled off the futon and scrambled to his feet.

"Are we stopping?" she asked as he stalked into the living room.

"Yes, we're stopping," he said testily, snatching up a stack of sheet music and positioning it strategically in front of his groin. "I'm done coaching you. I have better things to do than listen to you sing the goddamn scales."

Shan drew back, stung. "What's your problem?"

"My problem is that I'm sick and tired of being cooped up in this goddamn place and I'm sick and tired of you, too."

Shan watched, openmouthed, as he stomped out of the loft, slamming the door behind him.

Quinn was preoccupied during the subway ride from SoHo to his sublet in the East Village. When he switched to the F train at Washington Square, someone sat next to him and he didn't even notice.

He jumped when an elbow nudged him and when he turned, he discovered his neighbor Steve Markowitz. Steve was doing his residency at a clinic over near St. Vincent's and Quinn had gotten to know him a little when he'd gone to have a suspicious burning sensation checked out. He had an absolute horror of STDs and was relieved when Steve diagnosed a minor urinary tract infection.

"I said hi," Steve said, "but you seemed lost in thought."

Quinn shrugged. "Long day." He liked Steve. During his visit to the clinic, he'd gotten the third degree regarding sexual history and the young doctor had been taken aback at the number scribbled under PARTNERS. "As a doctor, I'm appalled," Steve had told him. "As a man, I want to know your secret."

They both disembarked at east Eighth Street. "I've had a long one, too," Steve admitted. "Think I'll stop for a beer. Want to join me?"

He indicated a tavern on the corner of Astor Place. Two women were getting out of a cab in front. One was a tall blonde, but it was the other woman who caught Quinn's eye—a petite brunette with curly hair almost the same color as Shan's.

"Sure," he said and followed Steve into the tavern.

chapter 10

Just as Shan slipped the tooter into her mouth, someone rapped on her bedroom door. She jumped, stuffing the foil back in the drawer and slamming it shut. "Yes?"

"You almost ready?" Quinn's voice. "Time to get moving."

"Be right there!" She waited until she heard him move away before retrieving the foil. She finished the hit, then reached for a bottle of Visine to camouflage the redness in her eyes.

"Just in time to watch us finish packing," Dan teased when she came into the living room "Just leaving it to us roadies, huh?"

"She always hauls her share," Ty defended her. "Besides, she looks real cute."

Quinn was carefully fitting the microphones into a cushioned box. There were a dozen of them, Beyerdynamic and Sennheiser. Shan had learned that they were specially ordered and quite expensive. The band had purchased them the year before at Quinn's insistence. They had another set of mics, as well, perfectly respectable Shures, but Quinn was a stickler about sound equipment. "It doesn't matter how well we play if the sound is bad," he'd lectured, more than once.

When Quinn finished arranging the mics, he glanced at Shan. "That new?"

"Yeah. What do you think?" She spun to model her violet slip dress. It was almost sheer, decorated with beaded fringes that gave it a twenties flair, and she'd acquired a pair of sexy spike heels to go with it. Her hair fanned out as she turned, revealing that the dress was backless. Ty whistled and Quinn slid a hand beneath her curls to run his fingers across her bare back.

"Hey!" She leapt away. "No groping!" Every so often, he'd slip out of his usual nonchalance and flirt playfully with her. She found it disconcerting, to say the least.

"You'd better not turn your back on me, then. That little number is way too hot." He began fingering the row of fringes that adorned her neckline.

Denise came out of her bedroom, resplendent in pink pleather and black mesh, and frowned when she saw Quinn's hand on her room-mate. "Go slobber on someone else," she told him, catching hold of Shan's arm and tugging her out of his reach.

The guys began inching the stack of equipment toward the door. Shan took up two of the guitar cases and waited while Denise gave her spiky red hair a last spritz. Together they descended the stairs. "You must be getting sick of hearing the same songs night after night," Shan said.

"A little, but Dan likes it when I come. Besides," Denise added, "it's entertaining to see what Quinn plans to drag home."

"He never takes any of them home, remember? He always goes to their places, so he can get up and leave when he's done."

Denise wrinkled her nose. "God, he's disgusting!"

As they reached the street, Shan noticed that Denise was still grimac-ing with distaste. "You really do hate him, don't you?"

"Yes," Denise said.

"Why?" Shan asked curiously. "I know Quinn can be tough to take sometimes, but your reaction seems way extreme. I mean, he's never done anything to you, has he?"

"I still can't stand him," Denise snapped, her face flushing. "He's such a dick, so rude and self-centered and full of himself." She scowled down at the ground, tracing the curb with the toe of her strappy san-dal. "I wish he'd go back to Boston and stay away from us, because—"

She broke off in midsentence and her blue eyes filled with tears.

"I'm sorry," Shan said quickly. "I didn't mean to pry."

"It's mutual, you know," Denise sniffed. "He hates me just as much as I hate him."

"I'm sure that isn't true," Shan said although she wasn't, entirely. Quinn and Denise sniped at each other constantly, a fact that had be-come even more apparent since he'd been spending so much time at their apartment. She'd noticed it was always Denise who started it, though.

"Yes it is," Denise swiped at her eyes. "Quinn despises me and he doesn't like that I'm with Dan, either. He seems to think I'm going to pull a Yoko and break up the band, but I'd never do that. I'm behind Dan one hundred percent, because he's the best thing that ever happened to me. I don't know what I'd do without him," she concluded with a sob, "so of course I have to go to every gig. Quinn always has so many girls hanging around him. That means they're hanging around Dan, too."

Shan pulled a tissue out of her bag to wipe the dots of mascara from under Denise's eyes. "Oh, Denise, Dan adores you. Anyone can see that. I've never seen him even look at another girl."

"Well, I still worry." Denise took the tissue and mopped her eyes. "Why can't Quinn just get himself a real girlfriend? Then he'd be more like a normal person instead of a slut magnet."

Shan laughed. "You'd better not count on that."

"I won't." Her eyes shot over Shan's shoulder. Quinn was coming down the stairs, laden with a stack of equipment. Her face hardened. "Just fuck 'em and forget 'em. That's all he can handle."

"Talking about me again?" Quinn inquired. "You're *way* too interested in my sex life, Denise. Does Danny maybe need a little instruction?" He smirked at her, but his grin evaporated when he saw the traces of her tears. "Hey, are you all right?"

"None of your business," Denise snapped. "Fuck off, Quinn."

He drew back, startled. "I'm just trying to . . . I mean, you look upset."

"Since when have you cared?" He frowned and opened his mouth to respond. "Just shut up and stay out of my face." She turned her back on him, climbing into the van and slamming the door behind her.

He looked at Shan. "What'd I do this time?" he asked, clearly mystified.

Shan shook her head. *What was up with this?* she wondered, then reached for the cymbal case that topped the pile of equipment in his arms. "Here, let me help with that."

By the time they got to the club, Denise seemed to have recovered. When they arrived, Quinn jumped out of the van and glanced around doubtfully. "What a crummy neighborhood."

Shan slowly climbed out behind him. Crummy was an understatement. The Fuego Club was on 111th Street, right in the heart of Spanish

Harlem. Jorge lived just a couple of blocks away. She hadn't seen any sign of him since that night, but to be this close made her uneasy.

The entrance to the club was between a dilapidated liquor store and a market with the word *Jódete!* spray-painted across its pull-down metal door. There was a sandwich board on the sidewalk. TONIGHT, it proclaimed in blue chalk, QUINGENTÉSIMO.

Shan pointed at the sign. "Doesn't that mean 'fiftieth'?"

"I think it means 'five hundredth,'" Ty replied, and looked to Quinn for confirmation.

Quinn was glaring at Dan. "It's a happening spot," Dan said as he started extracting the drum kit from the back of the van.

There was a group of seedy-looking characters milling in front, waiting for the doors to open. Shan recognized a couple of them from Jorge's place. She knew them only by their street names, White Julio and T-Bone. White Julio had a distinctly Native American cast to his features, so she had no idea how he'd earned his name. T-Bone at least was tall and skeletal, with limp hair and watery eyes. She remembered seeing him the last time she'd been at Desperado's.

She took the guitars then lingered, waiting for Quinn and Dan. "Yo, Shan," T-Bone said. He stretched his lips in a gap-toothed junkie smile.

Shan nodded briefly, running her tongue over her own teeth, and hurried down the steps into the club behind Quinn and Dan. "Friend of yours?" Quinn asked.

"Acquaintance," she said, the color rising in her cheeks. He looked dubious, but made no further comment. He proceeded down the stairs, which led to a corridor. Dan disappeared into a room marked OFICIO and Shan followed Quinn through the set of doors that led into the club. They went to the stage where Quinn deposited the pile of equipment before surveying the interior.

It was startlingly bright, a cavernous space lit by stark fluorescents that Shan hoped would be dimmed when they went onstage. The place had the look of a warehouse, with a cement floor and concrete walls coated with layer upon layer of sprayed-on graffiti. It smelled like an old basement, musty and damp, laced with the fumes of ammonia, cigarettes, and stale beer.

When Dan appeared, Quinn lit into him. "This place," he declared, "is a dump. You are *never* to book us again unless you check with me first."

"You wait. It'll be packed by ten," Dan said. "We'll make a bundle."

"That's not the point. When you book a gig, you have to consider the quality of the venue."

"Oh, sorry," Dan shot back. "I thought this was about making money." Denise nodded vigorously, slipping her hand through Dan's arm and glaring at Quinn.

"It's not *only* about money," Quinn said, ignoring Denise. "It's about image, too."

"Salsa clubs are hot these days," Ty said, but Dan looked crestfallen.

"Great," Quinn said. "We'll play the one Santana tune that we know over and over, all night long."

Ty tried again. "Look, we're here. Can we just play the gig?"

Quinn grumbled under his breath, but pulled out a handful of microphone cables.

By the time they finished setting up, the club had begun to fill. To Shan's relief, the fluorescents were shut off once they took the stage, replaced by softer illumination augmented by a strobe show. The flashing lights made the spray-painted walls shimmer, which Shan thought looked pretty cool. She had to admit the place wasn't all that bad, even with the stink.

Quinn turned out to be right about the crowd, though. They danced, but with a lack of enthusiasm that indicated a clear dissatisfaction with the music. They wanted Latin sound and the Quinntessence brand of hard rock did little to get them fired up. They liked the Santana cover that the band managed to jam on for a full twenty minutes and Shan got them grooving during a sprightly rendition of "Iko Iko," but, aside from those moments, it was a thoroughly uninspired night.

They finished to spotty applause and the whole band was despondent as they broke down their equipment. "I told you," Quinn said to Dan.

"We made a bunch of money," Dan said, "just like *I* told *you*."

"But the crowd hated us. None of these people will ever come hear us again," Quinn said. "If they talk about us at all, it'll be 'Quinntessence? Oh yeah, they were that band that sucked at Fuego.'"

"Don't cha mean 'Quingentésimo'?" Ty snickered.

Shan stayed out of it. She finished packing her guitars, then busied herself putting the mics away. She closed and latched the lid, then turned to the audio cables.

When she was done, she had a neat pile of items to be carried out to the van. She glanced around for Quinn and saw him at the bar hitting on some fake-blond Latina. Ty and Denise were outside and Dan was puffing up the stairs with the snare drum. Shan slid her purse over her arm, took up the mic box, and went out to the corridor that led to the exit.

Just as she reached the stairs, someone grabbed her, hard. Before she could react, she'd been dragged into a room marked HOMBRES. She blinked in the brighter light, then froze. The mic box slipped out of her hand, dropping to the floor with a *thunk*.

Jorge had her by the arm, his lips twisted in an ugly sneer. "I been on the lookout for you."

Shan didn't respond. She felt herself shaking and knew he could feel it, too.

"Nobody's seen you in so long I thought maybe you took off," he said, "but then my man T-Bone told me he seen you playing here tonight."

She found her voice. "Jorge, I know I owe you money."

"You bet your sweet ass you do, *querida*." He gave her arm a painful squeeze.

"I can give you some of it now. Here." She fumbled at her purse with her free hand, pulling out the wad of bills that was her cut from tonight. "It's almost four hundred. I know it's not enough, but—"

"No, it ain't." He pocketed it anyway. "You owe me another two grand." His fingers were like a vice around her wrist. She could feel her bones grinding together.

"I . . . I can give you more in a couple of days. I'm making good money now." She stopped talking when she heard Quinn's voice out in the corridor.

Jorge was watching her. "Don't want them hearing, do ya?" His mouth spread in a sly grin. "I'm guessing they wouldn't be so thrilled if they knew you was a junk whore."

Shan could hear Quinn and Dan arguing and waited until their voices faded before she spoke again. "That's all I have. Take it or leave it."

"Maybe I'll take it and a little more." He gave her a sudden shove and she stumbled back against the wall. "I'm still willing to negotiate. How 'bout you work some of it off?"

When she smelled his fetid breath in her face, she raised both hands and shoved him, hard. Then there was a metallic *click* and she felt the sharp point of a blade against her stomach.

She didn't stop to think, just lashed out with her spike heel. She caught him in the shin and he faltered, just enough that she could pull away. She bolted for the door, kicking off her shoes.

Barefoot, she darted into the corridor and up the stairs. She could hear Jorge crashing out of the restroom behind her and she burst out onto the street just as Quinn was coming back inside. "Where've you been?" he said. "We're about finished."

"Good." She pushed past him and climbed into the van, taking the seat behind Denise.

"Nice timing," he grumbled, turning away to help Ty stow the last of the gear.

The street was very dark. Several lamps were broken and a slight mist had settled, but Shan could still see Jorge when he emerged from the club. She hunched down in the seat, but he spotted her right away. His eyes shot from her to Quinn and Ty, then to Dan who was just coming around from the side of the van as they finished the last of the loading.

Jorge, still lingering outside, grinned balefully at her. "See ya soon, *querida*," he mouthed.

Then he disappeared, melting into the shadows outside Fuego.

chapter 11

"Has anyone seen the mic box?" Quinn asked.

There was a crash as Shan dropped a crate of hand percussion instruments. Dan and Ty jumped as their collection of tambourines and shakers hit the ground with a dissonant clatter. A single maraca made a swishing sound as it rolled across the floor, coming to a stop in front of Quinn.

He was staring at Shan. "Anything wrong?"

"N-no." She bent to retrieve the scattered instruments. "I'm just clumsy."

"Are you sure?" he said. "You've been acting weird lately."

She shrugged without answering. Quinn looked doubtful, but went back to rooting among the various boxes and crates that comprised the band's equipment. It was spread all over the loft's living room, like it always was right before a gig. "I don't see it."

Ty fingered his goatee. "The last time I remember seeing it," he said, "was Saturday night at Fuego."

"Me, too." Quinn frowned. "Who loaded it out that night?"

Everyone looked at Shan. Because the mic box was one of the lighter pieces of equipment, it was something she usually moved. She shook her head. "I haven't seen it." She went back to picking up the percussion instruments, avoiding Quinn's eyes.

"We must have left it at the club," Dan said. "They probably have it. I'll call."

"Do it now," Quinn said. "In that dive it's likely to disappear, then we're out two grand."

Dan headed for the phone and the rest of them went back to loading. Shan continued to collect the shakers and maracas. They clinked and rattled as she repacked them, but all she could hear was the *thunk* that the mic box had made when it hit the floor of the men's room at Fuego.

The mics hadn't been found. The manager at Fuego promised to keep an eye out for them and, when they played that night, they had to use the Shures. Quinn was in a foul mood as they left for the gig. Shan figured he blamed her and could only hope that he would never discover just how culpable she was.

She had no doubt about the fate of the expensive microphones. In the three days since the gig at Fuego, Shan had seen Jorge everywhere. Amid the crowd in the Spring Street subway station. Loitering in front of the bakery next to her building when she went for a morning croissant. Lurking in the back of the Laundromat where she did her wash. Each time, she only glimpsed him. When she turned for a better look, he'd vanished.

It wasn't until the night she saw him on the ledge outside her bedroom window that she realized she was imagining things. She had leapt from bed in terror, only to find that the face she'd seen was a reflection of the Dylan poster on her wall. Jorge didn't know where she lived, she reassured herself, but she'd upped her dose a tad, just for the tranquilizing effect, then spent two hours playing on the roof to calm herself down.

In the van on the way to the gig, Shan hugged her arms and wished she'd worn a sweater. Quinn had instructed her to wear something witchy and she'd found a filmy black sheath at a vintage clothing shop on Lafayette Street. It was low necked and sleeveless, and the material was of the lightest gauze overlaid with beaded black netting. The effect was good, very Charles Addamsy, but it was a cool night and she was freezing.

Quinn noticed her shivering. "Here," he said, shrugging off his jacket and draping it over her shoulders. The leather was worn soft and smooth, and she caught a whiff of the citrusy, limey aftershave that he wore. She liked it.

It didn't take long to reach the club, which was near the Woolworth building in Tribeca. After he parked, Dan twisted in his seat to look at Quinn. "Dude, this place looks like a shithole."

Shan thought so too, sort of. The club, Prometheus, was housed in an ornate Neo-Romanesque building that must have been spectacular at one time, although it was now in a state of advanced decay. The marble facing was discolored and cracked, and in some places had crumbled away entirely to expose the plain brick underneath the façade. Two life-sized goddesses flanked the tarnished bronze entryway. They were in the same condition as the rest of the building. Juno's face was cracked and she was missing a goodly bit of her torso. Venus was mostly intact, but she'd been adorned with a spray-painted garter belt and stockings.

"I guess the venue isn't so important after all, hey?" Dan remarked. Denise smirked.

Quinn ignored them. As soon as the van stopped he jumped out, threw open the back doors, and began pulling out equipment. Shan took the crate of cables and lingered, waiting for him. After he'd filled his arms, she followed him into the building. Ty and Dan were close behind.

When they went inside, Shan gasped. It was an old theater, with an enormous stage curtained in red velvet and surrounded by magnificent arches with red glass insets. The illumination was provided by red lights fashioned to look like torches and the light caused the glass in the arches to wink and sparkle like flames. The shiny hardwood walls were inlaid with murals depicting bloody scenes from Roman mythology and the tables looked like executioner's blocks. Each one held a flickering candle in a red glass globe. "Cool!" Ty exclaimed.

"I think it's spooky." Denise wrinkled her nose.

"It's supposed to be," Quinn said. "It's Goth, and the door take averages two grand."

"I thought that didn't matter," Dan said, "and aren't you always saying the number of assholes rises in proportion with the number of people?"

Quinn shrugged. "They have decent security. Decent enough for Black Sabbath, at any rate," he added with a grin. "They played here last weekend."

Dan muttered under his breath, but unfastened the amp rack covers.

Quinn was right again. The place filled up fast with an assortment of black-clad patrons sporting eyeliner, black fingernails, and earrings in places Shan wouldn't have thought could be pierced. By eleven Prometheus was jammed. Several fights broke out, but the bouncers were more than adequate, a group of forbidding-looking fellows clad in executioner's garb.

Quinn had modified their list to play to the crowd—dark, hardcore stuff, never Shan's taste. Instead of the blend of hard rock and acid jazz she'd grown accustomed to, that night she was performing the punk and deathrock tunes Quinn had insisted they learn, covers of artists like Alice Cooper, the Cure, and Black Flag. The crowd roared.

In spite of her distaste for the music, Shan found herself responding to the enthusiasm of her audience. She loved performing in such an ornate venue, which appealed to her theatrical side. She vamped and shimmied around the stage, sneering like Wendy O. Williams.

During "Putting Out Fire with Gasoline," Shan thought she spotted Jorge. Since he knew the name of her band now, it would be easier for him to find her and she'd been afraid all night that he'd show up.

"*Feel my blood enraged. It's just the fear of losing you,*" she sang, narrowing her eyes against the lights to get a good look. The strobes kicked in, blinding her, and she blew a line, humming her way through it. She could feel the disapproval radiating from Quinn and when the strobes stopped, the man she'd seen was gone.

They finished at two. "What happened to you on 'Putting Out Fire'?" Quinn growled as they packed. "That's not even a new song. You know it backwards."

"There was some weird guy staring at me," Shan said, glancing over her shoulder. "He gave me the creeps."

"Everyone here is creepy. It doesn't hurt to be careful, though. He isn't still here, is he?"

"I don't know." She scanned the crowd uneasily. "I didn't get a good look at him."

"Just don't go wandering off alone. Here, put these in the box." He handed her a coil of audio cables and Shan went back to packing. She continued to scan the crowd, but she knew Jorge rarely left his neighborhood. She'd never known him to venture this far downtown.

Quinn and Ty were stowing the last of the gear as Shan climbed into the van.

She paused. "Crap," she said, climbing back out. "I left Quinn's jacket in the band room."

"Better hurry up," Dan said, "I want to get out of here before all those drunken Goths start looking for somebody to sacrifice."

"I'll just be a sec. I know right where it is." Shan dashed back into the building. She made her way through the still substantial crowd and slipped backstage. After pausing to give her eyes a chance to adjust to the near darkness, she went to the old dressing room still equipped with a stage mirror, milky around the edges and rimmed with white lights.

She groped for the light switch and the mirror blazed. She spotted Quinn's jacket immediately. It was right where she'd left it, hanging on the back of a chair. She slipped it on and turned off the light, then headed back down the passageway that led into the club. They'd turned on some canned music and the weird, Goth beat was pounding at an unbelievable volume.

Suddenly she stopped. She could see a figure in front of the door, bathed from behind in a red glow cast by the exit sign. "Who's there?" she asked, her heart in her throat.

No response, at least none that she could hear over the music.

Jorge. She'd known it was him. Why, why hadn't she trusted her instincts? Her hands involuntarily shot to her abdomen, where the point of his knife had left a bruise.

The figure moved.

Shan didn't wait. She turned and fled down the passageway, away from the entrance to the club. Her high heels impeded her but, when she tried to kick them free, she tripped and went sprawling. She rolled quickly, but he was already over her and she flinched, holding her hands in front of her face, already feeling the sting of the switchblade.

"What in the hell is the matter with you?"

She lowered her hands. It was Quinn, staring at her as if she'd lost her mind.

"I told you not to wander off alone." He extended his hand, frowning. "Are you all right?"

She found her voice. "I'm fine. I just freaked for a minute. I thought you were him. That creepy guy, I mean." She scrambled to her feet, wincing. She'd scraped both knees and they stung.

He was still eyeing her suspiciously. "Are you sure you're okay?"

"Yes," she assured him, limping a little as she hurried down the passageway. "Fine."

When they arrived at home, Shan grabbed the guitars and went upstairs. By the time they finished unloading, she was hiding out in the bathroom. Her hands shook as she dosed, blowing the smoke out the window. She listened to the voices in the living room. They lingered for a long time, longer than usual after a gig, but she stayed put and eventually she heard Quinn and Ty leave.

She opened the door. The apartment was silent. Dan and Denise must have gone to bed. Shan went to her room and took off the black dress. It was ruined now, badly torn when she fell.

What a jerk she was, panicking over nothing. She could imagine what Quinn was thinking. He hadn't said anything to the others, but kept giving her suspicious looks all the way home.

The H had calmed her down, but she knew she wasn't going to sleep anytime soon. She changed into a pair of jeans and a sweater, then took Joanie and headed for the roof.

She settled in her metal chair. Joanie was just slightly out of tune and she concentrated on adjusting the peg. A slight breeze ruffled her hair and she breathed in the cool air, feeling herself begin to relax for the first time all day.

Then, behind her on the dark roof, someone cleared his throat.

chapter 12

Shan turned. Jorge was leaning against the door into the building, casually flicking his seven-inch blade open and closed. He smiled.

"Hi, *querida.*" He started toward her. He seemed to be moving in slow motion. Shan's eyes were riveted to the knife in his hand, glimmering in the dim light of the rooftop. "Is it a good time to finish our discussion?" Even his voice sounded slow, like a record playing on the wrong speed.

She rose from the chair. Joanie slid from her lap, landing on the ground with a soft slur of notes. Shan backed away as Jorge continued to advance, one step at a time. It felt like they were doing a dance.

When he'd moved far enough from the door, Shan made a dash for the stairwell. She was almost there when she felt sudden agony across the back of her head as Jorge grabbed her hair. He used it to jerk her to the ground and, as she hit, she felt the gravel scraping against her cheek and hands. She got to her knees, wincing, then she heard the metallic click and the blade was pressing into the flesh under her chin. She froze.

His breath was against her ear. "*I want my fucking money, bitch.*"

"I have five hundred dollars," she whispered, feeling the point of the knife against her voice box. She knew it could slice through her flesh like butter. "Just let me go down and get it."

He moved the blade and she started to get up, then he swung his foot. When his heavy work boot connected with her tailbone she screamed in pain, dropping back onto the roof. He kicked her again, his boot slamming into her ribs this time.

She assumed a fetal position, which she knew from long experience was safest during a beating. She wrapped her arms around her legs and ducked her head, tensing for the next blow.

She stayed that way for what felt like an hour, but she knew in reality that it was only seconds. Cautiously, she raised her head.

Jorge was no longer standing over her. She couldn't see him at all, but she had a clear path to the door. She scrambled to her knees, ignoring the stabbing pain in her side. She looked around and gasped. *"Put that down!"*

Jorge was near the edge of the roof, one foot resting on the ledge. In his hands was Joanie.

"I see you're still playing your mama's guitar," he said.

She got to her feet, winced, gripped her side. "Give it to me, Jorge!" She moved toward him. Just as her fingers were about to touch Joanie's wood grain, he pulled it away and extended his arm, holding the guitar out over the edge of the roof, nine stories above the street.

"What else you gonna do for me?" he asked.

"Give me my guitar!"

He tossed it lightly into the air then caught it, leaning a little farther out into space. "How about you get down on your knees? Show me how grateful you are?"

"Grateful for *what?*"

"Grateful that I didn't cut your fuckin' throat," he replied, "or at least that I didn't give you more scars than you already got. I still might. I could slice your pretty face to ribbons. Then the big blond guy you're screwing won't want ya." Her face must have betrayed something, because he suddenly looked uglier. "Yeah, I seen him. I been watching you all week. He wouldn't be with you if your face was one big fucking scab, now, would he? "

"I'm not *with* him," she said. *Why do I have to keep explaining this?* she wondered irrationally, her eyes glued to the guitar in Jorge's hand.

"Don't care if you are," he said, swinging Joanie like a pendulum. He reached out with his other hand and caught Shan by the front of the sweater to yank her closer.

"Give us a kiss, *querida,*" he whispered, "then get down on your fucking knees."

Shan could see the gaps in his teeth, his scabbed skin, the bilious yellow of his eyes. She remembered what it was like to be in his bed, his hands all over her, his cock inside of her.

She drew her head back.

And spit in his face.

He looked shocked for a moment, then his face twisted. He let go of the guitar.

Shan flung herself past him, her arms stretching out over the edge of the roof. She thought she felt her fingers just graze the guitar's body, then she was watching Joanie soar through the air, tumbling end over end in a graceful downward trajectory.

Shan made a sound like an animal in pain but she only had a moment to mourn, because the next thing she knew she was sprawling across the roof with Jorge bearing down on her. His fingers closed around her windpipe. "Now let's work on that face, *querida*."

His grip on her throat tightened, but suddenly something flashed past and Jorge's head snapped back. He uttered a strangled sound and the pressure on her throat relaxed as he fell off of her. Her hands shot to her throat. She looked up.

Quinn was towering over her with a clenched fist and a dangerous scowl.

Jorge sat up, dazed, and in a split second Quinn was between them. "You wanna play, motherfucker? How about picking somebody your own size?"

Shan watched Jorge inspect Quinn with clear apprehension. She noted that they weren't even close to the same size. Quinn was bigger. A lot.

Jorge's eyes shot back to her. "*I treated you decent,*" he cried. "I took care of you when you had nothin', and now—"

Jorge lunged. He was quick, but Quinn was quicker, lashing out with his foot. Jorge caught it under the chin and suddenly he was airborne. When he landed, his nose and mouth were bloody.

Quinn took a menacing step closer, his fists doubling up, and Jorge scrambled to his feet. He fled across the roof, bursting through the door. His footsteps echoed through the stairwell.

Shan didn't realize she'd been holding her breath until she exhaled, then her entire body started shaking. Quinn knelt down and put his arms around her. He held her for a long time, until the tremors stopped. "What the fuck, Shan?" he said, when she was still.

She let him help her to her feet. "Where did you come from? I thought you left."

"I did, but I came back. You've been weird all night, then that shit backstage at the club? I knew something was up." He knelt to examine a shiny object on the ground. Jorge's switchblade. His face darkened. "I was about to come upstairs when I saw your guitar sail off of the roof."

Joanie! Clutching her side, she headed for the stairwell and hurried down the eight flights to the front of the building.

Joanie was in pieces. The headstock was mostly intact, with part of the neck still clinging to it. The rest was destroyed.

She sank to her knees, staring at what was left of her mother's guitar. She touched the bridge, which had detached from the body. The strings were twisted and gnarled but some of them still connected the small piece of wood to the smashed instrument, like an umbilical cord linked to a corpse.

"Shan." She turned. Quinn was standing beside her. He raised his hand, showing her the switchblade. "Come inside. We've got to call the cops."

"No!"

"But . . ."

"No cops, Quinn." She shook her head, pulling the pegs to release the strings from the bridge and taking it in her hand. "I'm fine. I just want to go to bed."

She marched upstairs without looking back, but he dogged her, coming up the stairs right behind her. "Fine?" he asked. "How can you possibly be fine, after that?"

She unlocked the door to her apartment and Quinn followed her inside. "Just because I ran him off doesn't mean he won't come back," he continued, turning the tumbler on the deadbolt. "You have to do something."

He turned and realized he was speaking to an empty room. He went into the living room. No sign of Shan, so he went to her bedroom, knocked briefly, and opened the door.

The room was dark. His eyes adjusted and he saw that she was in bed. Her eyes were shut, her breathing even, and she looked very small under the covers. "I know you're awake," he said.

She did not respond.

He watched her for a few moments, his lips tight. "This isn't over," he said finally. "Not even close." Then he left, pulling the door shut behind him.

As the door closed, Shan's eyes opened. She sat up and pulled her hands out from under the covers. She held the small piece of wood that used to be the bridge on her mother's guitar cradled between her palms. "I'm sorry, Joanie," she said softly.

The next morning she woke to the jangling of the telephone. She waited until the ringing stopped, then rolled over and flinched. The back of her head burned as if the scalp had been torn from her skull.

She climbed out of bed, wincing again at a sharp pain in her side, and went into the kitchen to make some coffee. While it was brewing, she returned to her bedroom, sniffling as she prepared a fix and lit the candle. After a couple of hits, she felt her morning jones begin to dissipate. Normally she stopped, but today she'd treat herself to an extra hit or two. She deserved it, after last night. She wanted to get stoned enough that she wouldn't be able to think at all.

Shan was floating as she went back into the kitchen and poured herself a cup of coffee, but a knock at the door made her tumble right off her cloud.

Jorge's back! she thought, snatching the butcher knife from the rack on the wall.

Another, louder knock. She crept to the door and pressed her eye against the peephole.

It was Quinn. He was standing with his arms crossed over his chest and a frown on his face. His blue eyes were somber.

She rested her head against the door, sensing that the protective insulation she'd woven to separate her two worlds was about to unravel. When he knocked again, pounded this time, she jerked her head up, startled, then undid the row of locks and opened the door. "Hi."

He looked at the knife in her hand. "Did I wake you?"

She shook her head, half to clear it. "I just made coffee. You want some?"

"Sure." He shut the door as she set down the knife and took a mug from the cupboard. "I tried to call," he said. "I didn't want to just bust in on you at this hour. Sorry."

"It's okay. Come on in." She led him into the living room. She was wearing a short nightshirt, so she curled up in one of the chairs with her legs folded underneath her.

He settled into the other chair, fixing his eyes on her. She returned his gaze impassively. She wasn't going to speak first, not even if they sat staring at each other all day long.

"Well?" he said. "What the hell happened last night?"

She kept her face carefully bland. "That was someone I used to know."

"With a switchblade?" He looked dubious. "A little extreme for an ex-boyfriend, isn't it?"

A humorless laugh stuck in her throat. "He's not exactly an ex-boyfriend."

Quinn's lips twisted a little. "I didn't really think he was. Frankly, I'd credit you with more taste. What was it about, then?"

She didn't reply.

He frowned. "Look, you're obviously in some kind of trouble, but I can't help if you won't tell me about it."

What was she supposed to say? She couldn't tell him the truth and she was feeling a little too fuzzy to make up a plausible lie. She shook her head, cursing those extra hits.

Quinn caught her hand. "You can trust me," he said, his tone unusually gentle. "You know that, don't you, angel?"

Maybe he really would understand. Her lip trembled and she caught it between her teeth.

He took her other hand and squeezed them both between his palms, his eyes maintaining their lock on hers. "Look, I'm not going to judge you. What are we talking about here?"

"Well, he's not exactly an ex-boyfriend," she said carefully, "but I did have a relationship with him, sort of. I mean, I slept with him. Lived with him for a while, I guess. But I didn't . . . I wasn't with him because I wanted to be."

His brows slowly knit together. "What do you mean?"

"I just . . . it was winter and I was living on the street. I didn't have any money and I needed some. I mean, I needed . . ." Her voice trailed off as his face changed.

"What are you saying?" He drew back, just a touch. "That you were a . . ."

She could see the word on his lips. "*No,*" she snapped. "I wasn't a hooker. I was . . . I was . . ."

Her words trailed off. She'd never thought of it that way, but what else was it? She'd slept with a man who disgusted her in order to obtain drugs. One service for another. What was that, if not an act of prostitution?

"I suppose," she corrected herself, "that *is* what I'm saying." And she turned away, feeling suddenly ill.

Quinn didn't say anything for a few seconds. "Well," he began, after a while, "like I said, I'm not going to judge you. But I take it you're not . . . involved in that line of work anymore?"

"No." She felt a dull heat spread over her face. "Not in a long time."

He shifted, clearly ill at ease. "Good." He hesitated. "Why is he after you now?"

She kept her eyes averted. "The last time I saw him, he tried . . . I mean, he *tried*. And I wouldn't. I fought him off and ran."

His voice went deadly quiet. "What you're telling me is that he tried to rape you."

"I guess," she whispered.

"When did this happen?"

"Last month. That first night I was supposed to meet you. Remember my no-show?"

"And where does he live?" he persisted.

"In Spanish Harlem, over on Second. Why?" She raised her eyes to his face and recoiled from the rage she saw there.

"Because I'm going to *kill the motherfucker*."

"No!" She shook her head. "I don't want to drag you any further into this, Quinn. Besides, you probably scared him off." Her voice softened. "Thank you, by the way."

He shrugged off her words. "You'd better get dressed."

"Why? Are we going somewhere?"

"Yes. The police station."

"*No!*"

"You have to do something, Shan. Either you can tell me where to find him and I'll have a talk with him or you can tell it to the cops. It's your choice."

"I *can't* go to the cops, and I won't get you involved."

"Don't be a fucking idiot," he snapped. "You can't just pretend it didn't happen. He beat the shit out of you. And what do you think he was planning to do with that blade? Cut your meat?"

"If I go anywhere near the cops, they'll haul me to juvie so fast you won't even see me going!"

He caught her hands again. "Why?"

"Because I'm a runaway! And I'm *not* going back. *Never*. I'd rather be dead. *He's* there."

He tightened his grip. "Who?"

"My father," she whispered, "and you *can* pretend it didn't happen. I always did . . . before. The stuff he used to do to me. He used to hit me. Beat me up. Sometimes he burned me."

She stared past Quinn as if he wasn't there, back into the blackness that was her childhood. "He said it was my fault that my mother died, so he punished me for it. I just pretended it never happened." She shifted, pulling her legs in tight against her chest.

After a time she noticed Quinn looking at them, his eyes wide, shocked, and she realized that the scars from her father's burns were clearly visible, blazing a white trail over her knees and thighs. She looked away. "I've never told anyone that before," she admitted, wondering why she'd told him now.

When Quinn touched her, she flinched as if he'd struck her, but he gathered her into his arms and drew her onto his lap. She let him do it, curling into a ball. He put his hand on her leg, covering the scars on her knees.

They stayed that way for a long time. After a while, Quinn felt a crick in his leg. He changed position to relieve the stiffness and smoothed the hair away from her face, then realized she'd fallen asleep. Her head lay on his chest, her breathing was soft and regular, and her hand rested on his shoulder.

He touched her cheek. It was dry. She hadn't shed even a single tear.

He gazed down at her, experiencing the most peculiar glow in his chest, then buried his face in her tousled curls and breathed in her scent, his arms tightening around her small body.

chapter 13

Quinn rubbed his eyes. They'd been working the same song for days, but it wasn't coming to life and he was sick of the sound of it. Maybe they'd be better off just scrapping it and trying something new, or maybe the magic they'd found together was all used up.

He eyed Shan dolefully. She was cross-legged on the wooden coffee table with her twelve-string across her lap. She'd been playing the same riff for twenty minutes and it was beginning to grate on his nerves.

As she began it again, he let forth a resonant sigh. Shan leveled a coolly inquisitive look at him. "Do you have a problem of some kind?"

"Not really. I'm just a little comatose from listening to you play the same guitar part over and over and over again," Quinn said. "You think you could maybe change a chord in it. Any chord will do, as long as it sounds a tiny fucking bit *different?*"

"I'm trying to figure out what's wrong with it, and you're no help. You've been sitting there like a lump for the last hour."

"Why should I say anything? You won't listen," he said. "I told you to leave it alone and work on a different part of the song. It'll come to you when you stop obsessing over it."

"Thank you, Paul Simon. Tell me, what do you usually charge when you coach amateur songwriters?"

"No need to get huffy. You're the one who keeps saying you still want direction."

"I haven't said that in a while," she retorted. "Besides, it's not like your direction has anything to do with helping me. You love having a little protégée to boss around, so you can reassure yourself how brilliant you are."

The annoyance simmering inside him began to reach the boiling point. "You know, I've had just about enough. Your raggy little tantrums are beginning to get on my nerves."

"Then get out of here and don't listen to them."

"Fine." He stalked through the kitchen, stepped into the hallway and got a firm grip on the door, intending to slam it hard enough to knock the plaster from the ceiling.

Then he stopped, his hand on the knob. This kind of thing was happening with increasing frequency. They weren't arguing any more than they always had, but the arguments had acquired a different flavor. More venomous, and the venom was coming from her, not him, this time.

He closed the door and went back into the living room.

Shan didn't turn around. She knew he was still there—he could tell by the stiffness in her back—but she kept her head down and stubbornly began to play the same riff again.

He glared at her. "Would you mind telling me what in the fuck is the matter with you?"

She stopped in the middle of a beat and looked up, a distinctly unfriendly expression on her face. "Nothing! Just get off my back!"

"Bullshit. You've been acting like a turbobitch all week. Now, I know I'm not the easiest guy to put up with, but I haven't done *anything* to deserve the kind of shit you're dumping on me. You'd better start talking. Fast. Or I *will* walk out of here and, this time, I won't come back."

Her eyes had grown huge. The angry look melted as she set the guitar aside. "I don't know what's wrong with me," she confessed.

He advanced a couple of steps into the room. "I just don't understand the hostility. You're acting like you hate me. What'd I do, for Chrissake?"

"Nothing," she said, "except help me. It's just that when I'm with you now, I feel so . . ." she made a gesture of futility, "naked, I guess. Exposed."

He sat back down. "Well, you told me a lot of stuff that you've never told anyone else, so I can understand that. Maybe you should find somebody else to talk to about it."

"You mean a shrink?" she asked, elevating her chin.

"Well, it wouldn't hurt. Or you could talk to one of your roommates, at least. You girls are good at that, right? Sharing your feelings, or whatever."

"I'm not." She frowned. "Besides, I can take care of myself."

He suppressed a grin. "I know, but you must have a friend you're comfortable talking to."

She reached over and touched his hand. "I think I'm talking to a friend right now."

"I don't know if I'm the best choice for unconditional understanding. I'm better when there's a problem that needs solving. And all of my friends are guys," he added. "I've never really had a woman friend."

"Of course you haven't." She got up and wandered over to the window. "You're too busy sizing up every female as a potential sex partner."

"Not *every* one," he said. "Only the ones with the right attitude."

"I know. Only the ones who play by your rules." Shan gazed out the window with her hands clasped behind her back. It was a sunny Saturday in June and Spring Street was packed with people. "Hey, let's go for a walk."

"This is supposed to be a writing day," he reminded her. "That's why I'm here."

"Well, writing isn't working. We're blocked or something." She caught his hand and dragged him toward the door. "Maybe the air will clear our heads."

He grumbled as they came out into the sunshine. People milled up and down the street and the odd buildings that typified SoHo's architecture rose above them like cast-iron sentries. "You New Yorkers sure spend a lot of time on the street," he said. "Even at three A.M. when we get done gigging there are people out walking. You don't see that in Boston."

"Well, Bostonians are supposed to be stuffy," she said, heading down Spring Street.

He fell into step beside her. "I'm not, but I'm not a real Bostonian, either. Just a temporary transplant."

"That's right." She glanced up at him as they cut through the SoHo Square Park, heading west toward the waterfront. "You're from California, like Dan, aren't you?" He certainly looked like a surfer boy, with his long blond hair and swimmer's build.

"Yes, and I can't wait to get back there," he said. "I hate the fucking winters here. One more year, then I don't care if I never see another snowflake."

"Dan said he grew up in the San Fernando Valley. Do you come from that part of California, too?"

Quinn shrugged. "More or less."

"Whereabouts?"

He stopped, shooting her an annoyed glance. "Why are you so inquisitive, all of a sudden?"

"Well, it's just occurred to me that I don't know all that much about you and that's weird, don't you think? Especially since we spend so much time together."

"You know how I compose and how I play. What else matters?"

"But you know everything about me." Well. Maybe not *everything*. "You know a lot about me now," she amended. "A lot of stuff nobody else knows. It makes me feel like I'm on the observation end of a two-way mirror."

He nodded slowly. "All right then, if it'll help you chill out. Yes, I grew up in Southern California, like Dan."

"Do your parents still live there?"

"My mother does, and my stepfather. My father is dead."

They were near the end of Spring Street. The West Side Highway stretched before them and, beyond it, the waterfront docks. "I'm sorry," she said. He didn't respond. "How old were you when he died?"

"Nine."

As they crossed under the highway, she said, "That must have been hard on you, Q. I thought I'd die myself when I lost my mom. Was it that way for you?"

He nodded again, silently.

"How about your mother?" she prompted after a while. "Are you close?"

"Hardly." His face was reticent, a scowl materializing as they paused on a bridge connecting two mooring docks. The water below them was murky and dark, the sunlight not penetrating more than an inch below the surface. It smelled dank and fishy.

"Why not?"

Quinn swiveled his head to glare at her. "Christ, you're nosy. All right. I might as well take this from the top. There's an entertainment law firm based in LA. Marshall-Merrick. It's fairly well known."

"I think I've heard of them. They're agents, right? And they handle Cyndi Lauper, don't they?" She paused and eyes widened. "You mean you're *that* Marshall?"

"No. *That* Marshall was my father. Now it's my brother. And they're not agents. They're entertainment lawyers."

"What's the difference?"

"An agent books your gigs," he explained. "An entertainment lawyer gets involved after the gigs are booked. They handle talent agreements. Synchronization rights. Intellectual property. Stuff like that."

"Oh." She had no idea what any of those things were. "So what's the story?"

He looked down into the water. "Well, in my family, you grow up knowing you're probably going to be a lawyer. There's an expectation. I was even prelaw at Stanford for a while. Family alma mater, don't you know."

"You'd make a good lawyer," she said. "It's not easy to win an argument with you."

"It was never my scene, though. I had this music thing going on, ever since I started piano lessons. I was about five and I can still remember how excited my teacher got the first time he realized I could harmonize melodies on piano. Nobody showed me. I could just hear it." He smiled a little. "Mr. Huxtable, his name was. He started introducing me to other instruments, too, and he about went nuts when he saw how easily I learned to play them."

"Your parents must have been proud," Shan said.

"My dad was. He played piano, too, although it was just a hobby for him. After he died it became even more important to me. It made me feel like I was still connected to him, in a way."

"I get that," Shan said softly.

"Once I was a teenager and started playing in rock bands, that was it. I knew I'd found the thing that I was going to do for the rest of my life."

"So how did you end up at Stanford?"

He shrugged. "I had no choice. My mother was paying the tuition and there was no way in hell she'd let me go to a music school. It was college or nothing."

"Couldn't you have gotten financial aid or something?"

He grinned at her. "I grew up in Bel Air, angel. My folks still live there, right down the street from Ronnie and Nancy Reagan. They don't hand out a lot of financial aid in our neighborhood."

"Oh." She'd never thought that having too much money could be a problem. "I'm still surprised you wound up at Stanford, though, if you didn't want to go."

"Well, I had a plan. I needed to bide my time, so I figured I might as well be getting educated while I was waiting. And there were other factors. I couldn't really move out on my own at that point."

"Why not?"

"It just wouldn't have worked." He looked uncomfortable. "Anyway, I stuck it out until I turned twenty-one, then I came into an inheritance, a trust fund that my father set up for me. I applied to Berklee and got accepted, and when I told Mom, she went ballistic. Big fucking scene. Told me if I didn't finish college, she was throwing me out without a cent."

"And?" she prompted.

He scowled anew. "I told her to go to hell, grabbed my keyboard, and walked out of the house. That was four years ago."

"You haven't talked to her since?"

"No, and I won't," he declared. "She's a domineering bitch who controls everyone around her. My stepfather and my brother are completely under her thumb."

"Doesn't she ever try to get in touch with you?"

"Not anymore. She's given up on me, I think. I'm the black sheep of the Marshall clan. Too much wine, women, and song."

She wanted to ask more questions, about his brother, his stepfather, but she could see that he was beginning to get annoyed, so instead she reached up and smoothed the hair out of his eyes. "Well, I think you're pretty terrific, Q," she assured him. "Wine, women, and all."

"Thanks, angel." He folded his arms on the railing, rested his chin on them, and smiled at her. "We *are* getting to be friends, aren't we? How weird is that? Friendship's not what I usually want out of a woman, you know."

She had a snappy comeback on the tip of her tongue, but a sudden thought struck her and her words froze. Apparently her face did, too, because Quinn raised his chin off his arms. "Hey, I was kidding."

"It's the bridge," she said and he looked around in confusion. "Not *this* bridge," she clarified. "That's what's wrong with the song. The *bridge*. It needs to be in a different key. It needs to go to D minor."

He nodded, light dawning in his eyes. "Not bad. It could make for a better transition into the verse. I told you it would come if you left it alone." She rolled her eyes and he grabbed her hand. "Come on. We've still got the rest of the afternoon to work on it."

chapter 14

"I'm sick of waiting for him," Ty said. "Let's order."

"Yeah," Dan seconded. "I'm starving."

"It's not like Quinn to be late," Oda said. "He *did* say he'd meet us, didn't he?"

Shan nodded. They were at the Cupping Room, a little bistro on West Broadway. The place served the best brunch in SoHo and had become a Sunday-morning tradition for the group. "I asked him last night, before he left with what's-her-name. He said he'd be here at eleven, same as always."

"Well, I'm ordering," Denise said. "It's almost noon. I'll have the buckwheat pancakes," she told the waitress.

Shan checked the door as the others rattled off their orders. Where *was* Quinn? His absence would screw up her routine. She could never decide between her two favorite items so she ordered the fruit-topped french toast and he got eggs Benedict, then they shared.

"I'll have the french toast," she told the waitress, still eyeing the door. Her face brightened when she spotted a familiar mop of blond hair. "And eggs Benedict," Shan added. "One more coffee, too, and another orange juice," she said as Quinn slid into the empty chair next to her. His hair was in disarray and his green T-shirt damp with perspiration.

"Morning," he said to the table in general. He gave a tug to the curl over Shan's eye, then snagged her orange juice and polished off half of it.

"Hey, quit that!" She retrieved her glass. "I ordered you one."

"I'm thirsty," he said. "I just ran five blocks."

"What happened?" Dan asked. "She wear you out so much you overslept?"

"No, right at the crucial moment, she told me I'm the one she's been waiting for."

"So what happened next?" Ty said, leering.

"I went home." Quinn snorted. "Just as well. She was costing me a fortune in drinks."

Denise wrinkled her nose. "You're *such* a pig."

"Why? I leave them smiling. I've decided that's my role in the master plan; to go around spurting happiness wherever I am. And I'm late," he continued, over their hoots, "because I was booking us a gig tonight."

A chorus of groans erupted. "Dude, this is the first time in a month we've had a Sunday off," Dan said. "What about our Yankees tickets?"

"And I have a date." Ty glared at him. "Why didn't you check with the rest of us first?"

Shan remained silent, but eyed Quinn morosely. She'd been planning to spend the evening chilling with a good book and a mug of tea.

Quinn grinned and gave her hair another tug. "Don't look so disappointed, angel. How'd you like to warm up for Jerry Garcia at Carnegie Hall?"

According to Quinn, Garcia's agent had caught them at the Bitter End and been impressed, apparently enough that he remembered them when their scheduled opener canceled due to sudden illness. They suspected a bad batch of street drugs, Quinn imparted. Anyhow, it left a gap and he'd gotten a call that morning.

They wolfed down their food and spent the next several hours in a flurry of activity. They had to track down Bruce, their regular sound man, and talk him into bagging his own gig at Wetlands. He'd only do it if they found a replacement, so they had to find another engineer to cover. Then they had to be at Carnegie Hall for sound check at four o'clock. The PA wasn't completely set up, so they had to wait for another hour and a half. When everything was finally situated and plugged in, they discovered a problem with the monitors. By the time they finished, it was six-thirty and they were scheduled to go on at eight. They had barely enough time to go home, change, and get back to Carnegie Hall for their spot.

On the way to the gig, Shan fretted over her attire. There'd been no time to even think about what to wear, so she'd opted for skinny jeans and a tie-dyed peasant top. She was hot and perspiring, though no one else seemed bothered by the temperature in the van.

When a cramp doubled her over, Quinn was suddenly attentive. "Are you okay?"

"It's just all the excitement." She was jonesing, she realized, because she was late for her fix. She always dosed right before they went out gigging, but the timing had been so tight this time that she'd decided to wait until they got there. She hadn't had anything since eleven that morning, but she had a stash in her guitar case, in the embroidered bag that held her picks and extra strings.

By the time they arrived at Carnegie Hall, Shan was shivering although her forehead was shiny with perspiration. Her legs ached and she had to repeatedly wipe her eyes.

Quinn jumped out of the van, leaving Shan to climb down behind him. Her legs were shaky as she stepped out and he turned just as her knees began to buckle. "Hey!" he exclaimed, catching her around the waist.

Ty and Dan drifted around the side of the van and gaped at her face, which was flushed and wet. Her limbs shook, but she pushed Quinn away. "I'm okay."

"You don't look okay," Dan said doubtfully. "Are you sure you can play?"

"Of course I can." She fidgeted under their scrutiny. "Stop looking at me! I'll be all right."

Quinn was regarding her with trepidation and she knew they couldn't possibly pull off a performance of this magnitude without her. It would take days of practice to restructure the arrangements so they could be played without a guitar. "I'm okay," she said again.

Quinn frowned, but turned away when Ty jostled his elbow with the snare drum. Shan lingered, waiting for them to unload the guitars. As soon as they did, she grabbed her Fullerton and went inside the building.

Backstage was chaotic. There were people everywhere, musicians tuning up, roadies shoving equipment around, girls so scantily clad they could only be groupies. Clutching her guitar, she pressed through the crowd until she found a restroom.

It was marked MEN, but she didn't care. She went inside, locked the door behind her, then sat down on the floor and opened up her guitar case. She looked for the blue bag, groping around behind her twelve-string. She couldn't feel it, so she pulled the guitar out of the case to look beneath it. All she saw were a couple of loose picks, her string winder, and an old playlist. The guitar slipped out of her hand and she grabbed for it, her shaking fingers brushing the strings with a dissonant jangle.

Strings. She'd meant to change them before they left, but there hadn't been time. She'd just taken a packet from the blue bag when Quinn banged on the bedroom door, yelling that they'd miss their spot if they didn't go right away.

She'd shoved her guitar back into the case and rushed out of the apartment. If she closed her eyes, she could picture the blue bag with her emergency stash inside, lying on her pillow.

Twenty minutes later, Quinn inspected Shan as they stood onstage. "You look like hell," he said. "Can you sing?"

"Don't worry about it," she said. Her eyes glittered like prisms in the stage lights and she was trembling visibly now.

He smoothed the curls off her shiny forehead. "It's only a half-hour set. Can you hold it together that long?"

"*Yes, all right?*" She pulled away. "Now stop bugging me, Quinn!"

His face hardened and he turned away without another word as the stage manager held his hand up. The lights brightened and the curtain began to rise; Shan's eyes drifted over the audience incredulously as they began "Big City Heat." There was a hum in the air, a pervasive buzz that could only be created by vast numbers of people, and she suddenly felt very small and insubstantial under the scrutiny of three thousand pairs of eyes.

She snuck a surreptitious glance at the rest of the band. They seemed unaffected, Quinn in particular appearing calm and unruffled, singing and playing with his usual self-assurance.

When they shifted to "Voluntary Exile," she took a deep breath. Her voice was true and only the slightest uncharacteristic flatness revealed her precarious state. They had the crowd and they kept it as they transitioned to "Iko Iko."

As Dan pounded out the opening drum solo, Shan's abdomen contracted. Her throat closed and her stomach heaved; she shot an imploring look at Quinn, who brought his mouth to the microphone immediately, assuming the opening vocals as the audience shrieked their approval.

They took their bows to hearty applause, beginning to dismantle their equipment as the curtain dropped. Shan stumbled off the stage, nearly colliding with one of the Garcia roadies, a tall, gangly guy with short orange dreads and a pierced lip.

"Hey, sweetheart," he said, catching her by the arm to steady her. "What's your deal?"

Shan stared at him. Behind her, she could hear her bandmates hauling their equipment off the stage. "Do you know if anyone here is holding H?" she whispered.

The roadie grinned. "Sweetheart," he said, "this is your lucky day."

Fifteen minutes later the members of Quinntessence were watching the curtain rise on the Garcia band. Quinn looked around as Jerry opened with "Mission in the Rain."

"Where's Shan? I can't believe she's missing this," he said to Dan, whose attention was riveted to the stage. Quinn watched for a few more minutes, then headed for the greenroom in search of her.

He opened the door and stopped dead. She was in there, all right, facedown and motionless, halfway between the floor and the sofa. A pierced, dreaded white guy was attempting to lift her.

"Hey!" Quinn advanced on them, his fists doubling up. "Get your hands off her, you fuck!"

The guy let go of Shan and held up his hands. "Hey, it's cool! It's cool, man!" She slid the rest of the way to the floor, landing in a heap.

Cool? Quinn moved forward, scooping Shan into his arms and moving her to the sofa. Her head lolled like it was attached to her shoulders by rubber bands and he saw that her eyes were rolled back into her head. "What the hell did you do to her?"

"Nothing! She wanted it . . . *paid* for it! She just ain't used to China White, that's all." The guy dug in his pocket and produced a baggie of blinding white powder, then scratched his head ruefully. "I think it mighta been her first time shooting it, too."

Smack? Quinn wanted to kill her, and at the same time he was terrified that she might have already accomplished that on her own. She was a mess, not unconscious but close to it, mumbling incoherently. She couldn't even hold her head up.

Should he take her to an ER? He hesitated, recalling her reaction when he'd pressured her to call the cops on that sleazy creep on the roof.

There was a phone on the coffee table. He grabbed it and dug in his wallet for a number. "Steve? It's Quinn Marshall. I've got a fucked up girl on my hands and I think it might be an emergency . . . I'd rather not, if I don't have to. Can you meet me in about twenty minutes?"

He hung up, went to the door, and hailed one of the roadies. Yanking a ten out of his pocket, he handed it to the kid. "I need a cab at the back entrance. Fast."

The cab let them off in front of Quinn's building. He carried Shan upstairs and found Steve Markowitz waiting at his door, a black bag in his hand. Quinn struggled to balance Shan's weight while he extricated his keys. Steve took the keys and unlocked the door.

Once inside, Quinn dumped Shan unceremoniously on the couch. "She's really wasted," he said, trying to quell his rising panic. She was a fucking mess. "Smack, I think."

Steve knelt, checked her pulse and breathing, then reached into his bag for a penlight. He lifted one of her eyelids, shone the light into it, and did the same with the other.

"Latest addition?" he asked conversationally, pulling a stethoscope from his bag.

"Just a friend. A *good* friend," Quinn added after a pause. "Do I need to get her to a hospital?"

"She doesn't need one," Steve said, after listening to her heart. "A detox would be more appropriate. Do you know what she took?"

"China White. Heavy shit, right?"

"Right." Steve began repacking his bag, a disgruntled look on his face. "She'll be okay."

"It's not an OD? The guy who shot her up said she'd never done it before."

Steve pushed up Shan's shirtsleeves and examined the insides of her arms. "He's right," he said, after a moment. "I don't see any tracks. Just the one," he pointed to a pinprick in the crook of her elbow. "This is fresh. Probably from tonight."

"You think it's true? That she never did smack before?"

"I didn't say that," Steve said. "Just because she never shot up doesn't mean she isn't a junkie. Most of them don't shoot up anymore. They snort it, or smoke it."

"I've never seen her high," Quinn said, but his eyes were narrowing.

"Maybe you've never seen her straight. Junkies are on all the time, you know." Steve shrugged and Quinn nodded. "You'll be able to tell tomorrow, when this wears off. If she wakes up twitchy with watery eyes and a runny nose like she has the flu—well, then you'll know."

"Hey, wait!" Quinn said as Steve closed his bag and stood up. "What do I do with her?"

"Just ride it out. She'll probably stay this way through the night." Steve closed his bag, stood up, and headed for the door. "There's an inpatient detox at the clinic. You can bring her if she wants to try," he added, not sounding hopeful. "Call me if you get nervous."

"Okay. Thanks," Quinn said, his eyes still on Shan. Steve departed, shaking his head.

A junkie? She couldn't be. Could she? Suddenly he recalled the way she'd start sweating, how her eyes would get glassy after a long practice or when a gig ran late. The way she'd head for the bathroom, saying she needed to splash some water on her face, then look perfectly normal when she returned. And that scumbag from the roof, a lowlife drug dealer if he'd ever seen one. "Son of a fucking bitch," he whispered.

It was true. He knew it, and couldn't believe he hadn't seen it. He glared at her, still prone on his couch, which was also his bed. She was nodded out, he saw, floating in a semiconscious state, so he decided to leave her where she was rather than struggle with moving her to unfold the convertible sofa. He took off her shoes, spread a blanket over her, then retrieved a comforter and pillow for himself.

It was only about eleven-thirty, but he was exhausted. He snapped off the light and, with one last scowl at Shan, stretched out on the floor.

chapter 15

When Shan opened her eyes, the light from the window invaded her corneas like a million tiny needles. With a moan, she squeezed them shut. *Dope hangover,* she noted. She'd never slammed before, but works were all the roadie had with him. Obviously she'd done too much.

She lay motionless for several minutes, then cautiously pushed herself up on her elbows. She was lying on a couch in a sparely furnished studio apartment. She saw a bathroom to her left and another door straight in front of her that opened into a kitchenette. The last thing she remembered was her blood draining from the syringe while the red-haired roadie shot her up. Where was she now, and how had she gotten here?

Then she spotted Quinn's leather jacket hanging over the back of a chair. *Oh, shit.*

A moment later, Quinn himself appeared in the kitchen doorway with a cup of coffee in his hand. "How're you feeling?"

Like she'd been run over by a train. "Better," she lied. "Must be a twenty-four-hour bug."

He vanished into the kitchen, reappearing a minute later with a second cup. She accepted it with shaky fingers and took a bracing sip. "Is this your place?" she asked.

He nodded, watching her with the oddest expression.

"Can I use your bathroom?"

"Sure." He inclined his head in the direction of the bathroom, and she winced as she stood up. Even the soles of her feet hurt. As she shut the bathroom door behind her she saw that he was still watching her, his habitual half smile markedly absent from his face.

Quinn wondered if she was in there fixing, but realized she hadn't as soon as she emerged. She was whiter, shakier, sweating like an ice cube in the sun, and he could see the hunger in her eyes, now that he was looking for it. It wasn't the hunger of a first-time user.

"I'm sorry to be so much trouble." Shan put on her shoes, then edged toward the front door. "Thanks for helping me. Again," she added, attempting a smile as her hand found the knob.

"Don't leave," Quinn said. "I want to talk to you."

Shan hesitated, then returned to the couch. Her fingers found the bottom of her shirt and began twisting it into knots.

He was gazing fixedly at her. "So you're feeling better?"

"Yes, I told you," she said irritably. "I really need to get home though. What do you want?" She continued to tug at the hem of the shirt repetitively as her knee jittered up and down.

She was coming undone right in front of him. "What do you suppose made you so sick?"

"I told you it must be some bug," she snapped, starting to rise. "I need to get home, so . . ."

In a flash, he was on his feet and towering over her. He put his hand on her chest and shoved her back down on the couch. *"Don't you fucking lie to me!"* he roared.

Shan recoiled. No wonder. He'd never raised his voice to her before, let alone put his hands on her. Never once, in all their arguments.

"So tell me," he inquired, "how long have you been chasing the dragon?"

She cringed as if he'd struck her.

"Answer me!"

She threw her hands out in supplication. "What do you want me to say?"

"I want you to tell me the *truth*," he shot back. "What did I tell you, right at the beginning? No booze, no drugs when we're gigging. So what the hell was that last night, onstage, in front of three thousand fucking people? Do you know the trouble you could have gotten us into? Not just yourself, but me, and Dan, and Ty? *Do you have any fucking idea?*"

"Stop yelling!" She clapped her hands over her ears. "I couldn't help it!"

She was quivering like a vibrating string. He scowled, resisting a sudden stab of compassion. "You had an obligation to tell us you had a drug problem, if it was going to affect the band. You are *sixteen* years old. And *I'm* not winding up in jail because *you're a fucking junkie!*"

She pulled her hands away from her ears. "*Yes, I'm a junkie!*" she cried. "You can consider every one of our gigs a lie, because I've been using every time!"

"Using *smack?*" She nodded, eyes wild. "And you've been doing it *every fucking day?*"

"More like three or four times a day, so go ahead. Fire me." Her voice broke.

He relinquished his aggressive stance, flopping beside her to regard her silently. "You could have told me," he said finally. "Maybe not in the beginning, but now. We're friends, right?"

"It's not your problem. It's mine. I'll deal with it."

"Don't tell me you can take care of yourself, because you're obviously not doing a very good job." She glared at him. "I'm not going to kick you out of the band, but there's a condition. You have to get treatment. I don't even want to hear it," he said, as she began to protest. "People die doing what you're doing, Shan. Don't expect me to stand by and watch. Now, tell me how this happened," he continued. "I mean, I thought I knew you pretty well, and *this* doesn't seem like you."

She stared at him silently for a moment. Her face was pale, her eyes and nose beginning to glisten with moisture. "You don't know me at all," she said. "I'm not who you think I am."

He leaned forward, resting his arms on his knees. "Well, tell me who you are, then."

She pulled her knees in against her chest and huddled in a ball, staring down at the floor. "You know I lived on the streets for a while," she began, "and that was when I met Jorge."

"You mean that guy from the roof? The one who tried to—"

"Yes. I told you that he let me crash at his place sometimes, and we'd party. He's a dealer."

"So, when he was letting you crash, he was helping you acquire a nifty little habit, too, is that it?" Quinn's face darkened. "I wish I'd killed the motherfucker."

"It's not his fault, Q. I can't blame him because —"

"Bullshit. He was in it for something. What was it?"

She hesitated, then spoke very slowly. "One day he told me he couldn't keep feeding me dope. It was too expensive, he said, but he thought we could work out a deal."

Her voice trailed off as his face changed. "Are you telling me you fucked him for drugs?"

She turned away. "I . . . I didn't know what else to do. You don't understand what it's like, Q. When the dope is gone, it goes bad so fast. You feel like you're going to die, like you'll crawl right out of your skin, so when someone says they'll give you what you need if you just . . ."

Her voice broke and then Quinn was circling her with his arms. "I do understand, and I'm so sorry, angel." His voice was gentle. "So, so sorry."

She ducked her face against his shoulder. "I don't want you to be disappointed in me," she whispered. "What you think matters to me, Q. So much."

"I think it's a miracle you managed to survive at all, after everything you've been through, but you can't keep this up. You have to stop."

"I don't know if I can. Stop, I mean. I've tried."

"I'll help you," he said and drew her closer, suddenly assailed with that warm internal glow.

And he did. He dragged her, kicking and screaming, to the clinic near St. Vincent's that very day. She protested continuously, becoming louder and more insistent as they approached the place. Her eyes were wide with stark terror, or maybe it was just that her pupils were dilated to huge black circles.

When he reached for the door she yanked away, but he caught her wrist and jerked her back to his side. "*Listen,*" he barked. She flinched, but a trace of lucidity crept through the panic in her eyes. "You said you trusted me, didn't you?" She nodded mutely. "Then do it. Trust me. I'll take care of you. I promise."

He pulled open the door and towed her to the front desk. "I need to see Dr. Markowitz."

The receptionist looked up. "Do you have an appointment?"

"No, but he'll see me. Tell him Quinn Marshall is here, okay? And tell him I brought a friend." He turned his blue eyes on her and the receptionist smiled. She was a pretty blonde with big brown eyes, but he didn't give her a second glance as he led Shan to a couch against the wall.

A few minutes later, Steve emerged and knelt in front of her. "We met last night, Shan. Do you remember?"

She wiped her eyes. "No. Well, maybe," she ventured, taking his proffered hand gingerly.

"Why don't you come into my office so we can talk?"

Fear sliced through the dullness on her face. She yanked her hand away and pressed against Quinn's side, hostility radiating from her green eyes. "Quinn can come, if you want," Steve said.

"Sure," Quinn agreed, standing and hauling Shan to her feet. She reluctantly followed Steve down the corridor, but wavered when he paused outside an office. Quinn gave her a shove to propel her through the door. "Stop pushing me," she said, her eyes glimmering like wet glass.

"Then *move*," he hissed, giving her another nudge.

When she was ensconced in an armchair, Steve sat down behind his desk. He focused his attention on Shan. "Why don't you tell me why you're here?"

"Because Quinn dragged me here."

Steve kept his eyes on her. "Why do you suppose he did that?"

She swiped a hand over her perspiring forehead. "I think he's worried about me."

"And why is he worried?"

She met his gaze reluctantly. "Because I have a drug problem."

Within fifteen minutes, he'd coaxed most of the information he needed from her. She was fairly cooperative, until he asked her age. Then her face slammed shut, but Quinn spoke up. "She's sixteen, and she's a runaway." She glared at him. He glared back. "She's afraid you'll turn her in."

Steve kept his gaze on Shan. "Shan, this isn't a detention center. Our program is completely confidential. Now, when are you going to be seventeen?"

She bit her lip and groped for Quinn's hand. "September second."

"Well, legally you'll only be a runaway for a couple more months, then. In the meantime, we can start you on the program today. The first step is detox. You had your last fix last night at around ten?" She nodded. "Then you're probably feeling some withdrawal symptoms. The worst of that will pass over the next day or two."

"It takes a lot longer than that," she corrected him. "I've tried this before."

He inclined his head sympathetically. "Well, there are a few medications that'll make it easier to get through the first few days, but that's really the easy part."

She regarded him doubtfully. "I wouldn't call it *easy.*"

"I hear you, but getting off heroin is one thing. Staying off it is another. Ours is an outpatient program, once you get through detox. You're responsible for coming in every day for the medication. What we prescribe is methadone, which is really just a substitute for the smack. Over time, we'll decrease the dosage and I hope you'll eventually be drug free."

"I will," she said resolutely, "but how long will it take?"

"We want you off heroin for at least a year before we address the methadone dependency."

Her throat swelled in horror. "*A year?* I was thinking, like, a month."

"I wish that were the case, but you have to do this at your own pace. And you should know up front that a lot of addicts never get off methadone. It's not much different from a diabetic needing insulin."

"But I want off," she insisted. "I hate living this way, always worrying about the next fix."

"We'll do everything we can to help you get there," Steve promised, "but it really comes down to motivation and strength of character, and that's completely in your hands." She thrust her chin out and Steve grinned. "I'm glad to see you have some chutzpah. You're going to need it." He placed his hands flat on the desk. "That's the program. You think you can handle it?" She nodded. "Good. I'm assuming you don't have insurance?"

"No, but I can pay, at least some." Quinn shot her a questioning look. "I've been saving for a new guitar," she explained, "and I don't need anybody's charity. I can—"

"I know." Quinn rolled his eyes. "You can take care of yourself."

"Okay, let's get started," Steve said, standing "One of our nurse practitioners will give you a physical exam, then I'll refer you to one of the rehab doctors, okay?"

Shan looked at Quinn. "Do you have to leave?"

"Yes," Steve cut in. "He does. You need to concentrate on getting better now."

Quinn held her gaze. "I'll come and get you when you're ready to leave, okay?"

As the nurse led her into the examining room, Shan shot one last yearning look at him over her shoulder. She looked lost and terribly small.

Quinn watched until the door swung shut behind her. "I hate to leave her here alone."

Steve clapped him on the shoulder. "She's not," he said. "She's with people who can help her, but you can be there when it's time for her to face the outside. She'll need some support and you'd be a good one to give it. I get the feeling she's very attached to you."

Abruptly Quinn pulled away. "I'll call you in the morning," he said.

"Hey, did I say something wrong?" Steve called after him, puzzled.

Quinn did not reply, just headed out the door. When he hit the street he headed for the subway, to take the A train to Spanish Harlem.

chapter 16

Five days later, a pale, shaky Shan emerged from the clinic. She'd been assisted through the withdrawal process with a host of chemicals and had begun the treatments that would transform her from a heroin addict into a methadone addict. The methadone was creepy stuff. It came in an ampoule, a tiny bottle filled with thick, orange liquid that had an odd sort of solidity to it. Imagining what it looked like once it hit her stomach had made her vaguely uneasy as she chased it with the requisite glass of water.

When Shan came into the reception area, Quinn was waiting, looking over the plethora of Narcotics Anonymous propaganda tacked to the wall. She approached him with a mixture of relief and embarrassment but, when he turned toward her, she was momentarily distracted. There was an ugly purple bruise under his left eye.

When he smiled, she noticed his lip was swollen, too. "Are you okay?" he said.

"Yes. Are *you*?" she asked and he nodded. "What happened to your face?"

"Nothing much," he shrugged. "You hungry? Want to go somewhere for lunch?"

She shook her head. "All I can taste is methadone. But, Q, your eye—"

"Doesn't sound too appetizing," he interrupted smoothly. "I'll take you home, then."

He had the van and drove her home. She was silent, but kept sneaking glances at his eye. He was quiet during the ride as well, and, when they got to the loft, she went into the living room and wearily dropped into a chair. Finally she spoke. "What did you tell everyone?"

"That you were sick. They think you were at my place." He grinned. "Be prepared to get the third degree from Denise. I'm sure she thinks we've been screwing our brains out."

"What about our gigs? Did you play them without me?"

"No, I found replacements. No serious harm done."

She tried to smile, but couldn't quite pull it off. "I'm so sorry you got dragged into this."

"It's okay, Shan."

"It's not. And I'm not who you thought I was," she said miserably. "I hoped you'd never have to know. I lied to you, over and over."

"I can see why. You were scared, and that's my fault."

"It's not your fault. I lied to everybody, not just you. I'm so sorry, and I understand if you don't want me around anymore."

"Now you're being an idiot." He reached for her hand, but she pulled away.

"All I've been is a giant pain in the ass ever since you met me," she said, hanging her head, "and I don't want you feeling like you have to stay here and take care of me now."

He was silent for a long time, then, "Where'd you learn to have so much faith in people?"

She looked up to find him glaring at her. "Q, you've been amazing, but I don't want you to feel like you're obligated—"

"I thought we were friends." He was scowling. "To me, that carries an obligation."

"But . . ." She couldn't bring herself to meet his eyes and her voice was so low he had to lean forward to hear it. "I don't know why you'd want to be my friend, after the things I've done."

"Well, you were right when you said you weren't who I thought you were, that's for sure." She winced, but he went on. "You're a lot tougher. I've been thinking about you a lot over the last couple of days," he continued, reaching for her hand again. "I haven't thought about much else, to tell you the truth. All the shit you've been through . . . I can't believe you survived it."

She kept her head down, but gripped his hand. "It doesn't take much to survive."

"That's where you're wrong. I think most people would have given up, but you got through it. You even held on to your talent, kept it alive. I don't know how you did it. I couldn't have."

"You'd never hit bottom like I have," she said. "You're so together, and so strong. The strongest person I know."

He was silent for a long time. When she looked at him, she saw he was frowning down at their clasped hands. "What is it?" she asked.

He looked up, studied her for a moment, then shrugged. "Nothing. Want to play for a while?"

"Yes," she said. "That's exactly what I want to do." She waited, because he seemed like he wanted to say something more, but when he dropped her hand and got up to undrape his keyboard, she went for her guitar.

She made it only as far as her bedroom door and froze. She stood there for a long time and, eventually, she spoke. "Q, could you do something for me?"

The words were strained, enough to bring him to her side. She was still frozen, staring at the dresser. She pointed at the top drawer. "In there."

He squeezed past her and opened the drawer. His eyebrows shot up.

"Would you get rid of it?" Without a word, Quinn took what was left of the heroin rock and went out the front door.

He returned about ten minutes later. "All gone. Got any more stashed?"

"No." Her voice was still tense. "What did you do with it?"

He chuckled. "There'll be some happy rats in the sewer tonight."

"Thanks, Q."

"No problem. What's a friend for, if not to take your dope?"

"I mean it." Her voice shook. "I couldn't do it myself. I thought I could, but . . ."

"It's okay, Shan. I understand how you feel." He touched her shoulder.

She flinched. "No, you don't. You don't know what this feels like at all."

He studied her silently. She was still frozen, like she was perched on the brink of something. "Look, grab your guitar. Let's go to my place."

She eyed him with surprise. "Really?" He'd never suggested that before. In fact, that night after the Carnegie Hall gig was the only time she'd ever been there.

"Sure." He shrugged. "We can play there as well as we can here. You'll have to listen to my Yamaha keyboard, which doesn't sound half as good as the Kur, but it'll be easier, won't it?"

It would, she realized. The counselor at the clinic had warned her that it might be stressful for her to be in her home at first, because the craving could be triggered by the environment. "I don't want to intrude . . ." she began, but he went back into the bedroom and fetched her guitar.

"If it was an intrusion, I wouldn't ask. Let's go." He caught himself. "Unless you don't want to. Would you rather be alone?"

"*No,*" she said. "I mean . . . I don't want to put you out, but I'd like to be with you."

He grinned. "All right, then. Ready?"

"Only if you answer a question first. What happened to your face?"

He shrugged. "I paid a visit to your buddy in Spanish Harlem."

"I knew it was something like that." Her eyes widened in alarm. "I just knew it! Oh, Q, I told you I didn't want you getting mixed up with him."

"He had our mics," Quinn reminded her. "They cost over two thousand dollars, Shan. There was no way I was just going to let them go."

"I could have gotten them back. He's just holding them because I owe him money. I can pay him most of it now—there's almost enough in my guitar fund, although I had to spend some on the clinic stay and the methadone . . ." Her voice trailed off when she saw the look on his face.

"If you ever go near him again, I'll kill you myself."

"But I have to pay him," she insisted. "He'll never leave me alone until—"

"I did. With interest."

Her mouth fell open. "You settled my drug debt?"

"Yes." He smiled faintly. "It took some negotiating, but he's a businessman, after all. He won't bother you again."

"But he's *dangerous*, Q. He's—"

"Not going to bother you, I said. I guarantee it," Quinn said firmly. "I told you, I negotiated with him. It took some doing, but he finally saw the light. And if you think I look bad, you ought to see *him.*"

Shan went over to Quinn's place, but made a stop at the bank in order to withdraw enough from her guitar fund to pay him back. He argued furiously with her, telling her to use it on a guitar, but she insisted he accept the sixteen hundred dollars she'd managed to save. Afterward she had only twelve dollars left in her account, but she figured it was money well spent.

After that, Shan began spending a lot of time at Quinn's. They did their writing there, although band practice was still at the loft. Eventually it became easier for Shan to be at home, as she developed new routines that didn't revolve around fixing. She went to the clinic every day for her methadone, attended sessions with a clinic-assigned counselor, and went to NA meetings, although she was having trouble with the whole "higher power" thing.

Shan wasn't an atheist, exactly, but she wasn't a believer even though she'd been raised Catholic. Her father had been outwardly devout, going to church even when he reeked of the alcohol he'd consumed the night before. She supposed that was the basis of her own lack of faith, that God-fearing man who prayed in church, then burned her with cigarettes when he came home.

She confided this to Quinn, but he insisted that the meetings were critical. "You have to be around other people who know what you're going through," he told her. "Nobody else really understands." She was dubious, but he offered to go with her and, when he did, it was easier.

The craving still burned, but most of the time she was busy enough to push it away. Her evenings were taken up with gigging, since the Quinntessence schedule was jam packed. They played four, five, sometimes six days a week, just as Quinn had warned her in the beginning. He hadn't been kidding about his rule that they never turned down a reasonable gig, *reasonable* defined as a decent venue, good exposure, or significant bank. Preferably all three.

He proved that he was capable of bending the rules in late July, when he announced that he'd given away a lucrative Saturday-night gig at the Grotto so they could all watch a televised performance of Pink Floyd's *The Wall.* The concert was headlined by Roger Waters, Floyd's former bass player and principal songwriter, another of Quinn's personal heroes, and was taking place at the former site of the Berlin Wall, which had fallen some eight months before.

The band congregated at the loft to watch the show, which featured more superstars than Shan had ever seen on one stage. Sinead O'Connor, the Hooters, Thomas Dolby, the Scorpions, Van Morrison, Levon Helm, and Garth Hudson all performed. Shan cried out in delight when Cyndi Lauper appeared, but even that excitement was eclipsed when Joni Mitchell took the stage, singing "Goodbye Blue Sky."

Shan went misty as she watched, wishing her mother was there to see it, and when Joni returned for the finale, Quinn winked at her. "Prog rocker Waters and folk queen Mitchell sharing a stage," he said. "Who would have thought?"

She smiled, thinking they were about as likely a duo as Quinn Marshall and Shan O'Hara.

Before she knew it, the summer was almost over. Quinntessence spent a week in August recording a new demo and Shan was excited to find herself in a real studio for the first time. She hounded Quinn to let her participate, even after they finished recording. He was doubtful, but she insisted she wanted to experience every step of the process, and he acquiesced after instructing her that she was to watch silently without commenting or interfering in any way.

She promised, only to be treated to a dose of boredom so excruciating it made her want to scream. For days Quinn hunched over the mixing board with Bruce, debating each miniscule edit and blend with a focus bordering on obsession. Sometimes she found it impossible to refrain from comment, especially since none of the tweaking had any noticeable impact on the way the songs sounded, but anytime she opened her mouth Quinn silenced her with the threat of expulsion.

Finally, they finished and settled back to review the master. Afterward, as they sat there congratulating themselves, Shan decided to speak up. "I think there's too much bass."

"You think there's too much bass because you're sitting in the back of the room where all the lows build up," Quinn said without turning. "If I actually cared about your opinion, you'd be sitting up here with us."

"Oh yeah?" she bridled. "Well, I think all the keyboard solos are too loud, too."

Quinn was gritting his teeth as he swiveled his chair to face her. "Look, when you asked if you could be here for the mixing I told you you'd get bored, but you insisted. And I said okay because you promised me you'd sit there and absorb it, and shut the hell up."

"It's *my* demo, too, and I'm entitled to say what I think."

"I don't care what you think, little girl. We'll listen to it as a group and, if everybody thinks we need to make changes, then Bruce and I will come back and remix. *Comprende?*"

"Don't call me 'little girl,'" she shot back. "I hate it when you talk down to me."

"I don't mean it that way. You're physically a small person, that's all."

"So is Bruce," she said, "but I don't hear you calling him 'little boy.' No offense," she added to the five-foot-four-inch engineer.

"None taken. I'll leave you guys to fight while I go make a copy of this," Bruce said. "Interesting observation about the keyboard solos," he speculated aloud as he left.

Shan pointed her nose in the air as Quinn turned his back on her. "You are *so* annoying," he said, snapping his notebook shut.

"I don't see why *you* get the last word," she said, wandering over to the mixer.

"*I'm* the producer, that's why." He watched for a moment as she toyed restlessly with the sliders. "Having an edgy day, are we?"

"No, I'm not. I just don't agree with you on the final mix."

"Okay, you've stated your opinion. Now keep it to yourself until everyone else gets a chance to hear it." Shan muttered something about egomania under her breath and Quinn heaved a deep sigh. "And, yes, you *are* having an edgy day. Do you really think I can't tell by now?"

When she spun around and glared, he shrugged. "It's okay. You're entitled to that, too."

She gazed at him for a moment, then hung her head. "I don't mean to take it out on you."

"It's okay, I said. I'm used to it."

She put her arms around him and hugged him hard, then drew back to regard him with tender eyes. He grinned amiably in return and rested his head against her shoulder to look at her slant-eyed and teasing. "Why do you look so mushy?"

"I was just thinking what an incredible person you turned out to be," she said warmly. "You know, when I first met you, I thought you were an arrogant asshole."

"I knew that." He smirked. "It was way obvious, but I feel compelled to correct you. You didn't think I was an asshole until I hit on you, so I figured you were gay."

She sniffed, releasing him as Bruce returned. "Of course. The fact that I didn't immediately fall all over you couldn't possibly have anything to do with *you*," she said. "Besides, I was partly right. You *are* arrogant. It rings out as loud and clear as those keyboard solos."

Quinn rolled his eyes as Bruce held up a CD. "Loud as the keyboards may be," Bruce said, "here, pending final approval, is the official Quinntessence demo, summer 1990."

Quinn reached for the disc. "And what a summer it's been." His eyes met Shan's over the mixing board. She nodded, smiling.

chapter 17

Shan popped open the ampoule and gulped down her dose, then grimaced. Even after six weeks, she couldn't get used to the taste of the methadone. She tossed the ampoule in the trash and reached for a bottle of spring water.

Oda was at the stove, cooking up a pot of oatmeal. "Here. You're still too thin," she observed, handing Shan a bowl. Both Oda and Denise had known the truth for some time now; Shan had told them shortly after completing her stint at the clinic. She had confessed to Dan and Ty, as well, and their response had surprised and touched her. All had expressed support, instead of the scorn she'd anticipated.

Shan went into the dining room to eat. Oda was right, but she was starting to put on a little weight. The craving still jabbed, but she no longer woke up with a jones. She felt good.

Today she felt particularly good. It was her seventeenth birthday. Her first thought on waking was that no one could force her to go back to her father's house ever again.

She hadn't mentioned the significance of the day to anyone. Just the fact that she was free was birthday present enough, although the day was tinged with sadness as well, since it was Quinn's and Ty's last day in New York. They'd be leaving for Boston the next morning and Shan was going to miss them terribly, especially Quinn. He'd become such a central part of her life that she wasn't quite sure how she was going to get by without him.

"What are you and Quinn up to today?" Denise asked as Shan finished her oatmeal.

"We have to pick up the demos and then we're going to run them out to the clubs," Shan said, scraping the bottom of her bowl. "He wants to do it before they leave."

"Really?" Denise wrinkled her nose. "I figured you'd at least be doing something fun."

"He's a workaholic to the end." Shan paused. "I am a little disappointed," she admitted. "It would be nice to do something special, especially since all of us aren't getting together tonight."

"I wish we could, but Dan's sister is in town. We couldn't get out of it."

"And Ty has a date. Well, I can't blame him for that, either. I'm just glad Q doesn't have one." Just then a knock sounded from the front door.

"You ready?" Quinn said when Shan opened it. "We have a lot of ground to cover."

"It's only ten o'clock. You want some coffee?" He shook his head, hovering in the doorway. "I don't see why we're hand delivering them anyway."

"It's good PR. How many times do I have to tell you this?"

"Whatever. See ya, guys," she called as they departed.

"Besides, I might spring for dinner, even though it's your turn to pay," he said as they trotted downstairs. "Want to hit Salaam Bombay tonight?"

"You bet," she said. "Especially if it's on you."

That evening they climbed wearily back up to the loft. "I'm stuffed," Shan moaned. She handed Quinn a stack of discs and dug for her keys. "Well, we got most of them distributed. I can deliver the rest next week." She opened the door and he followed her inside. "It's only a little after seven. Want to rent a movie?" She walked into the living room, reaching for the light switch.

"SURPRISE!"

She jumped. The room was filled with people and decorated with balloons and streamers. A big, hand-lettered banner hung above the window. HAPPY 17TH BIRTHDAY, SHAN! it proclaimed.

"How did you . . ." she began and stopped, completely overcome. She turned, intent on escaping into the kitchen, and collided with Quinn, who was watching her with an enormous grin.

She inspected his self-satisfied expression and her eyes narrowed. "*You* did this."

"Guilty." His smile widened.

"How did you know it was my birthday? I didn't tell anyone."

"Yes, you did," he corrected her, "when you checked into the clinic."

Dan handed her a glass of champagne. "Happy birthday, princess." She looked him. "Your sister . . . ?"

"Is in California, where she belongs," Denise finished.

"It's a good thing we had Quinn to keep you busy," Ty said. "Did he run you ragged?"

"Yes." Shan nodded. "I should have known. Since when do we deliver demos by hand?"

"Since never," Ty said, his deep voice full of laughter, "but we figured you wouldn't be suspicious of an anal-retentive, time-consuming errand if it came at the behest of the Q-man."

Ty raised his champagne flute in Quinn's direction with a knowing smirk. Quinn winked at Shan and tapped his glass against Ty's.

Oda had baked a big carrot cake. Shan blew out the candles while everyone sang, then they forced her to sit in the middle of the room and presented her with gifts. Denise and Dan gave her a gorgeous Indian scarf and she received a dainty silver ankle bracelet from Ty. Bruce's gift was a stone jar filled with guitar picks and Oda's was a cool tie-dyed backpack. When she'd finished unwrapping, the coffee table was covered with birthday cards and wrapping paper.

Denise was examining the gifts. "Quinn, didn't you give her anything?" She frowned at him with disapproval.

Shan laughed. "He's not the sentimental type, remember?"

Quinn cocked his head. "Is that so? Well, it just happens I *did* get you something." He reached behind Shan's chair for a long, brightly wrapped box that he set on the floor. "Careful," he said. "It's heavy."

Shan stared at the package. It was almost as big as she was. She looked up at Quinn, who was settled against the window sill with a cat-that-got-the-canary expression.

She slid out of the chair and dropped to her knees. She loosened the wrapping paper and pushed it aside, revealing a heavy-gauge cardboard box. When she opened it, her eyes widened. Securely cushioned in a bed of tissue paper was a black vinyl guitar case. Shan looked up at Quinn again. A ghost of a smile was materializing on his face as she flipped back the lid.

She gasped. "Holy shit!" Ty exclaimed. She heard a swift intake of breath from Dan, and a low whistle from Bruce.

A Martin.

Not just *any* Martin. It was a Martin HD-28, the acoustic dream machine she'd lusted after for years. She recognized the spruce body and tortoise pickguard from the catalogue.

"Have you lost your mind?" she blurted. "This is a three-thousand-dollar instrument!"

His grin got bigger. "I got a deal on it."

She snorted indelicately. "So you got it for twenty-eight hundred? Come on, Q. This is the nicest thing anyone's ever done for me, but it's too much and I won't accept it."

"Too late," he said. "I had it personalized, so you can't return it."

"Personalized?" She examined the guitar more closely. She was almost afraid to touch it.

Then she saw it. There, on the headstock, a tiny inlay, no bigger than a guitar pick, directly between the machine heads.

It was an angel. A tiny, stylized angel with flowing hair and dainty weblike wings.

It was insanely extravagant and over the top, but so thoughtful and personal and lovely, the most wonderful gift she had ever received. Her throat closed and she was unable to utter a single sound.

"I thought she looked like you," Quinn murmured when she got to her feet and put her arms around him. "You wouldn't refuse a gift I put so much thought into, would you?"

She shook her head, hard. "Oh, Q," she said, when she found her voice, "I lo—"

. . . love you.

She gasped, pulling away from his embrace before the words could escape her lips, but when she looked up at him, she knew it was true.

She loved him. Truly. Deeply. Completely. Quinn, with all his arrogance and bossiness and frequent flyers and stupid, arbitrary rules. She loved him.

He was the one. The only *perfect* one.

He was looking back at her, frowning a little now. "What?" he asked. "Don't you like it?"

"I love it," she said. "*Love* it. It's perfect, Q. Absolutely perfect." And she stepped back into his arms.

"Oh, break it up," Denise sniffed.

"Yeah!" Ty agreed. "Are you going to *play* this baby or what?" He held out the Martin.

Shan released Quinn and took the guitar. When she ran her fingers over the strings, she noted that it was tuned to a T. As she began the opening riff of "The Only Perfect One," marveling at the rich, full-bodied sound, she could feel her arms prickling.

Quinn grinned and she knew he could see the goose bumps.

Several hours later, Quinn searched out Shan and found her in her room. She was sitting on her futon admiring the new Martin, which she'd placed in the metal stand that had always held Joanie.

"I'm glad you like it," he said. She turned around to regard him tenderly.

"I still can't believe you did this. Not just this," she motioned to the Martin, "but everything. Thanks for making it so special, Q. I . . ." She paused, searching, then shook her head. "I don't have any words."

He sat down beside her and looked around at the familiar furnishings, the shelves under the window overflowing with books and CDs, the futon with its colorful Indian blanket, the posters on the walls: Dylan, the Grateful Dead in Haight-Ashbury, a Monet print from the cathedral series. His gaze took in the objects scattered on top of her dresser, guitar picks and packets of strings mingling with earrings and necklaces, a framed photograph of her mother, a small amber bottle of the essential-oil blend she always wore. He noticed a new photo tucked in the corner of the mirror: a picture of the two of them that Denise had snapped one day at a Village street fair. They were cheek to cheek and their smiles were enormous.

"I'm going to miss this room," he said, a trifle wistfully. "I've spent more time here than I have at my own place this summer." He reached for her hand, then looked down at it. "What's this?"

When she opened her fist, he saw that she held a small piece of wood. He took it, examined it. It was a guitar bridge. "From Joanie," she said softly. "I was just . . . saying good-bye to her."

"Maybe not," he said. "This one could be Joanie Two."

Shan shook her head no. "This one's name is obvious, don't you think? She's the Angel."

"The Angel and the Kur. They'll make a good couple." He set the bridge on the milk crate Shan used as a nightstand, then stood up. "We're going to head home, I think. It's getting late."

She rose, too, and put her arms around him. He hugged her back, resting his cheek on the top of her head. The scent of sandalwood tickled his nose. When he felt his body stir, he drew back.

She compensated by pressing closer and felt so nice that he was unwilling to let go of her just yet. Maybe she wouldn't notice how much he liked the way she smelled.

She made a small, inarticulate murmur, then slid her arms around his waist.

Uh-oh. She'd noticed, all right.

He buried his face in her hair and let the hypnotic fragrance draw him in. The soft swells of her breasts were generating twin circles of heat that penetrated deep into his chest. He felt her tugging at his shirt and a moment later she was touching the skin of his lower back. Almost of their own volition, his hands slipped down her body and inside the waistband of her jeans. He murmured when he encountered the velvety cleft of her buttocks.

He was straining against her, pressing into her yielding form in an irresistible dance of intimacy. She was arching against him, responding with equal ardor, and his gaze traveled over her head to the futon located just behind them.

It would be the most natural thing in the world. Kick the door shut and tumble her back. Free her of her clothes, and glide his hands and his mouth and his cock over every inch of her.

He heard a sound behind him and turned his head.

Dan was in the doorway. "Er, we're heading out. Did you want to come or . . ." He trailed off.

Quinn hesitated. He felt Shan's arms compress around his waist and a tremor run down his spine as she pressed her lips into the hollow of his throat. He stared at Dan woodenly for a moment, then heaved a regretful sigh. "Yeah, I'm coming. Just give me a minute, okay?"

Dan nodded and backed out of the room, pulling the door shut behind him.

Shan raised her head and he saw that her laser eyes were smoky with passion. His gaze fell to her full, pink mouth. He raised his hand and traced her lower lip with his index finger.

"You know, there's nothing in the world I want more than to make love to you right now," he said, staring in fascination as she caught his finger between her teeth, nibbling gently. She murmured in assent and her tongue suddenly emerged to caress his finger.

He hastily pulled his hand away from her mouth. "We can't, though."

"Why not?" Shan rested her chin against his chest to gaze up at him. "We both want to."

"But there's a really basic disconnect here. You," he touched the tip of her nose, "are not an indulger in casual sex and to me there's no other kind. And so there we are."

"I see." Her eyes had darkened ominously. "Got to stick to those golden rules, right? God forbid you should *bend* them, just this one time."

"You're such an idiot," he said, giving her a little shake. "When have you and I ever played by the rules? But this isn't something we should just jump into, no matter how much we both want it. Besides, I'm leaving tomorrow. How are you going to feel when I'm gone?"

She pulled away and glared at him. He glared back for a moment, then turned toward the door.

"Q?" Her small voice made him pause in the act of slamming it. "Will I see you tomorrow?"

His scowl faded. "Do you think I'd leave without saying good-bye?"

She shrugged and he shook his head as he came back to put his arms around her again. She hugged him back, very tightly. "You really piss me off sometimes, Mr. Marshall."

He chuckled, then pulled away. "You'd better let go of me," he said, raising an eyebrow. "I might not be so noble next time. I only have a limited supply of morality, you know?"

Just before he pulled the door closed, he looked back at her. She was watching him, with her arms folded tightly across her chest and the most enchanting expression on her face. He felt a tremendous tug at his heartstrings. She was so fucking beautiful he could hardly look at her.

"Happy birthday, angel." The door clicked shut between them.

During the ride home, Quinn was pensive and silent. When they pulled up at a twenty-four-hour store and Ty went in for a pack of cigarettes, Dan cleared his throat. "You know, I wasn't sure you'd make it home tonight."

Quinn shrugged, keeping his gaze fixed out the window. "I got the feeling Shan wanted you to stay," Dan said.

Quinn remained stubbornly silent. "I could drop you back there," Dan persisted.

Quinn swiveled his head and scowled at him. "Lay the fuck off! You're worse than a broad, for Crissakes. Why are you pushing me?"

Dan shook his head with a small smile. "Because you're crazy about that little girl, dude. You've got it bad, and everybody knows it but you."

Quinn waved him off. "All I've got is a raging hard on."

"So why don't you do something with it?"

"With a bandmate?" Quinn shrugged. "It's no big deal. Just a simple case of fuckstration that creates some tension every now and then."

"Bullshit," Dan declared. "If you just wanted to get wet, you'd have done it a long time ago. I've never seen you like this before, and I think you *should* do something about it."

Quinn's eyes narrowed. "If you tell me I'm pussy whipped, I'll slug you, Danny."

Dan regarded him seriously. "I wasn't going to say that. It might be time for you to reconsider your priorities, you know? I think she's good for you. She suits you."

"Yup, she's a good friend and a great bandmate. End of story."

"That would be too bad." As Ty emerged from the store, Dan imparted one final comment. "It would be a damn shame, in this case, if the only perfect one was the one that got away."

The next morning they came over for breakfast and the mood was deliberately light. When the hour of departure arrived, Shan, Denise, and Dan walked Ty and Quinn downstairs.

As they lingered on the street, Quinn glanced at Shan. She was visibly upset, her lips tight and her eyes glittering with pain. "Will you keep in touch?" she asked.

"You know, I'm not dropping off the face of the earth," he told her. "I'll call."

"Will you write me?" she persisted.

"I'm not great at that stuff, but I'll try. Or better yet, you write. I'll read, and I'll send music." She nodded gravely and he felt a twinge of pain. "Please stop looking at me like that. You're killing me. Why are you so fucking bummed out all of a sudden?"

"I feel like I'm losing my best friend," she said and he frowned.

"You're not. Okay?" She nodded, but her face was wreathed in sorrow and he groaned aloud. "Just don't cry. I don't think I could stand it."

"I won't." She shook her head. "I never cry. Ever."

That was true, he mused. He'd never once seen a tear in her eye, not even when she was coming off heroin. "It's time for us to roll, so give me a hug."

She did, and brought her lips close to his ear. "I love you, Q," she whispered. "A lot."

He drew back, a trifle alarmed, then kissed her chastely on the forehead. She reached up to smooth the hair out of his eyes, but he turned away. "Let's go," he said to Ty, refusing to look at Shan. He gave Dan a light cuff on the chest and headed toward the car, then hesitated.

He was going to miss her. Christ, was he going to miss her.

"Come on, man," Ty said from the driver's seat. "We should have left an hour ago."

Quinn pivoted, grabbed Shan around the waist and swung her up in his arms. "What—" she began, but her words were muffled when he clamped his mouth over hers.

She stiffened, but only for a moment, then kissed him back. Her feet were dangling a good four inches off the ground, so she wound her arms around his shoulders and surrendered, secure in the strength of his embrace.

He let her body slide through his arms until she was standing on tiptoe, then moved his lips close to her ear. "It's a good thing I didn't do this last night," he murmured, "or it would have taken an act of God to get me out of that room." And he kissed her again, hard and sweet.

Then he let her go and smiled his boyish smile. "See ya." He got in the car, shut the door, and gave her a long, last look as they drove away.

Shan watched until the car disappeared around the corner. Her heart was pounding and she could still taste him on her lips.

For the first time that day, she wished she had a fix.

part two
1991

One good thing about music,
when it hits you,
you feel no pain.
—Bob Marley

chapter 18

In the van, Shan leaned forward, twisting around a pile of sleeping bags to peer out the window. "Is that it?" she asked, squinting at a small house just visible over a craggy hillside.

"We're looking for Echo Road," Dan reminded her, not for the first time. They had no air conditioning and he had his hair pulled back in a ponytail. Shan could see dots of perspiration on his cheeks and the back of his neck. "No, that's not it," he said, as they passed a sign identifying the small street as Ottie Road.

"I wish we'd get there already. We're getting so far from town," Denise said, fanning herself. The small diamond Dan had given her two weeks before glittered as she waved her left hand.

"Q said it was isolated," Dan said. "I guess he wasn't kidding."

Shan sat back, her hands drumming against her thighs. She wished they'd arrive, too. She could barely stand it, the waiting. She'd waited so long already.

They'd been on the road just over a week and it felt like they'd stopped in every random town between New York and Los Angeles. In fact they had not, although Denise insisted upon incorporating a few landmarks into their route. They'd seen the Sears Tower and Dodge City. They'd followed Route 66 through Flagstaff and, even in her urgency, Shan was enthralled by the beauty of the Grand Canyon. According to Quinn they'd be living in a canyon, Big Tujunga Canyon, and the vast walls and swooping descents of the South Rim captivated her, but even that only momentarily quelled her compulsion to keep moving.

She'd obtained her driver's permit for the trip and argued for traveling through the night, but Dan was adamant that they stop. He wasn't comfortable sleeping while she was at the wheel since she was a new driver, especially not with the U-Haul hitched to the back of the van.

The trailer made Denise nervous, so Shan and Dan divided the driving. They spent the nights at campgrounds, sleeping in tents since the vehicles were packed to capacity with Dan's drum kit, Denise's furniture and darkroom equipment, and Shan's guitars. In consideration for her traveling mates' privacy Shan had acquired her own small pop-up, which she pitched some distance from theirs. At night she could hear them making love and sometimes she touched herself, dreaming of Quinn.

She thought about him constantly, replayed the events of his last night in New York over and over again. When she did, she could practically feel his hands on her body, taste the kiss he'd given her before he left. When she wasn't remembering, she was fantasizing about the life they'd have when they were finally together again.

He'd flown out of Boston a few weeks earlier, right after graduation, to find a house where they could all live together. And that place, where the next phase of her life would happen, was somewhere ahead of them on this windy canyon road.

Their progression across the country had felt painfully slow to Shan, but neither as painful nor as slow as the passage of the ten months since he'd left New York. After his departure, she'd fallen into a funk from which she'd been unable to rouse herself. Her heaviness of spirit stirred the embers of her heroin jones. They had smoldered while Quinn was there to distract her, but flared with a vengeance once she was alone.

She remembered what she'd been told at the clinic, that the physical withdrawal was really the easy part. She hadn't wanted to believe that was true, but now she knew it was. What remained after the shakes and the sweats and the nausea subsided was far more sinister and, months later, it still hadn't gone away, the craving that percolated like a malignancy.

She turned to NA and tried to supplant her hunger for drugs with a compulsion to attend meetings. She went every day, sometimes twice a day, but like before found she couldn't embrace the "higher power" doctrine that was the backbone of the program. Still, the meetings helped. She made a few friends, listened to their stories, and knew there were lower bottoms than the one she'd hit. She'd never hurt anyone but herself, after all, and she was still alive and functioning. She knew she had Quinn to thank for it. It was torturous, having him so far away.

"I miss him so much," she told Oda. "My life feels empty without him."

"Well, you're going to have to fill it up," Oda said. "Quinn's not here to do it for you."

She couldn't think of any way to do that, especially with the jones and its insidious taunting. She tossed at night, her craving for heroin battling her longing for Quinn. Sometimes she didn't think she'd make it and her music provided the only respite. Her music, and his phone calls.

He called often and they talked for hours, amassing spectacular phone bills. They talked about everything, sharing their opinions on the war in the Persian Gulf (bad), the hole in the ozone layer (very bad), and the Milli Vanilli scandal (unconscionable). She soothed him when Cincinnati beat the A's in the World Series, although Shan knew very little about baseball, and mirrored his excitement over the development of something called the World Wide Web, about which she knew even less.

The one thing they didn't talk about was their relationship. Quinn never mentioned what had happened between them on his last night in New York and Shan didn't know how to bring it up. Instead, she waited for his calls and grew more and more dependent upon them, reveling in their growing closeness and relying on it to keep the jones at bay.

When she confided her fears about relapsing, Quinn had a practical solution. "Of course it's hard, but don't sit around and wallow in it. Do something, for fuck's sake. Why don't you take some music lessons?"

"Do you think I need more vocal coaching?" she asked.

"Absolutely not," he said. "I don't want anyone undoing the work I did on you. Some guitar instruction wouldn't hurt, though. Manhattan School of Music offers master classes."

"I'm pretty hand to mouth right now. The methadone is so expensive . . ."

"I'm sure there's a scholarship program," he said. "You're something special and that's what they want. Dan's got connections at MSM, so let's see what we can work out."

As it turned out, the artist in residence for the spring semester was Dexter Reinhardt. Quinn sent a demo, Dan talked to the school, and the next thing she knew she was learning from a master.

The sixty-seven-year-old Reinhardt was a music legend, an electric blues guitarist who hailed from the Louisiana bayou. He'd been among the first of the bluesmen to cross over into the rock arena and he was renowned for his razor-sharp sound. His bare-finger plucking style was his trademark, one that Shan occasionally emulated in her own work.

"You're a real guitar player's guitar player," Reinhardt told her. "Your fretwork—it's blistering, among the best I've heard. Sometimes, though, you're a little *too* splattery. You could use some discipline."

"Just be careful not to get too enamored with him," Quinn said when she bubbled over. "He's awesome, but you don't want to start sounding like a Reinhardt clone. Don't lose your personal style."

So she studied, and learned, and practiced with a newfound purpose. Her work was evolving, developing even more of an edge, and she adopted some of the avant-garde blues and funk that characterized Reinhardt's playing. Her gigs became forums for her experiments, and she was gratified by the reaction she earned from her audiences.

She'd always played guitar religiously, practicing every day, but now it became an obsession and she didn't realize how much until the last few days of the cross-country trip. When they first set out she played in the van often, but once in Colorado Dan had to swerve sharply to avoid a mountain lion. Shan was flung against the door and she heard the neck of her guitar hit with a sharp whack. The Angel was unharmed, but it scared her so much that she hadn't taken it out again while the van was in motion. By the time they reached the California state line, she was battling a guitar jones on top of all the others.

The most painful longing was about to end, though. Dan was turning off the canyon highway, starting down a bumpy trail with a dusty sign identifying it as Echo Road. At the bottom, she saw a rambling lodge-style cabin of faded clapboards. A stone porch with a couple of weathered Adirondack chairs decorated its front and parked outside was a shiny black motorcycle, the Harley she knew belonged to Quinn, and Ty's silver Mazda. Behind the house, Shan saw a windy stream meandering along the foot of a steep, brush-covered hillside.

As they approached the house, Dan laid on the horn. Almost immediately, the front door opened and there was Quinn, barefoot, in surfer shorts and a white T-shirt.

Shan was out and running before the van came to a full stop, her feet spraying gravel as she flew over the sandy ground. When she reached Quinn, she flung her arms around him with wild, reckless joy, plowing into him with such force that she felt him stagger backward.

"Q! Q!" she babbled, absolutely unable to form another word. "Oh, Q . . ."

She felt him catch his bearings, then enfold her in a massive bear hug.

She heard a screen door slam, then Dan's and Ty's voices as they greeted each other. After a time she drew back to look up at Quinn. His smile was enormous as he let go of her waist and took her face between his hands. "Angel," he said, gazing down at her warmly. "Damn, I missed you." He kissed her on the mouth, brief but hard, with a loud smack.

Shan's gaze fastened on him with rapt adoration. He was tanned now and his blond hair was longer, pulled back into a tail, but he was still beautiful, just as heart stopping as ever.

She heard Ty laugh softly. "Hey, you two, the rest of us are here, too, you know."

Without taking her eyes off Quinn, Shan reached in Ty's general direction. She felt him take her hand and squeeze it. "It's good to see you, Ty," she said, still gazing up at Quinn.

This time all of them laughed. Quinn released her and grabbed Dan's outstretched hand, clapping him on the shoulder in a manly, one-armed hug.

"Quinntessence," he said, "together again."

"And me," Denise chirped.

Quinn rolled his eyes, but smiled. "And you," he agreed. "Come on in."

They followed him into the house, which was roomy and rustic, with unpainted, rough-hewn walls and very little furniture. "It's not a palace," Quinn warned. "No air conditioning and the hot water runs out in ten minutes, but it's big and it's affordable."

"Kind of remote," Dan said. "I was surprised when you said Tujunga. It'll take at least half an hour to get into LA proper."

"More like forty minutes, depending on the traffic," Quinn said. He took them through the eat-in kitchen and tiny laundry room, which he commented might be a good space for Denise's darkroom, since they didn't have a washer or dryer anyway. Next he showed them the den, which had a stone fireplace, explaining that this would serve as their living room. He led them to the intended living room next, commenting that its sloped ceiling made it an acoustically suitable music room. He'd put down a carpet to further improve the sound; the room contained an array of percussion instruments, amplifiers, a four-track recorder, and a big console mixer in addition to Quinn's keyboard and Ty's collection of bass guitars.

Next Quinn led them up the stairs. "Ty's here," he said, pointing at the first door on the left, "and you two are across the hall." He opened another door to usher Dan and Denise inside.

"What about me?" Shan asked.

All across country she'd been fantasizing about this moment. She'd envisioned him throwing open a door to a romantic, ocean-view room with a sumptuous bed, saying, "Here, with me. We're together now, angel."

Instead he led her down the hall to a miniscule room that had a tiny window overlooking the creek. "This is your room," he said.

She was so disappointed she couldn't speak. When Quinn saw her expression, his face fell. "Don't you like it? We could swap, if you want. Mine is a little bigger . . ."

"No, this is fine," she said, recovering.

"I know it's small, but you don't have that much stuff. Your room in New York wasn't much bigger. And I'm right next door," he added, "which I thought would be convenient."

"For what?"

"For all the late nights we're going to have." He winked at her, then headed back down the hall. Shan trembled in anticipation of the activities she hoped they'd indulge in during those late nights.

The house had only one full bath, but there was also an outdoor shower. Shan and Denise took turns using the bathroom while Dan headed outside with a bar of soap. When they'd all showered and changed, they trooped downstairs where Quinn had burgers sizzling on a charcoal grill. Ty was tossing a salad and boiling ears of corn on the stovetop.

They gathered around the rickety picnic table situated next to the creek and Dan heaved a contented sigh as he sparked up a joint for a predinner toke. "Back in Cali," he said, taking a hit and handing the joint to Quinn. "Man, it's good to be home."

"I hear you," Quinn said, accepting the joint, hitting it, and offering it to Denise.

"We need more furniture," Denise said. She shook her head and Quinn passed the joint along to Ty. "I have some," she continued, "but not enough to fill the whole house."

"My folks are giving me some. Can you come with me to pick it up tomorrow?" Dan asked Quinn. "They'd like to see you again. I want Denise to meet them, too."

Quinn nodded and Shan regarded him hopefully. "Have you seen your family yet, Q?" She waved the joint past when it came her way, wondering if she, too, would have a chance to meet his parents.

"We stayed with my brother for a few days when we first got here," he said, passing the joint along without taking a second hit. "Had to get my bike. It's been stashed there while I was away at school."

"How is Ron?" Dan asked, reclaiming the joint. Just he and Ty were smoking it now.

"Same. It was good to see him, and the kids, too. They've grown a lot. They're four and six now and cute as hell. They remembered me, too," he said, his smile broadcasting his affection for his niece and nephew. "I thought maybe they wouldn't. I didn't get back last Christmas, and two years is a long time at that age."

"And the folks?" Dan said.

"I saw George last week," Quinn said. "He's fine and, according to him, my mother is still alive. That's as much as I care to know. Now can we talk business? I have gigs lined up starting the end of the month, so we need to get right down to it."

"Why so long? It won't take much to get back into the groove," Dan said. "We're not facing the same kind of issues that we did last year."

"I wish that were true," Ty mourned, taking another hit, "but the Q-man has other ideas."

All eyes turned toward Quinn, who nodded. "I want another guitar player."

What? For a moment, Shan couldn't breathe. "You're replacing me?" she choked out, when she was able to speak.

Quinn regarded her with disdain. "Right. I dragged you out here so I could fire you. I said *another* one," he clarified, "meaning two."

Hot words bubbled up. "That's bullshit, Quinn. I don't—"

"Oh, chill out." Quinn leaned over and put his hand over her mouth. She had to fight the urge to bite him. "Obviously you'd still play lead. I'm talking about a rhythm guitar. It would add some stability and depth to the music."

"It would also mean a pay cut for all of us," Ty said, dropping the sputtering nub that remained of the joint into an ashtray.

Quinn shrugged. "In the long run it will pay off."

"So we need to start auditioning guitar players again?" Dan groaned.

"No," Quinn said. "It just happens that Dave Ross is available."

"Dazzlin' Dave?" Dan's eyes widened. They were red and glassy from the pot. "No shit! What about the Stone Gurus?"

"On a break. They just came off a tour," Quinn explained, "opening for Jane's Addiction. Apparently there's some trouble in the band. He's looking for a change."

"We've got to grab him up," Dan said, obviously excited.

Quinn's smile widened. "My thoughts exactly."

Shan was still doubtful. "What kind of music does he play?"

"His training is mostly jazz," Quinn said, "but he's one of the most versatile players I know. Solid as a rock, and he does a cool flamenco thing that's pretty unique. He's the one."

Ty shrugged. "You don't have to sell me. I trust your judgment, at least about music. I'm just worried about the financial impact."

"It'll be positive in the end," Quinn told him. "I guarantee it."

Later that night, Shan followed Quinn into his room to hear some of his new music. She kicked off her shoes and lay across the bed, assuming what she thought was a fetching pose.

Quinn didn't seem to notice. He popped a tape into the cassette deck. "This is still a work in progress," he said, adjusting the volume. "It needs a bit of polish."

She stifled her impatience and forced herself to listen. After a few moments, the tune captured her attention. It was interesting, sharp and jazzy. She liked it. Still, it lacked the rough edge that characterized the music they'd written as a team. "It's good, but kind of mechanized."

"It's a drum machine and a sequencer," he bristled. "What do you expect?"

"Don't get defensive. I know that, but it's like taking the interstate instead of the scenic route. The ride is smooth, but the view is dull."

"I suppose you think you could do better?"

"Well, the main road is really cool. Wait a minute." She got up and went into her own room. When she came back, she had the Angel. "How about adding a scenic overlook?"

Shan sat down on the bed beside him and concentrated on the music. She strummed along for a few minutes to capture the chord progression, then said, "Scenic overlook coming up."

She sprang off into a choppy, reggaesque beat for a few bars, then smoothly transitioned back to the original rhythm. She beamed. "There! What do you think about *that*?"

"That's not a scenic overlook," he growled. "It's a ten-car pileup."

But she'd been watching his forearms and, when the goose bumps rose, she'd seen them.

Hours later, Shan put down her guitar. "I think I have to stop," she groaned, stretching.

Quinn glanced at the clock on his bedside table. "Holy shit, it's two-thirty," he said, setting aside his small Yamaha keyboard. "You must be exhausted after all the driving today."

"I am. I didn't expect we'd start in working so soon."

"Sorry, I didn't think about that. I was just so excited to have you here, finally."

She nodded. "Me, too. I love what we did with it. It's got some soul now."

"Yes, it's good. I'm glad we still have our connection. Sometimes when you're out of touch, things can change."

"We haven't been out of touch," she said. "We've talked two, three times a week."

"I know, but I mean the music connection. You're always evolving, you know. I am, too. Anybody who plays as much as we do is, or ought to be, and musicians can grow apart. I've seen it happen. I'm just glad it didn't happen to us."

"Me, too," she agreed, stifling a yawn. He tousled her hair as he climbed off the bed.

"Be right back," he said, heading for the bathroom.

She laid back on Quinn's bed. Maybe hers, too, soon? She could hope. She closed her eyes and snuggled her face against the pillow, smelling his lime aftershave as she drifted into sleep.

chapter 19

The next morning Shan woke in Quinn's bed, covered with a blanket, fully clothed, and alone. Apparently he'd behaved like a perfect gentleman. She sighed.

She rolled out of bed, used the bathroom, and then went to the kitchen for her methadone. Afterward she hunted up Quinn, finding him in one of the Adirondack chairs on the front porch, drinking coffee with Ty. He was barefoot in jeans, a black T-shirt, and sunglasses, blond hair loose around his shoulders. He looked like a rock star. "Morning," he greeted her. "I'm assuming you slept well, since you hogged my bed all night?"

"You could have waked me," she said pointedly, but he shook his head.

"Then I would have had to help you set up your futon. Easier just to let you sleep."

"Is there a plan for today?" she asked, boosting herself up to sit on the porch railing.

"I told Dan I'd go to Encino with him to pick up the furniture from his folks. Then I want to hit the Guitar Center on the way back."

"Me too," Ty said. "I need strings." The sun was hot already and droplets of perspiration were beaded up on his nut-brown skin. "Wait'll you see it," he said to Shan. "It's the ultimate shopping mall for guitar players."

"Cool! I want to go, too," Shan said, "and I'll have to bring my guitar. The Angel's case got broken on the trip," she added. "I'm using the soft one for now, but—"

"That won't work once we start gigging," Quinn agreed. "You need a new one."

"You can ride with me," Ty said. "We'll meet you there, Q. What time?"

Shan went inside for some coffee, leaving her bandmates to work out the logistics. As she poured, Quinn came into the kitchen. "Don't worry, I haven't forgotten that I said I'd help you find a clinic," he said, dropping his voice. "Did you get a referral?"

"Yes. There's one in Van Nuys. Is that close?"

"Pretty close. About half an hour." He was practically whispering and she smiled.

"You can talk about it out loud, Q. It isn't a secret, not with the phyamps in the fridge."

"But it's nobody else's business," he said. "I don't want you feeling weird about it."

"It's just as well everyone knows because I don't want to have to hide it. It's exhausting," she said and he nodded, squeezed her shoulder, then went upstairs in search of Dan.

Shan took her coffee out to the front porch. Ty had gone upstairs, too, so she was alone. She blinked in the bright sunshine, then leaned on the railing to survey the valley around her.

It was beautiful, in a rugged, desolate sort of way. Their house was tucked into a deep cleft in the mountain—Echo Flats, it was called, or so Quinn had told them the night before. The mountain was impossibly steep but, somehow, thick and twisted with trees and bushes that grew green and thrived in the rocky soil. The brush had a prickly, alien look unlike anything she'd seen before, even in the Rockies, which they'd crossed on their drive west. The mountains in the Berkshires where she'd grown up were mere hillocks compared with these.

The screen door slammed as Quinn emerged. "It's beautiful here," she said to him, "but it seems so remote."

"It is. The nearest neighbor is about three miles that way." He pointed back up the road they had traversed the night before. "I like that about it. There's no one to complain about the noise when we practice. Ready?" he asked as their roommates emerged from the house en masse. Dan and Ty were just finishing a joint.

Denise nodded. "Do I look all right?" she asked Shan. She was pretty in yellow and had toned down her usual punky makeup, wearing only light mascara and a sheer lip gloss.

"You look beautiful," Shan told her. "Very ladylike."

"I keep telling her not to worry about it," Dan said. He knocked the head off the roach, examined it to make sure it was out, then frugally preserved it in the small silver stash box he always kept in his pocket. "My folks are going to love her."

"They're pretty laid back," Quinn said, "just like Dan. They'll go easy on you."

"But they're my future in-laws," Denise fretted, smoothing down her dress. Her diamond sparkled in the sun. "I want to make a good impression."

"Of course you do," Shan said. "I'd feel the same way if I was meeting Q's parents."

Quinn looked uncomfortable. "They're the opposite of laid back, but don't worry. I'll never subject you to them."

Suddenly the sun didn't seem quite so bright to Shan. Quinn appeared not to notice. "Get there early," he said to Ty. "It will blow her mind, so make sure she has enough time to look around."

"I'd like to see Hollywood, too," Shan said, burying her deflation. "Will there be time?"

"Sure," Quinn said. "That's where the store is. But don't get your hopes up about Hollyweird," he added, boarding the van behind Denise. "It's not what you expect."

Shan found out what Quinn meant later that day, when she saw Hollywood Boulevard for the first time. She chattered excitedly, poking Ty and pointing as the HOLLYWOOD sign appeared on a distant hillside. She gasped when she spotted Michael Jackson outside of Grauman's Chinese Theatre, but a moment later realized it was just an impersonator. Hannibal Lecter, Edward Scissorhands, and a drag-queen Madonna all occupied the same block. Ty pulled over, anyway, so she could get out and look at the famous footprints in front of the theater.

It was a hot, sticky day and the boulevard was crowded with tourists. She saw they were milling on the Walk of Fame, but beyond the pretty pink terrazzo stars were tattoo parlors, shabby bars, and a couple of establishments advertising nude dancers. There were tour buses everywhere and each block seemed to house a different version of the same dingy souvenir shop. As they got back in the car, Shan wondered how this place had earned its reputation for glamour.

After a short distance, Ty pulled over again. "Here we are," he announced.

Shan got out of the car, shouldered the Angel, and looked up at an enormous building with a huge red guitar over its awning. She'd heard of the Guitar Center. Every musician had.

Ty had crossed the street and was standing under the awning, motioning her to follow. She did, and when she joined him he pointed down. "This is the RockWalk," he said.

She looked down and saw that the sidewalk beneath her feet was just like the one in front of Grauman's Chinese Theatre, except it was covered with handprints instead of footprints. She moved from square to square, looking at the names. "John Lee Hooker," she read. "Les Paul. Oh, look, Ty," she gasped. "*Eddie Van Halen!*" Ty chuckled as she dropped to her knees.

She was still there when Dan dropped Quinn off nearly half an hour later. He spotted her as soon as he got out of the van. She was down on her hands and knees in front of the shop, her guitar still strapped to her back. "Having fun?" he inquired.

Shan looked up at him. "B.B. King," she intoned with reverence. "But you know, Q, there are hardly any women."

"There are a few," Quinn said. "The Wilson sisters. Carole King . . ."

"But where are Joni Mitchell and Joan Baez?" she said. "Or Sarah McLachlan?"

"All good guitar players," Quinn agreed, "but they don't particularly rock."

"Bonnie Raitt, then. And how about Joan fucking Jett?" She looked affronted.

"There just aren't that many awesome girl rock guitarists out there, which is what makes *you* so special. Once your handprints are here, you'll lead the way for the rest of them. Couldn't you find a case?" he asked, switching gears as she rolled her eyes.

"What? Oh," she said, remembering her reason for visiting the store. "I didn't look yet."

"Have you even been inside?" She shook her head. "Christ," he said, taking her arm and leading her into the store. "We're going to be here all day."

She followed Quinn, but stopped dead just inside the door.

There were guitars, hundreds and hundreds of electric guitars festooning every inch of floor and wall space. Guitars of every conceivable brand and model and color and size. Gibsons and Fenders and Kramers. Telecasters and Flying Vs and Explorers. The Gretsch Black Phoenix like Brian Setzer. The '63 Strat hybrid like Stevie Ray Vaughn. And—

"The Gibson Lucille!" It was set up and plugged in, just waiting to be played, and Quinn laughed as Shan sprinted to it.

"Just like B.B. King," he said as she lovingly took the guitar into her hands.

"This is *not* a music mall," she called to Ty, who was himself playing a Gibson Thunderbird over in the next row. "It's guitar nirvana."

Some time later, Quinn found Shan in the vintage section. "Have you found a case?"

"Nope." She didn't look up, as she was concentrating on the solo from "Stairway to Heaven," which she was playing on a late-fifties Sunburst like Jimmy Page.

"You're beginning to annoy me," he told her. "This place isn't going anywhere, you know. You don't have to play every fucking guitar in the store today."

She let him take the guitar out of her arms. "I want them all."

"For now, you should take care of the guitar you've already got." He carefully set the 'Burst back into its metal display stand. "The cases are up there," he said, pushing her through a door and pointing up a flight of stairs, "along with the rest of the guitar trimmings. Do I have to go with you, or can you manage to take care of this on your own?"

She pointed her nose in the air and marched up the stairs. Quinn waited to make sure she didn't get sidetracked again, then headed back to the keyboard zone, shaking his head.

At the top of the stairs, Shan discovered a loftlike space as jampacked with equipment as the rest of the store. Instead of instruments, the walls and display racks were covered with picks, straps, capos, and a plethora of other guitar accoutrements. Before her, in front of a wall bedecked with packets of strings, was the sales counter. The clerk was deep in discussion with a tall, red-haired man, so she looked around as she waited. Almost immediately she spotted an array of guitar cases toward the back of the room. She headed that way.

She tested one hardshell case after another and finally narrowed it down to two. Neither looked particularly sturdy, but they were the only ones in her price range.

"They probably have the proper case for that out in back," someone said behind her.

She turned and discovered the customer who'd been at the counter, a giant of a man, easily six four, wide shouldered and buff in a skin-tight purple T-shirt. His eyes were a striking deep blue and his coppery hair tumbled halfway down his back. A gold hoop glittered in one ear and spidery tattoos snaked up both arms. Pretty hot in a California rocker way, she noted.

She realized he was examining her as well. In fact, he was giving her a very definite once-over. "Are you a guitar player?" she asked.

He pulled his gaze from her breasts up to her face. "Yes. Why, do I look like one?"

"Well, you seem to have opinions." He nodded, grinning.

"I wouldn't use one of these cheap shit cases, especially not with a guitar like that," he said. "Nice axe. A Martin, right?"

"Right, and thanks. What's yours?"

"My main one's a Gibson. A Les Paul."

"Also nice," she acknowledged. "I was just playing one downstairs."

"Are you in a band?" he asked, just as Quinn materialized with a bagful of audio cables under his arm.

"There you are," he said to Shan. "Have you found . . . hey!" he exclaimed, catching sight of the red-haired man. "Where'd you come from?"

"Well, hey there, Q," the man said, his face lighting up in a big grin. "Why am I not surprised to run into you here?"

"So you met?" Quinn asked, gesturing at Shan.

The red-haired giant looked puzzled for a moment, then comprehension dawned on his face. "You mean *this*," he looked down at Shan, "is the angel?"

"Well, *this* is the Angel," she corrected him, tapping her guitar. "*I'm* Shan O'Hara."

"And this is Dave Ross," Quinn said, clapping a hand on his shoulder. "Also known as Dazzle."

Dave was regarding Shan with a new respect. "I've been listening to your chops," he said, "working up some rhythm parts to go with them. You're one hell of a guitar player, Shan."

"Thanks. I haven't heard yours yet, but Q's been raving about you."

"Yes, you have heard him," Quinn said. "Dazzle's on at least three of the CDs in your collection. He's been a session sideman for years." Quinn's gaze shifted to the guitar cases on the floor beside Shan. "You're not buying one of those cheap pieces of shit, are you?"

"It's all I can afford until we start gigging," she said, flushing when Dave chuckled.

Quinn pulled out his wallet. "Get a decent case," he told her, handing her some bills. "You can owe me for it," he added as she began to protest. "You shouldn't fuck with that guitar."

Shan hesitated, then shrugged and moved toward the counter.

Behind her, she heard Quinn talking to Dave. "All set for our first practice? I think the two of you will be dynamite together, if the chemistry is right."

Shan glanced back over her shoulder. Dave was looking straight at her. "I look forward to exploring that," he said, with a little smile.

Later that night, Shan and Quinn were back in his bedroom, fine-tuning the song they'd worked on the night before. After a couple of hours, they had an arrangement they were both pleased with, and they christened it "Echo Flats."

"I'm done," Shan announced at about eleven o'clock. Her hair was bundled into a knot and she pulled out the pencil she'd used to anchor it in place. "I have some ideas for lyrics, but let's work on those tomorrow." She shook her hair out and struck what she thought was a sexy position, tresses flowing over one shoulder.

Apparently it was, since Quinn reached for a handful of her curls. "Okay," he said, winding his fingers through the ringlets. "I like that we're back in the same city. Long-distance composing just doesn't work. "

"I'm just happy we're together again." Her eyes met his. "I missed you so much."

"I missed you, too." He let go of her hair and stretched out on his back, lacing his hands together behind his head. She waited for a few moments, but he didn't say anything more.

"I thought about you all the time while you were away," she confessed. She shifted closer to kiss his cheek, then raised herself up on one arm to gaze down upon him.

He grinned amiably up at her. His hair was loose, spilling over the pillow like a splash of sunshine and his eyes looked blue as a summer sky. She'd never get used to it, how beautiful he was. She hesitated, then lowered her head to kiss him on the mouth.

His lips were pliant, but he didn't exactly kiss her back and, when she lifted her head, she saw he was no longer smiling. "Angel," he said softly, "what are you doing?"

His eyes were serious but, deep inside, she could see a glow, like a spark on the verge of flaring. Its promise fanned the warmth inside her. She took a deep breath and rolled on top of him.

She kissed him again and this time he pulled his hands from behind his head. Then his arms were around her, holding her tight, and she kissed him harder, opening her legs so she was astride him. When she felt his erection she arched against it, experiencing a throb deep in the pit of her groin.

He muttered and his hands found her ass, giving it one long, appreciative squeeze. Then he released her ass, took hold of her chin, and turned his face away. Shan's tongue popped out of his mouth, flailing around like a sperm in search of an egg.

"Shan." His voice was expressionless.

She pulled her chin out of his grasp and dove toward his chest, burying her face against the little bit of hair visible over the V-neck of his T-shirt. "Look at me, Shan."

She hesitated for a moment, then raised her head.

"So now you want to fuck," he said in the same bland tone. He could have been talking about the weather. "Is that it?"

How romantic. She didn't know what to say.

"Well?" He raised his eyebrows.

She could feel his erection between her legs, almost painfully hard. She knew he wanted her, no matter what he was saying, and that gave her courage. "Er . . . make love?"

"Whatever," he said, still annoyingly expressionless. "You've changed your mind, then? We can screw each other's brains out and, tomorrow, everything goes back to normal. No questions asked, no strings attached. Is that what you have in mind?"

She stared at him, eyes wide. *I love you,* she wanted to cry. *Please, please love me back.* She knew if she uttered a word that's what she'd say, so instead she said nothing.

He continued to watch her for a beat, then, "Not a fucking chance."

He twisted and she hit the bed with a thud. Her face burned. "All you have to do is say no. You don't have to shove me off like I'm contagious."

He rolled away so he was out of her reach. "Apparently I do. This is the same thing that happened last summer. I had to practically peel you off of me."

"That was mutual, as I recall, and things are different now!"

"What's changed?"

"We moved past the friend stage a while ago, but when you went back to school things were put on hold. So now that we're together again, I thought . . ." her voice trailed off, because the look on his face was something approaching horror.

"I don't know what you've been thinking," he said, "but I never had any ideas beyond picking up where we left off and we left off as friends."

A cold, hard knot was beginning to form in her stomach, displacing the liquid heat that had resided there just moments earlier. "I guess we left off in different places, then."

"Oh, shit." He ran a hand through his hair. "Don't do this to me, Shan. You know how I feel about attachments. I've been straight with you from day one."

"But we have a connection. You said so yourself. I feel like I've been in a holding pattern."

"A holding pattern?" He looked incredulous. "You don't think I've been living like a monk since last summer, do you?"

She winced. "No. I know you better."

"Good, because I haven't. I care about you a lot, as a *friend,* but if you're thinking we're going to set up house here and live happily ever after, then you'd better think again. You have to stop bringing it up, too. It'll affect our friendship if you don't, if it hasn't already."

A wave of indignation burst through the pain his words had wrought. "You're such a dick sometimes, Quinn. When have I ever brought this up before? But it's there between us all the time. I thought the mature thing to do would be to get it out in the open."

"Fine," he said curtly. "It's out in the open. And I don't want to hear about it again."

She scrambled off the bed and headed for the door. She slammed it with satisfying force, but the drama of her exit was cut short when she realized she'd left her guitar behind. She marched back into his room and snatched it up.

"Infant," she heard him snort as she stormed out once again.

chapter 20

The next morning Shan woke in a foul mood. She was cranky and cross, and her back hurt. Since her futon still wasn't set up, she'd spent the night in her sleeping bag. She took a long time showering and dressing in capris, flip-flops, and a blue halter top, but eventually her jones kicked in.

She went downstairs to the kitchen and dosed. Denise, Dan, and Ty were at the table, the guys sharing a post-breakfast joint while Denise marked up the Help Wanted section of the *Los Angeles Times* with a yellow highlighter. There was no sign of Quinn.

"There's some eggs left on the stove," Denise said. "What was all that racket last night?"

"I almost forgot what it was like listening to the two of you fight all the time," Ty added. "Let's try to keep it to a dull roar, okay? At least at bedtime."

Shan escaped to the front porch, where she stopped dead. Quinn was outside, tinkering with his motorcycle. He glared at her and she retreated back into the house, her nose in the air. A few minutes later, she heard the roar of his engine as he departed.

Dan took Denise out job hunting shortly afterward, brightly annotated *Times* under her arm. A little while later, Ty poked his head into her room. "I'm headed into town. Do you want to come along?"

Shan declined politely, although she was low on shampoo. She was dangerously close to broke. Quinn had offered to cover the rent until they started working, but she'd refused, unwilling to accept his help again. Now, she supposed, it was just as well.

After Ty left, she surveyed her new bedroom. Space in the van had been precious, so Shan had left behind her bureau and most of the few other bits of furniture she owned. All she'd brought was her futon, the stool she used for practicing, and a small bookshelf.

She set about unpacking. She unrolled her futon and made it up with her only set of sheets. She emptied her various bags and boxes, stowing her clothes in the tiny closet under the eaves. She unpacked her library of books and CDs, set up her small boom box, and hung her posters of Dylan and the Dead and her Monet print. She arranged her remaining possessions on top of the bookshelf: her brush, a bottle of sandalwood blend, her jewelry box, a few other odds and ends.

Then she unwrapped a newspaper-swathed bundle. It contained two framed photographs. One was of her mother, which she set on top of the bookshelf. The other was the photograph of her and Quinn. She glowered and stuffed it back in the box, then shoved the box into the closet.

She went downstairs and wandered through the house, which was quiet as a tomb, not even the sound of a passing car to break its silence. She went to the back door to gaze out at the creek.

Coyote Creek, as Quinn had called it, was picturesque against the scrubby hills. A large, flat rock just downstream from the house captured Shan's attention. There was a folding chair set up on the rock. A big California sycamore growing beside the creek cast some shade over it.

It looked like a nice place to play. She retrieved her guitar and headed downstream.

Hours later she was still there. It turned out to be a fine place for composing, her chords ringing sweet and silvery against the hillside. The music was demulcent for her troubled mind as she worked on the lyrics she'd conceived for "Echo Flats," and she was so absorbed that she never heard the others when they returned.

> *Somehow I know I'm home though I've only just arrived*
> *The way my feet meet the earth makes my body feel alive*
> *I've been looking for a place, the place where I belong*
> *And I think that place is here—I feel strong, strong, strong*
> *Been a force of one forever, always on my own*
> *But here at Echo Flats, I'm finally not alone*

"Nice."

She looked up, startled. Quinn was under the sycamore tree, listening. "I like it," he said. "A lot. I can really feel those lyrics."

She didn't reply, just kept playing. "I see how they've captivated you," he continued. "I've been standing here for ten minutes. You didn't even hear me come outside."

She played louder, to drown him out. The notes were jarring in the quiet.

Quinn heaved a deep sigh and climbed onto the rock to sit down beside her chair. She stopped long enough to shoot him an unfriendly look, then began playing again.

He reached out and grabbed the neck of the guitar near the twelfth fret, effectively muting her. "Look, I get it, okay? I'm not stupid, you know, and I'm not completely insensitive, either. I see how it is between us."

"And how is that?"

"We have this thing," he said. "An attraction . . . connection . . . whatever you want to call it."

She'd call it love, but she knew better than to say that.

"It's intense, whatever it is," he continued, "but you have to take it for what it is and not try to turn it into something more."

She drew back. "What do you think I'm trying to turn it into?"

"You want a mate," he told her. "Something stable. A home, probably a wedding someday—all that happily-ever-after jazz, and you want me to be the one to make it happen."

"I've never said anything of the kind. *Never.*"

"You don't have to say it. I just know, because I know you. And I can understand why that kind of security would be important to you. There's never been a single solitary thing in your entire life that was safe and lasting, and that you could believe in."

"There's you," she interjected softly, but he only looked sad.

"That isn't who I am. I'd do almost anything for you, Shan, but I can't do that. I'd end up hurting you and I couldn't live with myself if I did. You've been hurt enough."

She turned her face away again. "Why am I here, then?"

He took the hand holding the guitar pick and squeezed. "Because of the music, angel. It's why we belong together and why I'm going to make damned sure that we stay together."

"You don't need me to make music."

He smiled at her, although his eyes were still solemn. "I do, though. What you and I have—it's magic. Extraordinary, like Becker and Fagen. Jagger and Richards." She made a face and he laughed. "Garcia and Hunter?"

She smiled a little, in spite of herself. "Lennon and McCartney, you mean," she said, the one songwriting team whose greatness they actually agreed upon.

He nodded. "Someday they'll include Marshall and O'Hara in that lineup. We're going to make it, the two of us together, and I'm not about to fuck that up just for a piece of ass."

She lifted her chin. "Is that all it would be?"

"For me it would," he said. "I mean, I'm not saying it wouldn't be awesome. If I thought it was something you could handle, I'd do you in a second. For you, though . . ."

"I get it," she said. "You're saying you don't want anything more than what we have and I couldn't get by with anything less. You're my family, Q. The only family I've got. So . . ."

"So we stay right where we are for now."

She stared at him. "What do you mean, 'for now'?"

"I mean that we're friends, and roommates, and bandmates," he said. "We leave it at that."

"But you said 'for now.' Does that mean things might change?"

"I don't have a fucking crystal ball," he said, beginning to look irritated. "Who knows what will happen down the road?"

"But," she persisted, "do you think that someday . . ."

He put a finger over her lips. "We'll find out when someday comes, little girl. Now let it go."

She frowned, but held her tongue. He waited a few moments, then let go of her lip.

"Okay," he said. "Now that we have that settled, let me hear those lyrics again."

That night when Dave arrived for their first practice, Shan was still smarting. No matter how Quinn had tried to smooth it over, the fact remained that she'd blatantly thrown herself at him and he'd rejected her. Quinn, who'd had more women than anyone she'd ever known.

She tried to ignore her humiliation and focus on the music. She was looking forward to showing the guys some of her new guitar tricks and she knew that her voice had improved, too. She'd done her exercises faithfully, worked to stretch herself vocally, and she had a chance to demonstrate when they practiced a Queen cover that was a standard part of their repertoire. Despite everything, it felt good to be back with her boys and she opened up and sang her heart out.

They sailed along with tremendous energy until Ty got tangled up and hit a clanger on the climb. It was jarring enough that they stopped, everyone laughing except Quinn.

"Hold up," he ordered, when the mirth had died down. He focused his attention on Shan. "Sing this," he said, and struck an F2 on the Kur.

She complied and he had her keep singing, playing higher and higher notes until he stopped at F6. "You've come into your full voice," he told her, "and it's damned close to four octaves." He didn't make any further comment, but she could see the goose bumps.

He was less pleased by her guitar stylings. During "Wanderlust" he stopped them again with a swift raising of his hand. "What the fuck do you think you're doing with that solo?" he asked her.

Shan eyed him quizzically. "I'm playing it in G minor."

"What are you doing *that* for?"

She stared at him. "What do you mean? I'm in the right key."

"It's supposed to be a *solo*. Why are you playing what I'm playing?"

"I like it," Dave offered. "It's tight as a drum. I'd play it the same way."

"Of course *you* like it. If I wanted the solo to sound like Dazzle," Quinn told Shan, who was beginning to burn, "I would have had him play it. Have you lost your touch?"

"No, I haven't," she shot back. "In fact, I think I've improved. *Markedly.*"

"You sound like you belong on a Muzak recording," he said. "Where's the flash?"

Her fingers tightened on the neck of her guitar. "All you've ever done is complain how I'm too rough! Now I'm too smooth? What are you, schizo or something?"

"The rough edge is what makes your playing special. Reinhardt hammered you on it, didn't he, and you knuckled under. *I told you not to let that happen.* You can learn the technical stuff without giving up your personal style. When the fuck are you going to learn to think for yourself?"

"Fine." She was shaking with outrage. "I'll give you a goddamned rough edge."

They went back to the song and, this time when they got to the solo, Shan sprang off into a wild eruption that noodled frantically around the tight rhythm parts. When they finished, she was perspiring and turned around, ready to jump in Quinn's face when he lit into her.

Instead, he was grinning. "That's my girl!"

Dave grinned also, raising an eyebrow. "Well, *that's* a departure."

"You couldn't play that way if you tried," Quinn agreed. "I'm not saying you did it *well*," he said to Shan. "It was a splattery wreck, but you've got the idea. I'll work with you on it."

She didn't respond, but took off the Angel and scrounged around inside her guitar case.

"Why are you packing? We're not done," Quinn said. "You've got intensity, but now there's no structure. What I want is the psychotic angel we know and love. You're on the right track but, instead of Lizzie Borden, we're getting Rain Man."

"I'm not packing."

"Then what are you doing?" She continued to fiddle around inside the case. "What's your problem? Have you gotten so soft you can't take a little constructive criticism?"

She shot him a deadly look. "I broke a string. Is it all right with you if I change it?"

Quinn smirked. "I'll do some one on one with you," he said, "and show you how to get volume without damaging the equipment." Shan ignored him, lifting a bottle of beer to her lips. "That guitar was expensive. You shouldn't be treating it like a goddamn drum kit."

She whirled and flung the bottle across the living room. Quinn ducked and the bottle bounced off the wall behind him, spraying him with Corona. "You might be a magician on that keyboard," she snarled, "but you're not nearly the guitar player I am. Not by half, and *you're not going tell me how to play!*" She shoved her guitar into the case and yanked the top closed. Snatching it, she marched upstairs. "Screw you, Q," she yelled before slamming her bedroom door.

Quinn stared after her, his face frozen in shock. Dan and Ty exchanged incredulous glances and, behind them, Dave laughed softly. "Well," he said, "I guess she told *you*."

They practiced every day for the next two weeks as the band adapted to their new member. Shan's concerns about being pushed aside turned out to be groundless, as it became clear early on that Dave had no interest in competing for her spot.

Not because he couldn't play lead, because he could. When Dave soloed, he wove melodies that were strong and shimmery, an arresting contrast to her own edgier riffs. But his strength was in the rhythm and in the silver-toned tremolo chords that illustrated how he'd earned the nickname Dazzle.

It made the music more complicated, especially given the presence of the keyboard. Quinn soloed often, even more than she did, but Dave didn't compete with him, either. Shan suspected this had as much to do with his recruitment as his skill, since Quinn would never stand for anyone challenging his role as the musical pilot of the band.

He was a pleasant, easy-going sort of bandmate, a genuinely nice guy who fit right into the group. Thoughtful, too. As they set up for their first gig at a small LA rock club called Bluenote, Dave produced a handful of guitar picks, a whorl of bright colors in a tie-dye pattern. "Here." He dropped them into Shan's hand. "A little something to celebrate our first gig together."

"Too cool!" Shan exclaimed, examining them. "Thanks, Dave. That's so sweet of you."

He smiled when she looked up at him. "Don't be nervous. It's going to be good."

Shan was indeed nervous. Apart from the fact that this was her first gig in a new city and with a newly configured band, she and Quinn were still on the outs and she wasn't looking forward to sharing a stage with him. She couldn't shrug off the shame of that night and it clearly bothered him, too. Outside of band matters he'd barely spoken to her, even though they were continuing to develop their new material. Now they worked in the music room instead of his bedroom.

She didn't realize just how much he'd been holding back until she went outside to the van where Quinn was handing out equipment. "This gig is costing us a fortune," he was ranting at Dan.

"Well, we knew that was how it would be until we got established," Dan said, accepting the bass amp. "It don't happen overnight, dude."

"I know, but fifty fucking tickets! We only sold thirty, so we won't break even unless we pack the place." He handed Dan the cymbal case, closing his mouth when he caught sight of Shan.

Dan looked over his shoulder, saw her, and stopped talking, as well. He took the cymbals, hoisted the amp, and sped inside the building. "Quinn, is this a pay-to-play gig?" she demanded.

Pay-to-play was an avaricious system that LA clubs used as insurance against poor turnout. Bands had to prepurchase some set number of tickets, then sell them on their own to earn back their money. The cover tonight was ten bucks, so if they'd paid for fifty tickets . . .

"You had to lay out five hundred dollars?"

Quinn shrugged. "Everybody chipped in."

"Everybody except me, you mean." A fresh floweret of humiliation bloomed inside her, staining her cheeks red. "Damn it, I'm part of this band, too. Why didn't you tell me?"

He was still inside the van and he crouched until he was eye level with her. "What good would it have done? You're broke."

"Not completely. I could have kicked in *something*, at least."

"I've got eyes, Shan. You haven't eaten anything but ramen noodles for two weeks and your methadone stash is almost gone."

She couldn't think of anything to say, because he was right. She'd been counting on tonight's take to replenish it. She snatched her guitars and went inside.

She plugged in her Peavey and began tuning up, avoiding everyone's eyes as they set up around her. She felt like an utter failure. Here she was again, the weak link who couldn't hold up her end of the band responsibilities. She stayed quiet during sound check and, as soon as they finished, escaped to the bar to order a club soda.

After a few minutes, Quinn slipped into the seat beside her. "I'm sorry," he said quietly. "I didn't mean to embarrass you. I mean, that's what I was trying *not* to do. I know you're almost out of cash, so

I covered your share. I figured it would be better if you just didn't know."

When Shan turned to face him, she took one look at his sheepish, contrite expression and fell in love with him all over again. He was trying to protect her, she knew he was, but the wave of tenderness that swept her was firmly contained by a bank of residual indignation. "I know you think you're helping, but I need you to stop treating me like I'm a child. I'm a big girl, Q. Okay?"

"I'll try," he said reluctantly, "but I can't help worrying about you. You never say anything when you get into trouble. You just keep your mouth shut and suffer."

"What can you do? You're almost broke, yourself," she said and he shrugged.

"I've got plastic. Please don't starve and go into methadone withdrawal just because you're too pissed off at me to ask for help."

"But I'm *always* taking help from you! It was different when I first got here, when I thought we were going to be . . ." she hesitated.

"A couple?" he finished and she flushed again. "We are, in a way. A couple of friends. *Good* friends. I told you before that I'd do anything for you and I will. I've got your back, angel."

His words were so heartfelt, his eyes so earnest, that she melted. "I know that, Q," she said, "and I'm so glad, because I don't know what I'd do without you."

She leaned closer, intending to kiss his cheek, but he drew back. "No kissing," he said, a wicked sparkle in his eye. "I'm afraid you might lose control and jump my bones again."

The blood slammed into her face. "I take it back. You're a dick!"

He chuckled. "Oh, get over it, for Crissake. I've had girls hit on me before, you know. Now you think we could go make some music, so this town can find out how awesome we are?"

She nodded and, as she did so, she felt the pall of the past days lifting. It was going to be okay. Q said so and he was always right.

The crowd was spotty when they took the stage, but they started right off with "Summertime Blues," which they did nearly a cappella, with Dan tapping out a bare bones cadence on the tom rack and Shan's voice soaring up over a complex background harmony sung by the rest of the band. She performed it with a serpentine shimmy that was part Tina Turner, part Axl Rose, and it grabbed the attention of the crowd. They kept it when they swung next into "Come Sail Away" and, by the time they followed up with "Wanderlust," the place was rocking.

Their audience eventually grew to about eighty, far from a packed house, but they were loud and appreciative. It was enough to recoup their original investment and clear a little besides, and Shan knew they'd have no trouble booking future gigs at Bluenote.

And she was right. Pleased by both the audience response and the amount of alcohol consumed by the thirsty crowd, the manager booked them for three more gigs. Quinn had a decent schedule mapped out already, since he'd been hustling the smaller clubs nonstop since his arrival, but their word of mouth was good and before long they were getting gigs at some of the bigger venues. In Shan's eyes, they reached the pinnacle when they played the Whisky a Go Go on the Sunset Strip just two months later.

True, it was pay-to-play and they were at the absolute bottom of the gig food chain. They went on at seven, first in a lineup of six bands that got progressively more famous as the night went on, but even that couldn't dim her excitement. She was performing on a stage that had been graced by the Doors, Van Halen, and Led Zeppelin!

The crowd was small for their spot, but they were well received. Afterward the band and Denise claimed a table up on the second floor to watch a few of the other bands, none of whom were as good as Quinntessence. Even the headliner lacked their star power.

It was nearly midnight when they rose to leave. From the bar Quinn saw them and made his way back to the table, leaving behind the hot blonde he'd been flirting with all night.

"Heading out?" Quinn asked, the mic box under his arm. He never let it out of his sight at gigs since the theft at Fuego. When Dan nodded, he handed it over.

"Aren't you coming?" Dave asked and Quinn shook his head.

"I've got my bike. Besides, I plan to be busy later." He grinned and jerked his head at the blonde back at the bar. Dave chuckled.

"See you all in the morning," Quinn said, and aside to Shan, "Nice job tonight, angel."

He touched her shoulder, but she shrugged it off. "I got another shock from my mic," she said, nodding at the box in Dan's hand. "I thought you'd fixed it."

"I forgot," Quinn frowned, "but I'll look at it before the next gig. Are you okay?"

"Yes, but it really hurt." She touched her lower lip. "It was like a bee sting."

"Be careful," Dave said. "We don't want any marks on those pretty lips."

She tittered, then motioned to Denise. "Let's run to the ladies' before we leave. 'Night, Dave," she said, seeing him gather up his guitar.

Dave gave her a little wave and Quinn watched Dave's eyes follow her across the room.

"See you tomorrow," Dave said to the rest of them, but Quinn snagged his arm.

"Wait a minute." He motioned to Dan and Ty as the girls disappeared into the restroom. When they convened around him, he cleared his throat. "I am setting a rule," he announced. "No fraternization within the band. You fraternize, you're out. I won't tolerate that kind of bullshit."

Dave looked puzzled. "What do you mean, fraternize?"

Dan chuckled. "He means no messing around with Shan. Right, buddy?"

"Right," Quinn said.

"How's that any of your business?" Dave said, with the beginnings of a frown.

"It's common sense," Quinn told him. "We have one hell of a band here, just like I knew we would, and I can't see risking that if one of you gets the hots for the guitar player."

Ty hooted. "Are *you* willing to abide by that, my friend?"

He waved Ty off. "If I was going to make it with Shan, it would have happened a long time ago. Okay, it's a rule. No fraternizing within the band. Which means, gentlemen, no diddling the guitar goddess."

chapter 21

That Saturday night Quinntessence was booked at Pulse, a retro dance club in the Valley. As they were running chord to hook up the mics, Shan pulled out her regular one but paused before plugging it in, recalling the nasty shock she'd gotten at the Whisky.

When she turned to ask Quinn if he'd fixed it, she noticed a girl approaching him from across the dance floor. She had the requisite long legs and big boobs and she was pretty, too. And not in the bar slut way that most of Quinn's girls were. This one actually looked wholesome, with a heart-shaped face, wispy reddish blond locks and a light dusting of freckles across her nose.

The girl stopped just below Quinn. He was kneeling on the stage plugging in the monitors and she reached up to lay her hand on his back. Quinn turned his head and a smile spread across his face. He jumped down to kiss her full on the mouth. "Julie, what are you doing in LA?"

The girl smiled back. "I sent a demo to Arista and they invited me out for a showcase."

"That's fucking cool," he said, obviously impressed. "You think you'll get signed?"

"Well, they paid to fly me here," she said. "Can you spare some time for an old friend?"

"You bet," he said immediately and Shan watched the girl kiss Ty on the cheek next, then the three of them moved to the bar. Quinn ordered shots of tequila, which they downed. Dave hadn't arrived yet, so Shan and Dan finished setting up while the others lingered at the bar.

Ty returned to the stage when they started sound check. Shan shot an annoyed glance at Quinn, who was still at the bar. The girl was hanging all over him, sitting too close with her big boob unmistakably pressing against his arm. "Ty," Shan asked, "who is that?"

"That's Julie Janssen. We went to Berklee with her. She's a pianist," he said, "and a kick-ass singer. She was telling us that Arista's checking out one of her demos."

"Isn't that great," Shan said without enthusiasm. "She knows Q pretty well, huh?"

Ty shot a calculating look at her. "Well, yeah. They used to see each other."

Goddammit. She knew there was something different about this one. "But he never sees anyone on a steady basis. Isn't that one of his rules?"

"Not in this case. They dated on and off for a couple of years. Nothing exclusive, but it was a more or less regular thing for a while." Ty nodded toward her microphone. "Why don't you start the monitor check?"

Shan moved to the mic stand, her eyes trained on the pair at the bar. As she brought her mouth to the mic, a hard shock zapped her lower lip. "*Ouch!*" she spat, slapping a hand over her mouth. She was frozen for a moment, her lip tingling painfully.

"*That* had to suck." She looked down from the stage to find Dave gazing up at her, guitar in hand. "Are you okay?"

"Yes," she said, removing her hand, "but how am I supposed to sing into the damned thing?"

"It could be something simple. Here, let me have a look at it."

"Would you?" she asked. "Quinn was supposed to, but I guess he forgot."

Dave nodded, beginning to examine the amplifier her guitar was plugged into.

"I didn't get shocked from the guitar," Shan said. "It was the mic that did it."

"No, it wasn't. Your guitar charged you up and *you* zapped the mic. These old Vibrolux amps are notorious for it." He pulled the plug. "You're missing the ground pin," he said. "I can fix it right now." He pulled a Leatherman from a case on his belt, unfolded it, and cut the old plug off the chord. He carefully stripped back the wires, then dug into the pocket of his jacket and withdrew a handful of metal gadgets. He examined them, then selected a three-pronged plug.

"What are you," Shan laughed, "a walking repair shop?"

Dave chuckled. "Well, I like to be prepared. Nothing worse than starting a gig and finding out you have a wire crossed somewhere." He screwed the wire into the new plug, then pushed the plug back into the socket. "All set."

Hesitantly, Shan reached out and touched the mic with one finger. When nothing happened, she beamed at Dave. "You," she said, "are a handy man to have around."

"I never neglect a pretty lady in distress." He extended a hand. "How about a drink before we get started?" He helped her down from the stage, then placed his hand on the small of her back to lead her over to the bar.

Back on the stage, Dan looked at Ty, raising his eyebrows.

Ty pressed his lips together and shook his head. "Mm-mm-mm," he said.

After the gig, Shan searched the room for Quinn. He'd barely spoken to her all night and now was at a booth with Ty and that girl. She'd come up to do a couple of numbers with them, tunes Shan usually sang. It vexed her to hear this interloper sing tunes that she and Quinn had written together, but took some grudging satisfaction in the fact that Julie's voice wasn't nearly as good as hers. It was pleasant and technically correct, but lacked the power that was Shan's signature. Shan turned her back on them and stared into a tie-dyed chest. She looked up.

Dave was grinning down at her. "Think I might go out for breakfast. Want to come?"

"It's awfully late," she said. "And then you'd have to drive me home after."

Dave shrugged. "I'm used to getting home late."

She looked past him at Quinn. He was sitting very close to Julie, playing with her hair. She whispered something in his ear and he laughed out loud, then planted a kiss on the tip of her nose.

Shan looked back at Dave. "Okay," she said. "Let's go."

Shan was the first one up the next morning, despite the fact that she hadn't gotten to bed until nearly three. She hadn't slept well. Dave had treated her to breakfast, then taken her home. He'd mentioned that he was getting tickets to an upcoming Neil Young concert and asked if she wanted to go. She'd been noncommittal, although she adored Neil Young.

She liked Dave and was glad they were becoming friends, but there was a vibe between them that made her a little uneasy. She was pretty sure that friendship wasn't what he had in mind and the last thing she needed was a romantic complication, especially with a bandmate.

Well. With *that* bandmate. She glanced at Quinn's door as she headed down to the kitchen for coffee and methadone.

The house was quiet and the coffee wasn't made. That was weird. Quinn was an early riser, no matter how late he got in. She never got up before him. Once the pot started brewing, she swallowed her methadone, then went upstairs and tapped on Quinn's door. "Q? You okay?"

No response. She turned the knob quietly. The bed was unoccupied, the blue comforter smooth over the white sheets. Apparently his golden rules didn't apply to Julie fucking Janssen.

Shan went back downstairs, trying to ignore her sudden disquiet.

When the rest of her roommates got up, they told her they were going to the beach and asked if she wanted to come. Shan declined and Denise looked at her sympathetically, but didn't comment as they packed up their towels and water bottles and departed for Santa Monica.

The day passed slowly. Her eyes kept sliding toward the clock. By two Quinn still wasn't home and Shan wished she'd just gone to the beach. At three she changed into sneakers, packed the Angel into its soft case, and set off across the creek, hiking up the mountainside.

When she came back a couple of hours later, she was relieved to see Quinn's bike parked outside the house. She ran up the back stairs, then let herself in through the kitchen door. "Q?" she called.

Julie Janssen was sitting at their kitchen table, drinking a glass of wine and leafing through a copy of *Keyboard* magazine. "He's in the shower," she said. "You must be Shan. I'm Julie."

Shan set down her guitar as Julie rose and went past her to the refrigerator. She was nearly as tall as Quinn, Shan noted, and it was all leg. Her strawberry-blond hair was pulled smoothly into a silver barrette at the nape of her neck, not a hair out of place. Shan pushed the tumbled curls off her own forehead and surreptitiously sized up Julie's figure. It was fantastic, trim and athletic and clad in a snug dress of periwinkle blue. Shan felt small and dumpy next to her.

"Do you want a glass of wine?" Julie asked, taking out a bottle of chardonnay.

Making herself right at home, isn't she? "Sure." Shan got up and took a wineglass from the cupboard. Julie filled it, then put the bottle back in the refrigerator and returned to the table.

"The house is nice," she said. "Not exactly a place I'd expect to find Quinn, though."

Shan slipped into the seat across from her. "Why is that?"

"I'd think he'd want to be in town," she said, crossing one endless leg over the other, "closer to the clubs, like the place he had in Boston. I spent a lot of time there."

Shan gripped the hem of her T-shirt. "Ty mentioned that you went to school together."

Julie nodded. "Yes, we're old friends."

Shan's grip on her shirt was so tight her fingers ached. She couldn't think of anything to say, so she took a sip of wine, then grimaced. She hated chardonnay.

Julie was watching her as fixedly as a cat watches a mouse hole. "I thought you lived in New York. What made you decide to come out to California?"

"It was Quinn's idea," Shan said, gulping more wine.

The tight smile was still plastered across Julie's face. "He tells me the two of you aren't a couple, though."

Shan's fingers were growing numb. "No. We're friends."

"Good," Julie said, and suddenly the smile was gone.

Shan was saved from having to respond when Quinn came down the stairs. "Hi," he said to her. He took the wineglass out of Julie's hand and took a sip in a casually intimate gesture. "I don't think I ever introduced you guys last night. This is Julie Janssen, a friend from Berklee."

"We've met," Shan said, as he handed the glass back to Julie.

"Drink up, darlin'," he said, glancing at the clock. "I made the reservation for six and we can't be late, because I have to set up at eight." Quinn pulled on his jacket as Julie drained her glass. "Can you tell the others I'll meet you all at the club?" Shan nodded silently. Julie tucked a possessive hand through Quinn's arm and they headed for the door, but he suddenly turned back.

"I almost forgot. Dazz called for you. His number is by the phone." He frowned a little. "He wants you to call him, but you're going to see him tonight anyway."

"He's getting tickets to Neil Young," she said. "I told him I might go."

"Cool," he said, his eyes on Julie's legs. "He likes that folkie crap, too." He gave Shan's hair a careless tousle and she found herself staring forlornly at the door as it closed behind them.

She went upstairs to his room and pushed the door open. The comforter on the bed was rumpled and a couple of pillows were on the floor. She could see condom wrappers on the nightstand, too. Two of them.

He'd slept with her. Here. In their home, where she might have been right in the next room.

Shan slammed the door and closed her eyes. She stood that way for a long time.

As she showered and dressed, Shan carried on a continuous internal dialogue. Quinn could sleep with anyone he wanted, she reminded herself. And he did, all the time. He'd gone home with at least ten different women since she'd been in California.

But he'd never brought anyone to their home before. He'd never stayed away all night, either. He'd kept his sexual escapades away from her, until now. And, Shan noted unhappily, he seemed to genuinely like this girl.

For the first time, she realized that Quinn might just meet someone who mattered to him one of these days. She was deluding herself by continuing to believe he'd come to her when he was ready to settle down, and Julie Janssen obviously shared the same delusion. How many more women thought they'd get him in the end, if they only had the patience to wait?

She was quiet as she rode to the gig with Dan, Denise, and Ty. Dave arrived shortly after, then Quinn, with Julie in tow.

As she and Dave were tuning up, she smiled at him. "Does your invitation to Neil Young still stand?"

chapter 22

"We're good together," Dave said. "I think we have something special."

"I think so, too," Shan agreed, setting the Angel aside and stretching her arms up over her head. "I love the flamenco thing you do, Dave. I've never heard it done with our type of music."

"Sure you have." He stood up from the couch and stretched, too. "Plenty of rock songs have flamenco-inspired guitar parts," he said as he headed for the kitchen, presumably for another beer. "Your god Van Halen's done it. So has Queen, Triumph, Santana, of course, but some of the big prog rockers, too. ELP. Yes."

"I can see why Quinn likes it so much, then. He . . ."

Her voice trailed off as a wave of pain coursed through her. Quinn wasn't her favorite topic of conversation these days. Apart from their gigs, she'd barely seen him since Julie's arrival nearly two weeks before. He was never home now and she missed seeing him first thing in the morning, longed for the lazy afternoons she used to spend with him writing music by the creek.

Restless and at loose ends since Quinn's defection, she'd begun spending a lot of time with Dave. He was so easy to be around, with a carefree, happy-go-lucky quality about him that she found soothing. Nothing seemed to bother him, ever.

She'd gradually realized that his dope use had something to do with that. Dave apparently was respectful of Quinn's no-getting-fucked-up-during-a-gig rule because he was always straight enough while they were onstage and even during practice, but he usually snorted some coke after they finished playing. He smoked a lot of pot, too, and a few times he'd come by the house in such a light, dreamy state that she knew he was stoned.

All of her bandmates partied, but she hadn't realized how much until she started living with them. Dan was an archetypal California stoner, smoking pot on a daily basis, and Ty usually joined him. Even Quinn took a hit once in a while, despite his general antidrug stance. Both Dan and Ty liked an occasional line of coke, too, something Shan had never seen Quinn touch. He confined most of his partying to alcohol, for which he had an astonishing capacity. She'd never once seen him drunk.

She'd been thinking a lot about drugs herself, just lately. She'd even gone to a few of the NA meetings they held at the Methodist church in Tujunga because her mind kept drifting toward H, craving the marvelous way it had of evaporating pain. One hit and all this hurt—it would float away.

Hanging out with Dave helped, though. Tonight they'd been practicing for a couple of hours, just the two of them, since her roommates were all out. Ty was on a date with some actress he'd met at a gig and Dan and Denise had gone out to hear a band. Quinn hadn't been seen in two days and Shan knew he was off with Julie. She supposed it was better than having them here.

She pushed them firmly from her mind. "I'd like to learn flamenco," she said, as Dave came back into the room with two bottles. "Can you teach me?"

He twisted the tops off and handed her a beer. "Sure, but a flamenco guitar is different from an acoustic. The sound is brighter with less sustain. You can play notes that would sound muddy on an axe like the Angel."

"I know. It's more like a classical . . ." Her voice trailed off as she thought of her mother's classical guitar, the one Shan had left behind when she escaped from her father's house. She wondered what had happened to it.

"Well, it's different from a classical, too. I can teach you but if I do," he warned, "I guarantee that you'll be wanting a flamenco guitar of your own." He himself had a Cordoba Solista, in addition to two Gibsons, three Telecasters, and an Ovation.

She laughed. "Not any time soon. First on my list is a new electric. I have my eye on a vintage Strat at the Guitar Center."

"That white one I keep seeing you playing? Nice," he said. "Pricey, too, I suppose."

"Eleven hundred." She grimaced. "I'm saving."

"I'm surprised that's the one you're hankering after. Usually when we go there you head straight for the Gibsons."

"I love the hollow-body ES," she said, "but I don't have that kind of cash."

"Well, there's nothing more important than your instrument, now, is there?" She nodded in full accord and he beamed at her. "I do so enjoy our little chats, Shan. You're the only woman I know with a passion for guitar porn that matches my own."

She laughed as he sat back down beside her. "I think I'm finished for tonight," he said, taking a small box from his pocket. He selected a joint, which he sparked, and took a big hit. He held the smoke for a few moments, then exhaled and took another.

Impulsively Shan held out her hand. "Can I have a hit?"

"Oh. Sure." Dave looked surprised, but handed her the joint. "I didn't think you smoked."

"I don't usually," Shan said, taking a hit anyway. "I've had my issues with dope in the past. Stronger stuff," she added, "and it got me into trouble."

She handed back the joint, which he accepted. "I've seen phyamps in the fridge. Those are yours?" She nodded, shamefaced, and he shrugged. "Occupational hazard in our line of work."

"I'm clean these days, except for the 'done. It's been quite a while since I've done anything. Anything fun, that is," she amended. "Methadone is the opposite of fun."

Dave produced a conical silver container with a hole in one end. "Like this, you mean?"

Shan took it, then regarded it thoughtfully. "A snuff rocket," she said. "Coke?"

"Yeah. I do a little blow when I play once in a while," he said. "I like the energy it gives me. I keep it on the QT, though, because of Quinn. He's so uptight about drugs."

"Don't I know it. But I'm not complaining," she said, "because he held my hand every inch of the way when I was getting clean." She felt another pang of longing. She missed him so. "I don't think I could have done it without him. I owe him a lot."

"Well, he knows the drill, that's for sure. There's not much he hasn't seen, after all the shit he went through," Dave said, taking another hit off the joint.

Shan eyed him quizzically. "What do you mean?"

"All that time in rehab," he clarified. "He was in for such a long time."

"Quinn, you mean?" She still wasn't quite sure she was understanding him.

"Yeah," Dave stared back at her, beginning to look concerned. "Didn't you know?"

She shook her head, stunned.

"He had a pretty toxic coke habit, back in the day. His folks had him put away for a stint during freshman year. Some fancy fucking place," Dave added. "They could afford it. Anyhow, it worked. He never touches the stuff now."

Shan was staring at him openmouthed. "I can't believe he never told me!"

"Me, too. I figured you knew." Dave took another hit. "But he never has talked about it much. It can't be a pleasant memory, because he was royally messed up."

"Still, I'd have thought . . . after everything that's happened . . . or that Dan would have said something."

Dave looked thoughtful. "Dan might not know, either. He'd gone to New York by then. Q and I were in a band, the Accidental Evils. All of us did a lot of blow, but with him it was constant. He was the original snowman. Quinn the Eskimo, we called him. At first it was funny, then it got fucking scary." Dave shook his head. "I like blow, too, but I can handle it. Q, he can't."

"That just means it wasn't the thing that grabbed you," Shan said. She was both shocked and indignant at the revelation, but battling her hurt that Quinn had kept such a significant secret from her was a surge of tenderness toward this unexpected vulnerability in him. "If you've never been there you wouldn't understand, but I get how it happens, falling in love with a drug."

"Maybe you ought to pass on that, then," Dave said, nodding at the snuff rocket.

"Coke is something different, for me. I can take it or leave it. It's fun, though." It was, such a cheerful, happy sort of high. It felt like forever since she'd been merry and light, not weighed down under a gray pall of misery. She rolled the vial between her fingers.

"Well, there's a hit in there. You're welcome to it, if you want. I have more in the car." He frowned. "I don't know about blow when you're on methadone, though."

Shan hesitated. "No worse than a speedball," she said, and lifted the vial to her nose.

"Shh," Shan gasped, wiping tears of mirth from her eyes. "I hear a car." She tried to stop laughing and couldn't. She'd been laughing nonstop for hours. Her stomach hurt from it.

Dave peered out the window. "It's Dan and Denise."

"Oh no," she groaned. "What if they tell Q?"

"Fuck Q," Dave advised. "We're not gigging. What is he, your keeper?"

"No, but—" She scrambled off the couch and grabbed his hand. "Quick, let's hide."

Giggling, they ran upstairs to her bedroom. Shan eased the door shut. "I think they're downstairs," she whispered.

Dave leaned over her to press his ear against the door. A few strands of his long, burnished hair grazed her shoulder. "No, they're coming up. Shh." He caught her by the waist and put his hand over her mouth as she started giggling again.

She covered his hand with both of hers and laughed into it silently. She could feel Dave vibrating with laughter, too, and she kept laughing even when she realized that his hand was creeping under her shirt. His fingers on her stomach tickled, making her laugh even harder, until they dipped inside the low rise of her jeans.

Once she got over her surprise it struck her as funny and she began laughing anew, even as she tried to say no. But by then he'd gotten his other hand up her shirt and he was squeezing her breasts. He thumbed her nipples and she felt them harden under his touch..

She twisted out of his grasp and turned to face him. "Stop," she gasped. He looked so disappointed that she dissolved into laughter again. "I mean, jeez. You haven't even kissed me!"

"No, I haven't. Yet." Then he *was* kissing her. His lips were nice and firm and his tongue tasted of beer. He pulled open the snap on her jeans and slipped his hand between her legs.

She'd often admired how he fingered the strings on his guitar, with such confidence and skill. Now he was fingering her with similar skill.

She could feel how wet she was and it occurred to her that she was probably going to have sex with Dave. *That's a bad idea,* she noted, arching her neck as his lips nuzzled her throat. *It could get messy. I don't really feel that way about him, either,* she enumerated internally as his fingers swirled inside her. *Q is the one I really want.*

Like that mattered. It never stopped Quinn from having sex every chance he got, with anyone that caught his eye, and just now she couldn't seem to stop herself from rubbing against Dave's hand. She hadn't been touched this way in such a long time and it felt very nice.

He stopped kissing her long enough to pull her shirt over her head. "Hey!" She crossed her arms. He ignored her, fumbling at the buttons on his own shirt, which he let fall open, and she saw that he had a spidery tattoo on his stomach to match the ones on his arms. He pushed her hands away, slipped his hands behind her back, and pressed her bare breasts against his chest.

Her body erupted in gooseflesh and she wasn't laughing when he kissed her again. Her jeans dropped to the floor and, as her panties joined them, she realized that she was completely naked while he was still fully clothed. She began giggling again but before she could stop, tell him what was so funny, he'd dropped to his knees and his tongue was delving between her thighs. It felt exquisite and she moaned softly, laughter forgotten.

He turned her to face the wall, still exploring every inch of the terrain between her legs with his tongue. She didn't stop him, even when she felt his tongue in the crevice between her buttocks. He obviously appreciated that area, as he attended to it with gusto, his tongue flicking like a lick of fire. When he rose to his feet she heard a zipper opening, then something smooth and hard pressed against the spot that his tongue had been investigating so zealously.

That sobered her up a little. "Wait, Dave. I mean, I haven't . . ."

She heard his clothes dropping to the floor. "Let's take this over to the bed," he said and when she turned, he was naked. His body was a thing of wonder, all sculpted curves and long, graceful planes.

"You must work out," she said as he urged her down onto her back.

"Yup," he replied. He sat back on his heels, cock jutting from between his spread thighs like a sentry, and produced a condom. She watched him roll it on, thinking that it was the largest cock she'd ever seen, big as a Telefunken U-47 microphone. She giggled, singing the Zappa song in her mind.

Then, without further preamble, he was fucking her, filling her up so much that there was no room for anything but pleasure.

She woke the next morning with a pounding in her head and a sense of being dirty. She felt sticky and crusty as she rolled over to regard Dave snoring beside her.

They'd had sex for hours. They'd also done a whole lot of cocaine. She'd snorted rails off his erect penis and he'd rubbed coke on her vagina once it started get sore. Now that the numbness had worn off it felt bruised, rent, and it wasn't the only thing that hurt. She sat up and grimaced, shifting to take the pressure off the raw, mushy ache between her buttocks.

Dave opened his eyes. "Morning." He kissed her and her nose detected more than a tinge of rancidity in his breath. No wonder, she thought, considering some of the places he'd put his mouth.

Hers wasn't pristine, either. "Suck it," he'd groaned loudly. "Suck it good." She'd tried to tell him to quiet down, but her mouth was too full of cock to do more than mumble.

This morning he looked pleased, but Shan felt shy and uncomfortable with him. She wasn't ready to have sex with him again and searched for a way to put him off, then saw with relief that he was getting up. "I have to go," he said regretfully. "How about a little head for the road?"

There was that cock, huge as ever. He thrust it toward her and she turned her face away, suddenly assailed with another memory. He'd been pulsing in and out of her mouth, grunting for her to "suck it, suck it good," and he'd suddenly pulled away. She opened her eyes to see him yank off the condom and, when she opened her mouth to ask him why, was squirted in the face with a stream of semen. She'd laughed and laughed, but it didn't seem funny at all now.

"Hey. You okay?" Dave dropped down beside her, catching the bedclothes under his knee. The blanket shifted, suddenly exposing her to the waist, and she quickly tugged it to cover herself.

He moved his knee and caught up the blanket, wrapping it around her until she was securely swathed to the neck. "It's cool, you know,

Shan," he said. "I mean, it doesn't have to be weird. We're fine. Better than fine. Okay?"

She looked up and saw kindness in his eyes, and understanding. She bit her lip. "Okay."

He got up and pulled on his clothes, then stooped to kiss her on top of the head. "I have to go, but I'll see you later at practice. You sure you're okay?"

"Yes, I'm fine." She pulled the blankets a little tighter around herself. "I mean, you're right. It doesn't have to be weird. I don't want it to be, because I like you."

He regarded her warmly. "I like you, too. What did you think, that I'd stop liking you because I made love to you?"

"No, but . . ." She paused, then shrugged. "It's fine. We're good. You're a nice guy, Dave."

"Well, you're a nice girl." He winked, blew her a kiss, and then he was out the door.

She heard him go down the hall into the bathroom. She knew he was right; they'd be okay, but she still felt edgy and anxious. When her eyes went to the clock, she saw it was past noon and she realized she was late for her 'done. She sat up, unwinding the blankets from around herself, and heard the bathroom door open.

"Oh," she heard Dave say. "Morning."

A pause and then, "Afternoon."

Quinn's voice.

Shan gasped and fell back on the bed, flinging the blankets over her head.

When she finally got up, she peeked timidly into the hall. She saw it was empty and made a beeline for the bathroom. She scrubbed herself from head to toe, but she still felt dirty.

She went back to her room and dressed in capris and a pink Hello Kitty T-shirt, then regarded her bed. It was a rumpled mess mottled with suspicious stains. She pulled the sheets off, stuffing them into her wicker laundry basket. She wasn't going to the Laundromat until Friday when Ty went and this was her only set, so she'd have to borrow some from Denise. She turned toward the open door and stopped.

Quinn was standing there, watching her.

"Oh . . . hi," she said.

He didn't reply right away. They regarded each other silently for a few moments.

Eventually he spoke. "So Dave stayed here last night." It wasn't a question.

"Um . . . yes," she stammered. "We were up late, playing. I mean, practicing. He's teaching me some new stuff."

"I gathered as much. Did he teach you to suck it?" he inquired. "Suck it good?"

The blood slammed to her face. For a moment she couldn't respond.

He cocked his head. "Well?"

She found her voice. "What's it to you? I don't comment on the multitudes of bar sluts you date, or whatever you call what you do with them."

He didn't respond right away, just regarded her with glacial eyes, and she noticed a white line around his mouth. He was clenching his teeth so hard it must hurt.

When Quinn spoke, his voice shook. "Fuck you," he said, then vanished from the doorway.

Shan began to tremble.

chapter 23

Practice was torturous that day. Quinn was silent and withdrawn and glared at Shan sullenly, assuming an injured air whenever she spoke to him. "Julie's gone?" she heard Ty ask him.

"Yup," Quinn said without looking at him. "Flew out last night."

"Good thing." Dave chuckled. "You were becoming the Invisible Man."

Quinn didn't respond and remained uncharacteristically quiet. During a break he drifted outside. Shan followed and found him sitting under the sycamore tree, smoking a cigarette and gazing out over the creek bed. "Are you still mad at me?" she asked him.

"I'm not mad," he said, staring at the water. "I just don't have anything to say."

"I've noticed," she said tartly. "You're not even criticizing my playing, for once. I thought you were so committed to not letting anything personal interfere with the band."

"That's what I'm trying to do."

"Well, you're not doing a very good job," she said. "You won't even look at me."

"No, I won't," he agreed. "That's because the fucking sight of you is making me sick."

His words impaled her. She stared at him, frozen.

Quinn blew out a lungful of smoke. "I wish you'd go back inside and leave me the fuck alone, Shan. I really wish you'd do that."

Shan backed away, her eyes wide, then retreated into the house. When he came back inside, his face was completely blank. During the last hour of practice, he didn't look at her. Not once.

When they were done, she approached him. "Can we talk now?" she asked. Ty had a date and had departed speedily, and Dan was disassembling his kit in preparation for a gig the next day.

"Nope," Quinn said, busying himself winding chord.

Dave came back inside after loading his guitars and amp into his car. "Want to go for a bite?" he said to Shan.

She occasionally had dinner with Dave after practice, but tonight it didn't seem like a good idea. Her eyes were on Quinn, watching as his fingers wound the cable tight. Too tight.

"Maybe not tonight . . ." she began.

"Well, did you want to hang out?" he asked. "I can go get a pizza and bring it back."

Quinn stopped winding, standing stock still with the cable in his hands. He seemed coiled, ready to spring. "I changed my mind," Shan said quickly. "Let's go out for Chinese." She took Dave's arm and pushed him toward the door.

"Again? That's what we had last night."

"Indian, then," she said, almost shoving him out the front door.

"Do you want to bring your guitar? We could go to my place and play for a while," Quinn heard Dave ask as they got into his car. He lifted his head and glared after them with such murderous rage that Dan stopped breaking down the drums in midmotion.

"Man, you don't look good," he said.

"I'm fine," Quinn said, the muscles in his throat tightening convulsively.

"No, you're not," Dan corrected him. "I know that look. You'd better chill out, dude."

Quinn stared at him mutely for a moment. A bit of rational faculty seemed to be seeping through his fury. "A drink would help," he said, dropping the cables.

Dan followed him into the kitchen. Denise was at the kitchen table reading a copy of *LA Weekly*, where she'd recently landed a part-time job as a contributing photographer. She looked up with a smile that faded when she saw the look on Quinn's face. Quinn took out a bottle of tequila and sat down at the table, while Dan fetched a couple of shot glasses. When he turned back, he saw that Quinn was gulping the tequila from the bottle as if it were ginger ale.

Denise wrinkled her nose. "Quinn, don't you want a glass?"

"This is fine," Quinn replied, raising the bottle again.

Denise began to speak, but Dan placed a finger over his lips. "Why don't you go watch TV, sweet stuff?" He gave her a little nudge and

Denise acquiesced, taking the newspaper and withdrawing to the other room with a mystified expression.

When Quinn lowered the bottle, Dan slipped it out of his hand. "You know better than to guzzle Cuervo like that," he admonished. "Here, try a little of this." He sparked up a joint.

Quinn took three big hits before handing the joint back to Dan. They passed it back and forth, smoking silently until it was a smoldering roach.

Dan dropped it into an ashtray and examined Quinn, who now looked more fucked up than pissed off. "Want to talk about it?" Quinn stared at him blankly. Dan snorted. "Oh, please, dude. You look like you got run over by a freight train, just because your *roommate* is dating someone."

"Not dating him," Quinn corrected him sharply. "She's fucking him."

"I know." Dan grimaced. "I heard. But that's the main reason people date, in order to find somebody to fuck. *You* of all people ought to know that."

"I'm going to kill that motherfucker," Quinn said. "I'm going to reach down his throat and rip his balls out through his mouth."

"Don't talk crazy, man. This isn't about Dazz. It's got nothing to do with him."

"It sure as shit does. That douche bag is doing my girl."

"She's not *your* girl," Dan said, "and that's nobody's fault but your own. It's a wonder she didn't hook up with somebody a long time ago."

"But why now, after all this time?"

"Maybe two weeks of having your little fuck friend shoved in her face was more than she could take. And how do you think she likes watching you leave with a different girl after every gig?"

Quinn stared at Dan coldly for a minute, then, "You might be right. Not about the band broads. She knows they don't mean anything, but Julie might have got to her. She doesn't mean anything to me either, though. None of them do, really."

"Except for Shan, maybe?" Dan prompted.

Quinn rubbed his eyes. "Yeah," he said. "Except for Shan." He removed his hand from his eyes. "Gimme another drink."

Dan poured a couple of shots and slid one across the table. "Here's to you, man. It takes a lot for you to admit that. Don't think I don't know it."

Quinn drained the shot glass and set it on the table. "Do me another one, Danny." Dan refilled and Quinn downed it. Now his expression was one of abject misery.

"What's your problem now?" Dan asked.

"Now that douche bag has her and I didn't want to lose her." Quinn was beginning to slur his words.

"You haven't," Dan said. "You won't. You can shoot Dazz right out of the saddle. You're the one she wants. You know that. Shit, everybody knows that. Just tell her you love her."

"I can't," Quinn said. "Not yet. Gimme 'nother shot."

Dan poured. Tequila sloshed over the sides of the glasses. They gulped the shots and Dan let forth a copious, fiery tequila belch. "Why can't you fucking tell her?"

"Because if I do," Quinn said, swaying a little in his chair, "I'll have to make some kind of fucking commitment to her. She won't be happy any other way and I'm not ready for it."

Dan gave him a look of supreme disgust. "You're a stupid, stubborn fuck," he observed. "You have an awesome girl that you're crazy about. She's crazy about you, too. Shit, she worships you. Some guys would give their left ball to have what you've got, but *you're* whining about it."

"But I like having a lot of *different* women. How do you expect me to settle for only one?"

Dan snorted drunkenly. "It's not like you aren't hot for her. You've been after her like a stag in rut ever since the first time you laid eyes on her."

"I know," Quinn said. "I can't help it. She's fucking hot, and she looks at me like I'm king of the world. Besides, you're right. She's awesome. My awesome girl. But she's so young. Eighteen. Christ, she's a baby."

"Bullshit. Shan is hardly your average eighteen-year-old. She's been on her own for years. And she's been around the block—we all found that out last night."

Quinn's face twisted. "Don't talk about it."

"When she comes home, you should fuck her," Dan advised. "Just fuck her, for Chrisssake. You might find out she's enough for you."

"You know why I don't?" Quinn snagged the bottle away from Dan. "It's because I know that when I get into that luscious little pussy of hers"—he held up his hand, his fingers forming a round *O*—"*then I'll never fucking get out again.*" He snapped his fingers together, his hand clenching into a tight fist. "*Zap!* Just like a fuckin' noose."

He tilted the bottle to his face and took a long swallow, then set it down and stared into space. "I know it's going to happen, sooner or later, and that'll be that. I'm trying to put it off as long as I can. I figure there's time, since she's so young."

"Maybe not as much time as you thought," Dan said, "now that Dazzling Dave is in the picture. How is it that you didn't see this coming? She's exactly his type. More his than yours."

Quinn scowled. "Guys hit on Shan all the time. I figured she'd turn him down, and I wanted Dazz because he's perfect for the band. He's absolutely the best rhythm guitar player I know, and I knew his style would mate well with Shan's."

Dan snorted. "I guess it mated better than you expected."

"Could you shut the fuck up about it, please? I can't stand to think of him touching her." Quinn grabbed the bottle again and gulped at the dregs. When it was empty he pushed it aside and buried his face in his arms. He stayed that way for some time and, when he raised his head, his eyes had taken on a fuzzy dreaminess. "She's so beautiful," he said.

"She is," Dan agreed.

"And she has a great feel to her. The softest skin, just like velvet. The only thing softer is her hair. All those crazy curls. They don't look soft, do they? But they are. Soft as down. And those lips," he continued, swaying a little. "I have *dreams* about those sexy . . . fucking . . . lips." He pitched forward, his head landing on the table with a thud.

Dan struggled to his feet and staggered around the table. He lifted Quinn's head and squinted into his face, then smacked his cheek. "Q? Wake up, dude." No response. He gave him a good shake, catching the edge of the table as he stumbled and almost fell over himself. "Come on, man. You want to spend the night in the kitchen?"

Quinn mumbled inaudibly. Dan hauled him to his feet. Supporting Quinn's long, sagging frame against his own less than steady one, he struggled to relocate him to the living room.

Denise looked up from the recliner where she was cozily wrapped in a blanket watching television, her eyes widening as she watched her fiancé careen across the room and collapse on the couch with Quinn braced in his arms. They landed in a heap and didn't move again.

chapter 24

When Shan came downstairs the next morning, only Dan was snoring on the couch. She went in search of Quinn, encountering Denise in the kitchen. "Have you seen Q?"

"He was up and out early," Denise said. "Be glad you missed him. He looked mean as a rattlesnake. He must have a godawful hangover." She didn't speak again until Shan took her methadone, got some coffee, and sat down at the table. "Want to talk about it?"

"Not really."

"Oh, come on," Denise said. "It's about time you found a man, and Dave is *cute!* He's nice, too, and a guitar player, so you have a lot in common. Who cares what Quinn thinks?"

"I do," Shan replied. "He was so weird at practice, then I found him passed out on the couch when I got home last night. Q never gets drunk like that."

"So what? You've wasted enough time on him. I'm glad to see you're finally moving on."

"I'm not, really." Shan sighed. "I can't believe I even did this."

"Neither can I," Denise admitted, "and neither can Quinn, judging from his state last night. Why did you? I mean, after all this time."

Shan lowered her eyes. "We snorted some coke," she said after a moment.

Denise's eyes widened. "Is that smart?"

"Apparently not, since it made me screw a guy that I'm not even into. I like Dave, but I've never wanted him that way."

"How was it, though?"

"It was . . . dirty."

"But was it . . . good?"

"I guess so," Shan said. "I mean, he knows what he's doing. It felt good."

"Maybe it'll help you get over your fixation on Quinn. But you'd better watch the dope," Denise said. "I'm surprised at you, after you've been clean so long."

"I just slipped, and it's not like it was H. All I wanted was to feel good for a little bit. I guess that's why I slept with Dave, too." She watched Denise gather up her purse and camera bag, then realized it was her first day at her new job. "Good luck today. You'll do great."

"Thanks. I hope so." Denise took the van keys off the kitchen counter and headed for the front door. "Good luck to you, too. I think your hooking up with Dave will turn out to be a good thing in the end, Shan. You never know where it might lead."

They were playing at Gazzari's that night, a landmark club in West Hollywood. It would be a young crowd, Quinn informed them on the ride over, mostly college kids. Shan knew that was his favorite type of audience, because they were loud and enthusiastic and they danced nonstop.

It was her least favorite. By the end of the night, she knew she'd have her hands full fending off the amorous advances of drunken frat boys, who always seemed to get turned on by the sight of a guitar-wielding girl.

When they arrived at the club, Dave was already there. He came out to the stage entrance to help lug the gear and winked at Shan. Quinn saw and shot Dave a murderous glare, deadly enough to freeze him in his tracks. "Something wrong?" he asked Quinn.

Quinn did not reply, just took the snare drum from Dan and stalked into the club.

"He's hung over," Ty told Dave. "You might want to give him a wide berth."

Dan grimaced. "I am, too."

"Yeah, but you aren't scary," Ty said, and handed him a couple of mic stands.

While they set up and during sound check, Dave kept sneaking glances at Quinn. When he went outside for a smoke, Dave followed. "Everything okay, Q?"

Quinn didn't reply, smoking in stony silence, and after a minute, Dave tried again. "You were weird at practice yesterday, too. What's up?"

Again Quinn did not answer, just blew out a lungful of smoke.

"Okay, I broke your rule," Dave admitted. "I'm sorry. Now can you get over it, please?"

Quinn dropped his cigarette, ground it out with his heel, and stomped back inside the club. After a moment Dave followed and when they took the stage the tension between them was palpable. Shan felt it right away and she could tell that Ty and Dan were picking up on it, too. Dan seemed especially worried, eyes darting between Dave and Quinn with an air of foreboding.

It was a testament to the band's skill that they managed to sound good even with the undercurrents. Shan's vocals were a little subdued and Dave's tremolos a bit less lilting than usual. Quinn, despite the hangover, was solid as always.

The crowd liked them, bouncing and moshing with the kind of un-bridled energy only a cluster of twenty-one-year-olds was capable of. Shan had the dubious honor of being targeted by a passel of crewcut, muscle-bound thugs who looked like football players. They occupied a table near the stage, pounded shots of Jägermeister, and leered at her all night long.

Quinntessence finished to thundering applause. They came back for an encore, but Quinn started packing after just one song. The crowd groaned but Quinn did not pause. Dan and Ty headed for the bar and Shan tagged along to avoid being alone with Dave and Quinn.

Dave packed up his guitars, then approached Quinn again. "You're going to have to talk to me sooner or later, buddy," he said, beginning to fold up one of the mic stands.

Quinn ignored him, unplugging his Kurzweil.

"I can't take this," Dave groaned. "It's the same sort of shit that's happening in the Gurus."

"Why?" Quinn inquired. "Did you fuck somebody's girl in that band, too?"

Dave froze in his tracks. "What's that supposed to mean?"

Quinn scowled and turned away.

"You're jealous?" Dave persisted. "*That's* what this is all about?"

Quinn ignored him, stooping to disconnect the monitors.

"But you said there was nothing going on between the two of you," Dave said. "Besides, you fight all the fucking time. How am I supposed to know if nobody tells me?"

"There's nothing to know. I'm not jealous, I'm pissed that you're stupid enough to mess around with a bandmate just so you can get some."

"She's free and over eighteen," Dave said.

"But do you know how many bands have split over shit like this, you stupid fuck?"

"It's nothing that heavy and it's none of your fucking business besides."

"It *is* my fucking business because it's *my fucking band!* I don't want it screwed up because of an itch, do you hear me?"

Dave smirked. "Sounds like *you're* the one with the itch. And it also sounds like you're pissed because *I'm* the one who got the hot girl this time."

Quinn took a menacing step toward him. "You'd better shut your mouth."

Dave swatted at Quinn as if he were a pesky fly. "Oh, get over it, Q. I'll fuck anybody I want. You're out of line, *way* out of line, and—"

But Quinn was past caring what he had to say. "*Shut up,*" he snarled, placing both hands on Dave's chest and shoving, hard.

Caught off guard, Dave stumbled backward, catching his heel in one of the mic cables. He teetered at the edge of the stage for an agonizing moment, his arms pinwheeling wildly. Then as Quinn watched he toppled, landing squarely on the table of jocks.

"Fuck," Quinn muttered. Everyone in the club was watching. He could see the rest of his band over at the bar, staring openmouthed.

Dave scrambled off the table, apologizing profusely. The biggest, dumbest-looking jock got right up in his face, shouting and gesticulating like some kind of crazed motivational speaker.

"Fuck," Quinn spat again, with mounting concern. This was not cool. Not at all. The jock was big, but not as big as Dave. Sometimes that was a good thing. Sometimes not, especially if some moron thought he had something to prove.

This moron was still shouting, spittle flying from his flapping jaws, and Dave was starting to look disgusted. When the jock shoved his face to within an inch of Dave's nose, Dave grimaced, put his hand on the jock's chest, and gave him a firm push.

That was all it took. The jock pulled his fist back and popped Dave right in the face. Dave stumbled back and the rest of the frat jocks converged on him like zombies in a Romero film.

"*Fuck!*" Quinn yelled, and leapt off the stage right into the center of the fray.

When Dan turned to ask Shan what she wanted, his eyes widened. "What the hell?"

Following his gaze, Shan looked over her shoulder, just in time to see Dave land on the table. Moments later he was at the bottom of a pile and she watched, openmouthed, as Quinn dove off the stage into the melee.

"Oh shit!" Dan cried, as he and Ty charged over to help. In seconds it seemed like the whole bar was engaged in the brawl, with beer bottles and chairs flying through the air like something out of an old-time Western.

Shan couldn't believe her eyes. She watched Quinn snatch one guy off of Dave and toss him aside like he was a rag doll. When Ty and Dan got there, they plowed through the frat boys in short order and Dave emerged, looking ready to kill.

One jock leapt on Quinn's back brandishing a bottle and Shan gasped. She sprinted across the room and snatched the top of one of their wooden packing crates off the edge of the stage. "*Get off of him!*" she cried, bringing the board down on the jock's shaved head.

He let out a yelp and let go of Quinn, whirling to confront the threat from the rear. He hesitated for a second when he saw who it was. Half a second was enough and Quinn laid him flat with an uppercut.

Then he spied a couple of the jocks heading for the stage. "*Dan!*" he yelled, pointing. Dan saw, scrambled onstage, and grabbed one of the mic stands. Swinging it an arc, he managed to keep them away from their equipment until the bouncers could get their hands on them.

A screech erupted from the monitors. "The police are on their way," intoned a voice over the PA. It was the sound guy, who had wisely stayed behind his board.

The statement was like a magic incantation. The crowd evaporated like dew, leaving Quinntessence, a couple of bar staff, three bouncers, and a very angry club owner.

Shan watched Quinn and Ty disappear into the office to placate the owner. The place was a mess, with overturned tables and broken glass everywhere, but she couldn't spot any serious damage. Their gear was intact and the brawl hadn't made it as far as the sound board.

Dan appeared. "Here," he said, tossing her the keys to the van. "I'm going with Dave."

She caught the keys. "Going . . . ?"

"To the hospital," Dan told her, frowning. "He's hurt. I'll see you all back at the house."

Then he was gone and Shan was left wondering what in the hell had just happened.

The next morning, Quinn was sitting under the sycamore tree with a bag of ice on his right hand. The ride from the club had been animated, with Ty and Shan both still pumped up on an adrenaline high. He himself had been more subdued. Neither of them had witnessed his altercation with Dave, so they had no idea that it was all his fault.

Dan called shortly after they got home. Dave had a broken nose, he reported, and assorted bruises. Dan would drive him home, then crash at his place. Could they tell Denise where he was?

Quinn left that to Shan and went to bed, pausing just long enough to retrieve a bag of ice from the freezer. His right hand was killing him.

He swathed it in ice, wrapped it in an ace bandage to hold the pack in place, and slept with his hand propped up on a pillow. The bag leaked during the night and he woke up wet.

In the morning his hand was stiff, but the ice had kept the swelling down and he was relieved nothing appeared to be broken. He got a cup of coffee and a fresh bag of ice, then headed out to the chair by the creek, where he sat and smoked and moped.

Around ten, he heard a car pull up in front of the house. A few minutes later, Dave came out on the back porch, dressed in shorts, T-shirt, and sunglasses. "Hey," he said, sounding pissed.

"Hey," Quinn replied, dropping the ice bag into a bucket at his side. Dave descended the steps and crossed the yard to stand in front of him. His nose was swollen, but otherwise he appeared relatively unscathed. "You look okay," Quinn said.

"Do I?" Dave sneered. He removed his glasses, revealing two black eyes.

Quinn grimaced. "Sorry about that."

Dave's eyes, now rimmed with purplish black crescents, went to Quinn's hand. "What's the matter with your hand?"

"Not much." Quinn flexed his fingers. "A little stiff, that's all."

"Nice quality in a keyboard player," Dave said.

Quinn waved him off. "It's nothing."

"Put the ice back on the magic fucking fingers," Dave snapped. Quinn scowled, but retrieved the bag of ice from the bucket. When he had it positioned on his knuckles, Dave sat down in the other chair. Shan's chair. Quinn's lip curled.

Dave didn't waste any time. "What is it with you and this chick?"

"We've been over this. There's nothing."

"So I got my ass kicked over nothing? I don't buy it."

"I'm not the one who kicked it," Quinn reminded him. "I only shoved it."

"A technicality." Dave put his glasses back on. "Look, I have a feeling about this band. It's special. Besides, you and me . . . hell, Q. We go back a long way, and we've always had each other's backs."

"I had it this time, too," Quinn said. Dave's eyes flicked to the hand swathed in ice.

"Good thing," he said, "since it was your fucking fault."

"I said I was sorry," Quinn said defensively. "It's over. Can't you just let it lie?"

"It's over so long as I stay away from the guitar goddess, right?"

Quinn hesitated, then nodded. Dave frowned. "You said it was nothing heavy," Quinn said, "so what's the problem?"

"I do like her, though," Dave admitted. "I like her a lot. She's such a sweet little thing and we hang out easy together. Besides, I don't much like the idea of you dictating my sex life."

"I don't give a shit about your sex life," Quinn said, ignoring Dave's other comments. If he addressed those, he might well hit him again. "My concern is Quinntessence, which I have spent literally years assembling. I've put everything I've got into it and I can't think of a better way to rip it apart than exactly what you're doing."

Dave was still regarding him with suspicion. "So I'm supposed to believe that's what you're worried about? Disrupting the band?"

"What else would I be worried about?"

"I think you want this chick for yourself," Dave said. "Maybe you're too busy doing groupies to get into anything heavy right now, but I think you're keeping her on the back burner. A little insurance policy for when you decide you've done enough of them."

Quinn laughed to cover his chagrin. *Christ, am I that transparent?* "Right. That's just what I want, a fucking ball and chain right in my band. Have you met me, dude?" Dave hesitated, eying him with consternation. "Look, it's simple. There's a rule. No fraternizing inside of the band. Period. If you plan on mixing it up with my lead guitar player, then you're out. That's it. I'm not compromising on this, Dave."

Dave thought about it for a minute, then heaved a sigh. "I suppose you do have a point."

"All right, then," Quinn said, concealing a colossal rush of relief. "Fuck anybody you want, as long as they're not part of Quinntessence."

"So that means I can't do Danny either?" Dave said, forcing a smile.

Quinn grinned back. "I'd have thought Ty was more your type," he joked. "But no, you can't fuck them, either, Dazz."

chapter 25

Since Quinn's hand was stiff and Dave was in considerable discomfort, the band shelved practice for that day. Dave went home, Ty went out somewhere, and Dan left, as well, intending to drop Denise at work, then shop for a new splash cymbal at a drum store in Hollywood. After everyone departed, Shan came downstairs in search of Quinn.

She could hear him in the music room, experimenting with a different mix on a song they'd recorded the week before. He was at the mixing board, using only his left hand. The right, swathed in a bag of ice, was resting on his leg. She waited for a pause in the music. "Hey, Q," she said.

"Hey," he replied without looking up.

"Can we talk?"

"I'm kinda busy." His tone was cool and he still didn't look up.

She sat down next to him anyway. "I hate it when we don't speak."

He ignored her, fiddling with the sliders. "I know you're still mad at me," she said.

"I told you I wasn't mad," he said, beginning to sound testy.

"You are, though," she corrected him gently, "and I know it's about the thing with Dave."

He didn't reply, but he stopped moving the sliders. "I . . . I didn't know you were at home, Q. It wouldn't have happened, if I'd known."

"So you'll wait until I'm out of the house next time? How considerate of you."

"I meant that I wouldn't have been so . . . well, obvious," she said nervously. "I mean, I know it was kind of . . . um . . . loud. It must have made you feel uncomfortable, listening to that."

"Uncomfortable. Yup. That's how it made me feel, all right." He sniggered. "Just let me know in advance the next time you're planning a sex binge. I'll put on some punk ska to drown out your shrieks of ecstasy."

She stiffened. "You don't have to be so mean."

"*Leave me alone, then.* I told you I didn't want to talk about it."

"But I want to make sure you understand." She touched his arm.

He jerked away as if she'd burnt him. The ice slipped off his hand as he turned and she found herself looking directly into his eyes for the first time in days. His tone might be cold, but his eyes weren't. They were blistering, ablaze with barely suppressed fury. "Understand what?" he inquired. "Understand why you decided to rehearse a porno practically right in front of me? Or why you thought it was a good idea to get down and dirty with one of my oldest friends? Just what the fuck am I supposed to understand, exactly?"

"I . . . I don't know," she said miserably. "I'm just sorry, because I know that I hurt you. That's the last thing I want to do, ever."

He let out a snort of laughter at that. "It's true," she declared. "You're the most important person in the world to me. The thing with Dave . . . it was nothing."

He looked skeptical. "It sure sounded like something to me, Shan. It sounded like a whole lot of hot, sweaty something."

"It wasn't," she insisted, but he turned back to the mixer in a clear dismissal. She put her head in her hands, a sick, anxious jitter in the pit of her stomach. He was starting to scare her, beginning to make her afraid that permanent damage had been done.

She raised her head. "We did some coke," she said, after a moment.

He froze. "What?"

"We snorted some coke and wound up in bed together. That's all it was—crazy coke sex."

"What the fuck are you doing with coke?"

"Dave had it. I was in a lousy mood, and it was there and I slipped. Just a slip, Q."

"So you're down, and here's some guy with blow, and then you're vacuuming Bolivia's finest up your fucking nose?" His face was flushing with rage. "*Bad decision,* Shan. *Really* bad."

"It wasn't a big deal. It's not like it was H."

"I can't believe you could be so fucking stupid! And Dave—I'll kill that douche bag!"

"It's not his fault," she said. "I made my own choice. I'm a big girl, remember?"

"Right. A big, stupid girl making big, stupid choices. And you don't *have* to suck dick just because some guy offers you dope," he added viciously. "You have a choice about *that*, too!"

She blanched with a swift intake of breath. Her face went dead white.

He regarded her with disgust for another moment, then, "You know what? I'm done. I went through this shit with you once and I'm not going there again."

She gaped at him, eyes like saucers, then hastily cast them down.

"You can take care of yourself," he said. "That's what you always say. Do it, then. Find yourself a new band, and a new place to live, and dope yourself into a coma if you want. We'd both be better off if you moved out. You remember, don't you, that I told you a long time ago that I don't want an attachment? That I don't want a girlfriend? *That I don't want to be tied down?*"

The mere sight of her seemed to be making him madder and he turned away to direct his tirade at the mixing board. "But what do you care? You don't give a shit what I want. I haven't been able to get away from you from the first minute I set eyes on you. 'Take care of me, Q,'" he mimicked. "'Be my family, Q.' 'Make up for everything bad that's ever happened to me, Q.' If you stay here I'll have an attachment whether I want one or not, and a junkie one at that, because I'll have you hanging around my neck like a fucking lead weight for the rest of my life."

He reached for the sliders in a fury, forgetting his injured hand. He winced in pain and shot an angry look at Shan, who hadn't responded. Hadn't spoken. Hadn't even raised her head to look at him. Her knuckles had gone white from the force of her grip on the hem of her shirt.

His anger seemed to ebb as he stared at those white knuckles. "Hey . . ." he began.

Shan leapt to her feet and bolted, heading for the back door. Just as she pulled it open, he landed against it with all of his weight. She ducked her head. "Open the fucking door," she said.

"No." He grasped her chin and pulled her face around.

It was ashen and her eyes were huge. "*Get off of me, you—*" but the words caught in her throat. Her eyes brightened and he gasped as tears cascaded down her cheeks.

"Jesus, don't cry! You never cry. You never, *ever* cry. Don't. Don't. *Don't!*" He pulled her into his arms and she wrenched away, but he held fast until she collapsed.

He sank to the floor, holding her. "I didn't mean it, angel. You know I didn't." He rocked her like she was a child, but she covered her head with both arms, weeping as if she'd never stop.

She sobbed and sobbed. It was as if a dam had burst and she cried on and on, unable to quench the flow. Her muscles convulsed with each sob and he held her for nearly ten minutes before she showed any sign of slowing.

Eventually the sobs diminished to hiccups. "Are you finished?" he asked when she raised her head. She opened her mouth to answer, but was seized with a fresh onslaught of weeping. "Shan, please stop," Quinn begged. "You're breaking my heart."

But she couldn't, sobbing and choking for several minutes more. Eventually she swabbed her eyes. "Look at that," she said. Her voice shook like a maraca. "I got your shirt all wet."

His face was stricken. "I didn't mean it, angel."

She swiped her eyes again. "Oh, I think you meant it just a little bit." She climbed off his lap, opened the back door, and went outside.

Quinn scrambled to his feet and followed. Shan was picking her way across the creek. When she got to the other side she disappeared over a hill, never once looking back.

He set out after her and, when he crested the hill, saw her trudging up ahead. She obviously needed space so he kept some distance between them, but he was careful to keep her in his sights.

She trekked for a good, long time, easily a mile, probably closer to two. Eventually he caught up with her, after she'd flopped down on the mountainside. The view was stunning, a sweeping panorama of the canyon they lived in. "Is this where you come when you go out walking?" he asked when he reached her.

"Sometimes," she said, wiping her cheeks. There were still tears trickling from the corners of her eyes. "I like to sit here and play."

"You'd better be careful," he said, frowning. "I don't like the idea of you this deep in the woods by yourself."

Her lips pursed. "I can take care of myself, like you pointed out."

He sat down beside her and they were silent for a few minutes. Eventually Quinn spoke. "I'm sorry for what I said, about you being a burden. It was a shitty thing to say and it isn't true."

Her slight shoulders began to shake and he saw that she was crying again. "I've never felt that way about you," he persisted. "You . . . you're a joy to me, angel. An absolute joy."

She began to sob, pressing her fingers against her eyes as if to force the tears back into their ducts. He gave up talking and took her in his arms again. She was limp and slid through his hands until she was lying in his lap, her cheek against his thigh. He smoothed the hair off her face and let her cry. Eventually his leg was wet from her tears soaking through the fabric of his jeans.

After a while she pulled away and glared at him. "I'd better stay away from that area," she said. "You'll think I'm trying to suck you off for drugs."

He winced. "You know I didn't mean that, either. I think you're awesome, angel. Bright, talented, beautiful . . ." he paused, unable to come up with enough superlatives. "There's nobody I respect more than you."

She was watching him now, her face raw, painful. "You'll never let me in, though, will you?" He stared at her, a faint frown creasing his brow. "Sometimes I feel like I don't even know you, Quinn. Not in any real way."

"What are you talking about?" he asked, perplexed. "You know me better than anyone. I tell you everything."

"Tell me about the coke, then." He stared at her, clearly mystified. "*Your* coke, I mean. Your coke problem."

When he comprehended what she was saying, Quinn's eyes widened. "*What?* How did you . . ." He paused, and then, "Dave?" He looked utterly gobsmacked.

"Yes, but don't you dare get mad at him," she said, sniffling. "He didn't rat you out. I told him about *my* drug problem, how you helped me get clean, and he brought up yours. He figured I knew. It's a reasonable assumption, I think."

Quinn was silent for a long time, still looking stunned. Eventually he spoke. "I always planned on telling you," he whispered. "A dozen times I almost did."

"You *should* have told me. I can't believe you'd keep a secret like that from me." Her tears, which had never completely stopped, began to flow faster. "I'd like you to tell me now, please."

He hesitated, then nodded slowly. "All right. I don't know how much you know."

"Not much," she said, using the sleeve of her T-shirt to swipe her eyes and nose. "And that doesn't matter, anyway. I want to hear your story from you."

"Okay." He sat up straighter, clasping his arms around his knees. "I've told you how I got into my first real band when I was sixteen. The Accidental Evils. I was the youngest member."

"Just like me," Shan murmured, still wiping her eyes.

"Yes. I started out as a roadie, but pretty soon they figured out that I could play anything. They loved having me around, because I could fill in whenever one of them got too wasted to go onstage. Eventually the bass player got busted, so I started playing bass. A few months later, Gil, the keyboard player, ODed on smack and wound up in a coma. Then I was the keyboard player."

Go ahead and dope yourself into a coma, he'd snarled at her earlier. She sniffled.

"The drugs were everywhere. All kinds, too. Everybody had their own thing they were into. The candyman would come to our gigs with a briefcase full of little brown lunch bags, one for every band member. I was in the Evils for a year and a half and, during that time, I did just about every drug there is, except for smack." He shot a sideways glance at her. "Watching Gil turn into a brussels sprout kept me off the horse. Blow, though, that was a different story."

He sounded like he was reading a script and Shan realized he probably was. He must have recited his story a hundred times. She certainly had, at all those meetings.

"There were times it was weird, being the youngest. I could play as well or better than the best of them, but it didn't change the fact that the others were eight, ten years older than me. When I was coked up I felt like one of them, instead of the junior roadie turned keyboard player.

"Then I got really sucked into the whole scene. Having people come out, pay for a ticket to see us play, then getting the crowd high on that energy—there's nothing like it. *You* know. And the women . . ." he paused, shot a sideways look at her, then shrugged. "The women were everywhere, too. I was only sixteen years old, remember. I'd been having sex for a couple of years, but it was my first experience with groupies. I had so many women that I can't remember most of them," he continued. "If I met one of them on the street, I wouldn't even recognize her."

She knew that was still true today, but she tried to picture him at sixteen. Slighter, more willowy than he was now, and flawless as a young god, with his fair hair and ethereal eyes. The groupies would have eaten him alive, consumed him. "What about your parents?"

"I'd always been in one band or another, so they were used to my not being home much. My grades were still good, good enough to get me accepted at Stanford, so my folks didn't worry. I held it together, at least until that last summer when we went on tour."

"Your mother let you go on the road?" That didn't sound to Shan like the mother he'd described. Not at all. "What about school?"

"I was done, by then. I graduated high school early because I skipped the third grade. I was starting at Stanford for the fall and the tour was planned for summer, so my folks gave me the go-ahead. They trusted me, you see. I'd never given them any reason not to, as far as they knew.

"So off we went and it was open season, for me. I buried myself in blow—snorting all day, snorting to play, snorting and fucking all night. Fucking so much, sometimes, I rubbed the skin right off my . . . well. I don't have to tell *you*. You know, don't you, about crazy coke sex?"

He shot a sideways glance at her and she nodded hastily.

"I don't remember much about that summer," he confessed, "because I was fucked up one hundred percent of the time. And I barely remember anything at all about the night things came to a head. We'd played Jazz Alley in Seattle and I wound up in the bathroom with two chicks, snorting blow off their tits. I guess I finally hit my limit, or maybe it was some kind of extrastrength, pharmaceutical-grade shit. Or maybe it was cut with fucking Borax. Anyway I went down, smashing my head on the sink along the way. I woke up in the hospital with IVs in both arms, a tube up my dick, and a fractured skull. I still don't know much about how I got there. Dave can tell you more about that than I can."

"Dave?" she asked, puzzled, and Quinn looked nonplussed.

"Wow, he *really* didn't say much, did he?" She shook her head. "Dave was the one who found me," he explained. "He'd hooked up with us a few months earlier, after one of our guitar players went into rehab. The girls must have taken off when I passed out and, by the time Dave came into the bathroom, I'd gone totally code blue. He called 911 and did CPR until the paramedics got there. It's very likely that I would not be alive today, if not for Dazzlin' Dave Ross. He's the one who called my mother, too," he added, his face falling at the memory. "She was there when I woke up, her and George and my brother, all of them crying their eyes out.

"They kept me in the ICU for a week, to make sure I didn't have some kind of permanent brain damage, then they shipped me off to a treatment center. I was there for almost six months. When I came out, I was clean. I've stayed that way ever since."

He looked exhausted and Shan felt that way, too, overwhelmed by the enormity of what he'd told her. "My god, Q. Do the others know about this? Dan and Ty, I mean."

Quinn shook his head. "No. Dan moved to New York while I was on the road with the Evils. He knows something went down, because he knew me in my hardcore days, but he's never asked for details. All Ty knows is that I'm a holier-than-thou fuck about drugs. I know he and Dan both like a line every now and then, and that's fine, so long as they keep it away from the band and out of my face. Because *I* can't slip. It'll kill me. It almost did."

"Why can't you just tell them, then? They'd understand. They understand about *me*."

He shook his head again, more vehemently. "I don't like to talk about those days to begin with, and . . . well. It was hardly my finest hour. I wish nobody had to know."

He was worn out, obviously finished, but she had one more question for him. "Is that why you didn't tell me?" she asked softly. "Because you were ashamed?"

He was silent for a long time. When he finally spoke, his voice was low. "Yes." His arms were still clasped around his knees and he dropped his head against them. "You love me so much, angel," he went on, his voice muffled. "Nobody's ever loved me like you do. The way you look up to me, the way you look *at* me . . . it's everything, to me. I was afraid that, if you knew, you'd never look at me that way again."

She was crying again, her eyes so awash with tears that she could hardly see him. "But it just makes me love you *more,* knowing you made it back from something like that. I can understand better than anybody, don't you see?"

He didn't reply, but reached out with his good hand and laid it against her cheek, gently removing her tears with his thumb. She pressed her face against his hand as her tears came faster.

He sighed. "I really wish you'd stop crying."

"I can't," she sobbed. "It's a jag, or something."

He took her face between his hands. She closed her eyes and leaned into him, murmuring when she felt his mouth on her eyelid. He kissed one, then the other, absorbing her tears with his lips. "I love you, too," he whispered. "You know that, don't you? I don't say it, but . . ."

She nodded, still crying, her eyes squeezed shut. She no longer felt his lips against her eyes, but then she felt them against her mouth, soft and warm and moist with her tears.

Oh . . .

Quinn was kissing her, she noted with a sense of wonder, deeply, sweetly, in a way he'd never kissed her before.

Had she thought Dave was a good kisser? He wasn't. Nobody was, not like this, and she realized that she'd never really been kissed before. Not with this intimacy, or this yearning, or this tenderness, and she knew with complete certainty that she'd been waiting all her life for this kiss.

He kissed her over and over, then kissed her all over: her cheek, her throat, her forehead. Then he was lifting her T-shirt, kissing her breasts, burying his face between them, nuzzling the flesh over her heart.

She held his head, trembling, and then his hand was at her waist.

Time seemed to stand still as he pulled open the snap on her jeans, unzipped them, pushed them down, pulled them off. He reached for her panties, stripped those off, too, then pushed her thighs apart and kissed her between her legs.

She was flooded by a wave of heat more intense than anything she'd ever felt. She couldn't see his expression, he was bowed over her body with his back to her face, but she gripped his shoulder to pull him away, irrationally afraid that the raw forces swelling inside her would explode out of that opening. She felt thermonuclear and she could imagine it, her built-up longings erupting in a beam of white-hot heat that would incinerate him if he touched her there again.

But he didn't and instead she felt his lips against the inside of her leg. They moved gently, lovingly, and she realized that he was kissing the road map of scars on her thigh.

She started to cry again, softly, and when he turned to face her his expression was rapt, reverential. She reached for his pants but he already had them off, and she caught her breath when her hand encountered the firm, velvety head of his cock.

He moved between her legs, and his cock glided into her, and then was deep inside of her. Her body arched up and then he was moving, pushing and sliding and driving inside of her.

Shan already felt about to detonate and now she was building to an even higher, more unbearable pitch. She couldn't breathe; something inside was growing and it felt too big for her body, too big for the world, the universe.

When she came she cried out, her legs and arms constricting around him, and began to sob again, overcome by the sheer power and beauty and perfection of their fusion. He was plunging into her and almost immediately she felt the pressure building again, again, and she cried out once more before his body tensed and he threw his head back with a groan. "*Angel,*" he gasped.

"*Q,*" she whispered and they were kissing again, his body sinking into hers until they melded together.

She held him cradled in her arms, his face buried against her throat, until his breathing returned to normal. Tears were still trickling from her eyes.

Eventually he pressed a kiss against her breast and hoisted himself off of her. Shan made a small sound of distress when he slipped out of her, leaving her empty, spent. When he rolled over to lie at her side, he reached between her legs, gently cupping her vagina with his hand.

They lay together in silence for a very long time. Eventually Quinn pulled his hand away and Shan murmured, bereft without his warmth.

She turned her head to tell him that, but her words died when she saw the look on his face.

He was gazing up at the sky, too, looking stunned, chagrined, and, increasingly, horrified.

She stared at him silently, a cold, hard knot beginning to form in the pit of her stomach, displacing the sweet warmth that had filled her moments before. "Son of a bitch," she whispered and rolled away, tugging her T-shirt over her breasts.

Quinn looked at her, startled. "What . . . what's wrong?" His pants were still down around his knees and his eyes were as round as a deer in the headlights.

"Nothing, Quinn." She brushed the pine needles off her ass and pulled on her jeans. "Not a fucking thing." She jerked on her sneakers and stood up. Her panties were lying on the ground and she snatched them, stuffing them into her pocket.

Quinn had gotten to his feet and pulled up his pants. "Ready to go?" he asked, avoiding her eyes. His clothes still bore stains where she'd bathed him in her tears.

"Yup," she replied and he headed back down the trail toward the house. After a couple of steps, he became aware that Shan was trudging in the opposite direction. "Where are you going?"

She stopped and looked over her shoulder. "For a walk. I'm not ready to go home yet."

"Oh." He frowned, hesitating. "Do you want me to go with you?"

"No." She was regarding him coldly and, for the first time all day, her eyes were dry. "Don't worry, Quinn. I get it. It was a slip. Nothing more."

She turned away and set off up the trail. This time Quinn didn't follow, just stood still and watched until she disappeared.

chapter 26

"I brought you one of those cupcakes that you like," Quinn said, "from the bakery in Sunland."

"Hold on," Shan said into the phone and turned to face him.

Since The Act, as she thought of their slip on the mountain, Quinn had become almost her slave. He couldn't do enough for her, couldn't be more attentive, couldn't look more guilty. It made her want to kill him.

As a rule Shan rejected his overtures, taking an evil satisfaction in spurning him. His wretchedness pleased her, a counteraction for her own hurt and embarrassment, but the cupcake was blueberry butter-cream, her favorite.

She took it, sniffed her thanks, then stepped into the hall closet and shut the door in his face. "Another offering from Quinn?" Oda asked from the other end of the phone.

"Serves him right," Shan said. The location of the telephone afforded no privacy, so she often took the handset into this closet where she had to crouch among everyone's coats, Denise's tripods, and Quinn's spare helmet. "He should feel guilty, after the way he took advantage of me." Oda was the only person she'd told about The Act.

"Is that what you think he did?" Oda asked. "You don't think he just got carried away?"

"It doesn't matter," Shan insisted, taking a bite of the cupcake. "He should have had more self-control."

"Mmm-hmm. He sure should have." As usual, Oda made her opinion clear with a minimum of words.

There was a knock on the closet door. "Are you nearly finished?" Quinn's voice again, sounding sheepish and contrite like it always did now. "It's almost seven. We have to leave for the gig soon."

It was a Thursday in December, a few weeks after The Act, and they were playing the Troubadour in West Hollywood. They'd performed there twice, once as a Monday-night opener for a past-their-prime rock band and again on a Tuesday, number three of a six-band line up. Quinn had been lobbying hard for a better slot. "The Troub is part of the rock 'n' roll landscape in LA," he informed them. "A good Friday or Saturday night there is an indication of true star potential." Tonight they were opening for Roomful of Blues, one step closer to the coveted headlining slot. When they arrived to set up, the line down Santa Monica Boulevard was already forming.

They were supercharged onstage, buoyed up by the mystique of the club. Shan always found the energy of the place to be overwhelming. Dylan had played here. So had Bonnie Raitt. Neil Young, Bruce Springsteen, Guns N' Roses—all Troubadour alumni. It made her feel triumphant, like she'd made it, and, at the same time, like she never would, that her star could never shine as brightly as the legends that had graced this stage before her. When she learned it had been the site of Joni Mitchell's Los Angeles debut, Shan got misty, thinking of her mother.

The place was packed and by the end of their set they'd acquired a whole new group of fans, but there was no time to give them the encore they shouted for because Quinntessence had to break down and make way for the legendary blues band. "We blew them away," Quinn proclaimed as they loaded out. "And *you* kicked ass," he told Shan, who shrugged. Inside she glowed, since his recent obsequiousness had not extended to musical matters. It was remarkable, his skill at compartmentalizing.

Quinn had ridden his bike to the gig, as he often did, and wasn't yet home by the time Shan went to bed. Around three-thirty she got up to pee and encountered him in the hallway, obviously engaged in a walk of shame. He stopped when he saw her, his eyes wide with guilty consternation.

"Was it good?" she inquired before slamming her door in his face. She hadn't been entirely sure whether he'd continued with his frequent flyers since The Act. Now she knew.

Shan tossed and turned, then overslept the next morning. She woke cranky and jonesing, so she immediately went downstairs for her methadone.

She discovered Quinn in the kitchen. He was making a sandwich. "Hi," he said.

She ignored him and went to the refrigerator.

"You slept late," he observed. "I've been waiting for you to get up."

She didn't reply, just swallowed the 'done and poured a glass of water.

"I was thinking maybe we could spend the day together," he continued. "if you can stand to, that is."

At that, she turned around and looked at him. "Why?"

"Because things are weird between us. I thought we'd get over it, but . . ." He shrugged. "I don't like it. I miss you, angel."

Despite her mood, his words made her thaw, just a little. She knew what he meant. She missed him, too. Or, rather, she missed *them*— their easy affection and camaraderie. "What did you have in mind?"

"Nothing heavy. I thought we could just . . . have some fun." He gestured toward the sandwich. "A bike ride, then a picnic."

She regarded him dubiously, but the earnest, hopeful look on his face won her over. "Well, all right. I'd rather take the van, though."

"Can't," Quinn replied. "Dan's out somewhere. I don't know when he's coming home."

"Maybe we can borrow Ty's car."

"Nope," he said firmly. "This ride requires the bike."

"But . . ." she began, then paused.

"I know you think you don't like it, but you will. Just give it a chance." She still looked doubtful. "Come on. Don't you trust me?"

"It's not you," she said. "It's that bike. I don't like motorcycles, Q. I think they're dangerous."

"You have nothing to worry about. Seriously, angel," he said, his eye taking on a wicked glitter, "that bike is the safest thing of mine that will ever be between your legs."

She gasped, color flooding her cheeks, then burst out laughing. He grinned and gave her a little push. "Go on. Get dressed."

Half an hour later, they were gliding along the Angeles Crest, a windy mountain highway that led through the San Gabriel Mountains. The road twisted and coiled around jutting boulders and scrubby pines, its sharp turns revealing vistas of startling and unexpected beauty, spectacular views that Shan ignored.

She wasn't enjoying the ride. Quinn had often urged her to join him on his jaunts and she'd consented to a few short trips, but it always scared her. She wore a helmet, Quinn insisted on it, but she still felt vulnerable, exposed and helpless, completely without control.

So far this ride was no different. Whenever Quinn accelerated, Shan closed her eyes and waited to become a smudge on the pavement. Each time he leaned into a turn, her lips moved in silent prayer. She kept glancing over her shoulder. There was nothing between her body and the road but air. She imagined what it would feel like to hit it, to skid along the pavement, her skin sloughing off like a flayed fish, and she trembled.

When they coasted around a hairpin turn, she gasped, squeezed her eyes shut, and pressed her face against the back of Quinn's shoulder. She could smell his leather jacket, an earthy, masculine scent, and felt comforted, though her arms did not loosen their death grip around his chest. He gave her leg a reassuring pat.

They rode for a long time, more than an hour, and eventually Shan found herself acknowledging that she was in capable hands. Quinn was handling the bike with the same easy competence and skill with which he did everything else, keeping the ride smooth and the speed steady. She began to relax a little and realized that her hands hurt from the force of her grip. She flexed them to relieve the ache, laid them flat against his chest, and cautiously lifted her head from his shoulder.

The road snaked along the crest of the mountains and she could see for miles and miles, canyons, desert wilderness, and, in the distance, the unmistakable blue of the Pacific. It was spectacular. "Where are we going?" she shouted as they slowed for another sharp turn.

Quinn chuckled. "Your mouth is only about three inches from my ear, you know. You don't have to scream."

"Sorry." She lowered her voice a few decibels. "Where—"

"Someplace you'll like. You trust me, right?"

"Right," she yelled as he accelerated again. His hair was fluttering in the wind and the silky blond strands tickled her cheek.

Eventually they pulled off the road into a parking area, where he kicked the bike upright and dismounted. Pulling off his helmet, he grinned at Shan. "How was it?"

"Fun," she confessed. "It's still a little scary, but . . . I trust you."

"Told you so. How's your ass holding up?"

"Not too bad," she replied, but it was sore and she rubbed it. "I guess you get used to that, too, right?"

"Right." He was unfastening a saddlebag from the back of the bike, attaching a leather strap to it, and slinging it over his shoulder. "As long as you keep riding," he continued, "which I hope you will."

Just what he'd been bugging her to do for some time. As always, he'd gotten his way. She took off her helmet and dismounted, then he led her past a picnic area and up a trail. The ground was paved for a short distance but quickly gave way to a rugged dirt footpath that ran alongside a river.

Eventually he veered off the main trail onto a much smaller path. It was overgrown, nearly invisible. Shan would have walked right past without even seeing it. Five minutes later they reached a small, deserted swimming hole tucked into a canyon crevice.

It was a lovely spot, peaceful and serene. The mountain pool, fed by a small waterfall and surrounded by a fringe of brush, was clear as glass. Shan followed Quinn up the rocky grade beside the fall. When they reached the top he sat down under a tree and patted the ground beside him. After Shan sat down, he popped open the bag and took out the sandwiches. "We're here," he said simply.

She accepted a sandwich. When she unwrapped it, she saw it was peanut butter and honey, her favorite. She took a big bite, nodding her approval. He grinned, handing her a bottle of water.

They ate the sandwiches, then Quinn produced another treat, a bag of fresh, sweet strawberries. Neither of them spoke until they'd consumed every last one. "Tell me about this place," Shan said when they'd finished. "How do you know it?"

Quinn was collecting their empty water bottles and placing them back in the saddle bag. "I used to come here when I was in high school," he replied. "I still do, sometimes. There's a big party spot just up the trail: Switzer Falls. That's a nice spot, too. There's even a natural water slide, but it's always crowded. I like it better here. It's more private."

"Good place to bring frequent flyers?" The words burst out of her before she could stop them.

Quinn shook his head. He took a piece of crust left over from one of the sandwiches and dropped it into the water. They both watched a bass come to the surface to inspect it. "I've never brought anyone here before. It's a place I come when I need solitude."

"So why did you bring me?" she asked.

He shrugged. "It's like the bike, I guess. I love it here, just like I love riding. I wanted to . . . share it with you. Reconnect. I thought it would help." He kept his head down, watching as more fish surfaced to examine the bread floating on the water. "It bothered me when you said you felt like you didn't know me, angel," he said, after a while. "You do. More than anyone else does."

"Maybe I do," she conceded, "but that's not saying much, is it?" He looked up then and, when he did, she saw his eyes were troubled. "You're so guarded, Q, so closed off from everyone. Me included. You don't let anybody in."

He didn't reply right away, then, "I keep to myself, Shan. I always have. It's no reflection on you."

"It's a reflection on *us*," she corrected him. "On how one sided our relationship is."

"It isn't one sided. You're a big part of my life. Maybe even the biggest part."

"I don't see that, Q. I really don't. I mean, we've been living together for six months and I've still never met even a single member of your family. They only live half an hour away."

"So? I never see them."

"But I've met Dan's parents, and his sister, and Ty's father that time he was in New York. I've even met Dave's mother and father."

"All of those people have come to gigs," he insisted, scowling when she mentioned Dave. "Nobody from my family is likely to show up there."

"Maybe not your mother," she said, "but what about your brother or stepfather?"

"I don't particularly want them at our gigs," he said and she nodded.

"I know. Because you shut them out, too." He looked away, still frowning.

Quinn didn't say anything more for a long time. The silence between them was heavy. Shan was sorry she'd said anything at all.

After a time, she stood up. "I guess we ought to be getting back."

Without speaking, Quinn rose. He gathered up the last of the odds and ends from their picnic and put them in the saddle bag.

When he finally looked at Shan, his face was serious. "I hear what you're saying. This isn't always easy for me."

"What?"

"This." He pointed at her, then back at himself. "Us. This thing between us. I'm trying to . . . figure it out as we go along."

"Try harder," she said softly. He nodded, his eyes still troubled.

chapter 27

"Remind me why this is a good idea," Quinn growled through a mouthful of toothpaste. He leaned over the basin, filled his mouth with water, and swished it around.

Shan squeezed into the bathroom alongside him, mascara in hand, to survey her reflection in the mirror. It was Christmas Eve and her look was unusually formal: pumps and a black sheath borrowed from Denise, her hair pulled back in a french braid. "I think it's a *great* idea," she told him, "and I'm proud of you."

He let forth a ferocious snort and she was glad to hear it, because it sounded like the old Quinn, the normal Quinn, the one she hadn't seen much of since The Act. "I know this is hard," she continued, turning back to the mirror, "but it's the right thing to do."

She was attempting to flatten the errant curl that prevented her hair from achieving the sleek look she was after. "Leave it. It looks cute," he said, watching as she abandoned the unruly tress and gave her lashes a final brush with the mascara. "You're putting on too much makeup," he added. "And where's your nose thingy?"

"It doesn't go with my outfit."

"Since when have you cared about that kind of shit?"

"I'll feel out of place no matter what I wear. I don't want to make it worse."

"You don't have to fit in with them. You're not a goddamn sheep." He stomped out of the bathroom, reappearing with the scissors. "I guess I'll follow the flock, too."

Shan frowned as he drew his ponytail over his shoulder. "Q, don't be an ass." Her alarm mounted when he slid the blades around it. "You're going to cut your hair just to make a point?"

"Baa," he said. The scissors ground together and a few blond wisps drifted to the floor.

"Stop! I'll put it back in!"

He allowed her to take the scissors from his hand. "All right, then," he said. "If you insist upon meeting my family, I want you to look like *you*, not some fucking debutante."

Shan's eyes got progressively wider as they coasted down the driveway to his brother's Bel Air residence. By the time Quinn pulled over in front of the house, they were enormous. It was an actual mansion, with ivy trailing over white brick walls and a fountain bubbling in the middle of a stone walk leading to the front door. "You *are* rich," she told him, shaken.

"Not anymore." He slung his helmet over the handlebar and extended his hand to help her dismount. "Ready to face off with the illustrious Marshall clan?" He led her to the front door and rang the bell as Shan smoothed her dress and made some attempt to neaten her braid, which was disheveled from the ride. The door opened to reveal a man who resembled Quinn, although he was a few inches shorter, about seven or eight years older, and a lot more respectable looking.

He gasped, then grabbed Quinn in a delighted bear hug. "Holy cow!" After he released his brother, he beamed at Shan. "I don't know how you did it, but you're my new best friend."

It was the first time she'd met Ron Marshall although she'd spoken to him a few times on the phone. He called his brother regularly, most recently with an invitation to the annual Christmas Eve gathering, a Marshall family tradition. "I know Quinn won't come," he'd said fatalistically. "He's stubborn, my little brother, but I always invite him anyway."

She'd promised to deliver the message, then commenced a full-on attack. "You should go," she told Quinn. "It's not healthy, the way you avoid your family. I think it fucks you up."

"They avoid me, too."

"Bull. Your brother and stepfather call you all the time. I think you're awfully hard on your mother, too."

Quinn's face hardened. "I'm not, believe me. She doesn't respect me or anything I do."

"Maybe she's changed. You should go and see."

He flatly refused, but Shan was relentless. She wheedled and cajoled. When that didn't work, she told him he was an insensitive, withholding, self-absorbed dickhead who didn't care about anyone but himself. That didn't budge him, either, so she offered to go along for moral support. When he rejected that idea, as well, she accused him of being ashamed of her.

"You know better than that," he said, but she shrugged.

"So much for trying harder." And that was how they'd come to be here on this Christmas Eve.

As soon as they went into the house, Quinn was assaulted by two small creatures with apple cheeks and flaxen hair. "Hey, munchkins," he said, swinging a child up in each arm. "This is my nephew, Adam," he told Shan. The little boy, who looked about four, squirmed away as quickly as he'd appeared, so Quinn concentrated on the six-year-old girl who was climbing his body like it was a tree. "Alicia, this is my friend Shan."

The little girl had tow-headed locks and big blue eyes. "Do you like dogs?" she piped.

Shan smiled. "I *love* dogs. Do you have one?"

"I have *two* dogs." She held up two chubby fingers. "A black one and a yellow one. They're Labberdoors. You want to see them?"

Before Shan could respond, a supermodel lookalike appeared at Quinn's elbow. "Alicia," she admonished, "you're supposed to be in the nursery playing with your cousins until dinner."

"But I heard Uncle Quinn's bike," Alicia said. "I wanted to say hello, Mommy."

"All right, you've said hello." The supermodel took the child out of Quinn's arms and handed her to a matronly woman. "Take them back upstairs, please, Irene," she told her. "It's too crowded to have them tearing about like wild Indians."

"Bye, Uncle Quinn," the little girl called as she was borne up the stairs by the nanny.

"Bye, Alicia," Quinn called back, with a little frown.

"Ron, please have two more places added to the table." The woman said, turning to Quinn when Ron obeyed. "This is a surprise, Quinn. I hope the children weren't bothering you."

He regarded her with the same look he wore when he talked to Denise. "Not a chance. I'm always glad to see *them*. Too bad you had them rushed off."

She smiled tightly. "I don't think the cocktail hour before a formal dinner is an appropriate place for small children, although I see you've chosen to ignore the word *formal* in the invitation."

He looked presentable in black chinos and a charcoal blazer with a black, open-necked shirt, but formal was a stretch. Shan knew there were three suits in his closet, though.

"Sorry, my tux was at the cleaners. Shan, meet Ron's wife, Meredith."

Meredith Marshall had the kind of cool, Nordic good looks Shan had always envied. She was tall and slim, with ash blond hair that hung to her shoulders in a smooth sheet. Her understated black dress screamed elegance and diamonds sparkled at her ears. Aware that Meredith was examining her, as well, Shan pushed back her unruly braid, feeling like a rube in the presence of the royals.

Meredith looked at Shan's silver nose stud. Her mouth pursed. "Charmed, dear."

Shan was relieved when Quinn propelled her into the living room. It was filled with people, thirty or more, all smartly attired and as alike as the elaborate paper-doll garland that adorned the opulent Christmas tree. "I thought this was a family dinner," she whispered.

"It's a big family." Quinn was steering her across the room, nodding right and left, pausing briefly to introduce her to this aunt or that cousin, until they reached a portly gentleman whose creased face conveyed astonishment. To her wonder, Quinn embraced him.

When they separated the man kept hold of Quinn's arm, regarding him mistily. "Oh, Quinn. I'm so glad to see you here, my boy."

Quinn chuckled. "You're the only one in the world who still calls me a boy." He turned to Shan. "This is George Merrick, my stepdad."

George took her hand, but didn't let go of Quinn's arm. "Merry Christmas, my dear. It's nice to finally meet you. I've heard a lot of you, though. You have quite a voice."

"Thank you," she said warmly, realizing that this man knew his stepson very well. He'd brought up the one subject guaranteed to put him at ease: his music. "It's easy to sound good when you're singing Quinn's songs. He's so brilliant, Mr. Merrick."

"I know, and he says the same thing about you." He turned back to Quinn. "I must confess, I was quite impressed with the last piece you gave me, Quinn. I like all your music, of course, but this one . . . it's as good as anything on the charts. Better, in fact. Your mother liked it, too."

Quinn smirked. "I'll just bet she did. How is the grande dame?"

George shrugged. "Go and see for yourself. I think she's in the dining room."

"Quinn?" At the sound of the voice, Shan watched Quinn stiffen visibly.

Shan turned and there she was, Quinn's mother, staring at him like a castaway who'd sighted a mirage. She was so small, Shan saw with surprise, so slight and petite to be the lioness Quinn had described. But dignified, queenly, perfectly appointed from the tips of her buff-colored fingernails to her impeccable Chanel suit. Her skin was unlined, extraordinarily well preserved, but her hair was silver blond, coiled into a glassy chignon. Shan judged her to be around sixty.

Quinn's mouth quirked up in a half sneer, half smile. *"Mom?"* he said. It was impressive, how much hostility he could express with that single word.

She took a step toward him, hesitating when he drew back. "You're well?"

"I am," he replied, with an icy formality. "And yourself?"

"I'm fine. It's wonderful to see you. It's been such a long time." She was beaming at him, clearly delighted, and Shan experienced an unexpected pang of envy toward Quinn. How she wished that she could have a similar reunion with her own mother, whom she still missed every day.

Quinn did not respond, just maintained his frosty smile.

"I barely recognized you," she said, continuing to inspect him. "It must be all that hair. I suppose it's intended to be stylish. You're looking quite fit, though, regardless."

"You don't look bad either," Quinn replied. "Had some work done, haven't you?"

Her expression lost some of its warmth. "Well, I'm getting older, of course. As are you," she said, assuming a wintry smile eerily similar to her son's. "Far too old to have hair past your shoulders. It was acceptable when you were sixteen, but you're twenty-six years old."

"Twenty-seven," he corrected her. "In March."

"I'm aware of your age. I was present when you were born, remember." Her eyes slid past him to regard Shan curiously. "And this is . . . ?"

Shan experienced an odd jolt of recognition. Her eyes were exactly like Quinn's, crystalline blue and quite beautiful. It was the strangest thing, to see Quinn's eyes in someone else's face.

"Shan O'Hara," Quinn said, reaching behind him to haul Shan to his side. "Angel, this is my mother, Judith Merrick."

Shan shook the proffered hand and could feel her cheeks flushing, aware that she was being examined. "And how do you know Quinn?" Judith asked.

"We play together," Shan said nervously. "In the band, I mean. I play guitar."

"Oh, yes. That one." Judith did not look pleased, but Quinn rescued Shan soon enough, capturing her elbow and guiding her to his brother, who was at the bar.

"She didn't seem to like me much," Shan said to Quinn, who did look pleased.

"Nope," he said cheerfully. "Don't fret, though. She doesn't like me, either. Right, Ron?"

"You know that's not true," Ron said. "She misses you, Quinn. She just can't say it."

"That would make her just like you," Shan interjected, smirking at Quinn.

When she turned to order a drink Ron leaned closer to his brother, who looked annoyed. "Spunky," he said in an undertone. "Nice to see you with a girl who talks back, for a change."

"I'm not *with* her," Quinn corrected him. "We're friends."

Ron gave him a knowing grin. "You? With a female friend? Especially one who looks like that? *Ha!*" He nudged him suggestively. "You really like this one, don't you?"

"I like her fine," Quinn said, "as a friend."

"I like her, too. She even got you to come here tonight." He gazed speculatively at his brother. "Maybe this is the one."

Quinn escaped from his brother, retrieving Shan from the bar and steering her toward the dining room. "What's that?" he asked, noticing the cocktail in her hand.

"A martini," she said and grimaced. "It's awful."

"Why didn't you just order a beer, like you always drink?"

"I thought this would make me look more sophisticated."

"Oh, for . . ." Quinn rolled his eyes. He found their seats, then frowned at the place card beside his. "Well, this ought to be an interesting meal."

"Why?"

"Because I'm sitting next to my mother." He took the martini out of her hand and tossed it back before he sat down.

Dinner was a highly regimented affair. Shan had to watch Quinn to find out which fork went with each course. There was a smaller table at the end of the room just for the children. It was raucous with activity and laughter and she would have felt more comfortable there, especially since here she was seated directly across the table from Quinn and his mother.

The tension between them was tangible. Quinn was resisting all his mother's attempts to draw him into conversation, although he spoke readily enough to George, Ron, and all the assorted relatives at the table, excepting Meredith whom he ignored completely.

"You're living in Tujunga now, Quinn?" Judith asked him.

"Yes."

"I'm surprised you're not closer to the beach. You've always loved the water so."

"No."

Judith ignored his boorishness. "How is Dan? And his girlfriend?" A small frown crinkled her brow. "I can't recall her name. "

"Fine."

Shan felt a tug of sympathy for Judith. She knew firsthand how impossible it was to pull Quinn out of his shell when he chose to resist. "Her name is Denise. And did you know that they're engaged?" Shan said, kicking Quinn under the table.

"I hope they'll be able to manage," Judith said, selecting a squab with roast pear from a proffered serving dish. "It won't be easy to support a family on what he earns as a drummer."

"Actually, Quinntessence earns quite a bit," Shan said. "We're starting to gain a good following here. We just played the Troubadour, in fact."

Judith raised her eyebrows and turned away without responding. It was a familiar look, the same one Quinn assumed when he was being a condescending dickhead. Shan turned her attention to her plate, keeping quiet for the rest of the meal.

After dinner, the guests moved back to the living room, where Ron cornered Shan. He asked her about herself, but didn't push when she supplied only the sketchiest details. Instead he shifted the conversation to music, complimenting both her voice and her playing.

She decided she liked Ron immensely. He was warm and down-to-earth, despite his high-powered work and elegant home. Unlike his brother, he was to all appearances straightforward and uncomplicated, and she wondered how they could have possibly come from the same family.

Eventually Ron excused himself and she looked around for Quinn. He was nowhere in sight, so she went to the powder room where she attempted again to neaten her hair. As she struggled with it, she reflected how good a heroin hit would have felt. She still would have been out of place, but then she wouldn't care.

She headed back down the hall, stopping when she heard a familiar voice. "I knew this is how it would go." Quinn's words, hard as nails, were coming from behind a door that was slightly ajar. "I'm here for two hours and you're all over my ass already."

"Quinn, stop it." His mother, beseeching. "I can't help but worry, having you back in that environment. It's too much for someone with your issues."

"Mom, I'm *clean*. I have been for almost ten years."

"But for you to be back to your old stomping grounds—it's insane! It nearly killed you before."

Shan heard a snort and she didn't need to see Quinn's face to know how it looked. "They videotaped the Troubadour show, George," he said, "so I brought you a copy."

"Wonderful," Shan heard George say. "I played that last song for Brandon Terry and he was quite impressed. Quinn, I wish you'd take me up on my invitation to join us for lunch sometime."

Shan gasped out loud. Brandon Terry was CEO of Cardinal Records. She'd have endured crucifixion for a chance to promote Quinntessence to someone like that.

"Thanks for the offer," Quinn replied, "but I don't think it's appropriate. I wouldn't want your connection with him to be a factor in establishing a business relationship."

"It wouldn't matter, anyway," Judith said. "What does Brandon Terry care about a bar band? They're a dime a dozen on the Sunset Strip."

"That's because the Strip is where the clubs are, Mom," Quinn shot back.

"Stop acting like I don't have a right to be concerned. I can just imagine the people you're around, like the one you have with you tonight. You know, don't you, that she's an addict?"

Shan's mouth fell open, shocked. Forgetting that she was eavesdropping, she pushed the door open. "A *recovering* addict," she said, "and do you mind telling me how you know that, Mrs. Merrick?"

The room was dark and masculine, probably Ron's den. George, looking beaten, was sitting at the desk in the center of the room. Quinn and his mother were stationed at opposite ends of the desk, glowering at each other over his head.

Judith looked taken aback at Shan's sudden appearance, but quickly regained her composure. "It's a simple enough matter," she said, with a shrug. "Background checks are standard operating procedure at my husband's firm."

Shan was stunned. "You had me investigated?'

"No," Quinn spat. "They had *me* investigated, and you got caught up in the net. You're a piece of work, Mom, you know that?" And he glared at George, who wouldn't meet his eyes.

"I had to make sure you were safe, Quinn." His mother's words were obdurate, but Quinn shook his head. "I can't understand why you, of all people, would choose a profession where you're constantly exposed to drugs! Why won't you at least *think* about finishing college?" she added. "It will give you some options, and it's the only thing I've ever asked of you."

"He *has* finished," Shan said. "He has two master's degrees, for God's sake."

"Berklee is a music school, not a college," Judith said. "And I'd think you'd have gotten this nonsense out of your system after squandering your inheritance on those useless degrees."

Quinn's eyes went glacial and his face closed down completely.

"Berklee is the most respected music school in the country," Shan said. "It's one of the best in the world."

Judith waved a dismissive hand. "And most of its graduates are waiting tables during the day so they can play their second-rate gigs at night."

"But Quinn is incredibly talented! *Gifted,* and you should be proud of him!" Quinn's hand closed over Shan's arm, but she shook him off. "He's accomplished so much."

"And what, exactly, *has* he accomplished? He can barely afford the rent on that shack you're all living in. I wish you'd at least get a decent apartment in the city, Quinn, instead of living like some hippie in a commune in Tujunga. Who do you think you are, Wavy Gravy?"

"Wish I was," he shot back. "It'd be easier to get a record deal."

His mother rolled her eyes. "It's time you started thinking about the future and got a real job. I know that money is something you never really need to worry about, but—"

"Mom," Quinn said, "you can shove your bank right up your gold-plated ass."

"You didn't mind accepting it when it paid your way through Berklee!"

"That was Dad's money, not yours. When are you going to back off and let me live my own fucking life?"

"I don't appreciate the language," Judith said huffily. "You sound like a street thug. I'm entitled to tell you what I think. I'm your mother and I care about you."

"What you care about is the fact that I'm not living up to your expectations. It's the only thing you've *ever* cared about, when it came to me." He finished off his drink and set the glass on the desk. "Let's get the hell out of here," he said to Shan.

"Running away again?" Judith's face hardened. "Why can't you just face me, for once?"

Before Quinn could reply, Shan spoke up. "Because he has better things to do than listen to you dump on him. I think—"

"What *you* think is a matter of supreme indifference to me, dear. If you're like the rest of his girls, you'll be gone in an hour." Judith eyed her with the venom of a cobra preparing to strike. "Quinn's always had a weakness for a particular type of woman. Groupies, they're called in your profession. Is that how you met him?"

"Jesus, Mom!" Quinn exclaimed. "This is too much even from you! Come on." He grasped Shan's elbow. "Neither one of us has to stand here and listen to this bullshit."

"It's been a pleasure meeting you, dear," Judith called after them. "I doubt I'll be seeing you again."

Quinn tried to pull Shan through the door, but she hung back. "Nice to meet you, too. Now I see why he's so fucked up. How else could he be when he was raised by a ball-busting bitch?"

George winced and Judith's mouth fell open. Even Quinn looked briefly startled, but quickly regained his composure. "And on that note," he said smoothly, "I think we'll be leaving."

He hustled Shan down the hall, out the door, and shoved her onto the Harley. "That went well. Glad I let you talk me into it." He switched on the ignition, roaring the engine over her reply.

"Quinn, wait!"

When Shan looked over, George was on the front steps. Quinn glared at him, helmet in hand.

"I want you to go home, calm down, and call me tomorrow," George said, bellowing to be heard over the Harley. Shan reached forward and shut off the ignition, despite the withering look Quinn shot at her. "I'm sorry things didn't go better tonight," George continued, at a more reasonable volume.

"Whose fault is that, George?" Quinn donned his helmet.

"Actually, it's *both* your faults. Yours and your mother's," George said, coming down the stairs, "and I, for one, am sick and tired of this foolishness. Call me tomorrow and we'll talk. We're going to straighten this mess out once and for all."

Quinn sputtered and George cut him off. "Fine. Don't call. Just come for Christmas dinner," he said. "At our home, which is also *your* home. Your family's home."

"Last time I saw Mom, she told me to get out of that home and not to come back. I'm only respecting her goddamned request!"

"That was five years ago." George shook his head. "Good lord, I've never seen anyone hold a grudge like you do. You're so damned stubborn!"

"*I'm* stubborn? What about her? She's still trying to run my life. And so are you, apparently."

"I'm sorry about that, Quinn," George said. "I didn't enjoy invading your privacy, but your mother was frantic. We wouldn't have to resort to such measures if you'd just talk to us. We all love you, you know. Especially your mother." Quinn snorted and he sighed. "She misses you. She can't say it, but she does. She cries sometimes," he added gently. "She's crying right now. I think she's suffered enough."

Quinn looked down at the ground, frowning.

George reached out and laid a hand on his shoulder. "It's time to come home, son. I know you're still angry at her, but can't you do it for me?"

Quinn slipped out from under George's hand, mounted the bike, and fastened the straps on his helmet. The engine roared again.

"Christmas dinner," George persisted, shouting again. "Four o'clock."

When Quinn didn't answer, Shan slipped her hand under his jacket and poked him, hard.

Quinn gunned the engine again, hesitated, and said, "I'll think about it." Then Shan had to grab for his waist as he peeled out, roaring up the driveway in a most satisfying manner.

chapter 28

The next morning, Shan was up bright and early. Christmas hadn't involved any real celebration for her since before her mother died, so she was excited for this holiday that would involve some actual festivities. She had gifts for her roommates and Dave, as well as something extra special for Quinn: an African djembe drum that she'd seen him examine several times at the Guitar Center. It was a beautiful piece that cost almost three hundred dollars and she'd raided her guitar fund to pay for it.

She could hear that her roommates were up and about, so she went downstairs to the kitchen, where she found them preparing a pancake breakfast. Everyone was pitching in except for Quinn, who was nowhere in sight.

She knew he'd been upset last night. They'd gotten home around nine and he'd disappeared into his room almost immediately, not to be seen again for the rest of the evening. When she'd gone to bed, she could hear him in there, playing the Yamaha keyboard. She listened until the wee hours and she could still hear him playing when she finally fell asleep.

"Good morning," Ty said cheerfully. He was half filling glasses with orange juice, topping each with a healthy dollop of champagne. "Ready for a little good cheer?"

"Sure." Shan swallowed her methadone, chased it with a glass of water, then accepted a drink. "Merry Christmas," she said, taking a sip and nodding her approval.

"Methadone and mimosa," Dan laughed. "Talk about a happy holiday!" He was smoking a joint as he poured batter into the skillet over which Denise was presiding.

"Did Q go out?" Shan asked, moving to the stove to take charge of the sausage.

"Yes, but he'll be back anytime," Denise said. "He went out early, to . . ."

The front screen door slammed and Quinn himself appeared. "Good morning," he said, tossing the van keys to Dan.

"Mission accomplished?" Dan asked, catching them with a grin.

Quinn nodded. "What mission is that?" Shan asked.

Quinn didn't reply. "What can I do?" he asked instead, and Denise handed him the spatula.

After breakfast, they gathered around their small Christmas tree, which was woefully underdecorated. Dan's parents had contributed a box of green and red glass balls and Denise had a few ornaments, but nobody else owned any holiday decorations. Shan had fashioned some construction paper chains and she and Denise spent an afternoon stringing popcorn, so the tree was still pretty, in a Charlie Brown sort of way.

They all had modest gifts for one another. When Shan opened Quinn's gift to her, she discovered a shoe box filled with wire and hardware doodads, and she shot him a quizzical look.

"Keep digging," he directed. He didn't smile, but he'd been fairly subdued all morning.

She pulled out a handset. "A telephone?"

"Yup," he said. "I'll install it for you, in your room. That way, when you tell Oda what a dickhead I am, I won't have to listen. The closet door doesn't block the sound, you know."

Shan turned beet red, but the rest of them were laughing. Even Quinn's face bore the ghost of a smile and, when he opened her gift to him, he was astonished. "What were you thinking?"

"I got a deal on it," she said smugly, which wasn't true.

"Bullshit. I know *exactly* how much this cost, because I've been coveting it for months. You're supposed to be saving for a new electric, so you can get rid of that crappy Peavey." But he was untying the bow, pulling the drum from the nest of paper she'd swathed it in, positioning it between his knees. He experimentally slapped it once, twice, then he was banging out a riotous 6/8 groove that made the champagne glasses vibrate.

When he stopped, they all applauded. "Incredibly rich timbre. Needs tuning, though," he pronounced and beamed at Shan. "You had no business spending so much money, but I fucking love it. Thank you."

Shan tittered, pleased, and began to collect the scraps of wrapping paper that littered the floor. After a moment, she noticed no one was helping and looked up.

Everyone was watching her, including Quinn. "I have another present for you," he said.

A ripple seemed to go through the room as he put the drum aside. He settled her on the couch, instructing her to close her eyes. She obeyed, then heard him leave the room. "No peeking," Denise ordered when she opened her eyes.

Shan quickly squeezed them shut again as she heard the bang of the screen door. There was a chorus of *oohs* and *aahs,* then something was placed in her lap.

"Okay," Quinn said. "Open up."

She did, and her brain didn't immediately register what it was, besides a pile of warm black fuzz. When she touched it, a pink tongue emerged to lick her hand. "*A puppy!*"

Quinn was smiling. "She's a black Lab. Mostly, anyway."

"Oh, Q! I couldn't love anything more!"

"Haven't you always said pets were a pointless drain of money?" Dan said.

"Yeah, unless they eventually end up on a plate with steak sauce?" Ty added.

Quinn ignored them. "I thought you'd be safer on your hikes if you had a dog with you."

"I just *love* her!" Shan buried her nose in black fuzz. "She's the best thing anyone's ever given me. Well, one of the best," she corrected herself, recalling the Angel. "You do good presents, Mr. Marshall. But is it okay with everyone else?"

"Oh yeah. He cleared it first," Dan said. "We all voted in favor of a new family member."

Quinn reached out to scratch the puppy behind her ears. "She needs a name," he told Shan.

"I'm thinking Bertha," Shan said.

"*Bertha?*" Denise wrinkled her nose. "Yuck. She should have a pretty name. Besides, I'd expect something more esoteric from you."

"Do you think it's yucky?" Shan asked Quinn.

"A little, but I'm with you. It *is* esoteric," he said to Denise.

"I don't follow," Denise said.

"From the Dead song," Quinn translated, "written by Garcia and Hunter, Shan's all-time favorite song-writing duo. I have to agree with Denise, though," he added. "It isn't very pretty."

"Casey Jones, then," Shan said.

Quinn grimaced. "Please don't name her after a coke song."

"How about Corrina?" Ty said.

"That's pretty," Dan said. "Cool tune, too."

Shan shook her head. "Jerry didn't write that one."

The group pondered for a while. "How about Sugaree?" Quinn said finally. "He wrote that. And it was one of the first songs I ever heard you play."

And Sugaree became the puppy's name.

After the Christmas-morning carnage had been collected and disposed of, Shan fed the puppy her first breakfast in her new home, then took her outside to the creek bed. She sat down in the folding chair under the sycamore tree and watched Sugaree root among the stones. "Do your business," she told her. The puppy stared at her blankly.

The back door opened and Quinn emerged. "Any luck?"

"Not yet, but I'm patient."

"I'll help you with it. I'm glad you like her," he added, smiling.

"I *love* her. Thank you, Q. You've made this holiday really special for me. More special than it's been in . . .well. A long time," she said, thinking of her mother.

Her words seemed to hang in the air as Quinn sat down beside her, resting his hands on his knees. "I think I'm going to take George up on his invitation," he said.

Shan's eyes widened. "Really?"

"Well, the ice is broken now. Smashed, I suppose." He shrugged. "I don't know that it could go much worse than it did last night, so why not? I think he might be right. It's time."

Shan nodded. "They love you very much, you know. Even your mother," she added gently.

"Well, she has a hell of a way of showing it." He stood up. "Do you want to come?"

"No." She shook her head. "Not this time. You need to get to know your family again and, if I came, it would just complicate things. Especially after last night."

"I'm inclined to agree," he said, then frowned. "I hate to leave you alone on Christmas, though."

"I won't be alone." She looked at Sugaree, who was just concluding a pee. *"Good girl!"* She leapt up and scooped the puppy into her arms, covering her head with kisses.

Ty had no plans, either, so Shan spent the afternoon with him eating Chinese food, watching *It's a Wonderful Life,* and attempting to housebreak Sugaree. Dave came by later with a bottle of wine and a quarter ounce of grass, and everyone had the munchies by the time Dan and Denise returned with Christmas cookies and leftover pie.

Quinn still wasn't home when Shan retired to her bedroom with her puppy. He'd suggested that Sugaree sleep in the kitchen and the rest of her roommates had been fine with that, but Shan didn't want to leave her alone. The little dog came from the animal shelter in Glendale, Quinn had told her, taken there by someone who found her abandoned in a box by the side of the road. The story broke Shan's heart and she resolved that this puppy would never know another scared or lonely night.

She was playing her guitar and watching Sugaree chew on an old sock when Quinn knocked at her door. She called for him to come in. He was dressed for bed, in a ratty T-shirt and a pair of blue sweats with a BERKLEE logo on the thigh, and carried a small paper bag. "Hey," she said.

"Hey," he replied. "Can I come in and hang out, for a little bit?"

"Of course." She moved over to make room. Quinn flopped down on the futon and stroked Sugaree, who was rolling between them.

"I should have gotten her some toys," he said apologetically. "I'll take you to pick some out tomorrow, if you want. I brought her this, though, straight from the holiday ham." He pulled a bone out of the bag and offered it to the puppy, who fell upon it with gusto.

"How did it go?" Shan asked, over Sugaree's crunching.

"Not bad," he said. "Not great, either. It was a little intense. I'm still digesting it." He didn't seem inclined to elaborate further, so she turned the subject to less sensitive matters.

"I'm working on something. Just a fragment, really, but I think it could be the beginning of a song. Do you want to hear it?"

"Absolutely."

She took up her guitar and played the riff, and Quinn was intrigued enough to fetch the Yamaha. A couple of hours later, they had the bones of a new melody.

Shan yawned as she put their instruments away while Quinn took Sugaree outside. When he brought her back upstairs, Shan settled her on the bed and Quinn looked dubious. "You realize, don't you, that she's not going to be housebroken after just one day?"

"But I want to her to get used to sleeping with me."

He shrugged, still looking doubtful, and stretched out beside Sugaree.

"I'm going to bed now," she said, but he didn't move and, when his eyes met hers, there was something in them that caused the heat to start pooling in her belly.

"Stop looking at me like that," she said sharply, squashing the sensation.

"Like what?"

"You know. I'm not one of your frequent flyers." She frowned. "I know it's Christmas, but I hope you don't think I'm going to have sex with you just because you gave me this puppy."

He looked offended. "And I had to entice you with this puppy because it was so hard to get you to have sex with me the last time?" He waited until she flushed before continuing. "I'm not suggesting anything sexy. I just want to be with you. We slept together last Christmas," he added when she started to shake her head. "Don't you remember?"

"You were in Boston last Christmas."

"And you were in New York. But we slept together anyway."

Then she did remember. Oda had been upstate visiting her family and Denise was at Dan's, so Shan had been alone. Quinn was spending the holiday in a similar solitary fashion and, when he called her on Christmas night, they'd talked for hours. She'd fallen asleep talking. The next morning when she woke up, the phone was still beside her on her pillow.

She hesitated, then tossed him one of her Mexican blankets and turned off the light.

And turned it back on five minutes later, when Sugaree wet the bed.

"I warned you," Quinn said as they stripped the sheets.

She ignored him, going downstairs for rags and Lysol. She soaked up the small spot as best she could, then scrubbed it. They flipped the futon over and Quinn retrieved the comforter from his own bed while Shan remade it with the new sheets Denise had given her for Christmas.

When she finished, she saw Quinn fiddling with the little basket he'd given her along with the puppy. He removed its small cushion, lined the basket with a plastic trash bag, then covered the bag with a soft bath towel.

"What if she piddles on your towel?" Shan asked, amused.

He shrugged without answering and put the basket on the bed, then put the puppy in the basket. They got back into bed and Shan snapped off the light again. The puppy was between her and Quinn and she wasn't touching any part of him, but she was very aware that he was in her bed, next to her. She found the soft, even sound of his breathing comforting.

"Q?" she whispered, after a while.

"Mmm?" He sounded drowsy.

"Do you ever think about that day?"

He didn't reply right away. It was the first time she'd brought it up directly, The Act, and it occurred to her that he might not understand which day she was talking about.

"I think about it all the time," he finally said, no longer sounding sleepy, and she knew that he understood her perfectly.

"You never mention it."

"Neither do you."

She was quiet again, for a time, then, "Q?"

"Yes?"

"What *do* you think about it?"

He was silent even longer this time and, when he spoke, his voice was low. "I think that it was mind blowing. Earth shaking." He paused for an endless moment, then, "Life changing."

"Oh." Her voice was very small, but she thought he must be able to hear her heartbeat, which had accelerated to a gallop.

He wasn't finished speaking. "But, if you're going to change your life, you've got to make damn sure you're ready for it." He touched her, groping, and when he found her hand he took it. "You'll wait for me to be ready, won't you, angel?"

She didn't reply, but she grasped his hand like a lifeline. When she finally fell asleep, she was still gripping it.

chapter 29

Shan woke the next morning to an insistent knocking at the room next door. "He's not here," she heard Denise call downstairs, then there was a tap at her own door. "Shan," Denise said, opening the door, "do you know where . . ."

The words died on Denise's lips when Quinn sat up, blinking the sleep out of his eyes.

A moment later Dan appeared behind Denise, looking startled, as well, when he saw two occupants in the bed. "Er . . . phone for you, Q," he reported. "Sounds like a ball-busting bitch."

Quinn was nonplussed. "My mother?"

"She's the only ball-busting bitch I know," Dan said, heading back down the hall.

Quinn climbed out of bed and squeezed past Denise. "Excuse me."

"There is no excuse for you," Denise said, not moving an inch.

Quinn used his elbow to propel her out of his way. "Dan's wrong," he grumbled. "We all know about his thing for ball-busting bitches."

When he went downstairs, Denise turned on Shan. "Tell me you didn't fuck him just because he gave you that puppy."

"Do I look naked?" Shan said, scooping up Sugaree.

"Thank God. She's cute, but gratitude has its limits."

Shan heard him talking on the phone as they came downstairs. "No, it's okay," he was saying. "What's on your mind? . . . When? . . . Oh, wow . . . how did that come about?" He turned, saw Shan and Denise openly listening, and stepped into the closet, shutting the door behind him.

Shan took Sugaree outside and, when she came back in, Quinn was still in the closet. He emerged after about fifteen minutes and went upstairs without mentioning the conversation to anyone.

Eventually she heard him turn on the shower. Dan heard it, too, and looked at Shan. "This is huge, you know."

"I know," Shan said. "I'm so glad, although I can see how the whole situation evolved. She's a little scary, isn't she?"

"So is Quinn," Dan said. "He's just like her. That's why they don't get along."

Quinn wasn't scary that day, just preoccupied. He took Shan to the pet shop in Sunland as promised, where she selected some puppy chews, a ball, and a few squeak toys. He shook his head when she suggested lunch at their favorite burger joint and they were back home in an hour. He spent the afternoon wiring the new telephone, receiving several more calls, which he took in the closet, at least until he had the new phone working. After that, he commandeered Shan's bedroom. She could hear him in there talking and he didn't emerge until it was time to get ready for their gig.

That night they were playing Anti-Club on Melrose and, while they were setting up, he made an announcement. "I cancelled Thursday night at Bluenote."

"What?" Ty groaned. "That's New Year's Eve!"

"You can't cancel now," Dave said at the same time. "They'll never hire us again."

"I booked them a replacement," Quinn said, "because we have another gig."

Shan noted Quinn's cat-that-got-the-cream expression. "Where are we playing?"

"Disneyland."

Dave's nose wrinkled. "New Year's Eve at Disneyland?"

"They have bands on every corner on New Year's. Is that what we're doing?" Dan asked, not looking particularly thrilled, either.

"No," Quinn said. "It's a private party. At Club 33. We'll be opening for Valentine. Oh, " he added as everyone's jaws dropped, "and the host is Brandon Terry."

Dan and Dave went nearly catatonic. Shan and Ty were confused, but the others quickly filled them in. Club 33 was a VIP establishment located in the heart of Disneyland. It was members only, highly exclusive, and hideously expensive. The members could reserve the place for special events, like holiday parties.

Dan's eyes were like saucers. "How'd you pull this off, Q? Did your stepfather have something to do with it?"

"He did," Quinn admitted. "He and my mother are on the guest list."

Shan gasped. "I'm surprised your mom would let him score us a gig like this!"

"Actually, it was her suggestion. They watched the Troubadour tape with me on Christmas and it was the Valentine tie-in that gave her the idea. I don't think I ever mentioned it," Quinn added, "but Jerrika James and Carole Grayson are George's clients."

Valentine was big-time, a chart-topping, blues-rocking quintet that featured one of the industry's few female guitarists, Carole Grayson, who was among the best rhythm players in the business. Shan idolized her, but the band's real superstar was their charismatic lead singer, Jerrika James, a sultry blond bombshell lauded for her hard-edged, expressive voice. They were bona fide rock stars and Quinntessence was going to open for them, in front of an audience of music industry bigwigs!

Shan was elated and threw herself into the preparations as the band geared up for what was undoubtedly the most important gig they'd ever played. For the next three days the house was a cacophony of guitar chords, drum licks, keyboard trills, and singing as they practiced nonstop, both collectively and on their own. Quinn obsessed over the playlist, repeatedly changing and rearranging the lineup. Shan fretted over her wardrobe, trying on one outfit after another, and could barely contain her excitement as the gig drew closer.

Then, on the morning of New Year's Eve, she woke up with stomach cramps, a headache, and a wrenching, nerve-wrangling case of the jitters. *'Done jones,* she told herself, but the feelings didn't go away even after she swallowed her dose and she realized that she was in the throes of the worst case of stage fright she'd ever experienced. The feeling worsened and by midmorning when the band arrived in Anaheim, Shan was a nervous wreck, wishing she had a real fix to blot it out.

Their deal included access to the park, which they were free to enjoy once they delivered their gear. They set out to explore Disneyland, with instructions to return at four o'clock for sound check, and it was unbelievably crowded. New Year's was apparently a big event there and the atmosphere was loud and festive. Noisemakers were handed out at the entrance and there were bands everywhere, playing every conceivable type of music to crowds of people in party hats and mouse ears. Shan knew they'd never make it to most of the attractions, because the lines were interminable, and she was jostled and shoved as she followed her bandmates through the throng.

All day she was uncharacteristically silent, quietly freaking out within the confines of her mind. When they stopped for a snack in the Fantasyland section of the park, Dan checked his watch. "It's almost one-thirty and we still haven't gone on most of the rides."

"I vote for Space Mountain," Dave said.

Ty and Dan were in agreement, but Quinn hung back. When Shan walked past him, he caught her arm. "Go ahead," he said to the others. "We're going to check out the Haunted Mansion. There won't be time for both, so we'll find you later."

"You don't like Space Mountain?" Shan asked, just for something to say as Quinn steered her to a stately antebellum mansion gracefully flanked by weeping cyprus trees. The line looked infinite.

"Sure I do. It's awesome," he said as they took their place in the mansion line, "but this ride is really cool, too. Besides, it's much more your speed."

That irritated her. Why was it up to him to decide which ride she went on? Why was every decision always up to him? "You could have asked me first."

"Why?" He shrugged. "I knew you'd hate Space Mountain. It's a roller coaster."

"Maybe I like roller coasters," she said although she did, in fact, hate them. They made her sick, a weakness with which he was well acquainted since she'd thrown up on him once when they rode the Cyclone together after a gig at Coney Island. "Couldn't you at least give me the courtesy of deciding for myself?"

He stiffened. "Fine," he said, an edge in his voice. "Let's go on Space Mountain, then. Did I mention that it's high speed and entirely in the dark?"

Shan's stomach flipped over. "No, this is fine. I just don't appreciate you dragging me off without even consulting me."

"Well, I wanted a chance to talk to you privately. What is your problem today?"

"I don't have a problem," she said coldly as the line inched forward.

"Yes, you do. Your face is about as subtle as a signal fire, Shan."

She crossed her arms over her chest and pressed her lips together.

"Okay. Be miserable, then," he said dismissively. "Just don't try to bring me down along with you. We're at Disneyland, for Chrissake. It's supposed to be fun."

"That's right," she agreed, "and you're ruining my fun."

"I'm not doing a damned thing. You're the one acting like a spoiled brat."

"Oh, fuck off," she snapped. The lady in line in front of them turned around and glared at Shan, who flushed apologetically. "Sorry," she mumbled.

"Infant," Quinn snorted, not quite under his breath.

They maintained a mutual mute hostility, standing side by side without looking at each other for the next forty-five minutes, which was how long it took them to get through the line. Shan wasn't about to admit it, but Quinn was right, the attraction was really cool. Even waiting in the line was cool, because it wound past an atmospheric graveyard filled with elaborate headstones and sculptures of ravens and gargoyles. Tendrils of Spanish moss trailed down from the cyprus trees, brushing her hair when she passed underneath.

Once inside the mansion it became even cooler, with eerie, single-note organ music, shifty-eyed portraits, and a mysterious grandfather clock striking the hour thirteen. The sonorous tones of someone called the Ghost Host narrated their progression through the spooky manse.

A sudden clap of thunder made Shan catch her breath. The lights went out and a delicious shiver ran down her spine when she saw a skeleton dangling from a noose overhead, illuminated by flashes of lightning. Seconds later she jumped when the room resounded with a bloodcurdling scream. *Oh, this is* super *cool*, she thought, her spirits beginning to lift for the first time all day.

When they stepped back into the murky light, it was onto a moving platform shrouded in mist. "I thought we'd never get through that line," she said to Quinn, breaking their taciturnity.

"I'll pass your complaints on to the management," he said and, when she looked at him, she saw that he was still seething. "Anything else you'd like to bitch about?"

Shan pointed her nose in the air. "No," she said, climbing aboard the little black car apparently called a doom buggy. "I really don't have to say anything at all."

"Fine. Go back to the silent treatment you've been giving me all day," he said, getting in alongside her. They were private cars, so they could continue their argument uninterrupted as they were transported into the dark interior.

"I haven't been giving you the silent treatment."

"Yes, you have, and I'm sick and tired of it. Why can't you just grow up and tell me what's wrong?"

"I'm nervous, all right?" she blurted. "This gig is too big for us, Quinn, and you should have cleared it with the rest of us before you booked it!"

"I knew that was it." He slapped his hand against his thigh. "*I knew it!* You're wigging yourself out and it's made you crazy!"

"I'm not wigging out," she lied. "I'm mad!"

"I never consult any of you when I book a gig, so don't try and bullshit me. You *are* wigging and that shit ends right now. You get it together, Shan. Fast."

The doom buggy was carrying them past spectacular creepy displays. There were rattling suits of armor, a ghostly teapot pouring ectoplasmic tea, and a flock of holographic ghost couples waltzing through the air alongside them. The special effects were staggering, like nothing she'd ever seen, but Shan was too upset to enjoy any of it.

"You're right," she said in a shaky voice. "I'm not even mad, really. I'm terrified." She made a sound of panic. "This is totally out of my league."

"No, it isn't. Just relax, before you freak yourself out."

"I'm already freaking out!" she cried. Somebody in a neighboring car called to her to shut up so she lowered her voice, but it still shook. "This is huge, Q. Huge. It could change our lives. This could be our shot and you know what you said before, about being ready? What if I'm not?"

"You are." She shook her head. "Even if you aren't," he continued, "sometimes you have to just jump. This is what we've been working for, so don't fuck it up."

She made a low moan. He put his arm around her and she shifted closer, to bury her face in his shoulder. "I wish you could see yourself the way that I see you," he said softly. "You're so fucking amazing."

His nearness worked as a tonic, soothing her, and she could feel her trembling begin to still. "You're so talented," he murmured. "So special and so beautiful. There's a light that shines out of you, angel, so bright I think it'll blind me. Sometimes it does."

She experienced a wave of tenderness powerful enough to overcome the other emotions, the ones that had held her captive all day. "I . . . I think I'm okay now," she said, flustered. "Yes, I'm better. Definitely. Thanks, Q. I'm sorry for being such a basket case. "

She raised her head from his shoulder to give him a contrite peck on the cheek, but he turned his head so she encountered his mouth. Their lips met. And held.

It was no peck, this kiss. It was deep and sweet and sensual, like their kisses before The Act had been. Shan could dimly hear the monologue of the Ghost Host issuing from the speaker behind her head, the haunting voice nearly obscured by the pounding in her ears, and then she felt Quinn's tongue in her mouth.

She wasn't prepared for this now, today, and she pulled away, alarmed. "Wait," she began, but his lips clamped down again, smothering her words.

His mouth was like a drug and she surrendered to it, matching his ardor, kissing him again and again with an absolute abandon. He was brushing his lips over her hair, her neck, kissing any part of her that his lips came in contact with. She felt high on his taste, his scent.

Shan opened her eyes as a shaft of light appeared. Quinn was still dappling her face with fierce, burning kisses, now the corner of her mouth, her cheek, the bridge of her nose.

"The ride," she said, her voice shaking again, "is over."

He released her and as they rolled into the light. She ran her tongue over her lips, swollen and tender now, and snuck a surreptitious glance at Quinn. He was staring straight ahead, silent and pensive.

When their doom buggy came abreast of the rolling platform, he disembarked first, then turned back to offer her his hand. "Time to jump," he said. "Ready?"

chapter 30

"Ready?" Quinn asked, leaning close to look into her eyes.

Shan took a deep breath and nodded. Quinntessence was scheduled to go on at eight. It was nearly that now and they were charged up, in tune, and ready to play.

While there was no actual stage in Club 33, a riser had been installed in the northeast corner of a private function room. The gear was in place, although very little of it belonged to either them or Valentine. They had their guitars, but the rest was provided by the club: an elegant Pearl drum kit much nicer than Dan's Ludwigs, a Kurzweil even higher end than Quinn's, and an imposing Marshall stack that made the guitar players salivate.

If the equipment was impressive, the venue was overwhelming. They'd been transported to the present room via an antique elevator, a magnificent brass and glass contraption that the hostess referred to as a "French lift." Upstairs the club was resplendent, appointed with dark wood, crystal chandeliers, and Victorian antiques. Quinn was particularly captivated by a graceful harpsichord, which had reportedly been played by both Paul McCartney and Elton John. Even the restrooms were over-the-top sumptuous, equipped with gilded and caned toilets suitable for Cinderella herself. The club was bedecked for the holidays in greenery and red velvet, poinsettias, and shimmering lights. The effect was magical.

The lingering aromas of chateaubriand and butternut bisque made Shan's stomach growl, although they'd been treated to a perfectly delicious meal at the Cajun restaurant next door. The staff were clearing away the remnants of the feast, galloping about in a fashion that reminded her of the waiters in *Hello Dolly!,* which she'd seen on TV the week before.

As expected, Quinn's folks were in attendance. George greeted her warmly, but Quinn's mother's nostrils flared in dislike even as she critically eyed Shan's attire, a bright red and green tie-dye print with a handkerchief hem that floated when she moved.

Shan took up her guitar as Quinntessence prepared to take the stage, but she was distracted by a stir in the corridor outside the dining hall.

Ty nudged her. "Valentine," he whispered. When a flash of platinum hair and black lace confirmed that the headliners had arrived, Shan turned to Quinn, her eyes wide.

He frowned. "If you start to panic, I want you to sing to me, just to me. I don't even care if you have to turn your back on the audience. Pretend we're at home, singing together."

His gaze was so intense it hurt her to look into it. She turned her own eyes away to fasten the strap of her Peavey around her shoulders. When she looked up, Quinn was still watching her.

"Life comes down to a few moments. This is one of them. You're ready?"

She took a deep breath and nodded.

He reached for her chin, cupping it in his hand, and briefly traced her lower lip with his thumb. It felt like a kiss. "Time to jump, then. Make me proud, angel."

Flash your smile, the magic charm
That shelters me from certain harm
I'm coming back to your loving arms
They're home to me, baby
The only home I ever knew

Shan struggled to maintain the harmony that she and Quinn usually achieved so effortlessly. Her voice was traitorous and she could hear herself scooping on the high notes as he doggedly stretched his range to match her uneven vocals.

As they came to the end of "Shelter Me," she glanced at Quinn. He smiled, with an encouraging nod, and inwardly she cringed. She must have sounded pretty damned bad to get that kind of a response out of him. He rarely signified approval when they were onstage, even when she was at her best.

They were playing a short set, thirty minutes, all originals. For this performance Quinn had chosen not only their very best tunes but those that would showcase the skills of each individual band member. Everyone had solos, although the set was heavy with Quinn's keyboards and Shan's guitar.

Shan timidly checked out the audience as Quinn commenced the opening roll of notes of "Voluntary Exile." It was a relatively small group to be so intimidating, fewer than a hundred people. She'd played bigger crowds by herself, but the number didn't really matter. It was who they were that counted.

She looked over at the table where Brandon Terry presided. He looked in his late sixties, balding, a big man with a belly. His elegant suit was rumpled and he had the benevolent air of a grandfather, utterly at odds with his powerhouse reputation.

Terry was an industry legend, having founded the juggernaut Cardinal Records and presided over it for thirty years. The label had been born in the 1960s, when it played a pivotal role in the psychedelic rock movement, and since then had been a musical groundbreaker. Terry was a true innovator and over the years his artists had generated literally hundreds of hit records. Over 60 percent of Cardinal releases consistently made the national charts, Quinn had told them, an awesome figure in the bottom-line-driven world of popular music.

He was watching, but didn't seem particularly impressed. She knew he had an eye for female rockers; he'd been the one to pluck Valentine out of obscurity and steer them to their current pinnacle. There was no telling what he could do for Quinntessence, should he choose to.

The mere thought made her stomach jitter again. She tore her eyes from Brandon Terry, then found herself staring at Judith Marshall Merrick. Quinn had told her that tonight would be the first time in more than five years that his mother would see him perform live and she was transfixed. Her eyes, glued to her son, even looked a little misty.

Then Judith was looking at her and her expression changed, eyes narrowing. Her lips moved. *Do something!* she seemed to be saying to Shan.

Oh, screw you, too! Shan's lip raised in a sneer.

She grabbed on to that feeling and plunged into "Voluntary Exile" without a thought except to blow away that ball-busting bitch. She sang with something closer to her usual intensity and shot another glance at Judith. Her raised eyebrows signified approval, an expression so like Quinn's that Shan nearly laughed. She'd caught her attention and, just past her, Shan saw she also had caught the eye of Brandon Terry.

Shan's throat tightened as she was flooded with a panic attack of major proportions. Her hands shook. How was she supposed to form chords when all feeling had mysteriously vanished from her fingertips? As she struggled to regain her composure, she suddenly remembered Quinn's words. *Sing to me*, he'd said. *Just to me.*

She swiveled and fixed her eyes on his, willing away the club, the crowd, and especially the music mogul seated just a couple of tables over. Her surroundings gradually dissolved until all she could see was Quinn and she sang to him just like he'd told her to. It was a torcher, one of her favorites of his originals, and she performed it with a visceral intensity as she went into its chorus.

It's my way
It's my voice
And, though it hurts
It's my choice

When they finished, the audience was silent for a beat before they broke into a hearty wave of applause and then Quinn was swinging into the next song, "Big City Heat," a perfect showcase for his own considerable vocal chops. The song's chorus took his rich tenor into the stratosphere, while the arrangement incorporated some flashy drum licks, a thundering bass line, and a blistering guitar solo that Shan played like Yngwie Malmsteen.

After "City Heat" won even more enthusiastic plaudits, Quinntessence segued into "Echo Flats," which spotlighted Dave's lively tremolos, and then it was time for their finale. The last song was always the most critical and, when they swung into "The Only Perfect One," Shan was more than ready. She switched guitars, taking up the Angel, and launched into the rollicking melody that invariably enticed their audience out of their seats.

Prince-in-training at the beach building dreams out of the sand
Up rose a mighty fortress shaped by his own hands
But at the eleventh hour the waves of war rolled in
Smashed his dream to hell and took it back again
The only really perfect one
Is the one that got away

As always the song made her gyrate. Her dress was perfect to accentuate her lithe movements as she pranced, whirled, and shimmied around the stage. By the time she reached the final verse, the entire place was on their feet, grooving along with her.

They took their bows to thunderous applause, but had to clear out fast to make way for Valentine. Flushed and vibrating with gratification, Shan swept a low curtsy at the audience, then hurried offstage with the Angel. As she did, she ran smack into another guitarist. When their instruments brushed with a jangle of strings, she stepped back, but her apology froze on her lips.

Carole Grayson was smiling at her, signature black Rickenbacker in her hands. "Fab," she pronounced in a clipped British twang. "Nicely done, sister."

Shan, unable to form a single word, just stepped back to let her pass. She turned around to watch and encountered Quinn, looking dazed but grinning from ear to ear.

"Fucking-A fab," he said. Then he grabbed her, hugging her so tightly she couldn't breathe.

Valentine's performance lasted until close to midnight, at which point the audience dispersed for the final event of the evening, fireworks over Sleeping Beauty's castle. Some people went to the balcony to watch, but Shan escaped down the stairs into New Orleans Square.

There were few people there, the throngs having massed around the river for the show, but there were still too many for her overwrought state of mind. She made her way into a small courtyard that was charming, brick and pastel stucco with a spiral staircase painted periwinkle blue, and thankfully deserted. She lingered there, grasping at the brief moment of solitude.

"You okay?"

She turned to find that Quinn had followed her. "Yeah. Just a little . . . overwhelmed. I needed a minute, that's all."

He nodded. "I get that. Would you rather I left you alone?" She shook her head, sat down on the periwinkle steps, and patted the spot beside her.

He joined her on the steps and they sat together in companionable silence for a few minutes. "I wonder if New Orleans really looks this way," she remarked after a time, looking through the brick archway that led into the square.

"It does, actually," Quinn said, following her gaze. Disneyland's version of New Orleans was a pastiche of wrought iron, polished brass, and trailing ivy. There was even a steamboat churning away on a mini-Mississippi and strains of a Dixieland band wafted over on the breeze. "It's really something, the way they've captured it. All that's missing are the Bourbon Street bars."

"I've always wanted to go there. I'd love to see the Preservation Hall Jazz Band or catch some blues at Tipitina's."

"We'll do those things together," he promised, "when we headline there."

She smiled at him. "You think that will be anytime soon?"

"I think it just might," he said and she noticed that he wasn't smiling back. "I've talked to a lot of people tonight, angel. We're a hit."

She didn't know how to respond to that. These people could make rock stars, but could it really happen to them? It seemed like a fantasy, something so unattainable, like reaching for the moon. For just a few minutes while they were onstage it had felt like the dream was within their grasp, but now it felt like it had happened to someone else, the events of the evening already receding into a hazy, surreal memory.

She heard a muffled explosion. "The fireworks must be starting. Should we go out there?"

"I suppose. The others will be looking for us. My folks, too." He stood, extending a hand to help her up. His voice sounded normal, but his eyes sparkled in the moonlight, betraying his excitement. He was beautiful in his joy and she felt a tightness in her chest.

She let him pull her to her feet, but kept hold of his hand. "Why did you kiss me today?" she asked impulsively.

He paused, then shrugged. "Does there have to be a reason?"

"Well, it's not something you do, usually. You haven't kissed me since . . ." Her voice trailed off.

"Since that day on the mountain," he finished and she nodded. "I feel like it's a boundary between us, kissing. One that we probably shouldn't cross. I mean, look at what happened the last time I kissed you."

She saw his point and flushed. "But you did cross it today. Why?"

"Because you were freaking out." He looked sheepish. "And that was freaking *me* out. You had me worried, angel. I figured it would be good if you had something other than the gig to freak about."

Shan's smile faded. "Oh."

He shook his head. "Don't."

"Don't what?"

"Get tragic on me." He reached out and took hold of her chin, forcing her to look him in the eyes. "I'm not making light of it. It isn't light, this thing between us. That's why we've got to be so careful with it. Besides, you've got to know what it does to me when I kiss you." He traced her lower lip with his thumb.

"You could kiss me again," she said, after a pause.

He hesitated for what felt like an endless moment, then he leaned closer to brush his lips against her forehead. She raised her face to meet him, but he drew back. "Boundary," he reminded her. "For now. Come on." He caught her hand, tugged it in the direction of the square.

Shan let him lead her out of the courtyard, releasing his hand only when she spied their bandmates gathered by the river. She paused to look up at Quinn. He was watching her, the familiar blond lock drooping over his forehead. As she reached to smooth it back, she thought of the first time she'd ever touched him, back in the SoHo loft. That was the first time she'd felt it, the powerful current that ran between them.

He smiled and she was absolutely positive that he was remembering the same moment.

chapter 31

Shan spent New Year's Day watching the college bowl games with everyone except Quinn, who'd gotten on his bike and roared off before noon. Football bored her, but the ever present cloud of pot smoke was an effective anesthetic and she joined her roommates in rooting for Washington in the Rose Bowl and Miami in the Orange Bowl. He still wasn't back by the time she went to bed and she tossed and turned until well past midnight, when she heard his bike pull into the driveway.

It rained for the next two days so she spent them cooped up with her roommates, everyone except Quinn who continued to vanish early. Since the gig at Club 33 she felt perpetually off balance, nervous and jittery like a ceaseless jones, and being in the house with the others made it worse. They were jumpy, too, and hopeful, and the atmosphere was portentous, crackling with excitement and anxiety.

When she finally awakened to sunshine, she paused only long enough for methadone and coffee before setting off into the mountains with Sugaree and the Angel. After a time she found a good spot and situated herself with her back against a tree. Sugaree settled down to chew on a stick as Shan began to play. She played for a long time, choosing the songs of her childhood, musical comfort food. "Big Yellow Taxi." "Blackbird." "Diamonds and Rust." They didn't soothe her as much as usual, so she switched to another favorite, her old SoHo roof song.

All the manic, static
Slowly turning me deaf
They're all stressing out together
And that's why I left
I've got the cure
That's for sure
On the mountainside and dreaming

She was dreaming up a new chorus when she heard a shout. She paused.

"Shan!" Quinn's voice. "Where the fuck are you?"

"Here," she called back. Sugaree woofed helpfully and, a minute later, Quinn appeared over the ridge. When he saw her he hunkered down, breathing hard with his hands on his knees, and she saw that his T-shirt was soaked with perspiration. "Are you all right?" she asked.

"I've been running all over this mountain looking for you. Why do you have to hike so fucking far from the house?"

"What's going on?"

"You have to come home," he said. "Now. We have a gig to get ready for."

"Tonight? Since when?" She frowned. "We didn't have anything scheduled."

"We do now. It's big."

"How big?"

"Monu-fucking-mental. I just got a call. We've been invited to perform at a showcase. Tonight, at the Troubadour. And the invitation came from Brandon Terry."

"Is this all right?" Shan asked, walking into Quinn's bedroom.

He was brushing out his long hair. "If you don't learn how to knock, you're going to walk in on me naked one of these days."

"So?" she smirked. "I've seen it before."

He snorted as he set down the brush and pulled his hair back into a tail. She fidgeted until he gave a final twist to the elastic, then turned away from the mirror. *"Wow!"*

She began a slow rotation. "I've had this for a while, but I've been afraid to wear it. I thought it looked all right in the store, but I've been worried it makes me look . . . well . . . slutty. It might be right for tonight, though. I mean, it'll make a statement, don't you think?"

He didn't answer right away. He was too busy feasting his eyes on her slim figure in the backless black dress, which fit snugly to midthigh then flared out in diaphanous fringes that hung to her calves. A deep plunge under each arm revealed a curve of breast as she turned and his eyes got even bigger when she completed the rotation, displaying a magnificent triangle of cleavage.

She saw his expression and groaned. "I knew it. It's awful."

"It's not awful," he said. "It's fucking awesome, but I'm not used to seeing so much of your skin. Christ, your bikini covers more of you than that does." He was still examining her, beginning to look a little dubious. "You're comfortable performing in that?"

"Why do you ask?"

"Because you look hot. *Really* hot. Dirty hot. Every guy who sees you in that is going to want to rip it off of you. If you're okay with that, then rock it. If you aren't . . ." he shrugged.

She hesitated, pondering his words, and he raised his gaze from her chest to her face. "Well, we've established that your body looks great. How's your head?"

"Scared," she said. "What if I flub the lyrics? What if I screw up the solo on "Black Mile,"like I did last time? What if . . ."

"What if you shut up before you freak yourself out?" he suggested. "You were awesome on New Year's. Fab, remember?" She caught a fringe of her dress, worrying it between her fingers. "Come on," he said in a more businesslike tone. "If you're sure you're ready, then get your axe."

Shan hovered backstage, watching the band that was on before them. She'd changed her clothes and now wore low-rise jeans with a floaty white, poet-style top. It bared both her shoulders and her navel, which sported a dainty belly ring that she'd gotten in Hollywood a couple of months before. Her hair was loose and sparkly chandelier earrings swung from her ears.

The band was good, though she didn't care for the vocalist's style. Her voice was grating and she mumbled, but the music was fresh and original. All bands they'd heard tonight were good, each with some unique quality that set them apart from the thousands of groups that teemed through the LA club scene, but Shan didn't think any of them were better than Quinntessence. They'd shine in this forum, assuming she stayed cool.

"We're next," Quinn warned, examining her face for signs of freakiness.

"I know. I'm glad I changed my clothes. If I hadn't," she added, "I'd look like that." She nodded at the singer, who was slinking around the stage in a skintight, wet-looking number that exposed her camel toe.

Quinn chuckled. "You couldn't if you tried. You're too dainty." He glanced at her outfit, which was her usual boho-chic style. "You look really pretty," he added, his eyes softening.

She looked up and, when she saw his expression, she wondered if he'd touch her lip, like he had before their Valentine gig.

He didn't. Instead he began to lecture her. "Remember what to do if you start to freak. Just look at me—" he began, but she shook her head.

"I won't have to. Funny, but I'm not nervous now, Q."

"That's because you just did this, angel." Then he did touch her lip. "Time to do it again."

When they hit the stage Shan was radiant, Quinn commanding, and Dave's tremolos had never shone more brightly. It took no time at all for Quintessence's front members to get everyone in the packed venue out on the dance floor. They modified the set they'd played at Club 33, pulling "Voluntary Exile" and "Shelter Me" and adding "Sweet Addiction" and "Wanderlust." By the time they wrapped with "The Only Perfect One," the audience was in a frenzy.

Troubadour down at the coffee shop, pen poised in the air
Just about to nail down that tune when she stunned him with her stare
But out the door those big eyes went
His heart was broken and his song was spent
He knew the only really perfect one
Was the one that got away

Afterward Shan was forced to network, never her strong suit. She stayed close to Quinn, who was employing his formidable skill at charming people, and followed him around until he turned around and barked at her to "mingle, for fuck's sake!" Everyone seemed to want to talk to her and she did her best, smiling modestly when people complimented her performance or raved about her guitar chops. She lost sight of Quinn for a while, then spotted him in the bar with a tall, light-skinned, exotic-looking black woman who was vaguely familiar. He spent an inordinate amount of time with her and was still there talking to her when the rest of the band left around midnight.

Quinn pored over the LA newspapers during the next few days, combing the *Times* and the *Daily News* and *LA Weekly* for mentions of the showcase. He found several, reporting that Quinntessence had been singled out for glowing accolades. He was beginning to get calls from clubs and agents inquiring about the band, but nothing as exciting as an offer from a record company. Shan wondered what they were supposed to do next, how long they'd have to wait before something happened.

Not long, as it turned out. The following Monday, a black Lexus pulled into their driveway. The car looked incongruous in front of the weathered cabin, but not nearly so much as the sleek, elegant woman who emerged from it. Shan recognized her as the one she'd seen Quinn talking to after the Troubadour showcase. She had sharp, intelligent eyes, shoulder-length hair styled in a smart shag, and wore an ensemble that was saved from the label "power suit" only by its hue, a screaming shade of fuchsia. With it, she wore strappy Jimmy Choos with spike heels that sank into the sandy ground as she picked her way up the driveway.

Quinn came downstairs, looking surprised as he opened the door for the stranger. "Hi, Lorraine. What are you doing here?"

"We need a conference," she told him. "I've been trying to call you for two hours."

He shot an annoyed glance into the living room at Shan, who flushed. She'd just gotten off one of her marathon calls with Oda. "It's time you met everyone, anyway," he said, holding open the door for her. "This is Lorraine Slater," he said to the rest of them. "She's our new manager."

"Why do we need a manager?" Dan asked Quinn. "You've always handled the bookings."

"The role of a manager isn't really to book the gigs," Lorraine said, before Quinn could respond. "That's an agent's job. I'm going to see that you get one of those, too, but *my* interest is in guiding your career."

"So far, we've guided our own careers," Ty pointed out, "and it's been fine. We don't have to pay ourselves a percentage, either."

"That's about to change, I think. You need someone to handle your contact with the record companies. I have an idea of what you can expect as an offer from Cardinal and I can negotiate the deal for you. Once you're signed they'll want you in the studio right away, so I'll engage the technical personnel, like producers and engineers. Road managers and instrument techs, too, when it comes time to tour. I can put you in touch with the best in the business." She turned to Quinn. "I've received a call on your behalf, but we do need to formalize our arrangement prior to beginning any negotiation."

All eyes turned to Quinn, who nodded. "I'll call Dazz, get him over here." He headed for the phone and their new manager was left standing in the foyer with Ty and Dan, who both seemed speechless.

In the living room, Shan was sitting on the floor beside the couch, dressed in a T-shirt and shorts, the Angel in her lap. She didn't get up. She couldn't. While she'd gradually grown accustomed to her roommates seeing her scarred legs, she wouldn't expose herself to this impressive woman. "Uh, please come in and sit down," she called, blushing to the roots of her curly hair.

"Thank you. I will." Lorraine Slater replied, taking the armchair across from the couch and focusing her attention on Shan. "It's lovely to meet you. I enjoyed your set, very much."

"You were at the Troubadour?"

"Yes. I heard you at Club 33, as well." That's was why she'd looked so familiar. Shan recalled her velvet sheath and the smooth, upswept hairstyle that exposed ruby earrings the size of guitar picks.

Dave arrived within the hour. Quinn was in possession of a contract, which he'd apparently already had vetted by Marshall-Merrick. All of them read and signed the lengthy document. It appointed Lorraine Slater as their manager and, by the end of the conversation, Shan's head was spinning with terms like *intellectual property*, *partnership agreements*, and *publishing royalties*. She felt overwhelmed, confused, and in over her head.

After Lorraine left she took Sugaree and escaped to the creek bed, but found it already occupied by Quinn, who was smoking and moping. "Are you okay?" she asked.

"Fine," he grumbled.

"You don't look it," she said and sat down beside him. "I'm weirded out, too," she said. "It just feels too fantastic, like it would be stupid to get excited. I mean, is this for real?"

He nodded. "It is, Shan. Didn't I always tell you we'd get here?"

"I never believed it, really," she confessed. "I mean, there are a gazillion musicians trying to make it. Why us?"

"Because we're special. *You're* special. You worked hard for this, angel. Go ahead and get excited."

"You don't look all that excited," she said.

"I am," he acknowledged, "but . . ." He didn't finish, just fell silent, and Shan fed Sugaree a bit of biscuit, then tossed a stick for her to fetch while she waited him out. "I swore I'd never take anything from them," he said finally. "I knew I could make it on my own, on my talent, and I was willing to do the work, whatever it took. I didn't need their help, that's what I always said. Look at me now, though."

"You *are* making it on your own," Shan said, understanding immediately that he was talking about his family. "No one's worked harder than you have. All your folks did was set up a gig. And if you'd refused it," she added, "you'd be dead. We'd kill you, me and Dan and Ty. Dave, too. It'd be a lynching, Q."

He laughed. It was a good sound. "So what do we do next?" Shan asked.

"We wait," Quinn replied.

They didn't have to wait long. The following week, Lorraine got another call. Cardinal wanted their body of work. They packed up every one of their demos and handed them over to Lorraine.

A couple more weeks, then another call. Cardinal wanted something new, to see how quickly they produced. Shan and Quinn spent a couple of days camped out in the music room, coming up with an intense tune called "Sinner's Blues." The band spent a day in the studio recording it, then sent the disc off.

Another week passed and the following Saturday they were performing at the Music Machine in Santa Monica, a venue Quinn usually loved because of the excellent sound system, but he was out of sorts as they set up. They all were, really. The waiting was hard.

Shan turned as Quinn emerged from behind his keyboard. "Should we do 'Sinner's Blues' tonight?" It would be the first time they performed it in public. He didn't reply. Shan followed the trajectory of his gaze across the room and saw Lorraine approaching. Her smile was blinding.

"Good evening," she said. She reached into her purse and produced a small black box, which she handed to Quinn. "A present for you."

He took the box. "A pager? Why?"

"Because I'm tired of not being able to reach you. I've been trying to call you all day," she said. They'd been incommunicado because they'd played another gig during the afternoon, an unplugged AIDs benefit at Venice Beach. They'd come directly to the club without going home. "I have some news," Lorraine continued, still smiling.

Quinn gave a sign to Ty over at the bar and waited until he, Dan, and Dave congregated around them. "What's the news?" he asked.

Lorraine's smile widened. "I've received an offer from Cardinal. And it's a good one. A *damned* good one."

Four hundred thousand dollars. *Four hundred thousand dollars!* Even Quinn was speechless. And this was just the beginning. There would be royalties, and tour revenues, and personal appearance fees. This was an advance, Lorraine explained, against the profits of the albums they were expected to produce, six, according to the offer.

They were elated and ready to sign right away, everyone but Quinn. He wanted artistic freedom and he wanted it in writing. "They could dictate our creative direction, soften us up," he insisted when the rest of them freaked. "Our sound is unique, so we can't let ourselves be force fit into some preexisting niche. I won't settle for anything less. I'd rather go with an indie label."

Lorraine worked hard to change his mind, but Quinn was obdurate. He wouldn't budge, even when Cardinal countered with a higher offer. By then the buzz surrounding them had spread and other labels were developing an interest, sending out feelers.

Before long, a third offer was forthcoming. Four albums, two hundred and fifty thousand dollars, and full artistic control for the band. Songs and compositions. Producer approval. Video concepts. Everything.

Quinn was jubilant, the rest of them less so at the reduced figure. At Lorraine's suggestion, the bulk of the money was banked to cover the expenses they would incur while recording their debut album. Studio time was costly, she reminded them, and she was negotiating with high-end producers. After two hundred thousand was salted away and she presented each of them with a check for ten thousand dollars, though, the complaints dwindled.

Shan didn't complain at all. Ten thousand dollars, all hers? She was dazed.

What would she do with it? She needed so many things. A new electric guitar. A car. A real bed, but she was afraid to spend any of it, as if they might take it back. She was used to getting by with very little, so she deposited the check and guarded it like a miser. Her resolve lasted until the next time she went to the Guitar Center and saw the rows of electric guitars. Then and there she decided to spend some of her money on a new electric, but which one?

She'd always lusted after a Gibson, the hollow-body ES, but it was bulky and she liked to move when she played. The vintage Stratocaster she'd been eying was smaller, but heavier. Electric guitars were always heavy, though. Even the Peavey made her shoulder hurt after a long set and this model was lighter than most. It was so pretty, too, cream and chrome, and its tone was fantastic, ringing out clear and glassy on the high end.

The ES had a completely different character. The sound was thicker, more like an acoustic, with clean highs and gritty lows. Its fat, rich timbre was perfect for mournful tunes like "Sinner's Blues" or "Wanderlust," but she preferred the Strat for shredding.

What to do? She'd wanted a new electric for years, but now that she had the means she couldn't make up her mind.

Then she remembered. She had ten thousand dollars! She bought them both.

Just like that, more than a third of her money disappeared. She was a little embarrassed when she arrived home with the two beauties and expected Quinn to scold her, but he was delighted.

She couldn't wait to begin playing them and she didn't have to, because Lorraine was right. Cardinal wanted Quinntessence in the studio immediately. They needed a producer and met with a series of them, all of whom Quinn nixed. He had a different reason for each rejection. Different vision. Lack of chemistry. Too commercial. He finally approved one, but insisted upon visiting the studio where they'd be recording before he would sign anything.

Shan was dazzled by the space, all chrome and slanted glass windows with the biggest console she'd ever seen. Not Quinn, though. He ignored the fancy equipment, instead walking around the bright, shiny studio space, pausing here and there to clap his hands.

After he'd finished, he came into the control room, where the rest of them were looking over the console. "Who chose this space?"

"I did," said the hapless producer.

"You're fired. Sorry." Quinn turned and walked out, leaving the rest of them gaping.

When his bandmates protested, he was scathing. "Every room has its own sound that becomes part of the music, almost like another instrument. *That* room doesn't. It's an anechoic chamber. We record anything in that, it's going to sound dry and tasteless, crappy as dehydrated dog shit."

The next producer that Lorraine presented to them was Michael Santino, a soft-spoken man with olive skin and long curly hair. They'd all heard of him. He was one of the top guys in the industry and he cost a fortune. Just to get him in the studio would eat up half their advance, but Lorraine lobbied hard for him. He was the best, she said, with a reputation for bringing in nothing but winners. His skill at dealing with temperamental artists was renowned, too, she added when Quinn was out of earshot.

Santino owned and operated his own studio, Limelight Records, which Quinn insisted upon visiting as well. It was a big, dark, ugly room with layers of thick waffle board and heavy black fabric coating the walls. It looked like a haunted house.

As before, Quinn ignored the equipment in the control room and headed directly for the studio. He moved from the vocal room to the drum booth and back to the larger common area, clapping his hands. He spent a long time in there, longer than any other place they'd seen.

Eventually, Santino flipped a switch. "So, what do you think, Quinn?"

He turned around. He was smiling. They had a producer.

Two weeks later they were in the studio. A month after that, they'd finished preliminary recording on their debut album, *Quinntessence:*

Innocence. By April the project was complete and in June the album was released.

Shan poked her head into the house. "Come and look at it!"

Chuckling, Ty accompanied her outside. Dan and Denise followed and found her capering with excitement as she pointed out all the features of the forest-green Jeep parked in the driveway.

"It's got four-wheel drive and a car phone and look at these speakers! The stereo didn't have great sound, so I ordered a whole new system. What do you think?"

"I think it's great," Ty said. "It's time you finally got your own set of wheels."

"I had to do something with all this money! Do you know that, when my alarm went off this morning, 'Black Mile' was playing on the radio?" she said, her sneakered feet doing a jig on the driveway. "I went and dragged Quinn out of bed to make him listen to it."

As they went back into the house, Shan glanced into the music room. "Lorraine says we need to find another place to practice. She thinks the space is limiting us."

"I think she's right," Dan said. "How long are we going to live in this shack, anyway? I'm sick of the hot water running out after two minutes. Besides, if the album does okay, I'm thinking Denise and I might buy a house."

"I think you can start looking," said Quinn. He was leaning against the doorjamb, his forearms crossed over his chest and a magazine tucked under his arm. He was wearing jeans, a Rush T-shirt, and the biggest shit-eating grin Shan had ever seen.

"Why? What did you hear?" she asked him.

"Nothing I didn't expect. Just that *we*" —he slipped the magazine out from under his arm and they saw it was a copy of *Billboard*—"are on the motherfucking charts. 'Black Mile.' Number fifty-six. *With a bullet*," he added, just before he was drowned out by a rebel howl from Ty.

part three
1992–1994

Girls have got balls.
They're just higher up, that's all.

—Joan Jett

chapter 32

Shan pushed the suitcase closed, then attempted to engage the lock. The sides of the suitcase wouldn't meet over its bulging contents. "This is *not* going to work, Suge."

Sugaree wagged her tail in response. She was reclining on Shan's futon, no easy feat since it was rolled up and tied into a shape resembling a burrito. She fit atop it nicely, though. They'd celebrated her first birthday a month before, but she was still petite. She'd grown into a lovely dog, slim and graceful, with a shining black coat and a long, aristocratic snout that pointed to some greyhound in her lineage, or maybe whippet.

"I think you need your own bag," Shan told her, extracting a collection of squeak toys, a water bowl, and two partially chewed Nylabones from the suitcase. One of them caught on the cup of a lacy bra and Shan paused to unwind the thread from the bone.

Quinn poked his head through the doorway. "The movers are here," he said. "Aren't you ready yet?"

"Almost, but I'm having trouble fitting Sugaree's things in my bag."

Quinn snorted. "She's a dog. How many things does she need?"

She held up the toys in one hand and the water bowl in the other. Quinn went back to his own room, rooted through a box, and returned with a backpack into which he stowed Sugaree's toys, brush, food bowls, extra leash, and a box of treats. After that he rolled up her dog bed, maneuvered it between the pack's shoulder straps, and handed the bag to Shan.

Then he turned his attention to her suitcase. He flipped items left and right, extracted and rolled a few pieces of clothing, replaced them and fastened the bag closed. "Packed," he pronounced. She knew that the items in his own bags, already neatly stacked in the downstairs hallway, would have been arranged and stowed with the precision of a Tetris game. He was anal that way, but he'd become even more so since they began spending most of their lives on the road.

It felt like the members of Quinntessence had only just gotten back from their first tour, but already it was time for the second one. Shan knew it would be a crazy, confusing kaleidoscope of concert halls, hotel rooms, restaurants, and highways, just like the first tour had been.

When *Quinntessence: Innocence* was released nearly nine months before, it had performed quite well. "Black Mile" had achieved hit status, rising to an impressive number sixteen on the national chart, and Cardinal had been quick to pluck another single from the album, "Voluntary Exile." They'd commissioned a video, at which point Quinntessence was assigned a production manager and a rep from the artist and repertoire department, then turned over to a team of stylists tasked with creating a "brand" prior to the shoot. All of them received a makeover and Quinn insisted upon personally approving every suggestion made by Rachel, their A&R rep. He had only cursory comments about the looks proposed for any of the male band members, even his own, but he had strong opinions about Shan's.

"She's the face of the band, so she shouldn't look too girly," he said. "Not trashy, either. I don't want her coming across as a Madonna or Cyndi Lauper clone. As a musician, Shan has an edge. She's unique and her look should reflect that." And it did, when the stylists were finished with her. They'd primped, plucked, and waxed her to within an inch of her life. They'd made her get her teeth fixed, put her on a regular regime of facials to improve her skin, and tinted her hair, giving it a purplish sheen that she thought looked cool.

Next they turned to her wardrobe, fastening on to the hippie boho style that she favored and suggesting enough quirky touches and accessories to give her a look all her own. She now wore her favorite hot-pink baby doll dress with Doc Martens and oversized sunglasses, her hair rolled up into a high, messy bun to reveal chunky turquoise earrings. She performed in a flowing, cambridge floral print with gladiator sandals and a long linen scarf. She was photographed for a *Spin* interview in low-rise denim shorts and a brief, lacy tank, with her hair cascading from the back of a black leather baseball cap and studded ankle boots on her feet. She loved the clothes, although she felt like she was in costume every time she went out.

Quinn's look didn't change much. His preference in clothing was simple, good cuts and muted colors, and he still dressed that way, although his stylist had outfitted him with a dozen pairs of soft leather pants that made his derriere look like a sculpture. Dan suffered from the heat onstage, so he preferred Jams and wife-beaters, or going shirtless altogether. This was permitted, but Rachel produced a collection of funky vests and engaged a personal trainer to give some definition to his abs. Ty's look fell somewhere between hip-hop and beatnik while Dave, the peacock of the band, acquired an array of bright scarves and studded belts that he wore with tight jeans and spandex T-shirts snug enough to reveal his killer physique.

"Voluntary Exile" debuted at number thirty-two, leapt to the twelve spot when the video hit the channels, and Cardinal sent the band on tour. It meant four months on the road, Lorraine explained, although they were expected to be back in California no later than October 1 to begin recording their next album.

Four months? "What about Sugaree?" Shan had asked Quinn.

He frowned. "I don't think we should bring her, Shan. Maybe next time, but she's too little to be stuck on a bus for that long. Let's see if Denise will keep her."

Denise was delighted to dog sit. She'd been recently promoted to a full staff photographer position at the *Weekly* and had no desire to give it up in order to follow the band around. Since she'd be the only one in the house while the others were on tour, she was happy for some company.

The tour commenced with Quinntessence playing a series of openers, R.E.M. in Philly, the Smashing Pumpkins in New York, and the Spin Doctors in Charleston. They appeared alongside Siouxsie and the Banshees and Liz Phair, even played Lollapalooza with Jane's Addiction and Nine Inch Nails.

For four months the tour bus was home, a forty-five-foot coach complete with a shower, kitchen, well-stocked bar, even a laundry room. It comfortably accommodated all five of them as well as the driver, a curmudgeonly fellow named Fred. Most nights they stayed in hotels that ranged from the five-star Carlyle in New York to the downright scary Peach Bottom Inn in Mobile, Alabama. Their Tulsa show coincided with an aerospace convention, so they wound up at a fleabag where the accommodations included a herd of cattle in an adjacent feedlot that bellowed all night long and a used condom that fell out of a bath towel Shan was unfolding.

She called Quinn's room. "I can't take a shower!"

"Why not?"

She told him. "It's lying on the floor, like a snake. I can't bring myself to touch it!"

He was there in a flash to dispose of the offensive object for her, but had a good laugh later when he regaled their bandmates with the story. Condom jokes were a guaranteed hit these days, since the bus held an apparently endless supply. There was a big bowl of them, all colors and varieties, on the coffee table in the common area. They turned up everywhere, on the counters, in the bunks, garnishing the frozen margaritas Dave liked to whip up in the galley. Once Dan woke from a particularly savage bender to find his entire body festooned with them, like a safe-sex Christmas tree. Fred kept the blue bowl stocked, grumbling when he saw how rapidly its stores were depleted.

It was a matter of serious contention to Shan, too, how quickly the condom bowl was emptied. Her bandmates regularly utilized the bus to avail themselves of the groupies who materialized after every show. She'd raised it as an issue more than once. "I think it's disgusting," she told Quinn, Dave, and Ty. Dan appeared to be maintaining a monogamous state, at least in front of her. If he wasn't, she didn't want to know. "All three of you had girls in there at the same time after the Dallas show."

"We used different bunks, though," Dave assured her.

Shan wrinkled her nose. "That's just nasty, and I couldn't even come on board to change my clothes. It's so disrespectful, the way you treat those girls."

"They're not girls," Quinn said. "They're groupies."

"They're still people," she insisted.

"Barely. You ought to know by now that they're a different species. Groupies are like cats in heat. You can do anything to them and they beg for more."

Shan refrained from further comment, before he said anything more specific about what he did to them. She didn't want to know that, either. She already knew far too much about his sex life as it was. Quarters were adequate, but tight, and there were no secrets on the bus.

Occasionally they had to drive through the night to make it to the next show on time. As the only female, Shan was awarded the master stateroom, which boasted the most comfortable bed, a full-sized queen, as well as a loveseat that unfolded into an additional berth. There was a pull-out couch in the common area for sleeping, as well as four bunks curtained for privacy and a tiny compartment behind the driver's seat where Fred napped during the day.

The upper bunks were the least desirable sleeping quarters, especially after both Dave and Quinn were launched out of them in Minnesota, when Fred slammed on the brakes to avoid hitting a moose on the road. Whenever they had to spend the night on board after that, Dave slept on the couch in the common area while Quinn took possession of the pull-out in Shan's stateroom. He was in there all the time anyway, since they used the space for composing while they traveled from city to city, show to show.

It was also the designated drug-free zone, a haven where they could escape the rampant partying. The cloud of pot smoke was perpetual, the amount of alcohol consumed staggering, but it was the more powerful chemical usage that bothered both of them. Shan had discovered lines of coke cut out on the condom table, heard her bandmates giggling in what she was sure was a hallucinogenic state, and, just once, smelled a rich, vinegary tang that she knew was burning heroin. That night she locked herself in the stateroom and didn't emerge until morning, opening the door only to admit a grim-faced Quinn.

She'd felt guilty taking the only bed and had offered to share it with him. He'd declined, kindly but firmly, but that night he'd climbed in alongside her. He held her as she shook, overcome with a craving she hadn't experienced since before the tour when she'd unsuccessfully tried to wean herself off methadone, and the next morning she heard him upbraiding Dave.

"You will be out of this band if you ever bring smack on this bus again, Dave," Quinn was yelling, really screaming, "and I personally will break every bone in your fucking body!" Shan knew that Quinn didn't really have the authority to fire anyone anymore, not since they'd gotten signed, but Dave apparently still respected his authority. She never smelled H on board again.

During the tour Shan found herself clinging to Quinn more than ever, their relationship the one constant in the bewildering, constantly shifting montage her life had become. More than ever he was her family and that was how he treated her, familiar, comfortable, with an offhanded affection that was carefully devoid of passion.

Most of the time, anyway. Every so often he'd drink enough to catch a good buzz and, on those occasions, he touched her. A lot. He'd finger her lips, wind his hands through her hair, fondle her arm or shoulder or leg with covert, feathery strokes that brought goose bumps to her flesh and a painful neediness to her groin. It was still there, the heat between them, stewing and simmering, but these days he dedicated his energy to only two things: making music and having sex with as many women, excluding Shan, as he possibly could.

So she was still waiting, something that got harder and harder as time went by, especially after the shows when she'd watch him vanish into the bus with an anonymous groupie, sometimes more than one, and she hated him at those times, but needed him, too, and loved him no matter what he did.

She was glad when the tour ended and they could go home, but the breakneck pace let up only slightly even then. They had to be back in the studio immediately, to record the second of the four albums for which they were contracted. They'd produced a slew of material while they were on the road, heavy with themes of movement and journey and quest. The band set right in to learning, then practicing and honing the new songs, and by Thanksgiving they'd completed recording on their second album, *Quinntessence: Odyssey.*

Before it was even mastered, plans for the next tour were well under way, not to mention preparations of a different sort. Denise and Dan were finally getting married, a fancy holiday wedding strategically scheduled to occur toward the end of the band's hiatus so that the newlyweds would have time for a honeymoon before Quinntessence set back out on the road.

It was a flowery, festive affair, Denise having spent the better part of the past year, and most of Dan's advance, planning and funding it. Shan had to don a sea-foam frock for her role as maid of honor. Green was usually her best color, but this dress made her look like a piece of seaweed and she consoled herself with the notion that at least she'd get to walk down the aisle with best man Quinn, an event she knew was unlikely to recur during her lifetime.

The best part of the wedding was that Oda flew out for it. Shan had spent the night with her when the band played the Beacon Theatre in New York, but had to depart before seven the next morning. On the eve of the wedding, the three former roomies holed up in a suite at the LA Biltmore where the reception was taking place.

"One of you needs to loan me something," Denise said, examining her bridal costume. "You know, something old, something new . . ."

"Here, you can borrow this," Shan said, taking off a delicate silver necklace.

"How beautiful," Denise exclaimed, as Shan fastened the chain around her neck. It was a tiny eighth note carved out of jade. "Where did you get it?"

"Quinn bought it for me, at an outdoor market in San Francisco." She smiled slightly. "He said the color reminded him of my eyes."

Denise grimaced. "No thanks." She unfastened the necklace and handed it back to Shan. "Oda, can I borrow your pearl earrings instead?"

The wedding was lovely, if over the top. Dan and Denise flew to Puerto Vallarta for a weeklong honeymoon and, when they returned, they moved into the small house they'd purchased, a sweet bungalow in Pasadena. Ty was buying a home, too, a Santa Monica condo, which left only Shan and Quinn in the canyon house.

He'd insisted that it was pointless to keep the place when there'd be nobody living in it, so they'd given notice and now the movers were here. Their belongings were boxed, ready to be transported to a storage facility in nearby Sunland. Their bags were packed. The limo was outside, waiting to take them to the bus. They were ready.

After Quinn finished fussing with the bags, he straightened up and looked at Shan. "What's wrong?" he asked when he saw her melancholy expression.

"I feel sad," she said. "I'm going to miss this place."

"You've hardly been here during the past year."

"I know, but it's still been home. Even when we were on the road I knew it was here waiting for me, with all my stuff and Denise and Sugaree."

"You'll have a new home," he promised, "six or eight months from now, when we finish the tour. Till then your stuff will be in storage, home will be the bus, and Suge will be with us. Okay?" She nodded and he hefted her suitcase, heading for the stairs.

Shan slung her purse over her shoulder, then paused for one last look at her room. Out the window she saw the creek bed where she'd birthed so many songs, the trail where she and Sugaree had taken their hikes, the mountain where she'd once made love with Quinn. She'd been happy here, happier than at any time since her mother died.

Then she took up the backpack and followed Quinn down the stairs, Sugaree at her heels, ready for the next phase.

chapter 33

Shan could see that Quinn was edgy as the tour commenced. Their first album had been successful beyond her dreams, but it would really be its follow-up that would define whether they'd emerge as a full-blown force in music or be relegated to the discount rack along with the rest of the one-hit wonders. The curse of the second album was a well-known phenomenon and they were all tense as the debut drew near.

They were back on the same bus with driver Fred who, surprisingly, took a shine to Sugaree. He invited her into his curtained driver compartment, a place none of the rest of them were permitted to enter, where she rode shotgun, ears streaming in the breeze and tail wagging from side to side. Dave had grumbled at the dog's inclusion in their number, but her presence had such a positive impact upon Fred's mood that his complaints died.

They kicked off with a headliner in San Diego, then moved on to Phoenix and Albuquerque. Next the band traveled to Morrison, Colorado, for a festival at Red Rocks where they appeared alongside Tori Amos, Stone Temple Pilots, and Alice in Chains. They played Omaha, Topeka, and St. Louis, shared a bill with Cowboy Junkies in Lexington, Kentucky, and in mid-February headed for North Carolina to connect with Valentine, whom they were accompanying on the southeast leg of their US tour.

The two bands joined forces in Charlotte, where they performed before an enormous crowd, more than ten thousand people at a huge outdoor pavilion. The members of Quinntessence were greeted graciously by the headliners and Shan was thrilled to be appearing with one of her personal idols, Carole Grayson. She was tongue-tied each time they spoke, but there were few opportunities for conversation since each band traveled in an insular fashion with little crossover.

They sometimes fraternized after the bigger concerts, when Valentine would put out a sumptuous backstage spread for the press. "How come we don't get food like this when we headline?" Dan asked Quinn after the Atlanta show, helping himself to a hefty portion of smoked salmon and crème fraîche on endive. Shan accepted a caviar canapé, grimacing when the unfamiliar flavor hit her palate. She looked around for a place to dispose of it.

"Because then we'd have to pay for it," Quinn said, taking the canapé from Shan's hand and munching it. "You want to blow our profits on fancy hors d'oeuvres?"

"Particularly when we're happy to share, yes?" Shan looked around just in time to see Jerrika James lay her hand on Quinn's bicep.

During the odd occasions when the bands mingled, Jerri and Quinn always seemed to find a lot to talk about. These conversations, accompanied by what seemed to Shan to be an inordinate amount of physical contact, had become a source of painful anxiety for her. Jerrika James was exactly Quinn's flavor: tall, blond, and gorgeous. She was incredibly talented to boot, rock star royalty, and there was an unmistakable sexual vibe between them.

Shan could tell the attraction hadn't been consummated yet. Quinn's rules regarding women were basically unchanged. He confined his liaisons to hookups, casual encounters with nameless groupies who could be unceremoniously evicted once he was finished with them. Jerrika James would be something different, she knew, but she wasn't sure exactly what form that difference would take.

Her distress over the flirtation was briefly eclipsed when *Quinntessence: Odyssey* was released in February and became an overnight smash, selling nearly a million copies during the first week of its release. The single "Wanderlust" debuted at number forty-two, then leap-frogged into the top ten. When it landed at number six, the label launched its preplanned follow-up, a hard-rocking piece titled "Chasing the Dream." This one did even better, debuting in the top twenty, moving up quickly, and coming to rest at number four.

Shan's head was spinning. The critics were raving, *Rolling Stone* lauding them as one of the most talented American bands in decades. *Spin* concurred, stating that the enormous promise displayed in *Innocence* was achieved, even surpassed, by *Odyssey*. Shan was often singled out, her dense and slashing guitar solos and soulful vocals earning near universal acclaim, but the rest of the band received enormous praise as well, especially Quinn, widely acknowledged as the musical pulse behind Quinntessence.

On the twenty-fifth of February Lorraine paid them a surprise visit. They were in Little Rock and the show had sold out to standing room only. For the first time, Shan was beginning to believe it wasn't just Valentine drawing the crowds. "Nice job tonight," Lorraine said. "During 'The Only Perfect One' you had the whole audience on their feet, Shan."

Quinn winked at Shan. "I always said that was your best tune." He'd been dog-in-the-mangerish about "Perfect One," refusing to include it on the first album despite the band's unanimous opinion that it was their very best song. It didn't fit *Innocence*'s concept, he insisted at the time, but blended perfectly with the quest theme that unified *Odyssey*.

"Apparently the fans agree," Lorraine remarked.

Something in her tone caught Quinn's attention. "What do you mean?"

"I mean," Lorraine said, "that the advance copies of *Billboard* are in. Now, you know "Perfect One" has been getting some airplay."

"Right," Quinn said, "mostly on the college stations."

"Not just the colleges," Lorraine said, "because, as of this week, it's on the chart."

"Really?" Shan's eyes widened. "There wasn't any promotion, was there?"

"None," Lorraine said, "but it came in at number forty-three."

As they watched, the song zoomed up the chart. Album sales exploded, peaking at number two right behind Nirvana's *Nevermind*. The money, which had been coming in a respectable stream, turned into a flood and suddenly Quinntessence was hotter than Jesus.

On the night they played New Orleans, Lorraine called with the news that "The Only Perfect One" was the number one hit in the country. The members of Quinntessence went wild, whooping and howling, leaping about in jubilation. Ty hugged her and Dave planted a big, wet kiss on her lips, but Shan pulled away to search the backstage throng for Quinn, wanting to share the moment with him.

She found him on the bus where he appeared to be celebrating already, drinking a bottle of champagne and smoking a joint with Dan,

Jerrika James, and Curtis Strong, Valentine's drummer. Quinn was in the midst of giving Jerri a shotgun, leaning close to breathe the pot smoke into her mouth. Their lips were less than an inch apart.

When he finished, he settled back on the couch, his eyes lighting up when he caught sight of Shan. His lips immediately spread in a beatific smile that faded when she withdrew and hurried away without joining the celebration or saying a single word.

"To Quinntessence," Ty said two hours later. "The only really perfect band!" He had a groupie on his lap and a flute of champagne in his hand.

They were still celebrating, now at the bar of their riverfront hotel. They'd ordered a bottle of Cristal which everyone was drinking except Shan, who'd gotten carded despite her rock-star status. She clinked her glass of ginger ale along with the others, but Quinn took it out of her hand and raised his own flute to her mouth.

"You're breaking a rule," she said, "since this is technically a gig."

"The gig's over. And it's a good time for this rule to be broken," he said, feeding her a long tipple. The champagne was delicious, but all her attention was focused between her shoulder blades where Quinn's hand was resting on the bare skin exposed by her skimpy top, a square of lace secured by three cotton ties across her back.

Quinn dumped the ginger ale into a potted plant and kept her glass filled with Cristal. Soon she had a pleasant buzz and so, she suspected, did he. He'd followed her when she left the bus, been glued to her side ever since, and now was in one of his tactile moods, tucking a loose curl behind her ear, resting his hand on her lower back while they stood at the bar, once even lifting her hand to his mouth to drop a trail of kisses over her fingertips.

Before long she was starting to feel drunk. "I need some air," she said to Quinn, and he led her outside to a terrace overlooking the Mississippi.

She leaned her arms against the railing and lifted her face to the light wind coming off the river. It danced around her, causing her gauzy hippie skirt to flutter in the breeze. There was a steamboat chugging by and she could hear the sound of it churning through the water over the strains of the jazz playing inside the hotel.

"I'm having a flashback," she said, "to New Year's Eve at Disneyland. This is just like that, isn't it?"

"Not really," he said. "That was a just an illusion, a really good imitation of New Orleans. This is the real thing. I told you we'd get here."

She nodded, turning to look at him over her shoulder. The combined acts of nodding and turning made her slightly dizzy and she swayed, so he put a hand on her waist to hold her steady. "I'm getting bombed," she confessed, "from all the champagne you've been plying me with."

"You're entitled, tonight." The breeze was ruffling his hair and his eyes glimmered, the giveaway that he'd had a little too much to drink himself. He looked so happy with his wide smile, eyes sparkling in the moonlight, and her heart swelled with love for him. "We have a lot to celebrate, angel. All our dreams are coming true."

Not all of them, she thought, and suddenly she felt like crying.

As always, he saw. His smile faded. "What's wrong?"

She shook her head, turning away, but he pulled her into his arms. "You know you can't fool me. Tell me what it is, Shan."

She felt the tears burning her eyes. *I'm drunker than I thought*, she realized and swallowed them, but they caught in her throat and, when she spoke, her voice was ragged. "Sometimes I think I'll never be really, truly happy, Q. That I'm not meant to be. I feel like I'll never have the things that really matter and, without them, all the rest are just—trappings. Illusions, like you said."

His arms constricted around her. "Don't say that. How can you even think that? You're going to have the best of everything, angel."

"But I've never really cared about that." She pressed her face against his chest, so her words were muffled. "I know it's important to you, the money and the fame and all that stuff. I understand that, I do, but those aren't the things that matter to me. All I want is . . . a home. A family, maybe. Someplace where I belong." She thought of her mother and a dry sob caught in her throat. "I feel so alone sometimes."

Suddenly she couldn't breathe because he was holding her so tightly, impossibly close. "You aren't alone," he said. "You'll never be. You have me."

Usually she found comfort in his embrace. This time, his touch was painful, a bare fragment of what she needed and was becoming increasingly certain she would never have. "But I don't," she whispered. "I've never had you, really. It would be easier if I didn't love you so much," she added, almost to herself, "but I do and it hurts. It hurts a lot, sometimes."

He was silent for a long time and, when she looked up at him, she saw his face was stricken. Every trace of the joy that she'd seen there was wiped away, obliterated, and she experienced a wave of remorse that made her hurt even more.

So much for the celebration, she noted. "Look, it's nothing. I'm drunk, so I'm maudlin. I just need to get some sleep, Q. I'll see you in the morning." She forced a smile and gave him a peck on the cheek but he didn't reply, just watched silently as she disappeared inside the hotel.

Quinn stood on the terrace for a long time, gazing out over the river with a troubled visage. When he went back inside he avoided the others, instead making his way through the hotel and out the front entrance, then across the street to the lot where the bus was parked.

He climbed on board, went directly to the bar, and poured himself a neat Tanqueray. He tossed it back and poured another, a double this time, and snagged a pack of cigarettes off the condom table. It was nearly empty, containing only a nice, fat joint.

"That'll do," he muttered, flopping down on the couch and lighting up, closing his eyes as he took a deep, mind-numbing hit.

"Just who I was looking for."

His eyes flew open. It was Jerrika James, picking her way up the steps into the bus, stepping carefully in her high heels. "I had the same thought," she said, gesturing at the joint in his hand, "but it seems one of my bandmates has cleaned out the stash. May I join you?"

"Sure." He held out the joint and she sat close, too close, her thigh nudging his.

The invitation she'd been transmitting was overt, one he was clearly intended to notice. He had, of course. A guy would have to be dead not to notice Jerrika James. He passed the joint to her and she caught his hand, bringing it to her mouth. Her lips pressed against his fingers as she inhaled, casting him a smoky glance from beneath shadowed lids.

Then the ruby lips parted in sultry smile. "Alone at last, hey?" She took the joint and dropped it into an ashtray, then twined her fingers through his.

He looked at her, smoking hot with her white-blond hair, long legs, and creamy, copious set artfully displayed in a low-cut leather corselet. Teenage boys everywhere jerked off over her image in *Rolling Stone* and *Creem*, on MTV. She was a rock 'n' roll fantasy come true, the real deal right here for the taking.

But he shook his head. "I can't," he said. "I'm sorry, but I can't do it, Jerri."

She drew back, startled. "Do—what?"

"You," he said bluntly. "I know we've been heading in that direction, you and me, but I can't. I'm . . . I'm *involved,* you see," he added, realizing that he had never before made such a pronouncement. The words, though unfamiliar, felt fine, right. Overdue.

Jerrika looked flummoxed. "Since when?"

"A long time," he said. "Longer than I even knew." He lifted her fingers, still entwined with his, to his mouth and placed a respectful, apologetic kiss on the back of her hand.

Then he let go of Jerrika James.

chapter 34

When they departed for Jackson early the next morning, Shan gazed mournfully out the window of the bus. "We never made it to Preservation Hall," she said to Quinn as the wrought-iron and pastel colors of the French Quarter receded from her view, "or Tipitina's, either."

"We'll be back," he said. "I promise."

An opportunity came up sooner than expected when their schedule suddenly changed after the Montgomery concert. During the show the spike heel of one of Jerrika James's five-inch stilettos became tangled in a mic cable. She slipped, fell hard, and managed to make it through the rest of the show balancing on one foot. By the end of the evening she was in considerable pain and a trip to the ER confirmed that she had a broken ankle.

The remainder of the southeast shows were cancelled and the members of Quinntessence found themselves with an unexpected break, nearly a week to spare before they were due to headline in Orlando. Dan flew home but, to the others, Cardinal extended an invitation for some R&R on Hilton Head. "They maintain a condo there," Lorraine told them. "You're free to use it."

Dave and Ty snatched the opportunity, but Quinn declined, announcing that he'd be flying out, too. "Are you going home?" Shan asked him, disappointed. She was mulling the idea of returning to New Orleans for a few days and had been planning to ask him to go with her.

"No, I'm going to Daytona Beach. The first week in March is Bike Week. It's going on right now."

She knew about Bike Week. He'd mentioned it before. One of the biggest motorcycle events of the year, and one he'd always wanted to attend. "Sounds like fun."

"I was hoping you'd think so," Quinn said, and grinned. "You're coming with me, right?"

Daytona Beach was a patchwork of motorcycles of every conceivable make and size, but Harleys dominated the oceanfront strip. The people were even more colorful than the bikes and Shan was especially intrigued by girls who wore chaps with Daisy Dukes shredded high enough to expose their butt cheeks. "Why do they bother?" she asked Quinn as they idled at a light on their rented Harley. "It's not like those chaps protect anything. If they wipe out, their asses will be road pizza."

"I don't think protection is what they're after." Quinn stopped talking as a woman crossed the street in front of them attired in precisely the manner Shan had described. She wore studded leather chaps and, as she passed, Shan saw that her posterior was almost entirely exposed. Her shorts must have started as a pair of cut-offs, although now they were little more than a denim thong, plus she had a set of Harley wings tattooed on one cheek. Quite a rear view.

Shan watched Quinn's head rotate in perfect unison with her passage. She nudged him. "The light is green," she said irritably.

As he accelerated, she contemplated her own clothing, jeans and a leather jacket. "I look like a tourist," she said. "I should get some biker gear."

"Well, let's go shopping," he said, turning the bike toward vendors lining Main Street.

"Let's go," Quinn called, later that afternoon when they were in their suite. "Why is it taking you so long to get dressed? It isn't as if . . ." his voice faded as the bathroom door opened.

"I wasn't sure I should venture out on the street like this," Shan said as she emerged, now wearing Daisy Dukes and a tie-dyed tank top under her leather jacket. She'd embellished the ensemble with a few newly purchased accessories: a studded belt, fingerless riding gloves, and thigh-length leather boots. "What do you think? Do I look like a biker bitch?"

"You," he said, gawking, "look like a Hell's Angel's wet dream."

He seemed to approve of her shorts, which were brief, but securely covered her derriere. "I'm glad you didn't go backless," he said, as they descended the stairs to the parking lot.

"I'm surprised to hear that," she replied, "since your eyes have been bugged out all day."

He switched on the ignition. "Of course I'm going to notice when a bare-assed chick walks right in front of me, but it's not really a look that appeals to me all that much. A little too skanky." He mounted the Harley, eying her with admiration. "You don't look at all like a skank. You're dainty and innocent looking, even in leather and studs."

"You mean I spent all that money trying to look sexy for nothing?"

"You don't have to try." He held the bike steady while she mounted. "You're sexy all the time, angel."

"But you just said I looked innocent."

"*That*," he emphasized, "is exactly why you're so sexy. Hang on!"

They spent the afternoon bar hopping through establishments renowned for their colorful clientele. First, they watched a banana-eating competition at the Boot Hill Saloon, where the contestants seemed to be doing everything possible to a banana short of eating it.

Shan giggled as a tough-looking redhead massaged the banana with her tongue. "No wonder you wanted to come here. You'd get frequent flyer bonus miles in this place."

"I'm not looking to. I wouldn't leave you alone. Not dressed like that, at any rate," he told her as they left the Boot Hill. "Where to now?"

Shan dug in her jacket pocket for the Bike Week calendar. "Let's see. At Dirty Harry's there's a wet T-shirt competition, complete with music from a Lynyrd Skynyrd tribute band. At the First Turn, finals for Miss Bare Chaps. At Gilly's, you can compete in an arm-wrestling contest."

"Pass," he said. "I wouldn't risk my hands just to prove my machismo."

"Well, how about a stump tug at Will's Honkytonk? And at the Cabbage Patch, there are a variety of bike events and coleslaw wrestling." She raised her head. "Coleslaw? Really?"

"Let's go there. The Cabbage Patch is famous."

He let her off in front and found a place to park among the sea of tents and motorcycles. He dismounted, then frowned. Although Shan's attire was modest compared to some of the other females in the place, she was surrounded already.

There was a custom T-shirt stand set up beside the bar's entrance. Strolling over to it, he pointed at a brief, camisole-style top. "That one," he said, grinning at the blonde behind the counter. "And here's what I want it to say."

After he made his purchase, he maneuvered his way to Shan's side. "Here," he said, handing her a bag. "Put this on, will you?"

She pulled out the shirt. *Property of Q,* it proclaimed in lyrically curved letters.

"I'd rather not get into any fights defending your honor," he explained. "Most of these guys will leave a lady alone, if she's marked."

"Like branding cattle? How red-necky." He chuckled as she disappeared into the bar. She put on the shirt then drifted back outside to catch the end of the keg-rolling contest. Quinn was already out there, his front wheel pushing the keg with his usual precision.

He placed third, winning a bottle of Jack Daniels. They walked around the campground passing the bottle back and forth between them. The JD interacted nicely with the beer they'd been drinking all day, enough that they were both pleasantly buzzed when they paused to watch a bout of coleslaw wrestling. They climbed a set of bleachers to get a prime view and Shan settled on the bench behind Quinn, resting one forearm on his shoulder.

"*That* looks *really* disgusting," she said as two topless women rolled in a field of coleslaw. "Imagine what it must smell like, in this heat."

Quinn was eyeing her top appreciatively, as he'd been doing ever since she put it on. "*That* looks *really* good on you."

"Thanks," she said and snickered. "A couple more threads and I'd have a bikini top."

He laughed, leaning back to maneuver his body between her knees. "But look. It got me in between your legs."

She regarded him with surprise. "I didn't think that was a place you wanted to be."

He dropped his hand onto her knee. "Look at you. Who wouldn't want that?" His hand drifted up her leg to stroke the skin exposed at the top of her high boot.

She couldn't believe how much it excited her, a little thing like that, especially when he slipped his fingers under the leather to fondle the flesh of her inner thigh. When he raised his eyes she saw they were smoky, hot, and she gasped when he gripped her waist to pull her onto his lap.

Then she felt his erection. "Are—are you drunk?"

He nestled her a little closer. "You know better than that. I don't get drunk."

In general that was true. She suspected it was because he didn't like to lose control. "Once you did," she said, recalling the time she'd found him passed out on the couch with Dan.

"An anomaly," he said, nudging aside the thin strap of her top. She froze when he leaned forward, burying his nose in her cleavage, and inhaled deeply. When he drew back, his eyes were riveted to her chest. There seemed to be something about the Q there that mesmerized him.

"Q, what are you doing?" He never touched her this way. Never. His lips curved up in a knowing smile and she flushed. "I mean, where's this coming from, all of a sudden?"

"It's hardly all of a sudden," he said, then nuzzled the fabric over her nipple. She felt it harden right through the cloth and experienced a mind-bending jolt of desire.

He was torturing her. She thought he might even know it. She didn't know what to do, how to respond, so she didn't. On the field the coleslaw wrestling had concluded and now they were setting up some sort of scaffolding. "What are they doing?" she asked, her voice shaky.

"Setting up for the Weenie Bite." His hand dropped from her shoulder to her lap.

She kept her knees firmly together. "What's that?"

"The guys ride slow as they can, with their girls on the back of their bikes. The girl has to try and take a bite out of a hot dog that's hanging over her head on a string. It's really hard to do."

"Let's try it."

He paused, nonplussed, his hand between her thighs. "Now?"

"Now," she said, climbing off his lap and tugging her top back into place.

"You really want to deep-throat a hot dog in front of this crowd?" But he allowed her to pull him to his feet. They climbed down and he fired up the bike. Shan got on behind him, watching as several pairs passed under the dangling franks. None of the girls seemed able to get a bite and they were hung higher than she'd realized. She got a grip on his shoulders and stood up on the pegs, wavering a little. "You be careful," Quinn warned her. "I don't want you falling off."

She tightened her grip on his shoulders. "I will," she promised. He chuckled and she kept her eye on the hot dog as they wheeled up to it. It was dripping with mustard. She opened her mouth as wide as she could and, when the moment came, she bit savagely at the wiener.

The crowd was shrieking and, as Quinn rolled to a stop, he looked over his shoulder.

Shan finished chewing and swallowed. There was mustard smeared all over her lips and dripping from her chin, and he could spot a half a hot dog dangling from the line behind her.

Much later, they staggered back to the hotel. The currents flowing between them were heavy with need and wanting and sex. Once, while they were sitting in a bar, Shan became fixated on Quinn's hands. They were so sexy and capable, his touch always so sure. She remembered what they felt like on her and the recollection became physical, until she wanted to squirm and rub against the seat. It got so bad he noticed and asked her what was wrong.

When she paused at the door to fish the key card out of her pocket, he slipped his fingers up the back of her shorts. The contact made her flesh break out in goose bumps and turned her knees to jelly.

She opened the door and stepped into the suite, turning to ask him what the hell he thought he was doing to her, but before she could he pulled her into his arms. His mouth was on her then and his hands, too, cupping her breasts, her ass, infiltrating between her legs. Her mind was woozy, the combination of alcohol and lust making it nearly impossible to keep her mind in any kind of a logical place, but she was aware that the way he was touching her now was different from how he'd touched her in the past. There was roughness, a raw, urgent need that she'd never felt from him before.

He squeezed the apex between her legs, then slid one hand into her shorts where it was hot and wet and slick. He groaned out loud, sinking to his knees, and she could feel the burning of his breath when he pressed his mouth against her crotch. She felt like she'd dissolve, melt away until there was nothing left of her but a steamy, liquid pool of desire.

Then he was on his feet, backing her toward her room, pulling off his jacket and his T-shirt and dropping them on the floor. He gave her a little push so that she was inside the room while he was still standing outside it and she froze, picturing him slipping away yet again. "Are— are you going to leave me this way?" she whispered.

"No," he said. "I won't leave you. Not ever again." He was nude to the waist now, clad only in jeans, and the top button on his fly was undone. She could see how hard he was, how swollen.

"You mean—" she began, then stopped.

His eyes swept her from head to toe, pausing to stare hard and long at the words *Property of Q* on her chest. "I mean that I'm ready," he said. "Here I am, angel. I'm all yours. If you want me."

She didn't hesitate, not even for an instant. She took a step back.

And pushed the door wide open.

chapter 35

Quinn scooped Shan into his arms and she went eagerly, so much that she surprised herself. He pulled her right up off the floor, and she coiled both legs around his waist as he carried her across the room and spilled her onto the bed.

His hands were all over her, stroking and squeezing, pulling off her clothes, and he kissed her over and over, hot, burning kisses that seared her flesh. She was writhing under his touch, arching and bowing when he pulled her top down to expose her breasts. He lowered his head to nuzzle each one and she felt her nipples rising to stiff peaks against his mouth. He slid his hands down her body and, when he encountered her panties, he tore them away with an impatient jerk.

Then he froze, his gaze riveted between her legs.

She winced, pulling her knees together. "The stylist did that. It's a bikini wax."

"You mean a Brazilian," he corrected her, still staring at it in a near catatonic state.

"Whatever," she snapped. "It hurt like hell, but it itches when it grows back so I've had to keep shaving it." He pushed her knees apart again and ran his hand over the velvety seam, watching with great attentiveness as it opened under his touch.

She squirmed again. "Stop it! You're embarrassing me."

"Oh," he said. "Okay." Then his mouth dove between her thighs.

Her back arched and she could feel her body building up to a fervent pitch. She gasped, clutching the bedcovers, helpless under the powerful sensations unfurling within her.

He pulled his mouth away. When she raised her head, she saw he was gazing up at her from between her legs and she instinctively started to curl in, to barricade herself from his gaze.

He spread his hand over her navel, stopping her. "Don't," he said.

"I—I'm embarrassed," she repeated, whimpering.

"Why?" he asked, with a touch of incredulity. "You're the most beautiful thing I've ever seen." He turned his head and bit the flesh of her inner thigh lightly, just enough to tantalize. "You're so fucking beautiful," he breathed and his mouth was back between her legs.

He slid his hand down until it rested on her sex, one finger gently teasing the tiny nub from which all the sensation emanated. "Come for me, angel," he whispered, then his tongue was on her again, whirring like a butterfly's wing.

She arched up against his mouth. Her hips took on a life of their own and she couldn't catch her breath as she gyrated against him. A sudden heat deep in her belly alerted her that she was going to come and she shoved and rocked herself against his mouth until the heat exploded.

She fell back, gasping. He struggled out of his pants, then his long, lean body was sliding against her. She wrapped her arms and legs around him, reveling in the feel of his flesh. When he kissed her, his lips were salty, musky, and she knew it was herself she was tasting.

She felt his cock between her legs and tilted her pelvis up to meet him. When he stopped, Shan opened her eyes. His face was very close and he was watching her. "Why are you stopping?"

"Savoring the moment," he said huskily. "I've been waiting a long time for this."

She looked up into his beautiful eyes. "Not as long as I have."

"*Exactly* as long," he corrected her, then slid into her up to the hilt.

Then he was moving and thrusting and kissing her. "Fuck me, angel."

She rocked back and forth, utterly lost in the feel of him inside of her. She felt her body swelling, building again, to an even higher, tighter pitch. She half gasped, half sobbed, and grasped at his back, hot and slippery, slick with sweat.

"Fuck, it's good," he groaned, bending her legs, twisting them, pulling them over his shoulders to push deeper inside of her. "Do you feel it, angel?"

She felt it, all right. "Stop," she gasped, squirming. "Please, Q. I can't. It's too much."

But he didn't stop, just pumped harder, faster. She couldn't move, she was immobilized as he pounded into her, waves of pleasure coursing through her. This was different, so different from the last time.

He'd made love to her then, but this was fucking, raw and savage, even brutal, but he was right, it was so fucking good, and when she climaxed again it was with a sound somewhere between a screech and a howl, her nails digging into his flesh.

"Me too," he gasped and a moment later he came, his body tensing as he threw his head back with an animal cry.

Then he stayed rigid, his eyes fixed over her head. He had the strangest expression on his face, something like astonishment mixed with rapture. "Are you okay?" she whispered.

He pulled his gaze from whatever vision held him captive and looked down at her.

"Holy fuck." He shook his head, staring at her with wonder in his eyes. He kissed her, then relaxed, his body sinking deep into hers.

Later, after they'd done it again, they lay entwined, dazed and spent. Quinn's face was buried against Shan's throat, his breathing slow and steady. She thought he was asleep, but he stirred when she trailed her fingers through his hair.

He rested his chin lightly against her breast, his lips curving into a languid smile. "Hi."

She smiled, too, grateful he didn't look horrified. "Sorry I woke you."

"I wasn't asleep. Just comfortable." He rolled over, propped himself against the pillows, and held out his arms. Shan scooted into them, burrowing her face into his chest.

He chuckled. "You're tickling me." He slipped his fingers under her chin and raised her head to regard her warmly. "You look cute all rumply and tousled."

"You're pretty rumpled yourself." She slid further beneath the covers and groped between his legs.

His cock was soft now, pliable, nothing like the stony, rigid shaft that had pounded into her a short time before. It wasn't the biggest one she'd ever seen, or the thickest. It was long and elegant, though, just like the rest of Quinn's body was, and it fit nicely in her hand.

Suddenly she realized that it was coming to life, stiffening and growing as she examined it. She looked up at him, surprised. "Again?"

He smiled in a most lascivious manner, then rolled over on his back and pulled her on top of him. As she began to move, he swept her hair forward so that her curls spilled around his face. "Just like a curtain," he said dreamily, "blocking out the world."

"What?" she asked, stopping, but he gripped her behind, moving her. He strained upward, matching her rhythm, until he tensed and emptied himself inside of her again.

Afterward he wound himself around her. He fit against her like a glove and a sigh of absolute contentment escaped her as she began to drift into an easy sleep.

Then she had a thought that woke her right up. "Are . . . are you going back to your own room?" she asked.

He opened one drowsy eye. "I wasn't planning on it. Why, do you want me to?"

"No," she said, feeling an odd little twinge, "but . . . never overnight."

He snorted a little, nestling his face against her hair. "When has that ever applied to *you*? You've always broken all my rules. Never underage. Never overnight. Never—"

His eyes popped open, all evidence of sleepiness vanished.

"Shit," he said. "*Shit.*"

"What?" she asked.

"Do you . . ." he began, and then hesitated. "I mean, are you—" He stopped.

"Am I what?"

"Never mind," he said in a resigned tone. "You aren't."

"What?"

"On the Pill."

"Oh," she said. "No, I'm not. I have a diaphragm."

He frowned. "I didn't feel anything."

"Probably not," she said, "because I'm not wearing it."

"Oh." He fell silent. She regarded him narrowly.

"What about you? You're the biggest safe-sex advocate I know."

"You're right." He nodded, rolling over and staring at the ceiling. "I'm never unprepared. I have a whole box of condoms," he added, "right in the next room."

"I'm sorry, Q." She was staring at him, her brow still furrowed. "I just didn't think."

"Me, neither. No point in worrying about it."

"I think it'll be all right," she said, calculating the days since her last period in her head.

Suddenly he was tugging the covers away to press his bare flesh against her again and she could feel him getting hard. "Again? We already did it three times."

"Let's make it four."

"On one condition. Go get those condoms, Mr. Marshall."

chapter 36

Shan pulled the comforter over her nose. She was loathe to emerge from the soft fuzziness of sleep. The blanket over her brain was as comfy and warm as the one wrapped around her body. She felt safe, and contented, and . . . and . . .

Raw.

Holy shit! Her eyes opened and shot to the other side of the bed.

It was empty. Quinn was nowhere in sight. He'd bolted.

Goddammit! She knew that would happen. *She knew it!* And here she was, alone again.

She was damned if she'd sit here and wait for him to come back all ashamed and repentant, with that disgusting, guilty look on his face. She scrambled out of bed and pulled a T-shirt over her head, then grabbed her cut-offs from the chair she'd tossed them on the night before. Spotting her panties trailing out from under the bed, she snatched them.

She stared at the shredded piece of silk in dismay, then let it flutter to the floor. She pulled on the shorts, shoved her feet into flip-flops, then cautiously inched open the door.

The sitting room was empty. *Thank God.* She needed a shower—she reeked of sex—but she had to get out of there before he showed up. She just couldn't face it, that guilty look.

She was halfway to the door when a sound froze her in her tracks. Her gaze traveled to the breakfast bar that led into the small kitchenette and she watched the top of a blond head come into view around the corner.

Quinn's crystalline eyes appeared next. "Good morning," he said.

She stared back at him mutely.

"Going somewhere?"

She found her voice. "Yes. I have to be someplace."

He looked dubious, but didn't ask where. "Don't you want some coffee?" She heard a splash and a mug appeared on top of the breakfast bar.

She hesitated, then approached the kitchenette and perched on one of the stools. She kept her eyes on the floor as she sipped the coffee. The hot liquid cleared the last of the fuzziness from her brain and she sneaked a glance at Quinn.

He was staring at her intently, arms folded on top of the counter.

She raised the mug to her mouth in an elaborate show of casualness. Her elbow struck the edge of the counter and her hand jerked, spilling a bit of the hot coffee into her lap. She winced.

He continued to watch her, one eyebrow rising in a questioning manner.

Her temper snapped. "*What?*"

"Just wondering how long before you start wigging out on me."

She elevated her chin. "I'm not wigging."

He eyed her for another moment, then turned away. "You are."

"I'm not," she insisted, as he emerged from the kitchen and climbed on the stool next to her. He regarded her with amusement and she attempted a glare, but his grin was so engaging, his eyes so affectionately teasing, that she could feel herself beginning to relax. "Oh, all right. Maybe I'm wigging a little. I'm not exactly used to this."

"Me neither."

"Bullshit," she said. "You wake up with a different woman every day of the week."

"It's rare for me to wake up with anyone at all. You know that. And waking up next to *you*? That's definitely something new."

She pointed her nose in the air. "No, it isn't."

"Fair enough," he conceded. "I've never woken up *naked* next to you." She flushed and averted her eyes again. "So," he continued, "how are you feeling this morning?"

"I'm all right," she said, "but a little confused. I mean, we didn't talk about this at all."

He rolled his eyes. "We've been talking about it for years."

She saw his point and smiled. "But we didn't talk before we did it. We just—jumped. "

"Well, that's the way we do things, you and me." He shrugged. "I always figured it would happen that way, although it didn't really turn out like I thought it would."

Her smile faded. "What do you mean?"

He grinned and wrapped one of her long curls around his fingers. "I didn't expect it to be so mind blowing," he clarified. "The last time was awesome, but last night—holy fuck!"

"You said before that it was mind blowing. Earth shattering." She paused and bit her lip.

"Life changing." He nodded. "But that was intense in a different way. Emotionally, I guess. Last night was about passion, don't you think? All steamy and sexy and hot. *Dirty* hot." His fingers slid down to her thigh. "It took me a little by surprise, that's all. I didn't expect it to be so . . . so . . ."

"I did," she cut in. "I knew it would be good, because we're good together."

"Yes. We are." His hand began stroking her thigh, very gently, then slid into her shorts.

His eyes shot up to her face and she thrust out her chin. "I couldn't put them on. They were in shreds. They—"

Suddenly she was off the stool and on her back on the carpet, and he was on top of her, tugging at her clothes. She began to speak but shut up when he thrust his tongue into her mouth.

Then she stopped thinking, because he was inside of her again.

Hours later Shan was back in bed, curled against Quinn with one arm thrown over his chest. She kissed his shoulder and shifted to kiss his mouth, but stopped when she saw the look on his face. "What's wrong with you?" she said.

He didn't answer right away, but she could tell he had something to say. He was never good at holding things in, so she waited him out.

"I always knew you were going to fuck me up," he blurted after just a few moments. "I knew it the very first time I set eyes on you. You should have had a hazmat label on your forehead." He let go of her, got out of bed, and stomped over to the window.

"You're mad at me?" She stared at him, mystified. "What did I do?"

"I'm mad at *myself*," he corrected her, keeping his back turned. "I should never have let you in the fucking band in the first place. You were too goddamned young and I shouldn't have gotten so involved in your problems, either, because *then* I felt responsible for you. And I definitely shouldn't have talked you into moving out to LA," he added. "Guitar players are a dime a dozen there. Why the *fuck* didn't I just let you stay in New York, where you belonged?"

She drew back, stung. "Why the *fuck* are you yelling at me, Q?"

He ignored her, still railing. "Then I decide we ought to live together. What the fuck was I thinking? And then that day on the mountain. Christ," he spat. "That was the worst mistake of all. Of all the things I shouldn't have done, that was the thing I shouldn't have done the *most*."

Oh, God. She got it. She totally got it. This was it, the jump. The thing she'd never thought would really happen. No wonder he was freaking. "Well, thanks for the recap," she said.

He snorted, turning, and it was difficult for Shan to suppress her smile. The late-afternoon sun was bathing his skin in a golden glow, his blond hair shining around his shoulders. He looked like a Greek god, and *he's mine*, a little voice in her head was beginning to sing. *All mine!*

Shut up, she instructed the internal aria. *He hasn't said that at all. But that's what he meant,* the little voice argued. *He meant that he's jumped, and now he's mine. Isn't that what he meant?*

He sighed. "We have a lot to sort out. After the tour we have to find a place to live and I have some definite requirements. There has to be space for a home studio."

She paused, confused. This was not what she'd expected to hear. "A studio?"

"Yes. And, another thing, if I'm going to put all that time and money into creating a recording space, then it has to be permanent. No starter house or anything like that, which means something on the water. It's where I've always wanted to live. I want a boat eventually, which means beach frontage and space for a dock, but California real estate prices? Fuck," he growled.

Oh. Okay. She was following him now. "So you want to live together."

He snorted. "We already do, remember?"

"But you want to buy a house?" She frowned. "Don't you think that's rushing things? Between us, I mean."

"What are you suggesting, that we date for a while?" He regarded her with disdain.

"*You're* the one who never wanted to be tied down," she said, "and this is heavy, Q. I mean, it's a huge commitment. Shouldn't we think it through?"

"I've already thought it through, and so have you. I know perfectly well that you've been thinking about it ever since that day on the mountain. Longer than that, really. Ever since we moved to California. Probably since New York. You've thought and you've thought and you've thought about it. You think too fucking much, if you want my opinion."

"But—"

"Don't start dancing on me now. You said you wanted a home, so we're going to get one."

"So we're together now? A couple, just like that?"

"Just like that." And then he was grinning. "You make it sound like it was so easy."

"Falling in love with you *was* easy," she said softly. "The easiest thing I've ever done. But loving you, day in and day out, well, sometimes that hasn't been so easy, Q."

His grin faded. "I know. It'll be different now. I promise." His tone became businesslike once again. "Start thinking about what kind of house you want. We'll need a real estate broker. I'll line one up, give them our requirements so they can start a search. It'll take time but, if something really promising comes up, we might be able to fly back for a day."

"*Wait!*" she cried, hands on her head. "Let's just get used to this, to *us* first."

"I'm used to it," he snapped. "Let's move on."

A surge of indignation erupted inside her. "You know, it's not up to *you* to decide that it's time for me to buy a house, Quinn. I mean, I have *something* to say about it, don't I?" He rolled his eyes. It ignited her anger as it always did and she scooped up a pillow and flung it at him.

He sidestepped it then grabbed her, ducking as she swung at him. He wrestled her down on her back, pulled her hands over her head, then captured her legs between his knees.

She glared up at him, immobilized. "This Neanderthal routine is really not attractive."

"Neither is the turbobitch act," he shot back and she thrust her chin out, since that was the only part of her that she could move.

Suddenly he was smiling and she melted. He had such a nice smile.

"No more arguing," he decreed. "Not now." He kissed her, then let go of her hands and pulled her into his arms. "I'm too tired. Let's take a nap, then we'll go out for some dinner, okay?"

"Okay," she said agreeably and snuggled into his arms. "Hey, Q?"

"Mmm?"

"You love me, don't you?"

He didn't answer right away.

"Don't you?" she prompted. He hadn't said it, after all. Just that one time.

"Shh." His arms tightened around her. "Have a little faith in me. I'm not going anywhere."

She thrust the doubts from her mind and fell asleep with his arms wrapped around her, feeling his heart beating under her cheek.

chapter 37

For the next few days Shan floated, starry-eyed and utterly enraptured. The holiday in Daytona was pure bliss, hours and days devoted to simply enjoying each other.

And making love. That first day they didn't leave their suite until dinnertime. The second day they never left it at all, putting out the DO NOT DISTURB sign and ordering room service, which they ate stark naked. Quinn placed another order later that night, a white chocolate gelato that he proceeded to smear all over Shan's body, then remove with long, tantalizing strokes of his tongue.

Eventually they ventured out. They inspected a display of custom-painted Harleys, watched a Hot Leathers fashion show where he insisted on buying her a buttery soft, lace-up corset, and went to an afternoon Molly Hatchet concert. Afterward they had a candlelit dinner at an elegant bistro in the historic district. Quinn ordered pasta for two, an exotic dish with salmon and pancetta, and a champagne that even Shan's inexperienced palate could tell was something special. Later they made love on the beach, swathed in sheltering darkness.

They whiled away one morning at the hotel pool, lounging on beach recliners and reading in companionable silence. At one point Quinn was quiet for so long—not even the crackle of a page—that Shan thought he was asleep. When she looked over, she saw he was watching her through his Ray-Bans, his sci-fi novel facedown on his chest. "What?" she asked.

He smiled. "I like this. That's all." He turned back to his book and she was suffused with a warmth that she knew wasn't coming from the sun.

It was the most idyllic, romantic week of her life. *Like a honeymoon*, she thought wistfully, and like a honeymoon it passed much too quickly.

"What do you think the others will say?" Shan said, as they packed up their odds and ends the night before they were due to report for the concert. For the two-hour drive to Orlando, they'd swapped the rented Harley for an extremely cool Mustang Shelby convertible.

"About what?" Quinn asked, struggling to zip her suitcase. It was a tight fit.

"About us. They're going to torture you once they realize we're together," she predicted, chuckling. "Especially Ty. I hope you're prepared."

Quinn looked up. "They can't find out. Not now, anyway."

She stared at him, taken aback. "How's that going to work?"

"We're going to keep it just between us." She frowned, but he was resolute. "It's the best thing, angel. There's no point rocking the boat in the middle of a tour."

"But nothing has changed as far as the band."

"That's not entirely true," he said. "What you and I do impacts everybody. If anything ever split us up, that'd be the end of Quinntessence."

"That's been true all along, though."

"I know," he said, opening the bag back up and extracting her motorcycle boots, "but there's a lot more potential for problems the way things are now." He looked up and noticed her troubled face. "Don't get freaky. Nothing is going to happen to us."

"Then why are you worried about it?"

"I'm not. I'm only worried about dissension in the ranks." And he zipped up the bag.

His insistence on secrecy bothered her more than she let on, but she went along with it. They rejoined the others in Orlando, where they played to a packed arena. Already high on love, Shan was incandescent and the sheer dynamism of her performance galvanized the others. They brought the house down, performing three encores before the delighted crowd would let them leave the stage.

Her bandmates were nearly as enthusiastic as her audience. She squeaked in surprise when Ty and Dan twirled her between them. Then Dave kissed her full on the mouth, proclaiming her the guitar glamazon of all time. Quinn observed the kiss narrowly, signifying his own approval with a surly nod, but later he made love to her for hours.

The tour continued, looping from Orlando to Tallahassee, up the coast to Atlanta then west to Birmingham, Jonesboro, and Kansas City. The cities blended together, since they were never in any one of them for more than a day.

Shan and Quinn continued to book separate hotel rooms. At first Shan was forlorn at the thought of sleeping without him, but he tapped on her door on the very first night, after the Orlando concert. She never said a word, never made any demand or expressed any expectation, but there he was, every night.

They spent hours engaged in protracted, delirious lovemaking. She couldn't get enough of Quinn's talented mouth, his lean body and sure, sensual touch, and he seemed equally bewitched by her. Often it was dawn before they fell into an exhausted slumber and when she woke he was always gone, back in his own room to dress and pack before they reconnected at breakfast.

Before long the lack of sleep was taking its toll and Shan took to napping on the bus. She spent so much of their travel time sleeping that Dave asked if she was okay.

"Fine," she replied, stifling a yawn. "I don't sleep well in hotels."

"You're not the only one," Ty said, nodding at Quinn sprawled out on the couch beside him. His eyes were closed but she saw the ghost of a smile materialize on his lips. When she looked up, she saw that Dave had noticed it, too. He was frowning when he went back to practicing tremolos on his Cordoba and kept shooting suspicious looks at Quinn the rest of the way to Denver.

As she dressed for the show, Shan reflected that the lack of sleep wasn't affecting her appearance. On the contrary, she knew she'd never looked better. Part of it was their success, she supposed. The concerts were heady stuff; people screaming her name, singing along with their music, roaring for encore after encore. They even had their own security squad traveling with them now, a group of guards tasked with controlling the crowds that formed around them wherever they went. She was still on a strict beauty regimen, too, but she knew that wasn't the only thing responsible for the glow in her skin and the shine in her eyes.

It was Quinn and the knowledge that he was *her* Quinn, now. She was overcome with love, flush and replete with it, yet in some ways their relationship was remarkably unchanged. They still fought over the set list, bickered when they composed, whiled away hours on the tour bus debating the musical virtuosity of Dream Theater versus Guns N' Roses. All that was the same as it ever was, easy and familiar and supremely comfortable.

And there was the intensely hot sex. It was a period of eroticism unlike anything Shan had ever experienced and she bloomed in it, acquiring a new sensuality that was fresh and earthy, her eyes holding a look of shared secrets. Quinn saw it, too. She'd catch him looking at her, his own eyes scorching, and it would be torture to wait until after the show, when they could be alone.

When they reached Reno, Shan's room had a panoramic view of the strip, a hot tub as big as a small pool, and a trampoline-sized bed with a mirrored ceiling. At lunch, she slipped into the seat next to Quinn. "Wait until you see my room," she said, speaking in an undertone even though Dave and Ty were up at the buffet.

"I know. It's the honeymoon suite. I requested it. I can't wait to see what you look like in that mirror," he added, "all spread out and wide open for me."

Shan felt every bit of heat drain from her body to converge in her groin. He was so dirty, sometimes, so hot and lusty and unabashedly erotic. It never failed to rouse her, his utter carnality.

Under the table, she felt his hand between her legs. He leaned close, bringing his mouth against her ear. "Just wait, angel. I've got plans for this luscious little pussy."

"Shan!"

She leaped and Quinn's hand speedily disappeared from between her thighs. Denise was charging across the dining room, hauling Dan behind her. She'd flown in for the show and she was laughing and chattering as she threw her arms around Shan. "Let me look at you." She held her back, hands on her shoulders, and frowned. "Why are you all flushed? Are you sick?"

"It's because of me," Quinn said. "I don't like the way she's been doing that solo on "Black Mile" again and she doesn't like me telling her what to do."

"Oh, get off her back! Let's go shopping after lunch. It will give you a break from Quinntila, which I'm sure you need," Denise said, taking the seat on the other side of her. When Shan looked at Quinn, he was frowning down at the *Wall Street Journal,* but again she spotted a trace of a smile.

"Wow!" Dan exclaimed when Shan walked into the greenroom. "New look, hey?"

Quinn looked up, his eyes widening when he saw the slinky black dress she'd opted not to wear for their Troubadour showcase more than a year before. "Where did that come from?"

"I asked Denise to bring it. I thought it was showgirly, appropriate for Reno." But, more than that, she knew it was sexy. For the first time, she felt comfortable with that. She spun, the gauzy panels of the skirt spreading like the petals of a flower. "What do you think?" she asked her bandmates.

"Hot!" Ty declared.

"Awesome," Dave said, his approval transmitted by a wolfish grin. Quinn frowned.

The crowd appreciated her attire as much as her bandmates did and she was electrified by its energy. She was soaked with sweat by the end of the show and headed backstage to freshen up.

She yelped when someone grabbed her, pulling her into an empty dressing room. It was pitch black and she felt a jolt of fear but only for a moment, because she recognized the hands, the mouth immediately. "What are you up to, Q?"

"It's such a turn on, knowing every guy in the place wants you," he breathed in her ear, "but that I'm the one who's going to have you." His lips slithered down her body and she felt his hands under her skirt.

"What if someone comes in?" she asked, even as she shifted to give him easier access.

"We'll be quick. You're not attached to these, are you?" His hands were between her legs, massaging her through her black hose. He didn't wait for an answer and she felt his thumbs pop through the nylon, tearing it open. She fumbled at his fly, then he was hoisting her into the air, her back braced against the wall, and with a powerful thrust he was inside her.

His hips swiveled as he rammed into her and the unbelievable pleasure of it made her gasp, bringing her knees up under his arms. Just as she felt a climax coming on the door burst open, then slammed shut as two squirming figures collided with them, obviously intending the same sort of act that she and Quinn were engaged in.

Quinn let go and Shan landed on her feet as he pulled out of her. "Do you *mind?*" she said sharply. "This room is taken." All movement ceased. For a moment, there was silence.

Then, "Shan?" A familiar voice.

Shan gasped as the lights came on, revealing Denise and Dan, and Quinn leapt away from Shan as if she'd burned him. Denise's mouth fell open and Dan looked startled, as well.

He was the first to recover. "Er, sorry. Didn't mean to barge in." When he looked at Shan, his eyes averted quickly and she realized that the top of her dress was pushed to one side.

As Shan tugged her dress back into place Denise opened her mouth, then closed it. Then she opened it again. Still, nothing came out. She appeared genuinely speechless.

"We'll find another room," Dan said, grabbing his wife and pushing her out the door. He reached for the light switch and they both saw his broad grin before the room went dark.

The next morning, Shan had to practically drag Quinn downstairs for breakfast. "You're acting like a five-year-old who got caught with his hand in the cookie jar," she told him.

"That would be better than where it was," he groaned.

Shan rolled her eyes and, when they arrived in the dining room, they found a fairly normal conversation under way. Ty and Dave were chatting about some baseball game. Dan and Denise were whispering and holding hands, all lovey-dovey.

Then Denise looked up, saw them, and went gimlet-eyed.

Quinn quickly focused his attention on the newspaper, but Shan smiled at Denise as Dan went up to the buffet for seconds. "Did you have a nice night?"

"Very," Denise replied. "Did *you?*"

"It was fine," Shan said, which wasn't entirely true. The sumptuous room had been wasted on her and Quinn last night because, for the first time since Daytona, they'd gone to bed without making love. "My room is really nice," she added, just for something to say.

"I'm surprised you noticed," Denise said. "Did you see any of it except the ceiling?"

Quinn slunk farther behind the newspaper, but Dave was suddenly attentive. "What's this?" he said. "Did our little glamazon get some action last night?"

"No," Shan said, frowning at Denise.

Denise lifted her eyebrows. "Really? That's surprising. I'd think sex would be about the only thing you'd get out of him. Right, Quinn?"

"Just for once," Quinn said from behind the paper, "could you mind your own business?"

"You never hold back," she said. "Why should I?"

Quinn lowered the newspaper. "I don't give a shit what you think, that's why."

"I couldn't care less about you," she told him. "It's Shan that I'm worried about."

Shan began to speak, but Quinn talked right over her. "Shan is perfectly fine," he said.

"I doubt that, even though you might have her sweet-talked into believing she is. We all know how thick you can lay it on when you want something bad enough. How fine is she going to be the first time you have a craving for one of your frequent flyers?"

"Shut up, Denise," Quinn said and this time his voice shook.

"How could you do this to her? I can't believe what a selfish prick you are, Quinn."

"And I," he shot back, "can't believe what a loudmouthed, meddling cunt *you* are, Denise."

"Stop it! Both of you!" Shan begged as Dan returned to the table, his plate piled high with waffles and eggs. He surveyed the uncomfortable scene and looked at Ty. "Did I miss something?"

"I think we all did," Ty said, looking mystified.

"Your best friend," Denise informed Dan, "just called me a cunt."

He looked at Quinn, a rare frown crossing his amiable features. "Dude, you called my wife a cunt?"

"She deserved it, sort of," Shan said. "Now, can we drop the subject, please?"

"I'd rather not," Ty said. "I hate to miss a drama."

"You're not," Denise said. "It's going on right under your nose." Shan winced and put her hand up, as if to deflect further attacks, but Denise was on a roll. "And you," she said to Shan. "What's wrong with you? How can you possibly sleep with *Quinn,* with all you know about him?"

"I knew it!" Dave burst out. "Goddammit, I knew it!"

Quinn closed his eyes, dropping his head against the back of the seat.

"I had a feeling that's what happened, that you waited until the rest of us weren't around and crawled into bed with her. What about the rule?" Dave demanded, his eyes narrowing.

"Which one?" Shan asked, going through them in her head. Quinn had so many of them.

"The one that puts you off-limits. No diddling the guitar goddess, to use *his* exact words." Dave jerked his thumb in Quinn's direction. "A rule that apparently applies to everybody else!"

"Oh, get over it, Dazz," Quinn shot back. "She never really wanted you to begin with. What makes you think she'd want you now?"

Dave's face went crimson. He rose, stalked out of the dining room without another word, and Denise stood as well. "Let's go," she said to Dan. A naked note of authority rang in her voice.

Dan trailed submissively after her, looking back regretfully at his full plate, as Shan turned on Quinn with blazing eyes. "Is that the truth? Have you really been dictating who I can go out with behind my back?"

"It's just logical, from a professional standpoint. I've heard you say yourself that you don't think it's a good idea to date a bandmate."

"Bullshit! You obviously don't have a problem with it as long as the one I'm dating is you! Now that you've finally got around to it, that is."

He paused and she could see that she had him there. "You're overreacting—" he began.

"Save it." She got up from the table and he rose, too, catching her arm.

"Oh, chill out, angel. There's no reason to go storming off."

"I need to get away from you," she said, pulling her arm out of his grasp, "because I could punch you, Quinn. I really could." He watched her escape into the lobby in the same general direction as the others, then turned as a deep chuckle emanated from behind him.

Ty was still sitting at the table, eating steak and eggs and observing with amused eyes. Quinn scowled. "I thought you went out with the mass exodus."

"Nope," Ty replied, slicing off another bite. "Hell, I'd have paid to watch this!"

Quinn beckoned a waiter for a Bloody Mary, then he regarded Ty with suspicion. "Well?"

"Well what?"

"Go ahead, let me have it. I know you'd never miss a chance to tell me what a dick I am."

"I don't think you're a dick. Well," Ty qualified, "you *are* sometimes, but I don't think it applies here."

"You hold the minority opinion." The waiter brought Quinn's drink. He took a long slug.

"Dan doesn't think so, either," Ty said. "He just won't say it while his old lady is so steamed up. And Dazz is jealous. You hit that one right on the head, although you could have stated it a little more tactfully. Tact," he added, "has never been one of your strong points."

"Give me a break. What kind of a loser would moon after the same chick for—how long has it been? Two years, almost."

Ty's face split in a delighted grin. "I don't know what kind of a loser would do that, man. Why don't *you* tell *me*?"

Quinn took another slug of his drink, refusing to take the bait. Then he regarded Ty thoughtfully. "So you're cool? You don't have a problem with this?"

"What difference would it make if I did? Would it change anything?" Quinn didn't reply. "That was always a good point you had about hookups inside the band, though. You might want to keep it in mind."

"It won't affect the band," Quinn said firmly.

"Sure it will, but maybe it'll be for the better. Can't wait to hear the tunes you guys come up with now." He grinned, lifting the final bite of steak to his lips. "It's about time you snaked her plumbing. How was it?"

When Quinn didn't respond, Ty's grin widened. "What is it, classified? Come on, dude, gimme the goods." Quinn remained silent and Ty whooped. "It must be too personal to share!"

Quinn speared him with a dangerous look, but Ty was still chortling. "Who woulda thought that little chicklet could ambush the wild man?" Quinn continued to glower and Ty snickered again. "I'm going to track down Dazz, chill him out some before we're all stuck on the bus. You want to come?"

"No. I'd better start with Shan."

"Yup. You keep that little woman happy." Quinn shot him another deadly look and Ty was still laughing as he left the restaurant.

chapter 38

Quinn checked Shan's room, then the bus. She wasn't in either place, nor in the bar or any of the hotel shops, so he headed for the swimming pool, a sumptuous enclave resembling a tropical lagoon with lush gardens, fountains, and waterfalls. He didn't see her there, so he began checking the alcoves that housed the various hot tubs and whirlpools surrounding it.

He was dismayed when, instead of Shan, he found Denise in one of the hot tubs. She'd changed to a swimsuit and a big sun hat and she was alone, sipping an orange drink from a tall glass. When she spotted him, her mouth twisted into a moue of disgust. "What do you want?"

"I'm looking for Shan," he said. "Have you seen her?"

"She's in the sauna." Denise said, jerking her head in the direction of a nearby cabana marked LADIES BATH HOUSE. "Hopefully sweating every trace of you right out of her body."

He scowled, relieved but annoyed to find Shan here, with Denise standing guard like some kind of hat-wearing, Mimosa-swilling Cerberus. "Is it possible for us to quietly coexist until she comes out?" he inquired. "I've already heard more than enough from you today."

"Dan always says you have the ears of a bat, but I don't think you ever hear anything that isn't exactly what you want to hear, Quinn."

"What am I supposed to be hearing? You've already shared what a selfish prick you think I am. Duly noted. I'd appreciate it now if you'd just shut the fuck up."

"I will not shut up," she shot back, "any more than I would shut up and watch someone step in front of a bus when all it would take to save them is a word of warning. I will keep talking until Shan hears me."

"Shan doesn't need to hear anything from you. She doesn't need saving either," he said, "but I wish someone would save me from your big fucking mouth. Where's Dan?"

"In the fitness center." She gestured vaguely in another direction.

That figured. Dan was under strict orders to work out every single

306

day they weren't on the road, the penance he paid for the privilege of going onstage half naked. He suppressed a sigh, but sat down on one of the lounge chairs to wait for Shan.

Denise started right in. "You know how much she loves you, right? You know, but you don't care. You're going to break her heart and she might never recover. What a self-centered asshole you are, Quinn."

His temper flared anew. "You know, Denise, I've never done a god-damn thing to you, not ever, but you have behaved like a complete bitch in every single interaction I've ever had with you. You're like a rabid dog."

She pulled off her sunglasses and he recoiled from the venom he saw in her eyes. "You're the dog, Quinn, and you've done plenty to me. *Plenty.* You damage every woman you touch. First you fuck them, then you fuck them up, and you do it without a second thought."

"I've never fucked you up," he insisted. "Or fucked you, either, for that matter."

She made a sound like she'd been punched in the gut. "*Yes, you have,*" she cried. "*On both counts!*"

"What are you talking about?"

She stared at him mutely for a few moments, then, "You still don't remember. Jesus Christ, Quinn!" She turned her face away. "*Away from the lights of the city, we're alone in the galaxy,*" she sang. "*Under the eyes of a million stars, there's only you and me.*"

A thunderbolt of realization hit him. "Where did you hear that song?"

"You sang it to me," she said.

He could barely remember the music festival where he'd written it. It was in D.C., a gig he'd played with the Accidental Evils and so experi-enced through a coke-fueled haze, but he did remember the girl who'd inspired the words.

He'd thought of her a few times over the years, always in a sweet light, the pretty blonde with the camera. She'd been his own age, sev-enteen, with a sharp, saucy sense of humor that he liked. They'd hung out, gotten high, and eventually wound up making out, then making love back at the campground where she was staying, somewhere over the river in Virginia.

Yes, he remembered her. She'd been sweet as a woman could be.

"My god," he whispered. "Why didn't you ever say anything?"

"Why? I'm just another chick you screwed, then ditched. When I saw you again, you didn't know me. You'd forgotten all about me." She pressed her lips together, squinting, and he understood, suddenly, how much he'd hurt her.

He hesitated, thought back. "You looked different, back then. Your hair was longer. Blonde, not red, and you wore it in braids. And your name . . ." He frowned. "It wasn't Denise."

"I went by D.J. then." She shrugged. "I thought it was a good name for a photographer."

DJ from DC, he recalled, experiencing just a flash of that sweetness.

"After I moved to New York, I saw a flyer for Quinntessence and remembered that was what you wanted to call your band someday. When I went to the show, though . . . nothing. Not a glimmer of recognition." This time her eyes did fill.

"I'm sorry, Denise. I really am." He shook his head, dazed. "I was fucked up back then. It wasn't about you." He reached for her hand.

She snatched it away before he could touch her. "Of course it wasn't about me! It was about *you!* Isn't everything?" She rose, grabbing her sunglasses and groping for her towel as she prepared to leave the hot tub.

Christ. There were no words to make this better. "Wait a minute," he said. "Dan doesn't know, does he?"

"God, no." She shook her head, hard. "I don't want him thinking he was sloppy seconds."

"He wasn't, right? I mean, you aren't still into me."

When her mouth fell open, he winced. What a stupid thing to say, because he already knew better. Denise despised him, always had, and now he knew why.

She slammed her arm into the water, creating a mini-tsunami that doused him from head to toe. "You are a *dick,* Quinn. A selfish, self-obsessed dick and, no, I am *not* into you. I'm sure that's hard for you to believe but, for the record, I happen to love my husband."

He winced again. "I know that. I'm so sorry," he said and meant it. "I wasn't implying . . . well, anything. And I never wanted to hurt you. I just . . . fucked up."

She sniffed in disbelief as she got out of the tub, pulled the towel around her hips, and shoved her feet into her flip-flops.

"Shan . . . she doesn't know, either, does she?" Quinn said. "About you and me."

"Why would I tell her? It would only hurt her. That's what you do when you love somebody, Quinn. You treasure them and take care of them and *you don't hurt them*. Try and remember that, dickhead." She marched out of the alcove, hat jerking with indignation, leaving Quinn alone, soaking wet and staring into the water, and that was how Shan found him when she came out of the sauna.

"I'm sorry," he said as soon as he saw her. "I'm so sorry if I've ever done anything to hurt you, angel. I don't want to hurt you, not ever again."

She stopped short and he saw the confusion on her face. "I'm not hurt," she told him. "I'm pissed. Did you really tell Dave that you'd fire him if he went out with me?"

"Oh. Yes. Yes, I did." He'd almost forgotten what had started the fracas, because his no-diddling-the-goddess rule paled to nothing beside Denise's revelation.

"That is so wrong, I don't even know what to say about it," she said.

"Well, what else was I supposed to do? I wasn't about to take the chance that you might actually hook up with him, or Ty, either, for that matter."

"But it's not for you to control what I do. I'm not some kind of trained animal." She glared at him. "Although that's exactly how you've been treating me, like a faithful puppy dog who'll sit around forever, waiting and waiting and waiting for you."

"I didn't think of it that way." He shrugged. "This thing between us . . . it's big for me. Huge, and I'm all in, one hundred percent."

"So am I! I've *been* all in, all along."

"But I had to be ready, like I kept telling you. I had to learn how to do this, had to . . . grow into it. In the meantime, I wasn't about to let somebody else scoop you up. Dazz is a good guy. The best, in fact, and you two hit it off right from the start. I wouldn't blame you if you fell for him, so I sure as fuck wasn't going to stand by and watch it happen."

Shan stared at him for a moment, then dropped her eyes. "You're such a dick, Q," she said, so softly that it sounded like an endearment.

"I know I am," he said and pulled her into his arms. "A dick who couldn't see what was right in front of him for all this time. But I see it now and I promise you something, angel. I will never hurt you. Never. You can believe in me."

"But I do," she said, still confused. "I always have, Q."

He didn't reply, just pulled her closer, vowing to himself to take care of her, this treasure that he'd been given.

chapter 39

After the first shock passed, the band adjusted to the new state of affairs. Dave smoldered, but not everyone was so negative. Ty and Dan found the situation uproarious and razzed Quinn at every opportunity. After a while, Dave's inherently sunny nature kicked in and even he joined his bandmates in speculating on the intimate aspects of the relationship when Shan was out of earshot.

"Wonder what the dirty stuff is like?" Ty mused. They were in Salt Lake, waiting for the roadies to finish setting up the stage monitors at the Delta Center.

"She's a sweet thing," Dave said, clearly delighted to have an opportunity to share his own knowledge of the lady in question, "but a little conservative, you know, from a booty standpoint." He grinned evilly at Quinn, whose color was rising.

"Only with the lights out, you mean?" Dan smirked. "Wonder how the Q-man likes that?"

"I'm guessing he doesn't," Ty said. "Not after the freaky slam hounds he's used to."

Quinn ignored the crude and horny bastards. "Extra monitors in front of the keyboard," he called to Stan, the head roadie. "How many times do I have to tell you this?"

"Won't even give us the details." Ty shook his head. "What happened to the old studhammer we all know and love?"

"He's still a studhammer," Dan said. "He's just banging on the same nail."

Quinn scowled at Ty and Dan. "You're pathetic, both of you," he said, not acknowledging Dave, whom he wanted to hit. "Take your nosy fucking questions and shove them up your asses."

"Hey, we're entitled to ask. Usually, you brag about your women," Dan said. "Or rather, you brag about what your women do to you. Or what you do to them."

"Or, sometimes," Ty added, "what they do to each other."

"Obviously this one is different," Quinn said icily.

"Because you're whipped," Ty clarified.

Dan nodded. "That's all we're saying."

Shan was spared this exchange, as she was making her monthly methadone pickup. Because she'd tested clean for so long, she only had to visit a clinic once a month, when she would receive twenty-seven take homes at a time. Obtaining them on the road was difficult, though.

Finding the clinics and scheduling the visits was something Jeff, their road manager, took care of. She was embarrassed, despite Lorraine's assurance that this was not an unusual practice for a touring rock band. "It would be easier to get it off the street," Shan complained to Quinn.

"I know," he said, because another of Jeff's duties was procuring the recreational drugs for their bandmates. "Don't you even think about it," Quinn added, frowning at her.

She hated the fact that, once again, the band had to make special accommodations for her. She wished she could just get off the stuff, but try as she might, she couldn't kick that last dose. She couldn't take the withdrawal. A methadone turkey was worse than coming off heroin.

One of the security guards drove her to the clinic, which was just outside Salt Lake City, in Midvale. She got in line with the rest of the nod squad and waited her turn. This clinic was more thorough than some, requiring a physical exam as well as the standard drug screen. Not even rock stars were exempt from the piss test, apparently.

She peed in the cup, endured the exam, and answered the questions without much interest until the counselor asked when her last period had been. She thought back. They'd been in Little Rock which was—

Nine weeks ago?

She collected her doses, pills now, much easier to manage on the road. On the way back to the Delta Center she had the driver stop at a drugstore, where she purchased a pregnancy test.

She tried to stay calm, reminding herself that opiates screwed up a menstrual cycle. Back when she was using she'd hardly ever had a period. She still skipped them sometimes, but never thought much about it since prior to the last couple of months she'd never had much sex.

They got caught in traffic and she'd worked herself into a near panic by the time she arrived at the amphitheater. The show began at seven, so she had barely enough time to change her clothes and gobble an energy bar before they were due onstage.

Her performance was a little stilted and afterward Quinn raised his eyebrows at her. "Not your best," he said. "Are you feeling all right?"

"Anyone can have an off night," she huffed, collecting her backpack containing the pregnancy test.

"Sure they can, but you're shaking like a leaf." He draped his leather jacket over her shoulders. "Maybe you're coming down with something."

She caught a whiff of his lime aftershave as she slid her arms into the jacket. It didn't soothe her like it usually did and she escaped to the bathroom, where she pulled the test out of her bag, unwrapped the plastic stick, then followed the directions.

She was waiting for the result, which seemed torturously slow in coming, when the bathroom door opened. She snatched up the stick and shoved it in her pocket.

It was Quinn. "Don't you ever knock?" she snarled.

He glared back at her. "You're in a charming mood," he remarked. "There's a crew here from *Spin*." He stood aside to let her pass. "You're definitely coming down with something," he added. "You're white as a sheet."

She suffered through an interview for the rock magazine, posed for a few photos, and hurried back to the bathroom as soon as she could escape. This time she leaned against the door before rooting through her backpack for the white stick.

It wasn't there. Then, she remembered. It was in the jacket pocket, where she'd shoved it. She'd taken it off for the photo shoot and left it on a chair in the greenroom.

She hastened back there. Quinn was just pulling on the jacket as he gave Stan a few last-minute instructions. "Those Sennheisers have a special case," he was saying. "I don't care who packed them. If I find them in that condition again, somebody's getting fired." Helplessly she watched Quinn put his hands in his pockets, still lecturing Stan, then glance down.

She saw that he had the white plastic stick in his hand. He held it up, perplexed, examined it, then stared at it. Stared hard, for a long time. A *very* long time.

When he finally looked up at her, his eyes were like saucers.

"I can't fucking believe this is happening," Quinn said later, when they were in their room. They were sitting side by side on the bed, both staring straight ahead at the wall.

"I'm sorry," Shan said woodenly. She didn't know what else to say, because she couldn't believe it either. They went through more condoms than a brothel, but they had slipped just a few times. They should have known better, both of them, because they both knew that one little slip could change everything. And now it had.

"Nobody to blame but ourselves. We've been irresponsible," he said, his gaze not moving from the wall. "I'm usually Jimmy on the spot, too. How could I have been so careless?"

"I'm sorry," Shan said again, more softly.

He shifted his gaze to the ceiling. "Can't it ever just be easy?" he inquired, seemingly addressing some higher power. "Why does everything we do have to get so fucking complicated?"

"I'm sorry," she repeated, nearly whimpering this time.

He swung around to face her. *"Stop telling me you're sorry!"* he shouted.

Shan snatched up a pillow and flung it at him, then dashed into the bathroom and threw up. She flushed the toilet, then sank onto the floor. She heard the door open. "Go away," she choked.

Instead she heard water running. Then he knelt to press a cool cloth against her forehead. "I'm the one who's sorry," he said. "I didn't mean to yell. I'm just—shocked, I guess. Confused."

"Freaked. Me, too."

"I know," he said and wiped her face with the washcloth.

She felt her stomach beginning to roil again. "Get out, Q." He shook his head, but she gave him a push. "Please? I don't want you to see me this way."

"I'm the one who made you that way," he pointed out and stayed put even when she threw up, gathering her hair into a tail to hold it away from her face.

Afterward she staggered out of the bathroom to collapse on the bed. "I guess it's morning sickness," she groaned, "but why is it happening now?"

"It *is* morning, technically," Quinn said and when Shan looked at the clock, she saw it was nearly five o'clock. They'd been sitting there for hours, just staring at the wall. "We should get some sleep," he added and she crawled under the covers obediently, curling into a fetal position. When Quinn got in beside her he rolled over so that his back was touching her. The little bit of contact comforted her and she fell asleep.

When she woke a couple of hours later, she was alone. It felt cold in the bed without him and she could see him sitting by the window, smoking. It was just getting light and he had the window cracked, holding the cigarette outside so none of the smoke escaped into the room. "What are you doing?" she asked.

"Thinking things over," he said and ground out his cigarette. "Mulling the possibilities. There are a few different ways we can handle this."

"Are there?"

His head swiveled. She knew he was looking at her, but all she could see was his silhouette, dark and dense and blank as the proverbial slate. "I think so. Unless you've already made up your mind." He paused. "Have you?"

"An abortion," she said. The word felt harsh, unfamiliar on her tongue. "What else?"

"Is that what you want?"

"What choice do I have?"

"Of course there's a choice. For both of us, I hope. There's abortion," he conceded, "or adoption, I suppose. Or we could . . ." He paused again. ". . . have it."

His words unlocked a torrent of emotions inside her. Fear. Doubt. Disbelief. And, deep down, a paralyzing flash of possibility that she immediately quashed. "You can't be serious."

"Don't tell me you haven't at least considered it." She shook her head, staring at him mutely. He rose and came to the bed, climbing in beside her. "I know we've never talked about it, but I always assumed we would have one. Not this soon, but eventually."

She remained silent, because she didn't know what to say. She lived their relationship one day at a time, without much contemplation of the future. It was the way she lived the rest of her life, too. All those NA meetings, she supposed. They'd left their mark, not to mention the fact that hoping and dreaming and planning—these weren't things she did. In the past, they'd mostly led to disappointment.

"It would be difficult," he was saying. "We have another two months on tour, so you'd have to deal with being knocked up on the road. We have to start on the new album as soon as we get back, then there'll be another tour and, somewhere in the middle of that, we have to find a house. The timing really couldn't be worse, but we'll make it work, if it's what you want." He caught her hand, squeezed it. "Is it? You said you wanted a family. Would it make you happy?"

Happy? She didn't know, had never thought about having a child with Quinn in concrete terms. It seemed like something impossible, a dream so far out of her reach that to ponder it would lacerate, and she'd firmly blocked any such musings before they could begin to bloom into fantasy or, even worse, hope.

And she wouldn't fantasize about it now, because there were other considerations. She pulled her hand out of his grasp. "It doesn't matter," she said sharply, "because I'm a methadone addict, Quinn. Did you forget about that?"

He shook his head. "No, I didn't forget."

"Then how can you even suggest this?"

"It isn't as cut and dried as that. There are options. We should see an OB and find out what they are." She shook her head, but he caught her face between his hands, stopping her. "Just think about it, that's all I'm asking. Wait to decide until we find out what we're dealing with."

She shrugged, dropped her eyes, then realized she was looking down at her pregnant stomach.

Quinn put Jeff on it, had him line up an emergency appointment with the best obstetrician in Casper, where they were bound for their next show, and the OB, Dr. Benner, spoke candidly to them. "If you choose to have the baby, I wouldn't advise trying to detox while you're pregnant," he said. "It can cause a miscarriage, if you do it too fast. Have you tried before?"

"Yes," Shan admitted, the old shame welling up inside. "I haven't been able to kick this last dose."

"Then don't try to do it now," he said. "All you'll do is put yourself under duress. That's more dangerous for your baby than the methadone is."

"But won't the 'done hurt the baby?"

"Not if you're careful. Stabilization is what's important during pregnancy, not dose reduction. If you deliver, though, the concern will be neonatal abstinence syndrome."

"Meaning the baby could be addicted to methadone?" Quinn asked. Shan went cold.

"Right. There's no way of knowing if that's the case until the baby is born."

"What's the least I can be on?" Shan interjected. "You know, for that not to happen?"

"It's hard to say. Some people are on eighty milligrams and it doesn't affect their child. Others are on ten and it does. It's individual and might change over the course of your pregnancy. You'll need to be monitored closely and, after you deliver, the baby will have to be watched for signs of withdrawal."

Shan thought about what a methadone turkey was like. The sweats and shakes and nausea. The utter exhaustion, feeling like she'd collapse if she didn't get some rest, but not being able to sleep no matter what she did. The anxiety that made her want to crawl out of her skin, the physical sensitivity that made everything hurt. Then she thought about a newborn baby going through that.

"I want an abortion," she said without looking at Quinn. "Can we schedule it today?"

chapter 40

Dr. Benner didn't perform abortions and apparently neither did anyone else in the state of Wyoming, so he referred her to a clinic in Nebraska, where their next show was scheduled. She and Quinn flew to Omaha, then rented a car and drove to Bellevue, where the facility was located.

First she had to undergo counseling. It was state law, Dr. Benner had told her, warning her that the session would likely rely heavily on information intended to discourage her from having the procedure. He turned out to be right, but the stream of propaganda declined sharply once she told the counselor about her methadone dependency.

"We don't advocate abortion here," the counselor told them, "but we recognize that it's sometimes the best choice. In some cases, life can be a curse instead of a gift." Apparently, the right to life carried less weight when the fetus in question could turn into a junkie baby.

She was required to wait twenty-four hours before they'd perform the abortion, so they checked into a motel near the clinic. Quinn was with her every second, even went to the counseling session with her, but he remained uncharacteristically quiet. She could barely bring herself to meet his eyes, they looked so troubled and guilt ridden and there was something sorrowful there that she didn't want to see.

The morning of the procedure she woke to find him sitting up in bed, watching her. "What if you never get off methadone?" he asked, once he saw she was awake.

She blinked. "What?"

"A lot of people never kick it," he continued, "and you have to think about what that would mean. You said you wanted a family. If you can't get clean and you won't get pregnant if you aren't . . ." He paused, then shrugged. "What happens to that dream, angel?"

She stared at him for a moment, then got up and went into the bathroom without answering.

An hour later they were in the waiting room at the clinic. When they called her name Shan rose to follow the nurse practitioner. She was at the door leading to the procedure room when Quinn was suddenly at her side, gripping her hand.

"You know that I'm with you, don't you, angel?" he said. "I might have made a different choice if it was up to me, but . . . I'm with you. You aren't alone." Again she saw that look in his eyes and she experienced a pain deep inside when she realized that what she was seeing was grief.

He kissed her and she dropped his hand, then followed the nurse into a little cubicle. She undressed, donned a gown, and was led into the procedure room. The nurse helped her climb onto the table and spread the paper sheet over her lap, then Shan lay back and stared up at the ceiling. It was very white, the fluorescent bulbs glaring, and she wondered why they didn't make it a little easier on the eyes since she assumed most of the patients in this room would be flat on their backs.

The doctor came in next, a tall woman with curly dark hair shot through with silver. "Hi, Shan. I'm Dr. Greene. Do you have any questions about the procedure you're having today?"

Shan mumbled a no. The counselor had been more than thorough in her description, but the doctor still went on to explain the intricacies of the method she'd be using to terminate the pregnancy, something called first trimester suction aspiration.

Shan let her mind wander during the discourse, remembering what Quinn had said that morning. What if he was right, if she never did get off methadone? Did that mean she'd never have a child, never be a mother? And what would that mean for her relationship with him?

It had never occurred to her that he might want children. She knew he liked them, he adored his niece and nephew, but she'd still been shocked when he suggested keeping this baby.

What would it be like, she wondered, to create a child with Quinn and raise it with him? They'd be a family, a real family, bound by blood and love and progeny. For the first time she let herself imagine the child they might have. A little boy who looked like him, maybe, or a little girl. She might have dark hair, like hers, but her eyes—they'd be blue as a summer sky, just like Quinn's.

I'd name her Abby, she thought, and tears welled up in her eyes at the thought of her mother.

The nurse handed her a tissue. "Are you all right?" she asked gently.

Shan nodded, but she wasn't sure that she was. She felt something rupture in her chest, actually felt it, her heart breaking. Her stomach was roiling, too. Maybe it was morning sickness or maybe it was the weird, wondrous thing that was suddenly causing her to expand from the inside out. The thing that, very soon, would cease to exist.

The doctor turned back from the sink, now enumerating the postoperative instructions. "You should rest for the remainder of today, avoid any heavy lifting, and no swimming or tub baths for the next week," she concluded, snapping on a pair of gloves. "Is there someone here to drive you home?"

Shan dashed her hand across her eyes. "Yes, my—"

Boyfriend, she was going to say, when she was struck by what an inadequate word that was to describe what Quinn meant to her. He was her best friend, her partner. Her muse. Her lover. Her family, now more than ever, fused to her by the small, fragile bump in her belly. A sob escaped her.

The doctor's smile faded. "Are you sure you want to do this, Shan?"

Shan opened her mouth to say yes but her eyes filled again. Then she was sobbing, so hard it felt like she'd never stop.

Quinn was drinking a cup of lukewarm coffee and staring out the window when Shan came back into the waiting room. He took one look at her red, ravaged face and leapt to his feet. "Are you all right?"

She shook her head. "Get me out of here," she choked. "Now. Please."

Wrapping an arm around her, he guided her out of the clinic, across the parking lot, and into the rental car. When he got in beside her, she was doubled over with both arms wrapped around her middle. "It'll be all right, angel."

"I hope it will," she said, "because I didn't do it."

He froze. "You didn't?"

"No."

"You're still pregnant?" He looked stunned.

"Yes."

He was silent for a long, long moment, so long that Shan's eyes filled again. "Oh no! You're upset. I'm sorry, Q. I didn't mean to—"

He held up both hands. *"Stop!"* he said. "I'm *not* upset. I just need a chance to—to catch up with you." He put his hands over his eyes and rubbed them, hard. "Why didn't you do it?" he asked, after a moment.

Her face twisted and her arms tightened around her stomach. "I want her."

"Her?"

She shrugged. "Or him. Whoever it is. It was different before, when she . . . he wasn't real to me. Now he . . . she is. She's ours and I want her."

"Oh." He was silent for another moment, then he lowered his hands from his eyes. When he did, she saw they were beginning to shine. "I guess we're having a baby, then."

Then he was pulling her into his arms, squeezing her so hard she could barely breathe. A minute later they were peeling out of the parking lot, speeding back to the motel. Once they got back to the room she pulled the T-shirt over his head, unbuckled his belt while he pushed her back on the bed and slid in beside her to embrace her and kiss her and fondle her.

Then he stopped. "Can we? I mean, will it hurt anything?"

"Oh no," she breathed. "I mean, no it won't. And yes, yes we can." Then she stopped talking, because he was inside of her.

Afterward his hand stole between her legs, fitting snugly over her vagina. She loved it when he did that. It was such a possessive gesture, like he owned that part of her.

"So," he said, "should we get married?"

"Fuck!" Quinn tore a sheet of paper out of his notebook, balled it up, and threw it on the floor of the bus. Sugaree raised her head, alarmed, and he scratched her behind her ears so she'd know it wasn't her he was mad at.

"Why is this so hard?" Shan groaned. The rest of their bandmates were up front playing poker, but they were in the master suite. They'd been there for hours, trying to write their vows.

"I don't know, but it is. Why can't we just say 'I do' and be done with it?"

"We can," Shan said. "I just thought it would make the ceremony more personal if we wrote the vows ourselves, since we have to get married in Vegas. We don't have to do it, though, if you don't want to."

The scowl had faded from Quinn's face. "We don't *have* to get married in Vegas, angel. It was just a suggestion. We can't put together a big shindig until after the tour and you wanted to do it sooner rather than later because of the baby, so I thought it made sense. We can change our plans, though, if you—"

"No," she said quickly. She wasn't about to rock the boat. She still couldn't believe that he wanted to marry her. "It's okay. It doesn't have to be a big thing."

"Well, it *is* a big thing." He regarded her thoughtfully for a moment, then, "Maybe we're going about this the wrong way. You and I aren't poets, after all." He climbed off the bed and left the compartment. When he came back, he had the Angel in one hand and his Casio in the other. "We're songwriters. Let's write a song."

They were married three weeks later, at the Graceland Wedding Chapel on the Las Vegas strip, and the place felt as packed as one of their concerts. All their bandmates were present, as well as Denise and Oda. Quinn's mother and stepfather were there along with Ron with his family, and also Jeff, Stan, and the assorted other techs and crew from the tour. Lorraine flew in for the occasion and even Fred the driver was present. He'd volunteered to take charge of Sugaree who was there, too, wagging madly at the end of her leash.

Shan smoothed her skirt as she waited behind a bower of silk roses for the canned wedding march to commence. Her dress was more traditional than the venue, an ethereal white frock that floated around her like mist. She wore no veil or jewelry, just the dainty engagement ring Quinn had presented her with, a perfect one-carat, heart-cut diamond nestled inside a swirl of green-gold garnets exactly the color of her eyes. "It's not too fancy or ostentatious," he'd said when he put it on her finger, "but it's unique. Beautiful. Special, just like you are, angel."

When the music began, Shan took the arm of the Elvis impersonator who'd be walking her down the aisle. Quinn had insisted upon that detail, much to the horror of his mother, his sister-in-law, and Denise, but Shan understood and wholeheartedly approved. They lived in the rock 'n' roll world, after all. How could they get married in Vegas and not have the King in attendance?

Shan's eyes went to Quinn as she made her way to the front of the chapel. He was handsome in a white cotton suit with a white, open-necked shirt and his eyes shone as he looked at her. Her heart expanded, felt too big for her chest, and she wondered just how it was possible to be so filled with love and still have room for the baby growing inside of her.

The ceremony was brief, to the point, and before long it was time for their song. They'd been planning to sing it a cappella, but Dave surprised them both by volunteering to provide the musical accompaniment. Shan could tell that Quinn was deeply affected by the offer. His friendship with Dave hadn't been the same since the revelation that they were a couple and she knew it was a sincere effort on Dave's part to extend the olive branch, one that they were touched and grateful to accept.

When Dave heard the song, he decided it needed to be played on a twelve-string guitar, which had a prettier, sweeter sound than a six-string. Quinn concurred, requesting that he use the Fullerton that had belonged to Shan's mother. "That way she'll be there with us, too," he told her and Shan could only nod, overcome by this thoughtfulness.

They turned to face each other as the opening chords of the song commenced and Quinn began to sing as haunting, lilting tremolos filled the chapel.

I told you I was ready
Now here with you I stand
I knew someday I'd be here
Prepared to take your hand
I found what I was missing
When you appeared that day
My perfect mate, my woman
You took my breath away

They'd created their individual verses separately. It was the first time Shan had heard them, the words he'd composed just for her, and her own voice wavered as she sang the words she'd written to him.

You're the one I've always wanted
My key, my heart, my home
You opened up my silence
And now I'm not alone
We're a family together
And it's time to take a leap
Into a happy ending
To have, to love, to keep

Even Elvis looked misty as they began the chorus, which they'd practiced over and over and over, until their voices blended so flawlessly that it was impossible to hear where Shan's singing ended and Quinn's began.

You're the one
We sing in perfect harmony
You're the one
The only perfect one for me

"I now pronounce you husband and wife," the chaplain said when they finished singing. Their friends and family burst into a wave of applause and even Denise was smiling as Quinn pulled Shan into his arms and she rose up on her toes to kiss him, the man she'd never thought she could have.

chapter 41

"This studio is coming right along," Dan said. "It's going to be primo, dude. You're putting in a drum booth, though, right?"

"Of course. A vocal booth, too. I'll treat that end acoustically," Quinn said, pointing at the southern tip of the room. "That way, we'll get surgical sound there, but it will be livelier here."

"Got your equipment picked out already?"

"Three ADATs and a Yamaha O2R," Quinn said. "That'll give us twenty-four tracks. Shan wants a Lexicon reverb, too."

"You must be working like a dog to get it finished so fast," Dan said.

"It's a welcome diversion. I need an occasional break from 'I'm so fat.'" Quinn's ear caught the sound of ponderous footsteps. He grinned. "Here comes the fat girl now."

Shan emerged from the stairway. She looked hot and irritable. And huge, Quinn thought, his eyes drifting to her stomach, barely covered by the bulky Indian dress she wore.

"The burgers are on," she announced and noticed Quinn looking at her. "What?"

"You look like a Weeble," he said cheerfully.

Shan made a pained sound, turning away, and Dan chuckled as Quinn grasped her arm. "Oh, come on, babe. You're nine months pregnant. Nobody expects you to be light on your feet. Can you watch the burgers?" he asked Dan, pulling Shan onto his lap and waiting until he went upstairs before speaking again. "Tell me what's wrong, angel."

She shook her head. "Come on," he said. "I can tell something's up."

She hesitated for a moment. "I feel strange today."

"How do you mean, strange?"

"Strange, as in not normal. Strange, as in not right. Just *strange*." She frowned. "Stop looking at me like that."

"Like what?"

"Like I'm a lab specimen." She grimaced. "I can't wait until this pregnancy is over with, so you can stop acting as if it was a science project."

"Do you want to call Dr. Taylor?" he asked, ignoring her editorial commentary.

"No." She shook her head. "Not until I'm sure something important is happening."

"Maybe we ought to, just to be safe."

"*No*, I said." She struggled to rise and he obligingly teetered her into an upright position.

She stomped up the stairs and Quinn followed, experiencing the thrill of possession that he felt every time he looked around their new house, where they'd been living less than two months. It was a graceful, Tudor-style villa in Mission Cove, a seaside hamlet about an hour south of LA. The place was spacious but not huge, nothing like the palatial estates that his parents and brother lived in. The property was breathtaking, though, right on the water, the house perched on a craggy overlook that gave the illusion of an island, with nothing but water and sky as far as the eye could see. It was everything he'd wanted, but the basement was really the pièce de résistance as far as he was concerned, a vast area that couldn't have made a more perfect studio space if he'd designed it himself.

Shan seemed dazzled by the house and he knew she never thought she'd be living in such a place. It was a palace compared to what she was used to, with five bedrooms, three bathrooms, a pool, a hot tub, and a guest house as well as a boathouse for the powerboat he planned to buy. He often caught her wandering from room to room inspecting them with a frown, like she didn't believe it really belonged to them.

Right now she was frowning at him instead. "I know my own body," she insisted, "and *you* don't know anything, because *you've* never been pregnant."

Quinn decided that silence was the best course of action. She was prone to these little fits of temper lately. Must be hormonal, he speculated, following her into the kitchen to get a beer before joining Dan on the deck, where he could bitch about the trials of having a pregnant wife to a sympathetic listener.

Denise was in there, making a salad. "I can finish this," she said, as Shan pulled out a knife. "Why don't you get off your feet?"

"It's better when I move around," Shan confessed and Denise made a sound of sympathy.

"You poor thing. Quinn, I hope you're doing everything you can to help her through this."

"Whatever she'll allow," Quinn said, opening the fridge, "but my very existence seems to annoy her of late." He treated Denise with kid gloves these days, although she was meaner to him than ever. He swallowed her rudeness now, accepting it as his penance.

"You're annoying in general," she concurred, "but less so than usual lately."

"Thanks," he said and meant it, since it was about the nicest thing she'd ever said to him.

"He's so fascinated with your pregnancy," she said to Shan. "I have to confess, he's surprising me."

"I can't see why. He's fascinated with anything scientific. I'm sure when the moment comes, he won't even talk to me. He'll have his head in between my legs, videotaping the grand entrance of his offspring. I've forbidden cameras in the delivery room, but you'll wait until I'm too delirious from pain to care and pull the Sony out of your pocket, won't you?" She scowled at Quinn as she tossed a handful of chopped chives on the salad. "Can one of you bring this out?"

Denise took it and went outside. Shan took up the knife again to slice some tomatoes, but instead gasped, gripping the edge of the counter. "What is it?" Quinn asked immediately.

She opened her mouth to reply but a second spasm seemed to strike, this time accompanied by a gush of water. She looked down. "I think my water broke," she said, as he gaped at the flood.

"You think we could maybe call the doctor now?" He grabbed the phone. "I can't believe how fucking stubborn you are." She moaned and he dropped the phone to catch her in his arms.

She clung to him, panting. "We'd better go to the hospital."

He didn't answer, just snatched the car keys off the rack. When he turned back, she was halfway to the bedroom. "What are you doing?"

"Changing my clothes. Would you wipe up the floor?"

"But—" The door closed in his face. For a split second, he considered physically dragging her to the car, but as quickly as the thought occurred he abandoned it. One had to be patient when one's pregnant wife went into labor. Clearly, they become irrational.

He grabbed a roll of paper towels and did as he'd been told. He was just straightening up when Shan emerged from the bedroom. She'd put on another tentlike dress, one he'd bought her during the last tour. It was a mass of tie-dye colors and she loved it but refused to wear it once she'd grown big, stating that it made her look like a weather balloon at a Dead show. He'd chuckled and agreed, but it pleased him to see her in it now.

"The food is getting cold," Denise said, coming in from the deck just as Shan hunched over with another moan. "Oh my God! Is she in labor! She's in labor! *Why are you just standing there?*" she shrieked at Quinn.

Quinn hurried toward the side door, almost colliding with Dan as he came in through the sliders. "What's all the yelling about?"

"The baby's coming," Quinn heard Denise say as he headed for the garage to get Shan's Jeep. He hated it and would have preferred to go in his new Testarossa, but she hadn't been able to get in or out of that for weeks now. He pulled it around front and jumped out to help her, but Denise was already easing her inside. He danced impatiently, sure he should be doing something, then ran back around to the driver's side. As he did, he heard Denise issuing orders to Dan.

"Go turn off the grill," she was instructing him as she squeezed into the back seat, "and bring Sugaree inside. Then lock up the house—you know where the spare key is, right?—and meet us at the hospital."

"I can take it from here," he said to Denise. "You can ride with Dan, if you want."

"Get moving," she told him and he frowned, but put the Jeep in gear and sped up the long driveway. He could hear Denise murmuring to Shan, encouraging her to breathe, reassuring her that everything was going to be all right, all the things he was supposed to be saying. He grabbed the car phone, plugged in the speed dial for Dr. Taylor, and reported the situation, pausing when asked how the contractions were spaced.

"Six minutes," Denise said. "I'm timing them."

"Six minutes," he snapped and hung up after being assured that Dr. Taylor would be paged immediately. He reached for Shan's hand, but found Denise already holding it. "Keep your mind on the road," she said.

"It *is* my wife and also my kid, you know, Denise," he said, braking for a red light. "I think I'm entitled to touch them."

"Right now your job is to get them safely to the hospital," Denise said, "so why don't you just shut up and drive?"

He bit the inside of his lip, actually bit it, hurting himself in an effort to suppress the angry retort that sprang to his lips. "Deep breaths," Denise was saying to Shan, and he took a few himself. "Can I do anything to make you more comfortable?"

Shan choked out a shaky laugh. "Do you think you could give birth to this child for me?"

"I would, if I could," Quinn said as they pulled up in front of the hospital.

"You couldn't stand the pain," Denise said. "No man could."

He considered a variety of responses, then a yelp from his wife drove Denise's obnoxiousness right out of his mind. By the time they arrived at the hospital, Shan was white, the look on her face was beginning to resemble agony, and he felt a tendril of panic invade his stomach as he jumped out of the car.

Shan got her feet to the ground, then made it no farther. "I don't think I can walk," she gasped. Quinn continued to tug at her arm mindlessly.

Denise hung over the seat. "Get a wheelchair," she hissed and he bolted inside.

When Shan was installed in the chair, he dashed alongside until he was unceremoniously halted at the door to the birthing suite. "But that's my wife," he insisted. He watched her roll away and, for a surreal instant, was transported back in time to the moment he'd watched the doors swing shut behind her at the clinic in New York. She looked defenseless, just as she had then.

"We have to get you scrubbed and suited," a cheerful orderly said, nudging him into an adjoining room. Quinn fell into the hastily provided scrubs and was heading for the door when the orderly blocked his way. "You need to tie back your hair."

Quinn regarded him in a blind rage. "My wife is in there giving birth and I'd like to be there when she does, if it's all the same to you."

"I'm sure you would," the orderly replied, still annoyingly cheerful, "but first we need you to tie back your hair."

Quinn considered punching the jovial smile right off the orderly's face, but instead pulled his hair into a ponytail and installed the cap on his head. Next he was instructed to wash his hands with foul-smelling disinfectant, then he was finally allowed to join his wife.

"I can always tell a first-timer," the orderly said. "You'll be fine. I'll take care of you. I even have smelling salts," he added, "in case you pass out. Lots of first-timers do, you know."

Quinn ignored him, catching Shan's hand and gazing tenderly into her eyes.

"Where the hell did you disappear to?" she groaned.

"They made me change—" he began and she suddenly clamped down. He winced, his hand sending out darts of pain where her nails dug in.

"I'm so scared," she whispered, and he pressed his lips against the back of her hand.

Just then Dr. Taylor bustled in, red faced and smiling, and disappeared behind the sheet. "Six centimeters," he reported and the assisting nurse beamed at Shan.

"Looks like you're in a hurry to get this over with, Mrs. Marshall."

Quinn blinked. Nobody ever called Shan that. Most people used her first name. She still went by her maiden name professionally, too, but guessed it *was* her name now. He'd never really thought about it. "Mrs. Marshall" had a nice ring to it. In fact, he liked it. A lot.

Mrs. Marshall let out an agonized scream and what followed was three and a half hours of the most excruciating ordeal he'd ever witnessed another human being experience. More than once his gorge rose and once, when he saw a gush of red between her legs, he felt the blood draining from his own head.

The cheerful orderly was right there. "Do you need to sit down, Mr. Marshall?"

"No." Quinn shook his hand off. "I don't faint at the sight of blood, for Chrissake." But it was Shan's blood and emanating from a place he was intimately familiar with. The thought of that soft aperture, which he'd caressed so tenderly and so often, being stretched wide enough to permit the passage of a baby was causing his own body to contract with sympathy pains.

He tried to imagine something similar happening to himself and the only comparison he could come up with was passing a turd the size of a butternut squash. A big one, maybe some kind of hybrid. He gasped and redoubled his admonitions to breathe.

During a brief respite she fell back gasping and he disengaged one cramped hand from her grip to wipe the sweat from her forehead. "I'm sorry," he whispered. "You must hate me."

She stared at him. "Why?"

"For talking you into this," he said. "It's all my fault."

"Shut up, Q. Just *shut up!*" Her groan turned into a gasp, then to a scream that was a higher decibel level than any she'd attained thus far. And, in its wake, another, smaller cry.

He raised his head. Was she screaming out the other end? How was that possible? "What—" he began, but broke off when Shan shrieked again.

Dr. Taylor was smiling. "It's a girl," he announced. "Would you like to cut the cord?"

Quinn gaped at him. He'd been so wrapped up in his wife that he'd nearly lost sight of the reason they were there. He'd even forgotten to pull the Sony out of his pocket, where he'd craftily concealed it.

He released Shan's hand for the first time in almost four hours and took the scissors. He severed the cord, craning his head to get a look at his daughter. She didn't look like much, just a bloody little mass, but he could glimpse a tiny foot waving in the air.

"Is she all right?" Shan cried, tensing again as she prepared to deliver the placenta. "Goddamn it, Q, *is she all right?*"

"I think so." He squinted over Dr. Taylor's shoulder. They were hosing off the baby and he could hear a nurse calling out the points of the Apgar scores as they foot printed her.

It took less than a minute, then they were placing the baby in Shan's arms. She was covered with goop, despite the hosing, and chunks of . . . of . . . *whatever.*

He wrinkled his nose. It sure wasn't like the movies, where the glowing new mother was handed a clean white bundle. They always talked about the sweet smell, too, but this baby didn't smell sweet. She smelled kind of rank, in fact. Shan wasn't glowing, either. She looked like hell.

"Oh, look at her," Shan gasped. "She's perfect. Look at her, Q!"

He looked.

And his heart turned over.

It was a little, tiny person, it really was, with fingers and toes and even infinitesimal toenails. He held out a finger and watched as a miniature fist curled around it. Her hair was dark, dark fuzz that looked like it was going to be curly and, even through the goop, he could see the light clear pink of her rosebud mouth.

"Look what we made," Shan said and her voice was full of wonder.

When Shan woke a few hours later, Quinn was examining their daughter with his science project eye. "She looks just like you, angel," he said, when he saw she was awake.

"Gimme!" She held her arms out for her daughter. "Happy birthday, Abby."

Quinn shook his head as he handed the baby over. "She doesn't look like an Abby."

"We agreed," she reminded him. "I want to name her after my mother."

"But she looks like *you*." When he looked up, he saw that she was frowning at him and he shrugged. "Look, I get it. You want to name her after the most important woman in your life. I guess I want to name her after the most important woman in mine."

As he watched, she melted. "That's sweet, Q. But we can't call her Shan Junior."

"No, but maybe she shouldn't be Abby Junior, either. She deserves her own name."

They were both quiet for a moment, regarding their perfect child. "She's so little, " Shan said, touching the baby's hair. She had a lot of it and it was fuzzy and soft.

"A little angel," Quinn agreed. "Maybe that's what we ought to call her."

"Another Angel?"

"Well, we've already got two of those hanging around. How about Angelica?"

"Angelica Abby O'Hara Marshall?" she said and considered for a moment. "Angel Abby. Yes, that's it. Good call, Q."

"I love you," he said suddenly and, when she looked up he saw she did glow, after all. "Mrs. Marshall," he finished, and kissed her.

chapter 42

Shan had been fanatically cautious during her pregnancy, eating nutritious food, getting plenty of rest and exercise, which wasn't always easy while they were touring, and committing to natural childbirth. She tried to do everything right, be an absolutely perfect expectant mother, even prayed to a god she didn't believe in to atone for the methadone she was ingesting every morning.

At first she thought it worked, because the baby wasn't born withdrawing. She was small, just over five pounds, but possessed a rosy skin tone once the ravages of birth faded. They were relieved beyond measure, but Dr. Taylor still advised keeping her under observation.

And, when Angelica was three days old, she began to scream. It was different from her usual crying, a jagged, pitiful, high-pitched squall. Then the tremors started, the sweating and diarrhea and vomiting. They moved her to the neonatal intensive care unit, where it was confirmed that she was suffering from methadone withdrawal.

She remained in the hospital for weeks after her birth, sequestered in the special section of the unit devoted to drug-addicted infants. It was a dark, somber place, quiet as a tomb except when one of the babies was crying, which was often, the shrill, piercing wail of the addicted.

"These newborns are hard to console," one of the special care nurses told them. "They're physically sick, like having a bad flu. *You* know," she said pointedly to Shan. Quinn bristled, but Shan nodded meekly, her lower lip trembling. "They're jittery and they generally don't sleep well, either. They need quiet, a dark and calm environment, and they need to be held and comforted a lot. That's what you can do for your daughter," she added, to both of them.

So they did. They held her and soothed her and sang to her. Shan learned infant massage, stroking and rubbing the tiny body tenderly. She bathed her when she perspired, then swaddled her in soft blankets and rocked her, for hours sometimes.

Still the baby screamed. She screamed and screamed and screamed. It made Quinn feel like crawling out of his own skin, sometimes, but Shan seemed immune to it. She was tireless in her ministering and never once complained, like she deserved to pay penance for her baby's misery.

It was an attitude clearly held by some of the staff who looked at her like she was scum. He'd expected better treatment, since addicted newborns were what the place specialized in, but he didn't even want to imagine the things these people had seen.

Then child protective services showed up and it caught both of them off guard. Apparently it was standard procedure when it was established that a newborn had drugs in her system, but Shan was hysterical, even after assurances that their intention was not to take their baby away. They'd be assigned a case worker, though. Strictly routine, the investigator told them, but it would have been nice to have gotten a fucking warning.

Angelica was a fussy eater, which was usual for babies suffering from neonatal abstinence syndrome, and it was another blow to Shan when the same nurse advised against breast feeding. "There would be traces of methadone in your milk," the nurse informed her, "and she doesn't need that, not when she's trying to detox. It's healthier for her if she goes on the bottle."

When Quinn consulted Dr. Taylor, he unequivocally disagreed. "That's absolutely not true. Breast feeding is the healthiest alternative. It will give your daughter the antibodies she needs and it's fine if there are minute traces of methadone in the milk. It might even help with the withdrawal."

When Quinn communicated that information to Shan, she shook her head. "I won't do it, not if there's even the slightest chance that I'm toxic for her."

Toxic? Christ. She was stretched tighter than a snare head and his role, he supposed, was to absorb some of it. He'd felt like he'd had quite a bit of practice with that, since she'd been as irritable toward the end of her pregnancy as the baby was now. At least then they'd been working on the new album—and fighting with her about the songs, yelling at her during the recording sessions was helpful, for him at least. It relieved some of his own tension and he knew Shan understood it. That was part of their relationship; it was what they did, and the normalcy of arguing over the work helped get them through that nerve-wracking time.

But now he had no outlet. She had him to take it out on and he could tolerate that, to a point. Patience wasn't his strength, though, and before long he could feel the pressure building up to an explosion.

Shan had a room adjacent to the neonatal intensive care unit and she was at the hospital 24/7, one hundred percent focused on Angelica. She hadn't touched her guitar in weeks and he thought that might have something to do with her anxiety, so the next time he went home he retrieved the Angel.

"Play to her," he ordered and, when she did, it seemed to help. Whether it was a case of music soothing the savage beast, in this case a detoxing infant, or because it calmed Shan, which in turn settled the baby, he wasn't sure. All he knew was that the music comforted all three of them. It was his turn to hold his daughter and he did it against his bare chest, skin to skin with a blanket spread over her back, something the charge nurse referred to as a kangaroo hold. Sometimes Shan was the one to hold her that way, nestling her between her breasts and singing with him while he played, but it really seemed that the music her mother made soothed Angelica best.

After nearly four weeks, Dr. Taylor pronounced the baby drug free and they were finally allowed to take her home. When they arrived there, Quinn had a surprise for them.

There was a bassinet for her in their bedroom, a pretty wicker and toile confection that was a gift from Quinn's brother. She would sleep there at night, but Angelica had her own nursery, too, a corner room with north- and east-facing windows. Shan had put an enormous amount of care into its furnishings. No blithe pastels for her child, she decided, instead creating a warm space of earthy, restful colors, greens and tans and blues. An enormous coast live oak grew right outside, its gnarly limbs and dark green leaves swathing the broad windows protectively. Together with the muted green walls, it gave the room the feel of a haven in the trees, a peaceful, calming place for a baby whose road into the world had been a rocky one.

While she'd been at the hospital Quinn had added a few touches of his own: a high border comprised of musical notes, a beautiful layette that reflected the same, even a sweet mobile of musical instruments that played "Rock and Roll Lullaby." Shan gasped when she saw it. "I hope you're not mad," he said hastily. "I know you put a lot of thought into this room, but she loves music, angel. It nourishes her, just like it does us, and she should be surrounded with it."

When Shan turned, her eyes were shining. "It's wonderful," she said. "It's perfect. I love it. I just love it, Q . . . and I love you, too."

He grinned, relieved. He was never quite sure how she'd react to things these days. Those damned hormones again, he noted as he lifted the baby from Shan's arms and checked her.

"Dry," he said, then tucked her into her crib. Once he had her situated, he bent to examine her. He did this often. He was enchanted with his child, so tiny and fragile, beautiful as her mother except for the blue eyes that were just like his own.

Those eyes were now closing and he felt Shan pressing against him. "Let's make love," she whispered. "Please?"

"Really?" He regarded her skeptically. "It's a little soon for sex, isn't it?"

"We can do other stuff," she said archly.

She didn't have to ask twice. They only made it as far as the hallway outside the nursery before he pulled her down on the floor.

Angie continued to be a fussy baby, so they both spent a lot of time rocking and holding and singing, but Shan's relief at having her daughter at home had done much to alleviate her distress. Their life returned to a semblance of normalcy.

Even normal felt strange to her, though. The beautiful house, her new family, her own status as a rising rock star and the seemingly endless stream of money—it felt like she'd somehow landed in someone else's life. She was suspicious of her good fortune and reluctant to embrace it, but when she allowed herself to feel it she was happier than she'd ever been in her life.

Except for the days when the case worker visited, when Shan's anxiety indicator shot up to critical levels. The visits angered Quinn, who didn't understand why they were necessary. Their child was safe, loved, well cared for, and Shan didn't fit the profile of a drug-addict mother. Except for the prescriptive methadone she never touched drugs of any kind. She wouldn't let anyone smoke a cigarette within fifty feet of the baby, for Crissake. She was financially well off, gainfully employed, involved in a stable relationship—what was the fucking problem?

Quinn detested the case worker, an officious bitch named Carolyn Prout who seemed to hold a personal grudge against Shan. The investigator at the hospital had assured them that the visits were a precautionary measure and they'd likely close the case soon, but Ms. Prout kept scheduling visits. He spoke with their pediatrician, who told him that cases like theirs were common. Addicted mothers were considered child abusers, even in cases like Shan's where the drug in question was doctor prescribed.

He even called Dr. Taylor, who was sympathetic. "There's so much focus on perinatal drug use these days, such an increase in fetal alcohol syndrome, crack babies, and so forth, that a lot of people have adopted a zero-tolerance policy. They want to see the mothers off methadone, even though we know it's often not possible or even advisable. There's no point in trying to educate those people," he added, "because, when we try, we hit a brick wall."

Ms. Prout was clearly one of those people and it seemed to Quinn like Shan was being punished for getting help. The woman was mining for a reason to nail them, but after three months of visits to their pristine home, squeaky clean drug tests, and excellent reports from their pediatrician she reluctantly closed the case and they rejoiced to have an unsullied opportunity to enjoy each other and their child.

It was short-lived, as the release of their third album was imminent. It was highly anticipated, Cardinal having poured significant resources into the promotion of *Quinntessence: Questions,* and the band members were gearing up for the tour, another six months on the road.

For the Marshall family, the preparations were more extensive this time. Quinn was working with Jeff to secure another vehicle that didn't need to be as huge as the tour bus, but had to accommodate the two of them, Angelica, Sugaree, and the nanny they were planning to hire. They were interviewing scores of people for that position, each of whom was rejected for one reason or another. Quinn was ruthless in his determination to unearth any flaw, but even the few who passed his muster were nixed by Shan.

"We need a special kind of person. Angie's difficult, sometimes," Shan said as they pored over yet another set of applications.

"She's adorable," Quinn said, bristling. "The most beautiful baby in the world."

"Of course I think that, too," she assured him, because he worshipped his daughter and refused to hear even the slightest criticism, "but she still needs a lot of comforting. I want someone restful and soothing, and very responsible. They need to like dogs, too," she added.

The departure date was looming when Quinn struck on the perfect solution. He made some calls and, a few nights later, their doorbell rang.

"I have a surprise for you," he told Shan.

"Oh?"

"Yes." He took her by the arm, propelled her down the hall, and positioned her in front of the door. "I hired a nanny," he said. "She's here."

Shan's eyes widened and her face went bright red. "*What?*" But he'd flung open the door and her anger was throttled when she saw the bright white smile in the very dark face.

Shan's mouth dropped open and she stared at Quinn. "You hired Oda?"

Oda laughed, a wonderful, deep-belly rumble that Shan didn't realize how much she missed until she heard it, and it broke her paralysis.

"Oh, Q! *You hired Oda!*" she squealed, throwing her arms around her friend.

"You said you wanted somebody soothing, restful, and responsible, and who liked dogs," Quinn said. "I thought it would be good if it was somebody who liked *us*, too. Besides, she makes a mean Bloody Mary."

"And we both figured you wouldn't have any objection to rooming with me again," Oda added with a laugh. Shan hugged her again, beaming over her shoulder at Quinn. *I love you,* she mouthed and he smirked, clearly pleased with himself as he reached for Oda's bag.

They had barely enough time to get Oda settled before it was time to depart. Jeff had engaged a luxury coach with enough sleeping compartments to accommodate them all on the odd occasions when they'd have to spend the night on the bus.

They set off on the road and the band was a little less enthusiastic than they'd been about their previous tours. Dan was never happy to be separated from Denise. Dave had just bought a house in the Hollywood Hills and grumbled about having to leave it. Ty was all hot and heavy with a model he'd begun dating and was glum about his new relationship being put on hold.

Shan was down, too, as they departed, even though she knew Quinn had made an enormous effort to make the trip bearable for her. Their coach was beautiful and she had her best girlfriend on board, not to mention her baby and her dog. They even had driver Fred at the helm, since he'd refused to give up his canine copilot.

The shows were just as packed as the last tour, especially when *Quinntessence: Questions* was released with great fanfare. Once again the media was everywhere and they were interviewed by *Creem*, *Keyboard*, and MTV, but the most exciting press by far was a cover story for *Good Vibrations*. It was one of the biggest music magazines in the world, second only to *Rolling Stone* in the United States. To be so highly featured, Lorraine told them, was a signal of impending superstardom.

During this tour, she'd arranged for them to be joined by Max Archer, one of *Vibration*'s top rock journalists. The reporter and his camera crew dogged them for more than a week, particularly Shan. Although she was uneasy at being the focus of such attention, she capitalized on the opportunity to cast some light on the challenges faced by female musicians.

"So you're a rock feminist?" Archer asked.

"That's not the point," she told him. "Calling me that just makes me a nonman. What I'm saying is that the hard rock landscape needs to be wide open to everyone, not just men, because gender doesn't have anything to do with making music. I'm sick of people acting like testicles are a requirement for playing a hot guitar lick."

"Case in point," he laughed.

"It's about talent, not balls," she said. "Right, Q?"

"Right," Quinn said, but his smile looked forced.

They were in Houston when the issue with the story was messengered to them, arriving the day before it broke on the newsstands. When Quinn pulled it out of the envelope, Shan gasped.

The picture on the cover was of her, only her, clad in tight, faded jeans and a lacy tank, confronting the camera with a challenging stare, hair flying wildly around her face and white Strat shielding her body like a talisman. NO BALLS HERE proclaimed the caption.

"*What?*" Shan said. "That is so *not* the message I was trying to give! And where's everybody else?" Dan didn't reply. Dave shrugged and Ty looked downright annoyed. Even Quinn's face was tight as he flipped open to the story.

"'It's no secret that rock music is under the dominion of men,'" he read aloud. "'From Mick Jagger, Jim Morrison, and Led Zeppelin right up to today's hypermasculine heavy hitters like Guns N' Roses and Mötley Crüe, the male mojo has been an essential ingredient in the hard rock crucible. But Quinntessence has changed all that. Their highbrow fusion of hard rock with a progressive edge, acid jazz, and hard-hitting blues delivered through the dynamic guitar stylings and silvery vocal chops of a supremely talented female rocker has birthed something entirely new, every bit as powerful and aggressive as cock rock, but without the injection of semen. All hail Twat Rock—the new sound of the nineties!'"

Quinn's smile vanished.

"Twat rock?" he said.

He raised his head and looked at her. "*Twat—fucking—rock?*" he repeated in disbelief.

Shan just stared at him, speechless.

chapter 43

"It isn't my fault," Shan insisted later that night when they were in their hotel room.

"You spent the entire fucking week shooting your mouth off about how women never get a decent break in the rock world," Quinn said. "It's no wonder that's what Archer zeroed in on."

"It's true," she declared. "Haven't you always said I should blaze a trail for girl rockers?"

"Yes, but not at the expense of the rest of your band. That article made it sound like we're nothing but your fucking backup, for Chrissake!"

That wasn't entirely true. The piece had devoted considerable space to Quinn's virtuosity on keyboards, his flawless technique, and unique musical vision. Every band member had been singled out for praise; in fact, Dan's expertly articulated drum syncopations were described as ferocious and huge, Dave's inventive, grooving rhythm style was extolled, and Ty was pronounced a master of intricate jazz melody. The article was about Quinntessence as a whole, not just her, although she had to admit that both her musicianship and her opinions were front and center.

"Well, I'm the lead singer," she said. "When they write about Guns N' Roses, they focus on Axl Rose. With Nirvana, it's Kurt Cobain. It's what the media does."

"Guns N' Roses and Nirvana are not categorized as twat rock," he pointed out icily.

"That's because they don't have a twat fronting them!" she shot back. He rolled off the bed, jerked on his clothes, and stormed out of the room. Shan glared at the closed door, steaming.

When he returned a few hours later, she'd worked her way into a righteous anger. She'd heard Valentine referred to in a misogynistic manner, and also Heart, Hole, and the Indigo Girls. The presence of vagina always seemed to overshadow the talent of the artist in the eyes of the rock press. It pissed her off and she was right to speak out about it, and she was more than ready to fight with Quinn about it, too.

When he appeared, though, she took one look at him and held her tongue. She could see he was still angry, *really* angry, and he reeked of gin. She knew there was no chance of a reasonable conversation until he cooled down, so she kept quiet as he paused to peer in Angie's portable crib. He dropped a brief pat on Sugaree's head, then stripped and fell into bed without a word to Shan.

He was still fuming the next morning and opted to join their bandmates on the tour bus for the next leg of the trip, a lengthy one from Houston to Jefferson City. "I guess this is the designated twat bus," Shan said to Oda, stroking Sugaree's soft ears. "I can't believe he's acting like such a dick."

"I can," Oda replied. She was sitting cross-legged on the floor, dangling a plush ukulele for Angie to grab at. "He's always seen it as his band and all this focus on you is threatening to him."

"It's their fault," Shan said. "Dan's and Ty's and Dave's. They've let him think that all along, when this band is about all of us, not just Quinn. Let them listen to him bitch."

"Well, in some ways, it is his band. He's the one who brought all of you together. Even now he picks the producers, approves the content. He's always been the leader."

"What are you saying—that his behavior is acceptable?"

"No, he's acting like a dick," Oda conceded. "All I'm saying is that it's understandable. Just leave him be and he'll chill out. He always does," she reminded Shan, who sniffed.

Quinn remained on the other bus until the show. When he accompanied her back to the hotel Shan was relieved, as she'd missed him dreadfully once she got over her annoyance. She'd grown so accustomed to having him constantly at her side that a full day and night without him left her needing him, hungry for his touch and the sound of his voice.

And he was clearly suffering from a jones of his own, which he demonstrated when he insisted on stopping at Oda's room to retrieve Angie after the show. "I missed her last night," he said, picking her up for a cuddle. She still rarely slept through the night, but with their schedule it made little difference.

"I missed *you*," Shan said, "and I'm sorry we fought."

"Me, too," Quinn said, "but that doesn't mean I've changed my opinion. The band is not the proper forum for your feminist issues."

"I don't agree," she said sharply. He moved Angie to his other shoulder, shooting an annoyed glance at Shan as he did so. "This business is loaded with misogyny," she continued. "Female artists don't get one-tenth of the respect that the men do."

"*You're* getting some respect," he said.

"Yes, being referred to as a twat rocker makes me feel all kinds of respected."

That wrested a smile out of him, finally. "I see your point," he said, settling Angie back in her crib. She was falling asleep, finally.

"This is a tough industry for women," Shan said, continuing their conversation in a lowered voice, "and I think I have a responsibility to speak out about that."

Quinn came to the bed and snagged the waistband of her sweats. "You can keep speaking out about twat rock or we can fuck and make up. Your choice."

After they finished, he snuggled his hand between her thighs. "Talk about rocking a twat," she whispered and he cracked up, burying his face in her hair to muffle his laughter.

After Missouri, they headed to Indianapolis, Baltimore, and Philly, then into the Northeast. They played Boston, then Albany, Columbus, and Fargo, then drove into Canada, to Winnipeg, Saskatoon, Edmonton, and Vancouver. Then back to the United States, to Spokane and Boise.

Quinntessence heaved a joint sigh of relief when they arrived in Vegas, which signified the beginning of the last leg of the tour. They proceeded next to Reno, after which they'd perform in Seattle, Portland, and finally California. Once they fulfilled their commitments in San Francisco, Sacramento, and San Diego, they were finished, at least until the next time.

Shan hoped a return to normal life would have a positive impact on Quinn's state of mind. His irritability had persisted through most of the tour, keeping her on edge, as well. She kept catching him eying her resentfully and she wondered what she could do to jolly him out of it.

After their performance, they went back to their hotel to find a screaming baby and a worried Oda. Angie was red faced and wheezing. She'd been battling a cold for the past few days so she was crankier than normal, but now no amount of consoling worked, Oda reported. When she'd taken her temperature it was 103 and she had a call in to their pediatrician.

When he called back, he instructed them to get Angie to a hospital. At the emergency room they feared meningitis or pneumonia, but it was finally diagnosed as acute bronchiolitis. The ER doctor kept her under observation for a few hours and when the fever broke he released her, instructing them to keep her quiet and watch her for breathing difficulties.

"What about antibiotics?" Quinn asked, but the doctor shook his head.

"This is a viral infection, so drugs won't touch it. A humidifier will help with her breathing, but mostly what she needs is fluids and plenty of rest."

When Quinn heard that, he pulled out his mobile and called Jeff, ordering him to charter a plane to fly Oda and Angie home.

"I'm going, too," Shan told him.

"You are not going. We have to be in Seattle tomorrow. Jeff's booking us seats on the red-eye." The buses with the rest of the band and the crew had departed hours earlier.

"I have to. I can't leave her when she's *sick*, Q." She thought about the times when she herself had been sick as a child. She couldn't remember a single time, not once, when her mother hadn't been there to take care of her.

"I'm not crazy about this either, but we don't have a choice. You heard the doctor. Angie's better off at home, but you and I can't just leave, not right before a show. It's not an option."

So Oda and Angie flew home while they flew to Seattle, Shan fretting the whole way. The doctor had told them that most babies recovered from bronchiolitis quickly, but that complications could result if they had underlying health issues. *Like methadone addiction?* she wondered.

It awakened all the anxiety and fear Shan had experienced when she was pregnant, the ever-present worry that she'd injured her daughter through her drug use, that she'd cursed Quinn with a damaged child to go along with his damaged wife, that her own weakness would inflict permanent harm on those she loved most. By the time they arrived in Seattle, she was a mass of ragged nerves. Quinn slept through most of the flight but Shan remained dead awake and terrified, heart pounding with the urgency she felt. The plane had barely touched down before she called Oda. She was reassured to hear that Angie was safe, finally asleep, but it did little to stem her compulsion to get closer to her daughter.

When they arrived at the Kingdome, the roadies were setting up. Quinn went to inspect the monitors and, when he turned back from the stage, he saw Shan huddled in the front row with her mobile glued to her ear. He could see her worried countenance from across the room.

He climbed down from the stage. "How is she?"

She was folding up the phone. "Her fever is back up to one hundred." Her eyes were wide and frightened. "She's had some Tylenol and formula, and now Oda's giving her a bath."

"The doctor said that might happen," he reminded her. "It means that her immune system is fighting the infection. It sounds like Oda has the situation under control."

She glared at him. "If this situation was under control, then we'd be at home taking care of her, not stuck here! Can't we just *go?*"

"No, we can't. Do you have any idea what it would cost us to cancel a show?"

"Whatever it costs, it's not worth more than your daughter!"

Dan glanced at them uneasily and Quinn dropped his voice. "You'd better calm the fuck down. We've got a couple of days before Portland, so we'll fly home in the morning. I'll charter a plane if I have to, but we can't go tonight, Shan. It's not an option."

"You can't play one fucking show without me?"

"*No,*" he snarled, his temper finally snapping, "*we can't.* Twat rock, remember?"

"Which you hate," she shrieked, "so, for once, why don't you try it without the twat?"

She flung her phone at him, snatched her purse, and headed for the door.

By seven o'clock, Shan was nowhere to be found. Quinn couldn't call her, because she'd left her phone behind. Eventually one of the roadies came backstage and handed him a note. She was long gone, on a flight bound for LA.

They limped through the concert, offering a story of sudden illness to explain the absence of their lead singer. They managed to piece together a show with Quinn singing lead, but it did little to appease the outraged audience, who booed them.

When the band got back to the hotel, Quinn parked himself at the bar. He'd curtly refused to speak to any of the press after the show and Dan watched with foreboding as he ordered the first of what was to be many drinks. His eyes were narrowed to slits.

Eventually Dan sidled up and quietly joined him. Quinn was on his third double T and T in less than an hour. "You okay?"

"I'm fucking great," Quinn sneered, "at least until the fucking papers come out and we get fucking crucified."

Dan didn't know what to say. Lorraine had flown in to meet with the promoter and she'd been with him all night, frantically trying to reach a compensation agreement. They were almost certain to wind up on the receiving end of a lawsuit, though, and, if they did, it wouldn't be Shan personally. It would be the whole band. She hadn't just fucked herself, she'd fucked them all. But mostly she'd fucked Quinn who, Dan could see, wasn't just angry. He was enraged.

He watched Quinn order another T and T. He was beginning to exhibit a crazed, maniac-on-the-warpath look, so Dan resolved to stay close, in case he blew his famous cool and decided to slug some innocent drunk who was unfortunate enough to look at him the wrong way.

After a while Dan noticed Quinn looking across the bar, eyeing a busty blonde who'd been checking him out all night. This wasn't unusual. The Q-man had maintained an appropriately monogamous state since taking himself out of circulation, but he still flirted playfully with the women who pursued him so relentlessly. Shan didn't like it, but she dealt with it. She'd confided to Dan that expecting Quinn not to flirt would be like expecting the sun not to shine. It was an ingrained part of his personality, and it was harmless.

Except that, in this case, it was looking less harmless than usual. He was returning the blonde's admiring gaze with something resembling the predatory expression that the old Quinn had always referred to as visual foreplay.

Eventually, the blonde worked her way around the bar. Her name was Janelle, she explained, and she was a *huge* fan. Dan watched Quinn turn on the charm and play her like an instrument. After a few minutes of casual conversation rife with sexual innuendo, she excused herself and went to the ladies' room. Probably to dry herself off, Dan reflected. It was uncanny, the effect the guy had on women.

He nudged Quinn. "What are you doing, man?"

Quinn's face was expressionless. "None of your fucking business."

"Don't get crazy, dude. I know you're pissed off at Shan. You have a right to be, but don't do something you're gonna regret just because you're drunk and pissed off."

Quinn's response was stony silence.

Dan gripped his arm. "Q, chill out. I'm serious, man. You're fucking with the band now. You screw that broad and Shan finds out, then you've screwed each and every one of us, too."

Quinn's head swiveled and his eyes were like chips of blue ice. "Get your hands off me, Danny," he said. "Right now."

There was a clear warning in his words and Dan hastily released him. The blonde returned, sitting even closer this time. Within minutes, Quinn had his hand on her leg, his thumb massaging her inner thigh in what had once been a signature move.

At one point, he raised his glass to his mouth and the blonde's gaze fastened to his wedding band. "You're married, aren't you? To Shan O'Hara?" Dan heard her ask.

Quinn followed the path of her gaze and he regarded his left hand speculatively. After a moment, he looked her right in the eye. "Is that a problem?"

Apparently it wasn't, because the blonde rushed to her table to tell her friends she was leaving and, when Dan looked around again, Quinn was gone.

The next morning, Quinn woke with a monstrous hangover. He ordered an extrastrength Bloody Mary and a pot of strong coffee, downed them both along with four aspirin, then staggered into the shower. After a couple of minutes, he began to feel human again.

As his mind cleared, he was assaulted with a sickness of a different sort. After a quick stop at the hotel shop, he'd returned to the suite with the blonde in tow, fucked her a couple of times, then thrown her out at four o'clock in the morning citing the fact that his wife might show up as an excuse. It was a good one, as she'd departed hastily.

It was the first time he'd touched another woman since he and Shan had been together. For better or worse, as the saying went, and it hadn't been a hardship, even though he'd been subjected to a little bit of the worst just lately. He still checked out the groupies, flirting with them in a teasing manner. It amused him that they still pursued him so doggedly, even when Shan was standing right next to him. As if, especially when none of them could hold a candle to her.

He could live without them because he'd known fidelity was part of the deal right from the start. If Shan ever caught him screwing around, he knew exactly how she'd interpret it. She wasn't worthy of him. She wasn't enough for him. It would destroy her.

But she was. She was *everything* to him, her and their daughter, and he'd never jeopardize their family just to scratch an itch. But now he had, in a fit of pique, with somebody whose name he couldn't even remember. Jane? Janet? What difference did it make, anyway?

By the time he climbed out of the shower, he'd convinced himself that it was no big deal. So he'd done a groupie. So what? He'd done scores of them, over the years. Shan would never know. He'd make goddamn sure of it, and he'd never do it again.

He toweled himself dry and emerged naked from the bathroom with clouds of steam hovering around him, then stopped dead.

Shan was in the room, standing next to the bed, with something clutched in her hand.

As she turned and he saw the look on her face, he swayed a little, suddenly realizing he was about to tumble over a precipice.

chapter 44

Shan had heard the shower running as she let herself in to the hotel room. She briefly considered undressing and climbing in there with Quinn, but just as quickly abandoned the idea. Better to wait him out.

By the time she'd arrived in Los Angeles, she'd come to her senses. What had she been thinking? She'd bagged a sold-out show. Quinn would be furious, not to mention the rest of the band and her record label. She knew she'd screwed up royally, so she called Oda, confirmed that Angie was all right, then immediately booked a return seat.

Quinn's clothes were strewn over the floor, an indication that he'd staggered to bed in a drunken state. Quinn was neat, as a general rule, neater than she was. When she undressed she tossed her clothes on a chair but he folded each item fastidiously, unless he was in a hurry to get her into bed. On such occasions their clothing flew like confetti.

She heard the shower turn off as she began collecting his clothes from the floor. Then her eye fell on the nightstand and she dropped the pants she'd been folding, moved around the bed, and picked up a couple of crumbled pieces of foil from its top.

Condom wrappers. Two of them.

Time seemed suspended as Shan stood and stared at the objects in her hand. She heard the bathroom door open and turned, clutching the wrappers in her fist. She watched Quinn emerge and freeze at the sight of her, then opened her hand and let the wrappers flutter to the floor.

They stared at each other across the room, her eyes wide and disbelieving, practically uncomprehending, his radiating shock and . . . something else. Guilt?

Shan broke the silence. "Say something," she whispered. *Say anything. Say Dave used the room, or Ty, or even Dan. I'll believe whatever you tell me. I'll make myself believe it.*

She could see the lie hovering on his lips, then he shrugged. "I don't know what to say."

His words came at her from a vast distance. She started to tremble and forced her suddenly wobbly legs to move. She walked to the door and paused to look back, her hand on the knob.

His eyes told her everything. There wasn't a trace of the anger she'd expected to find this morning. All she saw was the guilt.

The trembling in her limbs increased and she left the suite, pulling the door closed very quietly. He didn't say a word, just stood still and watched her leave.

When the tour bus arrived in Portland, Shan was already there. She skipped sound check and showed up at the arena thirty minutes before they were due onstage. She was cordial to Quinn in a distant way and installed herself in the greenroom where there wasn't the slightest chance they could exchange a private word.

After the show, he hurried back and caught her as she was gathering her things.

He hesitated. He still didn't know what the fuck to say to her. "Can we talk?"

"No," she said, snapping her guitar case shut. "I have a plane to catch."

"You're leaving?" His words caught in his throat. "*Now?*"

"Yes. I don't want to be away from Angie any longer than I have to." She collected a couple of packets of strings and stuffed them into her backpack.

"Well, I'll go with you. We're wrapped up here, so—"

"No," she said sharply. "I don't want you with me."

Quinn frowned. "You have a right to be pissed, but don't blow this out of proportion."

"Don't worry. I'm not." She gathered up her things.

He grabbed her arm. "Shan, you have to at least talk to me!" She shook his hand off and moved toward the door, but he was past her in a flash, holding it closed. "Don't leave. Please?"

She whipped her head around. "I don't have anything to say to you, Quinn. Quite frankly, the sight of you is making me sick."

Her green eyes were icy. Over the years, those eyes had radiated a whole spectrum of emotions in his direction. He'd seen them blazing with anger and wide with fear. He'd seen them sparkling with joy and liquid with passion. He'd seen them tender with love, but he'd never once seen the emotion emanating from them now.

They were narrowed with hatred.

Did she really hate him? How could she? He let his hand fall away from the door.

"I fucked up," he whispered. "I'm so sorry, angel,"

She laughed, a bitter, hollow sound. "I'm going. Don't follow me."

He didn't, just stood to the side and let her pass.

Quinn stayed on the bus, although he could easily have flown to LA. since they had a three-day break before they were due in San Francisco. When he called home, Shan refused to speak to him. "She told me to tell you not to come home," Oda reported. "She says she won't let you in the house."

"How bad is she?"

"Bad," Oda said. "You really fucked up this time, Quinn."

He stayed away to give her some space, but phoned every few hours. She continued to refuse his calls and he didn't see his wife again until she appeared just before they were scheduled to go onstage in San Francisco. She looked through him as if he wasn't there.

When they hit the stage, they started off with "Big City Heat" and Quinn hit a wrong note, on the climb. He floundered for a moment, struggling to recapture his rhythm. Out of the corner of his eye, he saw Ty glance at him sharply.

He made another mistake. Two in one song? That was unheard of, for him. He brought his mouth to the mic and paused, waiting for Dan's drum roll to conclude. He inhaled.

And froze.

He couldn't remember the lyrics.

Even as his brain blanked out, his hands took over and moved the music away and back toward the bridge. The rest of them stumbled, then caught up with him.

He brought his mouth back to the mic. It was just a momentary glitch. He'd cowritten the song. He'd sung it a thousand times. How could he possibly forget the words?

Except he had. His mind was completely blank.

A surge of panic gripped him as the music again approached the vocal cue. He shot a pleading look at Shan, with an almost undetectable shake of his head.

She immediately brought her mouth to her mic. "*You've got to be tough . . .*"

She had his back. Thank God. She was always there.

After the show he hurried backstage to find her, but she'd vanished like air. He headed for her dressing room, where the door was opened by a plump middle-aged man in a windbreaker. "Mr. Quinn Marshall?"

"Yes," Quinn replied, looking over the man's shoulder into the room. It was empty.

The man handed him a long manila envelope. "For you." He bobbed his head. "Have a good evening, Mr. Marshall." He waddled off, past Dan who was just coming down the hall.

"She gone?"

"I think so," Quinn frowned.

"She had a car waiting, I think. I guess she hasn't calmed down yet. You can't really blame her," he admonished gently. Quinn didn't respond, just followed him into the greenroom. Ty was in there, too, just cracking a beer.

"What's that?" Dan asked, nodding at the envelope in Quinn's hand.

Quinn glanced down at the envelope, which he'd forgotten about. He dropped into a chair and tore it open as Dave came in.

"What the fuck was up with you tonight, Q?" Dave asked, helping himself to a brew, as well. Quinn didn't reply. He was staring at the papers he'd pulled out of the envelope. "Good thing Shan was there to bail your ass out." He glanced around. "Where is she?"

Quinn had a document in each hand and was looking from one to the other. "Gone."

"Already? She must have lit out of here quick," Ty said. "Is your kid okay?"

"Yes."

"What is she, scared to face us? There's a settlement. It's not the end of the world, even though it's going to cost us a pretty penny." Quinn didn't respond and Ty frowned. "What's up, Q? A little trouble in paradise?"

"You might say that." Quinn looked up. His eyes were terrible. "In fact, I think paradise just got wiped out by an A-bomb." He dropped the bundle of papers on the table, grabbed his jacket, and disappeared without another word.

"Hey," Ty called as the door swung shut. He looked at Dan, who was looking after Quinn with a troubled countenance. "You know, I think I'm missing something here."

Dan reached out and picked up the packet of papers from the table. His brow furrowed. "A summons? Are we getting sued, after all?" He flipped it over and gaped. "Holy shit!"

"What?"

Dan held up the document so Ty could see the title.

PETITION FOR DISSOLUTION OF MARRIAGE.

chapter 45

Shan woke with a scream still on her lips. Quinn had moved out nearly a month before, but now another demon shared her bed. She woke screaming nearly every night, filled not only with nameless terror, but a painful, wrenching sense of isolation.

In the next room, Angie began to cry.

Terror was edged aside by guilt and self-reproach as Shan got out of bed. The nightly screams were traumatizing her daughter, who was disturbed enough by Quinn's absence. No daddy to comfort her now, just a twitching, nervous, train wreck of a mother.

"I'm so sorry, Angel-Abby," Shan whispered, lifting her sobbing child from her crib.

"Shan?" Oda was in the doorway, regarding her soberly. "Are you all right?"

"Fine." Shan forced a smile. "Another nightmare, that's all. I woke her again."

Oda didn't smile back. "I'll make you some tea."

It took a long time to soothe Angie enough that she could be put back to bed. When she was finally settled, Shan came out on the deck, took a cup of tea, and curled up in one of the lounge chairs.

Oda cleared her throat. "So," she began, "how long are you going to let this go on?"

Shan sighed. "I was wondering when I'd be in for one of your famous pep talks."

"This isn't a pep talk. I'm worried about you, Shan. You hardly ever get out of bed. You're not eating. You look terrible. I know it's hard, but it's been a few weeks and you should be dusting yourself off a little bit by now. I'm not saying you shouldn't grieve," Oda added gently, "but you still need to have some kind of a life."

"What are you suggesting, that I start dating?"

"You could bring Angie down to the beach or take Sugaree for a walk. Play your guitar. Do something, anything, to make yourself feel better. And *no,*" she added. "I don't think you should start dating. I can't think of a worse idea."

Shan elevated her chin. "Why not? Quinn is. Or whatever he calls what he's doing."

"Quinn is a different animal than you are. I think he's doing a lot of things just to keep numb. At least you'll let yourself feel the pain, but he's just burying it wherever he can."

"Yes," Shan shot back. "In women."

"In women," Oda agreed. "And booze, too, I think. He's a mess, according to Denise."

Shan turned her face away. "What he does is no longer my problem."

"He's your daughter's father," Oda said, "and you need to be able to communicate with him. You're letting your anger get in the way of what's best for Angie."

"How can you say that? I would never let my own problems hurt her. She loves Quinn, no matter how much I hate him, so I'll make sure that she sees him. And she does, all the time!"

"But you haven't taken a single call from him," Oda said. "You hide in the bedroom every time he comes to pick her up. You lock the door whenever he's in the studio."

"I don't want him in my house. I don't want to have to look at his lying, cheating face. And I'm touched by your concern for him, Oda, but what about *me?* I'm the one he left."

"He didn't leave," Oda corrected her. "You threw him out. Not that I blame you. Quinn did a shitty thing and deserves to suffer, for a while. I don't know that he should suffer for the rest of his life, though."

Shan assumed an expression of pained wonder. "Are you suggesting that I take him back?"

"That's up to you," Oda said carefully, "but it wouldn't hurt to recognize it as an option."

"I liked your first idea better. Maybe I *will* start dating."

"I never said that and, if you're asking my opinion, I think that's the worst thing you could do, because *you,* girlfriend, are still in love with your husband." Shan began to protest but Oda waved her off. "This is me you're talking to, honey. I've been there from the beginning. I saw you turn your whole life around from the minute you met him, and how long did I watch you pine over him? Then I listened to you promise to have him and love him and keep him, and I don't think those vows came lightly to you."

"They did to him, apparently." Shan shrugged. "It's my own fault. He told me over and over that he didn't want to be tied down. I should have listened. And all we ever did was fight, even at the best of times."

"That's true," Oda agreed. "It's been the language of the relationship all along. That and the music." Shan turned her face away. "But that's a not bad thing. You have to be able to hold your own with that one. You didn't pick an easy man, after all."

Shan sniffed. "I think there are literally hundreds of women who would disagree."

"Well. I don't have anything to say about that. You always knew what he was. Did it actually surprise you that his choice of a weapon was his penis?"

"What do you mean?"

"What do you think happened, that night in Seattle? You think he spotted the girl of his dreams and couldn't help himself?" Shan didn't reply. "That gun of his was aimed right at you, honey. Where he put it doesn't even matter."

"I guess that makes it all right, then." Shan glared at her. "How did he get you on his side? Did he sleep with you, too?"

Oda's face tightened, but her tone stayed even. "I'm not on anyone's side. I'm just trying to get you to face the truth. You have to, if you're going to make a wise decision. It's going to affect the rest of your life, and your daughter's life, too, so you'd better make it a good one."

"I don't know what you want me to say to you."

"You can say anything you want to me, but you ought to draw the line at lying to yourself."

"What am I supposed to be lying about?"

"Just stop it, Shan. Stop telling me how much you hate Quinn. Or at the very least, stop telling yourself. He hurt you and you're angry, but don't try to turn anger into hatred. You can love him and still let him go, if that's what you want. Bless him with your love and release him. You'll be releasing yourself at the same time."

Shan got up and went back inside without another word, leaving the tea behind.

When she reached the privacy of her own bedroom she closed the door, then sank down to the floor, pulling her knees in against her chest.

You, girlfriend, are still in love with your husband.

Like she needed anyone to tell her that. She was tormented by thoughts of Quinn, consumed with them. She missed him every day, every minute, longed for him with a potent, painful yearning, the most treacherous jones she'd ever faced.

Shan went back to bed, tossing and turning, absolutely unable to sleep even though she was exhausted. It was like the insomnia she got during a methadone turkey, the kind she knew had racked Angie during her detox. Shan remembered how miserable and inconsolable she'd been, how nothing they did soothed her until Quinn suggested the music.

She got out of bed. She hadn't touched her guitars in weeks, but she headed for the studio to retrieve the Angel, singing softly to herself, words that had given her solace so long ago.

Don't bother me
I don't care
I'm all alone and dreaming . . .

She unlocked the door to the basement and went down the steps. She made it as far as the threshold and not one step farther, because the sight of the studio was like a shot of acid to her heart.

Quinn's specter was everywhere. The Kur, plugged in and ready to be played. The stacks of hand-notated sheet music, which he would examine with his feet up on his desk and Sugaree asleep at his side. Worst of all was the sound board where he did most of his work, sometimes with Angie cradled in his lap.

She could see her guitars in their customary places on the wall, but now she didn't want to play them, or touch them, or even look at them. For the first time in her life, the thought of making music was abhorrent. It was so intricately enmeshed with Quinn that she knew they would torture her, the sweet sounds that in the past had only soothed.

She turned and fled back up the stairs, and didn't go down there again.

Weeks later Shan still hadn't found any respite from the pain that was with her every minute of every day. It was hell, pure hell, and, regardless of what she'd told Oda, she knew full well that the reason she'd been so frantically avoiding Quinn had nothing to do with hatred. On the contrary.

It was because she loved him so much, too much, beyond all reason and with an intensity that was all consuming. She'd love him no matter what he did, no matter how much he hurt her. The power of it terrified her, because she'd known that intensity before.

It was an addiction, plain and simple, to a person who in his way was more toxic than any substance ever could be.

She knew about kicking addictions, though. The first step was always cold turkey, so she'd systematically erased Quinn from her life. Banished him from her presence. Turned away from their music. Removed all traces of him from her house, but it still wasn't getting better and, after nearly two months, she was beginning to think it never would.

Well, turkeying never worked, really. When she was trying to kick heroin, all it did was make her sick. She hadn't kicked the H, *really* kicked it, until she replaced it with something else. She'd needed methadone to take away the jones.

And it was to the methadone that she turned, at first. She began playing with her dose, increasing it just a touch, looking for the blunting effect that she knew opiates could have. The pills were scored, easy to cut, and she experimented with an extra quarter tab.

Just that little bit caused the 'done to act as a sedative, taking the edge off her anguish. She could get out of bed. Play with her daughter. Take Sugaree for a short walk on the beach.

Before long, her body adjusted and the tranquilizing effect faded. She upped the 'done a little more, until it blanketed the acute anguish that accompanied her every waking moment with a dull, fuzzy patina. She'd thought Oda would be relieved to see her up and functioning, but she never said a word about it, just kept watch with her all-seeing eyes.

After a while she had to take two pills a day, eighty milligrams, to maintain the flat, murky haze. When she got up to three tablets a day, though, the effect of the 'done changed. It made her high. For the first time in months, she was up instead of down, feeling good instead of feeling suicidal or, at best, not feeling anything. The world felt right to her, finally, like she could go through this and come out the other side stronger and wiser.

But the well-being came with a price. She'd eaten deeply into her take-homes and she'd be fucked, just fucked, if she ran out. She tried reducing, but the withdrawal set in. The thirty milligrams she was supposed to be taking did nothing now and she couldn't get more from the clinic, not until her prescription warranted it. She'd forgotten, somehow, what she was: a junkie with an addict's tolerance.

She called Jeff. "I need something," she told him, after an exchange of pleasantries. "Can you help me?"

"Sure," he said without a trace of judgment. "Are you looking for 'done or dope?"

Methadone or heroin. He knew her preferences, of course. "'Done."

"Okay," he said. "I'm leaving on a tour tomorrow, but I can set something up before I go. Just one thing, Shan. I'd prefer it if Quinn didn't know. I'm pretty sure he'd fire me if he did."

"We're on the same page then." She tried to laugh, but it came out sounding like a sob. "What I do is none of his business. You know we're separated, right?"

"Yes, I do," Jeff said. "I'm sorry."

"Don't be," she replied. "Just hook me up."

"All right. Let me make a few calls."

Jeff called back inside of an hour. He had someone—did she want it delivered? Absolutely not. Shan stuffed her hair under a baseball cap so she wouldn't be recognized and drove to North Hollywood to meet her new connection, Big Black, who in fact was an average-sized white guy. She began meeting him every few days to pick up methadone. It helped for a time, but before long her mind was turning to something she knew was a surefire cure for whatever ailed.

A little piece of rock. A thin trail of smoke. One hit and all the pain . . . it would float away. She had a standing order with Big Black by then and, the next time she saw him, she changed it from 'done to H.

She was very careful. Oda was around constantly, watching her with those eyes. She had her own quarters in the guest house, but for a while she'd been sleeping in one of the spare bedrooms in the main building. Shan didn't comment, glad to have a responsible adult in the house for Angie.

When she thought about it, which she tried not to do, she was shocked by how quickly it had happened. All that work, nearly four years of being clean—gone, like the whiff of smoke that rose off the foil after she applied the flame. She couldn't believe she was back here, and so fast. She'd slipped, true . . . was that all it took?

But she knew it was. She'd known it all along, really. No one knew about slips better than she did but, regardless of what she knew, she was right back in the abyss: living for the next fix, planning her day around dosing, arranging her life based on the waxing and waning of the drug in her bloodstream.

In a way it was comforting, the systematic, hour-to-hour orchestration of her time. Without it, she'd still be foundering in a sea of pain and pointlessness. The H was stable, a predictable entity in the formless blob of her existence. It gave her structure and a focus, like funeral arrangements after a death.

She wasn't inclined to stop but, even if she was, she couldn't go to a clinic. She'd test dirty and the stakes were so high now. What if they called social services? And what about Quinn? If he found out she'd relapsed, he'd take Angie in a second; she knew he would. So she kept managing it, dosing just enough during the day to keep the withdrawal away. Her bedroom was redolent with the scent of incense, triggering an olfactory déjà vu of her old room in SoHo.

The nights were still bad, laden with knife-in-the-chest regrets. She ruminated about the love she'd lost, the music she wasn't making, the beautiful daughter whose care she now left largely to Oda, afraid to sully her with the same hands that boiled heroin. Just the thing, H, to numb the pain and the shame and the paralyzing fear of what the fuck she was supposed to do with the rest of her life.

That fear was always there, insidious as a percolating malignancy. Every morning when she woke, the jones was accompanied by remorse that cursed her for being a lame-ass junkie who'd had more good fortune than any ten people deserved and blown every bit of it.

It was when she spent time with Angie—when she held her and kissed her and cuddled her—that was when she hated herself the most.

She'd look down at her, her perfect little girl with her own face and Quinn's eyes, and be filled with shame by the love she saw there. There was a soundtrack in her head now, a constant looping chorus of castigation and self-loathing: *not good enough, never good enough, bad mother, bad wife, bad person, weak, stupid, worthless junkie . . .*

One Thursday night in September, Oda tapped at her bedroom door just as Shan was beginning her nightly dose. She jumped, startling Sugaree who was napping on the dog bed beside their California king. Just hers now, Shan supposed, as she stuffed the foil and tooter in the drawer of the nightstand. "What is it, Oda?"

Oda pushed the door open. She looked drawn, her brown skin ashy, without its usual robust bloom. She'd had some dental work that day and it looked like she was feeling some pain. "I need to run to the pharmacy before they close," she said. "I don't like using pain killers, but Tylenol just isn't touching this. I'll only be a half hour or so—will you be okay?"

"Of course. Go ahead." Shan blinked to clear the fuzziness from her eyes.

"You sure?" Oda looked at the stick of incense burning in the wooden holder. "I can put Angie in the car seat, take her with me."

A shimmer of annoyance penetrated her H-induced well-being. "I can take care of my daughter for half an hour, Oda. Just go. *Go,"* she emphasized, as Oda hesitated again.

After Oda left, Shan lit a candle, then retrieved the foil and tooter from the nightstand. She cut a chunk off the rock, dropped it on the foil, and held it over the flame.

It seemed like seconds later that Oda was shaking her. "Shan, wake up! *Wake up!"*

She floundered out of the H-induced fugue, crawled her way back to consciousness.

And smelled the smoke.

She'd knocked over the candle, somehow. It had rolled off the nightstand, onto Sugaree's cushion, now a smoldering pile emitting puffs of foul-smelling smoke. She could hear her dog whining under the bed.

Shan ran for water. By the time she made it back to the bedroom, Oda had beaten out the burgeoning flames with a blanket. Underneath, the hardwood floor bore a roundish black scar.

"The smoke alarm should have gone off," Oda said. Sugaree, un-harmed, sniffed dubiously at the remains of her bed. "We should have it checked."

Shan was silent. She knew why it hadn't gone off. She'd pulled the battery, afraid that the smoke from the candle and the incense and the H would set it off.

"I'm not going to nag you, or yell at you, or try and persuade you," Oda told her, after they'd cleaned up the mess and opened the balcony doors to let in some air. "I know it won't do any good. You let me know when you're ready for some help." Then she went to bed and Sugaree followed, leaving Shan alone in the toxic-smelling room, her guilt and shame even more cloying than the fumes.

She went to her nightstand and retrieved the rock of heroin. Then she went onto the balcony and threw it as far as she could out into the water.

A few hours later, she was a sweating, shaking mess. She had a little 'done left from her last prescription, but it was like a breath mint now. She searched through her drawer, found a sliver of rock. She lit more incense to camouflage the smell, then smoked it. It wasn't enough, so she scraped bits of foil, searched through her pockets and drawers, hoping to scavenge enough for a real hit.

She used her mobile to call Big Black, got his voice mail, and left an urgent message. Then she crawled around the bedroom floor, finding and examining little bits of crud, praying to find just a pinprick of heroin.

In the nursery, Angie began to cry.

The sound sliced through Shan like a white-hot knife. She clenched, rolled into a ball, squeezed her eyes shut. She heard Oda go into the nursery and make soothing noises. Still, Angie squalled. The sound lanced through Shan, assaulting her nerves like molten lava.

Shut up. She pressed her hands against her eyes, hurting herself. *Shut up, before I give you something to fucking cry about.*

Oh, Jesus!

She cried out herself then, in horror, and covered her eyes again to block the image that suddenly materialized. But she still saw it, the burning ember, felt its heat coming toward her, waited for the bite as it branded her flesh.

When she began to scream, she was even louder than Angie.

A sound caused Quinn to lift his head from between the thighs of the frequent flyer spread across his bed.

There it was again. A knock, at three o'clock in the morning? He pushed aside the other blonde, the one that was sucking his cock, so he could go see what was up.

He saw them through the peephole, Shan and Angie, right outside his door. *What the fuck?* He retrieved his jeans, pulled them on, and opened it. "What's wrong?"

It was clear something was. Shan was flushed and wild-eyed, her hair soaked with sweat and clinging to her forehead in snaky strands. "I need you," she whispered. She was holding their daughter tight. Too tight. Angie was squirming, making mewling sounds of protest. "*She* needs you. Please, Q."

"Wait." He shut the door. "Leave," he said to the two women tangled together on the bed. He searched for their names, couldn't remember. "Sorry, but leave. Now."

A few minutes later he pushed both of them out into the hall, half dressed and still protesting. Shan's mouth curled into a grimace. She moved to the side to let them pass, averting her eyes until they boarded the elevator and disappeared.

Quinn grimaced himself. "Sorry about that."

She didn't reply, just stepped forward to place Angie in his arms, cupping the little face between her hands to kiss her over and over. "I love you, Angel-Abby," she murmured, kissing her once more before stepping away. "Take care of her, Quinn."

Quinn was suddenly scared. "What is it?" he asked. "What's happened?"

She looked up at him and he saw it all, the pinned, glassy eyes, the tremors, the sweat beading her forehead. "I'm using again. I don't want her anywhere near me." Her face broke as she turned away.

"Shan, wait." He took a step toward her, reached to touch her. "What can I do?"

"You've done enough." She backed away like he was a poisonous snake. "All you can do is make it worse. I'm falling apart. I'm a fucking mess, Quinn, and it's because of you."

At her words, something inside him coiled up and died. "Let me help. Please. I'll do anything you want. Anything you need."

"Take care of her," she said, "but stay the fuck away from me. Just leave me alone, Quinn."

"I can't leave you alone," he said helplessly. "Not when you're in trouble. I don't know how to do that."

A movement down the hall caught his eye. It was Oda, waiting by the elevator. "I may be in trouble," Shan said, "but I'm not alone." She took a step closer, kissed Angie once more, then vanished into the elevator. She didn't look back.

chapter 46

Shan instructed Oda to drive her to a rehab randomly selected from the phone book, but Oda insisted on taking her to some holistic treatment center in the San Gabriel Mountains, more than an hour from Mission Cove. Shan was in no condition to argue.

The place, Mountainside, was beautiful and came with a whole slew of New Age remedies: acupuncture, Reiki, massage, macrobiotics—all the trends, all the fads, but its luxurious, spa-style trappings and peaceful, wooded grounds couldn't conceal the condition of its occupants, recovering addicts in one or another stage of detox.

Shan barely noticed the sylvan surroundings. When she checked in she'd been adamant that she didn't want methadone, so they treated her with a cocktail of other drugs to get her through the initial withdrawal. None of them did much and, after a couple of excruciating days of shakes, cramps, spasms, and utter misery, they stuck her in a sweat lodge where she was instructed to sit and sweat and let the drug residues leak out of her body, along with the metabolites that triggered cravings.

Still, it was torturous. She endured days, then weeks of clawing and scratching at herself, kicking, feeling like her muscles and sinews and nerves were going to burst right through her skin. Then one morning she woke up and it was over. She looked in the mirror, into her own eyes, and realized that she was drug free for the first time in five years.

Her stomach settled, her vision cleared, and now they plied her with vitamins, herbal supplements, electrolyte drinks, and a macrobiotic diet that didn't taste half bad, now that she could keep it down. They wanted her to exercise, too, another way to stave off cravings. She had her choice of yoga, qigong, or tai chi, followed by a massage. She obeyed, though all of that did little to stem the craving that dug at her with white-hot pincers, to quiet the little voice whispering that all she needed was H, just a little bit of H and all this agony would vaporize. She started going for long hikes, trying to outrun the voice. That did help, a little, but the trails around Mountainside were a lot like the ones near the old canyon house and it felt wrong, somehow, to be hiking them without Sugaree.

Then the talking started. Drug and alcohol classes. Drug and alcohol counseling. Drug and alcohol group therapy. Twelve-step meetings. Not much variety, but she went and listened, reciting her own story when prompted, the oft-repeated phrases coming back like the foreign-language dialogues she'd had to memorize in high school. She had a new bottom now, nearly burning the house down over her eleven-month-old daughter's head, and welcomed the scourge of shame she experienced every time she told it.

By the end of the second week, she was allowed visitors and Oda brought Angie every day. It was awkward the first few times they came. Not with her daughter, who was pitifully happy to see her, but with Oda and her all-seeing eyes.

Shan knew she looked awful. She'd lost at least ten pounds. Her skin was sallow and papery, her lips dry and cracked. She'd been picking her face, too, and her chin was covered with scabs. "You're clean?" Oda asked.

"Mostly." Shan shrugged. "They have me on antianxiety meds because of this." She touched her chin. "And sometimes I need a sedative to help me sleep. No methadone, though."

"Good." Oda took her hand, held it. "I'm glad to see you getting healthy again."

"I've never been healthy since you've known me, Oda," Shan confessed, keeping a tight grip on her friend's hand. "The 'done just turned me into another kind of junkie. Taking it was like trying to put out a fire with gasoline." She turned her face up to the sun to let its warmth hit her injured chin and closed her eyes. *"Feel my blood enraged. It's just the fear of losing you,"* she sang softly, almost to herself, then opened her eyes and smiled. "We used to play that song, remember?"

"Sure I do. I could bring your guitar. You can play it again." Shan shook her head and Oda didn't push. "Everyone's asking about you. Denise. Lorraine. The guys in the band. And Quinn, of course," she added gently. "When you're ready, you'll have lots of visitors."

She wasn't ready, not for a while, but after a couple more weeks she told Oda that people could come, if they wanted to, everyone except Quinn. Denise arrived the very next day.

They sat by the pool drinking decaffeinated coffee and Denise talked very fast about a wonderful book she'd read and wonderful movie she'd seen and a wonderful dress she'd bought. "You haven't asked about Quinn," she said, after a while.

Shan hadn't asked about anything, since she hadn't been able to get a word in edgewise. "How is he?" she inquired, since that's what Denise seemed to want her to say.

"Not good," she said and Shan knew right away that this was the top item on Denise's agenda.

"I don't want to talk about him."

"You're right to be pissed, Shan. You've really raked him over the coals and he deserves it. I have to hand it to you. Torture time is lasting a lot longer than I thought it would."

"I'm not trying to torture him," Shan said.

"But you are and it's working. You should see him. It would break your heart."

"He did that already," Shan snapped. "I'm not about to give him a chance to do it again!"

"Well, you're not giving him a chance to make it up to you, either," Denise said, "and that's not like you. You've always forgiven Quinn, for everything. Why can't you forgive him this time?"

"Denise, I don't understand you. You've never approved of me and Quinn, not even when you stood up for us at our wedding. Why all the concern, now that it's over?"

Denise frowned. "I'll admit I never understood why you adored him so. He's such a dick, so bossy and overbearing, and he has that nasty sarcastic streak. And I hate the way he treats women," she concluded, her face twisting. "Most of them, anyway, as if they're worthless, disposable."

"All right, then. You were right about him."

"But I wasn't," Denise insisted. "It's taken me a long time to figure out what you see in him, but now I think I get it." She reached out and took Shan's hand. "He's different since you've been together, Shan. He's so devoted to you, and to Angie. When he's with you I can see it, why you love him so much. It's like . . . like you complete him. You make him into the person he's supposed to be. And that person—it's a good one. Even I can see it."

Shan stared at her. "I can't believe you're defending him."

"I'm not. He did a terrible thing, but you know it didn't mean anything to him. He just—fucked up." She squeezed Shan's hand, hard. "The guilt is killing him. I'm worried about him. So is Dan."

"You don't even *like* Quinn," Shan reminded her. "You never have."

"You're right. Sometimes I don't." Denise let go of Shan and folded her hands in her lap, then looked down at them. "But we've been together for so long now. All of us. We have a history. We're family, so we have to take care of each other. And, even if I don't like Quinn sometimes, I guess I've grown to love him a little bit, too."

Shan didn't have an answer for that, so she stayed quiet. What could she say, after all? She knew, like no one else did, how easy Quinn was to love once he allowed it.

She'd been at Mountainside just over a month when her counselor, Elizabeth, suggested that she might be ready to have Angie come and stay with her. "It would be good for both of you, Shan. If your daughter is here, you can focus on overcoming your addiction instead of constantly worrying about where she is and how she's doing."

"Her father would never permit that," Shan began, despite the sudden longing that suffused her. She missed her child every moment, her smell, her touch, the sound of her babble. It was a full-on baby jones.

"Let's ask him," Elizabeth said. "It's time we brought him in for a session, anyway. Repairing your family is the next step for you."

Some things were beyond repair, she knew, but the prospect of having Angelica with her was enough to spur her to action. After the session she went to the office and called Quinn's mobile. "My counselor thinks we need a family session," she said when he answered. "Will you come?"

Dead silence. She hadn't spoken to him on the phone him in months. "Wow. I didn't expect it to be you." He sounded jarred, off balance. She concentrated on that, instead of the liquid warmth that suffused her when she heard his familiar voice.

"Well, it is me. Will you come?"

"Of course I will," he said. "I'd have come sooner, if you wanted me."

"I didn't," she said. "I don't now, either. This isn't my idea. It's part of the treatment plan. My counselor will call you to set up a time. Her name is Elizabeth."

"I'll be there," he said. "I promise."

"Thanks," Shan replied. "Good-bye."

"Wait! Are you all right?"

"More or less. I'm clean. Mostly, anyway," she added. "No methadone."

"I'm glad." His voice was hesitant, uncertain. She hated the way it was making her feel, all aglow and quivery inside. "I've been so worried about you."

"Don't be. I'm fine."

"I can't help it," he said. "I hate having you there, even though it's what you need right now. I know what it's like, how alone it feels." He paused. She didn't say anything. "I think about you all the time, angel. And I miss you," he added quietly.

"Screw you, Quinn," Shan said, her voice shaking. She hung up the phone.

When the day came for the session, Shan had worked herself into a state of self-protective anger. At the appointed time she stalked to the counselor's office and threw open the door. "Let's get this over with," she snarled at Elizabeth, who was seated at her desk.

She rose, a buxom, pretty woman with dark, curly hair and intelligent eyes behind silver-rimmed glasses. "Good morning, Shan. Your husband is here." She nodded at Quinn, who was standing by the window, looking out.

There he was, her cheating prick of a husband whom she still, inexplicably, loved. His face looked drawn, gaunt, and his hair was longer than he usually wore it, past his shoulders. He looked pale, too, but she could see the flush of a new sunburn across his cheeks. "Hi," he said.

Shan nodded and sat down on the couch. She couldn't answer him, because her heart had leapt out of her chest and into her throat. "Nice place," he remarked.

Shan coughed. "Is it like the place you went?" she asked, after a minute. It seemed like a safe topic, their mutual detoxes.

"No." He shook his head. "That was in Malibu."

"On the water. That figures." She sat a little straighter. "I prefer the mountains."

"I know." He moved toward her, as if to sit beside her, but the look she shot him clearly transmitted her displeasure. He sat down across from her, instead, and looked down at his hands. She saw that he was still wearing his wedding band. She'd taken hers off, months before, although she still wore the pretty garnet and diamond ring he'd given her.

Elizabeth joined them, choosing the flowered loveseat between the couch where Shan sat and the chair that Quinn occupied. "Thank you for coming, Quinn."

He shifted, keeping his eyes down. "Absolutely. Whatever she needs."

"The only thing I need from you," Shan said, "is my daughter."

He looked up then, surprised. "I'm not keeping her from you. I never would."

"But I want her *here,*" Shan emphasized, "with me. Living with me."

"Here?" He looked nonplussed. "At the rehab?"

Shan glared at Elizabeth. "I told you he wouldn't let me do it."

Quinn still looked confused, so Elizabeth filled him in. "We have accommodations for parents who wish to keep their children with them while they're in treatment, Quinn. It's helpful, sometimes, because it takes a long time to recover from an addiction. It can't be rushed, either."

"I know that," he said. "Firsthand, in fact."

She nodded. "For mothers especially, separating them from their children can make them anxious to get through the program as quickly as possible. When the kids are here, they're likely to stay longer, which helps make the treatment more successful."

Quinn frowned. "Do you feel like you're ready for something like that?" he asked Shan.

"If I wasn't, I wouldn't ask. I'd never put her in danger." *Except when I almost burned the house down over her head.* Another surge of self-loathing filled her and she ducked her face.

Quinn was still frowning. "I'd like to hear some of the details."

Shan snorted, but Elizabeth was already launching into a description of the program. Private quarters for families. Certified child care staff for times that Shan would need to be away from Angie, for counseling sessions or meetings. Play groups. Story hours. Field trips.

"Sounds like summer camp," Quinn said, but his frown had cleared.

"We try to make it as positive an experience as possible," Elizabeth agreed. "The kids need to be safe and happy, so that their mothers can focus on getting well."

"What if she stays with you during the week," Quinn said to Shan, "and I take her on weekends? That way she'd still be in her home, at least part of the time."

"Your hotel isn't her home," Shan corrected him sharply.

"I'm not there anymore. I've been staying in Mission Cove since you've been here," he said, frowning anew as her eyes widened. "Didn't Oda tell you?"

Shan shook her head. The thought of Quinn back in their house filled her with alarm. It scared her because it sounded so right, like that was the way it was supposed to be.

"I thought it would be better for Angie. More normal. It's hard on her, being away from you. Don't worry," he said, correctly interpreting the look on her face. "It's temporary. I'll leave when you're ready to come home."

That was scary, too, how well he knew her even now.

By the end of the session, they had Angie's schedule worked out. Shan still didn't want Quinn visiting her, but they'd see each other when they passed Angie back and forth. Elizabeth wanted to meet with them weekly to work on healing their family dynamic, although Shan stated flatly that she had no interest in resuming their marriage. Quinn didn't comment, just looked sad, and at the end of the hour he asked Shan if she'd walk him to his car. "Please," he added, when she hesitated. "I have something for you."

She squared her shoulders and followed him out to the parking lot. "You're doing the twelve-step thing again?" he asked, along the way. "That never much worked for you before."

"It still doesn't," she confessed without looking at him. She kept her arms tightly crossed over her chest, as if to block his access to her heart. "But I'm trying everything. Group therapy. Acupuncture. Macrobiotics. Even a sweat lodge," she added. "It smells like a dirty hippie."

He laughed out loud. It sounded like a rusty gate opening. She herself hadn't laughed, really laughed, since before that morning in Seattle. From the sound of it, neither had he. "Good plan," he said. "Even the NA thing. There's really something to it, that higher-power stuff."

"Oh, please. You're an atheist."

"I said higher power," he emphasized. "Not God. It's not the same thing. Your higher power is the thing that guides you, keeps you on course. It will save you, too, if you let it."

"It can also destroy you," she shot back, experiencing a potent, virulent spurt of rage. She didn't want any guidance from him, not now or ever again. "And if you're not careful, it can take your heart and soul and shred them into a million pieces. It can destroy every single thing that matters to you, until there's nothing left. You'll never be my higher power again."

He stopped dead and, when she looked up at him, she saw he was paralyzed. The pain in his brilliant eyes was so deep and raw and stark that they looked colorless.

She looked away. They'd reached the parking lot. She saw his Testarossa, parked in the shade with the windows rolled down. "I have to get back. What did you want to show me?"

He didn't say anything, just went to his car and pulled open the door. When he did a black shape streaked out, heading straight for Shan. She gasped.

"Sugaree!" She dropped to her knees and was immediately knocked flat by the dog, who flung herself upon her person with insane, irrepressible joy. Shan wrapped her arms around Sugaree's neck and let her face be bathed in sweet, sloppy kisses. For the very first time since she'd been at Mountainside, she felt a lightness in her heart.

Shan took her out on one of the trails, which felt healing and restorative with Sugaree at her side. They had a short hike, including a stop at the pond where Suge went for a dip. After a bit, they returned to the parking lot. Quinn was sitting in the car, head down.

Shan was smiling when she opened the door. "She's all wet," she warned, laughing as Sugaree leapt inside, spattering drops like a summer rain. But the laughter died on her lips when Quinn looked up and she saw his tears.

She'd never seen him cry, ever, didn't think he was even capable of it, but his eyes were wet, red, and there was something in them that made her heart twist into a knot. "All I ever meant to do was take care of you and make you happy," he said. His voice shook. "The last thing I ever wanted was to hurt you. I'm sorry, angel. So fucking sorry."

She backed away from the car. Seeing him was hard enough, hearing him, but this? It was enough to annihilate her. "I've got to get away from you," she said, her voice quivering like a fiddle string.

"Wait." He jumped out of the car, swiping his fist across his eyes, and unlocked the trunk. "*I'm* not your higher power, Shan, but you do have one. It's been inside you, all along. What's killing you now is that you've turned away from it."

"*Don't tell me how I feel!*" she cried, her voice scaling up. "I'm sick of you always telling me what to do, how to be! *How the hell do you know what's inside of me?*"

"Because I've been right where you are," he shot back, shouting too, now. "Only I wasn't stupid enough to throw away the one fucking thing that held me together!"

He yanked open the trunk and pulled out a guitar case. "Take it. *Take it,*" he ordered, shoving it into her arms even as she was shaking her head. "Do something to help yourself, instead of bitching about what a fucking villain I am or whining about what a fucking victim you are."

"Fuck you, Quinn!" she shrieked, clutching the guitar case.

"*Fuck you too, Shan.*" He got back in the car and drove away, and then she was alone, except for the angel in her arms.

chapter 47

Shan took a deep, bracing breath of the sea air, lifting her face to the sun. Her hair shone, her skin was clear, and the marks on her chin had faded to light-pink specks she knew would eventually fade. It was a gorgeous day in Mission Cove, sunny and warm, the sky as blue as her daughter's eyes. Or her husband's.

Ex-husband soon, she supposed. Now that she was back at home, it was time to finalize the divorce. It would be good to get it over with, she reflected, because that day, with its confirmation that she and Quinn were finished once and for all, would unquestionably be one of the very worst days of her life. But it would be good, too, in a way. She needed the closure, the incontrovertible proof that her marriage was dead so she could scatter the ashes and move on.

And she was doing that. After nearly five months at Mountainside, she was clean and healthy, back in her home with her daughter and her dog.

And her guitars.

Shan was making music again, producing a stream of fresh, new material, all on her own this time. She didn't have Quinn to bounce her ideas off of, correct her mistakes, or provide her with inspiration. She had all the inspiration she needed, deep in her heart.

It had been there all along, really. He'd been right again. Once she let it out, the music saved her, giving her the strength she needed to take her first steps alone into a new life, the same strength that was giving her the courage to confront the last of her demons, the one she'd been avoiding for some time.

Oda joined her on the deck. "I'm taking Angie down to the studio," she said. "Quinn just called, from his car. He'll be here in a few minutes."

"Don't," Shan told her. "Just keep her here for a bit, okay?" Then she marched to the door that led to the studio, unlocked it, and vanished down the stairs.

Quinn had vacated their home as soon as she told him she was ready to come home and hadn't set foot in the house since. He was back living in the hotel and they'd reverted to their old system regarding the time he spent with their daughter. Oda took her down to the studio when he picked her up, following the same routine when he brought her home. Like before, he and Shan avoided any face-to-face contact. The difference was that it was him, not her, who was insisting upon that restriction now.

He'd kept his promise to attend the weekly counseling sessions at Mountainside. For weeks he sat stone faced and silent while she pummeled him with acrimony and castigation and abuse. He maintained his stoicism even when she railed and shouted and threw things, told him he was cold and selfish and cruel. It wasn't until she insisted that he'd never loved her, that he'd married her only because she was pregnant, that he finally exploded, lashing back with so much rage and vitriol that she was stunned. Then he walked out, refusing to attend any more of the sessions. The violence of his response made her acknowledge, finally, that she hadn't been the only one hurt by their ordeal.

Although she'd found her higher power, she still had very little use for twelve-step programs. She did recognize the value of some of the steps, though. Especially step nine.

Making amends.

Shan generally stayed out of the studio. She'd gone down there only long enough to retrieve the rest of her guitars, her amp, and the old four-track they'd used in the canyon house. She installed it upstairs and recorded in the living room, respecting Quinn's request to keep out of his space.

When she came down the stairs, the first thing she saw was the Kur. She switched it on, sat at the piano bench, and hit an A note, appreciating the resonant sound the instrument possessed. She touched the keys, thinking how many times she'd watched Quinn's hands manipulate them, so skillful and capable, so rarely making a mistake.

When she heard his car in the driveway, she pulled her hands away from the keyboard and laced her fingers together. She took a deep breath as the doorknob turned and Quinn came into the darkened studio.

He didn't see her right away, going to his desk and switching on the light, then flipping open a file. He selected a page of notated sheet music, held it up, and frowned at it. Then he began humming lightly, tapping out a beat on the desktop with his knuckles.

Shan was motionless, watching him scowl at the music. His face had lost its hollow cast and it looked like he'd had his hair cut recently, the silky strands just brushing his shoulders.

She hesitated, then lifted her hand to the Kur. She ran her fingers across it, producing a smooth slur of notes.

Quinn raised his eyes. When he saw her, he stopped tapping.

"Hello," he said. It was impressive, how much hostility he could express with that word.

"Hi," she replied.

He frowned. "Are you working on something? I told Oda I was coming, but she didn't say you'd be—"

"No, it's okay," she told him. "You're not interrupting anything."

He kept a wary eye on her. "Then why are you down here?"

"Because I want to talk to you."

"Is something wrong with Angie?"

"No. It's about us." He raised a skeptical eyebrow. "I won't keep you long."

His eyes shot to the clock over the mixing board. "You can have five minutes. Not one second more." He sat down at his desk and folded his arms on top of it. "What's on your mind?"

"I wanted to tell you that I'm sorry."

His eyebrows went up even higher. "Sorry?" His tone was dubious.

"Yes. Sorry for—" she stopped. She'd had a whole speech prepared, but in his presence it vaporized like mist in the sunlight. "Sorry for everything." That summed it up, she supposed.

He didn't reply, just continued to eye her suspiciously. She rose from the piano bench and crossed the room. The desk was between them, but she was close enough to reach out and touch him if she chose.

She didn't, since he looked utterly forbidding. "All those things I said—how I hated you, how you ruined my life—I didn't mean them." Her voice trembled. "I was so angry at you, and I wanted to hurt you. I know now that I did. I'm not very proud of myself for it."

She waited. He didn't make a sound; just watched her.

She hung her head. "I'm so sorry, Q. That's really all I wanted to say." And she moved toward the door.

As she reached for the knob, she heard his voice, very low. "I'm sorry, too."

She turned. The suspicion was still in his eyes, but now with a trace of sorrow as well.

"That means a lot to me." She paused, but when she spoke, her voice was still shaking. "I never in a million years would have thought that I could be capable of . . . of . . ."

"I never thought I could, either," he said, "and I never wanted to hurt you. I just . . . lost my way for a little while. I hope you can believe that."

"I can," she said, "because I know how it can happen. You can get carried away with the anger. And the pain. And the drama, too, I suppose."

"There's been a lot of mutual hurting, I guess. I'd like to find a way to put it behind us."

"That's why I'm here," she said, "to try and repair some of the damage I've done."

"You didn't do all of it. I started it, remember? And I regret that, Shan. I will until the day I die." His eyes met hers. She hoped he wasn't going to apologize again for the Seattle thing. They'd beaten it to death, over and over, in therapy. She didn't want to think about it anymore.

He didn't. "I loved you so much," he said, instead. "More than I ever thought I could love someone. I don't think you ever believed that, really, did you?"

"No. I didn't." She shook her head. "But that didn't have anything to do with you. That was me, all me."

"I should have said it more." He sighed. "I should have told you I loved you, every day."

"It wouldn't have mattered. I never thought I was worthy of it, your love."

"You were, though. You're an amazing woman, Shan. I always thought that. I still do."

She smiled then. "Actually, I think I might be doing some amazing stuff." He eyed her expectantly. "I'm writing, Q. A lot. And I think some of the tunes might be . . . well, sort of great."

"Yeah?" He smiled, too, for the first time. "I'd like to hear them. And the timing is good. We have an album to assemble and we're short on material."

She regarded him with surprise. "I figured you were taking care of that."

He grimaced. "I'm not having a great creative spell. For some reason, everything I write turns into a women-suck song."

She gasped, flushed, then doubled over as peal after peal of laughter erupted from her. In a moment Quinn was laughing, too. They stood there, holding on to either side of the desk, laughing together.

"Oh God," she groaned, wiping tears from her eyes. "This feels so good, that we can still be this way." Her words were enough to wipe the smile from his face. "That we can laugh, I mean," she hastened to add. "You know, we started out as friends. It's a good place to go back to."

"I hope we can, someday. I'm not feeling it yet, though," he replied candidly.

She waited for him to elaborate, but he seemed to be finished speaking. "How *are* you feeling, these days?"

"Honestly?" She nodded, biting her lower lip. "I don't feel much of anything. Especially about you."

"You don't feel anything about me?" Her chest began to hurt. "How can that be?"

"I'm not sure. I think there's just been too much angst. Too much shit. I'm numb." He passed a weary hand over his face. "But there's our work. We'll still have that, I suppose."

"Do you want to try writing together?"

"I'm not there yet, either. Maybe, after some time passes."

"I know." She forced a smile. "We have to be ready."

"Sounds like you learned something from me, after all." She nodded, and he turned away. "Could you ask Oda to bring Angie down?"

It was a dismissal, but she thrust her chin out. "No."

He glanced up. "No?"

"No," she repeated. "Come upstairs and get her. It's where she lives, after all." She headed upstairs. After a moment, he followed.

A little while later, Shan stood on the front porch and watched Quinn buckle Angie into her car seat, then waved until his car disappeared.

She went back inside the house and into the bedroom, where she closed the door and sat down at her dressing table.

I loved you so much, he'd said. Past tense.

She lifted a frame that was lying facedown on the dressing table's polished top, then looked at it for a long, long moment. This photograph had occupied a place on her dresser since SoHo. The city had changed, the room, even the dresser, but the picture remained.

She'd gradually divested her house of all the photographs of Quinn. She'd relocated a few to Angie's room and packed the rest away in a box, which she hid in the back of the closet.

This was the only one left. It was their first photo, the one Denise had taken at the street fair in Greenwich Village. She hadn't been able to bring herself to put it away, but she couldn't stand to look at it, either. So she'd compromised, by leaving it facedown on the dressing table.

She hadn't looked at it in a long time. Quinn's mouth was wreathed in that boyish smile that had captured her heart right from the beginning and a single blond lock dangled over one of his crystalline eyes. She ran her finger across the glass.

Silly. Of course she couldn't push it aside. It was only a picture, after all. Just a memory, captured forever behind a piece of glass.

She opened the mahogany jewel box on the dressing table. It had been a gift from Quinn, purchased at an antique shop in some anonymous midwestern town. She slid her fingers down inside of it, feeling for a tiny button. She found it, pushed, and a small door sprang open.

A secret compartment. Quinn had demonstrated when he gave her the jewel box, stating that it was a good place for expensive jewelry. When she'd pointed out that most of her jewelry wasn't that expensive, he'd grinned. "You can use it for a place to keep your secret treasures."

The compartment was empty. She'd never had anything she considered a secret treasure, until now.

She raised her left hand. Her diamond and garnet ring still adorned the third finger. She'd taken off her wedding band months earlier but, like the photograph on the dresser, she hadn't been able to bring herself to put away this circle of green and gold.

She grasped the ring and tugged. It came off with difficulty and, when she finally wrenched it free, it left a white impression in its wake. She gazed at the ring for a moment, then lifted the photograph.

She took one long, last look, then brought it to her lips to kiss the glass over the stray blond lock. "I'll always love you, Q," she murmured and slipped the photo into the secret compartment. She placed the ring on top of it and took hold of the little mahogany door, pausing for a moment to look at the treasures inside.

"Blessed, and released," she whispered.

She closed the door.

chapter 48

You know when we first met I was just a little girl
who thought she knew
how to be strong
You taught me everything and I followed you around
like a little puppy dog
You were the supernova that made my world shine and
kept me alive
I know you liked it that way, when you set up the rules
that steered my life
But I'm not a little pet now, I've got the right to get upset,
find my own way
around the world
I'm not a dog at all, I'm an angel who might fall but still can fly
With wings unfurled
Yes, I can fly
So very high

Quinn watched Shan press the stop button, then return to the conference table. She looked around at her bandmates. Denise and Oda were there in the studio, too, for moral support, he supposed. It was the first time the band was hearing her new tunes, the ones she'd written entirely on her own.

No one said anything for a minute. He was quiet, too, tapping the tabletop with his fingers. "Well?" she said. "What do you think? Are some of them good for the new album?"

"Hell, yeah!" Dan exclaimed. "All of them. It's a great collection, Shan. But this last one. You really want to call it 'Puppy'?"

"Oh, you can't change that," said Denise. "Girls will love it! And it's girly music, but with an edge, don't you think? Cyndi Lauper meets riot girl, or something."

"Definitely the grrrls," Ty laughed, "because I heard some punk in there. It's different, for sure—jazz-pop fusion with a punky edge. Cool stuff!"

"Hard-rock rhythms, though. Very cool," Dave said, grinning. "Nice work, Shan. I notice you left lots of room for harmonizing guitars. Not so much keyboard this time, though." He snickered.

Quinn hadn't said a word. He was staring at the tabletop, still tapping away with his fingertips. "Q," Shan prompted, "what do *you* think?"

Slowly, he raised his head. His face felt hot and he suspected it was very red. "I think that tune is well named," he said, "because it's as drippy and sappy and crappy as a piece of puppy shit. Unlike the rest of the tape, which is more like a pile of dog shit."

Shan gasped, but he noticed that the rest of his band didn't make a sound. Wise of them. "Uh, it's a little sentimental," she said, clearly shaken, "but don't you think it has commercial appeal?"

"No doubt," Quinn snorted. "Nothing like a little schmaltz to captivate the masses."

"It isn't schmaltz," Shan said. "This song was written right from the heart."

"I didn't realize the new album was the proper forum for airing out all the stained marital sheets. Since it is, why don't I throw in a few of my women-suck songs?"

"But I'm not airing anything," Shan said. "I'm just letting my emotions guide the music."

"Fine. We'll make sure the liner notes make it perfectly clear that *you* wrote this dreck. I'll see what kind of work I can do on the music. Some of it's salvageable, but the lyrics?" He shrugged. "I can't help you there. Shit is shit, no matter how much sugar you dump on top of it. You just wind up with sweetened shit."

"My songs are not shit!" Now she was the one with the flushed face, cheeks as red as a bad rash on a baby's ass.

"This tape is a thirty-two-minute-long dump," he decreed, "but if it's all we've got . . ."

"Maybe if *you* had a little more to contribute—"

"Sorry," he snapped. "I'm not as adept as you are at converting my personal tragedies into pop tunes."

Shan's face took on a frigid cast. She got up and went to the little refrigerator he kept down there for beer, removing a bottle of champagne. "I think we should have a toast," she said, "in honor of the new album."

"How festive," Quinn said as she filled flutes and passed them around. "Here's to the new album. Let's call it *Quinntessence: Excrement.*"

She ignored him, but the color on her cheeks was deepening as she raised her glass. "To Quinntessence," she began. Everyone dutifully picked up their glasses. "It's been a long haul, but here we are, together again. I'm excited to be gearing up for this new project . . ."

"Without the injection of semen," Quinn said, "a substance that apparently has been rejected in favor of vaginal secretions."

"Quinn, shut up and let her talk," Denise said, glaring at Quinn.

"*You* shut up, Denise," he shot back.

"You really should both shut up," Oda remarked.

Shan raised her voice, talking over all of them. ". . . and I'm especially proud of what we're accomplishing, blazing a new trail for women in music. Especially with this album, we'll be leading the way for other girl rockers to make music about the issues women face, both in the rock community and in society—"

"Oh please," Quinn said. "This band is not a platform for pussy."

Shan whirled on him. "Twat rock, remember?"

"Screw twat rock," Quinn sneered. "This music deserves a brand new name. How about tampon pop? A compilation of whiny, hormonal, premenstrual tunes performed by the most self-righteous, self-absorbed cunt of the century."

Shan's eyes narrowed as Quinn set down the untasted flute of champagne and headed for the door. She put down her own flute, then picked up the bottle.

Dan's eyes widened. "*Q, look out!*"

Quinn began to turn, caught a yellow flash out of the corner of his eye and ducked. The bottle smashed to pieces on the cement wall behind him, showering him with champagne and glass shards. He felt a sting as a large chip ricocheted off the wall, catching him just under his right eye.

He winced and touched the spot, then stared in disbelief at the stain of blood on his fingertips. "What in the fuck is wrong with you? Have you gone completely insane?"

Shan was coming straight at him and the old hatred was back in her eyes. "I'm self-absorbed? *I* am? What about you, you prick? *You took my fucking life away from me!*"

He opened his mouth to respond, but she punched him before he could utter a sound. Quinn's lips collided with his teeth and he cursed as he tasted more blood.

"Stop it!" he commanded, sidestepping to evade the fingers that streaked toward his face. Her nails raked his cheek as he hurriedly backed away. *Thank God guitar players can't have long nails!* "I'm sorry I called you a cunt! Stop hitting me!"

She kept right on coming and pounded his chest with her clenched fists. "Go ahead! Hit me back! It would hurt less than finding you fucking a pile of frequent flyers in a hotel room!" She aimed a slap at his face and he deflected it, throwing her off balance. She stumbled and, when he grabbed her arm to steady her, she knocked the wind out of him with a well-placed shot to the gut.

"Shan, knock it off! This is not fair! You know I would never hit you!" He succeeded in locking his arms around her and twisting her so she was facing away from him. "There! You'd better calm the fuck down, because—"

His words broke off in midsentence as she flung her head back, catching him squarely in the nose. He saw stars and was silent for a moment, clutching her with his chin jammed against her shoulder to prevent her from head-butting him again.

They were motionless and their combined heavy breathing was the only audible sound. Quinn snuck a glance at the rest of the room. Nobody was moving. Time seemed frozen.

He took a deep breath. "Are you finished acting like a turbobitch?"

She went slack in his arms and he caught her weight a little closer. His head snapped up and he regarded her with concern. Had she fainted? Then he saw that she'd pulled her feet right up off the ground, extending her legs straight out in front of her. He stared down at them for a moment, wondering what the hell she was trying to do.

Thwack! She brought back both her heels with every bit of force her hundred-and-fifteen-pound frame could muster. Quinn flung her away and sank to the floor, gripping his shins.

She swung over him, formidable as an Amazon warrior, and he flinched. "I give up! What do you want? I'll do it! Only stop hitting me!"

She wavered and, in that split second, went from giantess to Lilliputian, tiny and fragile and young as the sixteen-year-old child-woman he'd met in a SoHo loft four light-years before.

"You can't give me what I want," she whispered, beginning to tremble.

He got to his feet, wincing at the pressure on his injured shins, and regarded her with caution. Her face had gone a sick, cottage-cheesy color. "Are you all right?"

Her eyes brightened ominously.

"No! Shan, don't . . ." She collapsed and he caught her just before she hit the ground, completely overcome by the violence of her sobs.

"Stop it," he ordered, bracing her against his chest. "You never cry, remember?"

A sound came out of her that was something like a keen, a long, drawn-out wail of anguish.

"Maybe I was wrong," he heard Oda say. "It's possible she hasn't let herself feel all of the pain, after all."

Shan buried her face against Quinn's shoulder and howled like a she-wolf discovering the slain body of her only cub. It was the most heartbreaking sound he'd ever heard.

"Sounds like she's feeling it now," Dave said.

"I think the Q-man is the one feeling the pain," Ty said, "since she just kicked the living shit out of him."

Nosy fucks. "Shan, you've got to calm down," Quinn said. "You're going to make yourself sick." He looked around at their friends, all watching with interest, until he met Dan's eyes. "Leave, please."

Dan's paralysis evaporated and he jumped to his feet. "Yeah. Let's go, guys." Oda, Ty, and Dave made a beeline for the stairs, but Denise hung back.

"Not a chance," she chirped, her round, inquisitive eyes fixed on the drama before her as she reached for a handful of chips from a nearby bowl.

"Get the fuck out of here!" Quinn struggled to keep Shan in an upright position. No easy task, as she was blubbering uncontrollably and her body was as limp and amorphous as a glob of overcooked spaghetti. "Denise, I'm warning you . . ."

Denise scowled as Dan caught her arm and hauled her to her feet. "But—" He pushed her after the others. "We can't go *now!*" Dan gave her a firm shove, propelling her up the stairs. "For God's sake, Dan! Don't you want to see if they get back together?" she entreated.

"Christ, Denise, give them a little privacy. This isn't the Jerry Springer show!" Dan banged the door shut behind them.

Quinn sank to the floor and held Shan. She wailed and sobbed, and pretty soon he was drenched in her tears. He looked down at himself.

The front of his shirt was covered with blood.

"What—?" He pulled away and looked at her face, then heaved a resonant sigh and moved her off his lap. He propped her against the wall with her legs splayed out in front of her and her face buried in her hands, her shoulders quivering as the furious fit of weeping continued.

Quinn went into the tiny basement bathroom, returning with a fistful of wet paper towels. He knelt down, pushed her hands aside, and began to mop off her face. Shan opened her eyes and stared and stared at the blossom of red on his chest. "What . . . what's that?" she gasped.

"You gave yourself a bloody nose. Put your head back." She let it fall backward obediently, still sniveling. "I told you you'd make yourself sick, but you never listen." He pressed the paper towels over her nose. "Fucking women. None of you listen. You're as bad as Denise. She never listens, either, especially when she's in nosy, meddling bitch mode."

"She's our friend," Shan protested through the paper towels. "Don't call her that."

"She couldn't mind her own goddamned business if her life depended on it. Didn't you see the way Dan had to drag her out of here?" He removed the towels and squinted at her nose. "I think the bleeding stopped."

She lifted her head and touched her nose gingerly. "Maybe she does interfere and meddle, but only because she loves us."

"Loves *you*," Quinn said. "She hates *my* fucking guts."

"No, she doesn't," Shan said and sniffed. "She loves you, too. She told me so herself."

He snorted in disbelief, watching a tear slide down her cheek to the corner of her pink, trembling lower lip. "What, exactly, was the context of that conversation?"

"It was when I was at Mountainside. She was worried about you," Shan said, her voice quivering. "She said you needed me. That . . . that I make you into the person you're supposed to be. And that the person you are is a good one."

Quinn was too surprised to respond immediately. The tear was still clinging to the corner of Shan's mouth and he stared at it, experiencing a sudden, powerful urge to remove it with his lips. At the same time, there was a flicker of warmth in his chest. *Goddamned Denise,* he thought. *Nosy, loudmouthed, meddling, sweet Denise.*

Shan swiped a hand across her face. When she lowered it, the tear was gone. His gaze shot from her mouth to her eyes. "Do you suppose she might be right?" he said.

Shan stared back at him. "About what?"

"About us." He cupped her face between his hands. "Getting back together. It *could* happen. It could even happen"—his index finger moved over her lip gently—"right now."

She was unable to utter a sound.

"I think I'm still in love with you. I think I really am." His tone was wondering. "What do you think? Are we going to make it happen?"

For a moment, a wild hope flared in her eyes.

And, just as quickly, faded away. "No," she said, beginning to sob as she got to her feet.

"Why not?"

"Because I can't go back there, Q."

"We don't have to go back. We can go forward."

"We will. Just not together." He scowled and she held up her hands as if to ward off a blow. "It's too late. Nothing's changed."

"I still love you," he reminded her. "And, judging from the thermonuclear fit you just threw, I'd venture to say that you still love me, too. I think that changes things, don't you?"

"No, because we've always loved each other, whether we admitted it or not. But some people don't belong together no matter how much they love each other."

"All you need is love," he quoted, "according to the other great song-writing duo."

"They were wrong, though." She held up her hand again when he began to argue. "I can't talk to you anymore. Not about this. I need you to leave, okay?"

He got to his feet and reluctantly moved to the door. She followed, but stayed well out of his reach, as if she was afraid to let him touch her.

When he paused to look back at her, she was standing with her arms crossed over her chest and the most poignant longing on her face. He reached into his pocket, producing a CD. "New song?" she asked.

"Yes. I was going to play it today, but I decided not to, after I heard your stuff."

Her lip quivered anew. "The dog shit, you mean?"

"It's not. I'm sorry I said that. It's great stuff, Shan. It's hot and it's fresh and it rocks, and it's all yours." He smiled, a little sadly. "There's not a trace of me in it."

"That's not true. You'll always be part of my music, Q."

He hesitated for moment, then reached back into his pocket. He took out a Sharpie and flipped open the CD case, then scribbled something on the inside of the sleeve. He handed it to her and turned away. "Good-bye, Shan."

She closed the door on him, very gently.

She wiped her eyes and went back into the studio. She sat down in front of the console, opened the CD, and read the words he'd scribbled.

I wrote this for you, angel. I'll miss you forever. Love, Q

She took out the CD and inserted it into the player. She hit play, then drew her knees against her chest as a throbbing, haunting melody filled the room.

There was an angel who slipped in my heart
Rocked my life, changed my destiny

I never wanted a counterpart
But she didn't wait for an invite from me

Had Quinn actually written this? And yet, his dulcet tones were clearly recognizable, as familiar to her as the steady, measured rhythm of his composition.

She broke all my rules, took away my control
I fought against getting drawn in too deep
But when I had her, what I didn't know
Was that she was a treasure I couldn't keep

She squeezed her eyes shut and began to tremble.

Angel fallen from the sky
I'm reaching for you day and night
But the closer I get, the higher you fly
And I know that part of me will die
If I don't keep you in my sight
My Rock Angel

She broke and slid to the ground, pressing her face against the carpet. She cried and cried, and couldn't hear the closing chords of the song over her sobs.

chapter 49

Quinn gave up, switching off the Yamaha. He'd been tinkering with a new song ever since coming back from Mission Cove, but it wasn't jelling.

His stomach rumbled and he was mildly surprised to realize he was hungry. A couple of hours earlier, he'd felt like he'd never eat again. He lifted the phone and dialed room service. "Room three-twenty. A pepperoni . . ."

No way. He couldn't face a pepperoni and mushroom pizza. All it would do was make him think of the dozens that he and Shan had shared over the years. It was their standard song-writing fare, because they could never tear themselves away long enough to cook or even eat out when they were on a good run. She used to joke that people could tell they'd had a prolific spell by the number of take-out cartons stacked by the trash can.

"A burger. Medium. Thanks."

A little while later, a knock heralded the arrival of his dinner. He opened the door.

It wasn't the burger, though.

His soon to be ex-wife was standing on the threshold.

"I listened to your song," she said, "and I have some feedback."

It suddenly felt like he had a buzz saw lodged in his esophagus. He coughed. "What?"

"Do I have to deliver it from the hallway?"

"Oh, sorry." He pushed the door open. "Come on in."

She walked in, sat down on the couch, and looked around. "Nice suite."

"It's fine," he said impatiently. "What's your feedback?"

"That song is amazing, Q. It's the best thing you've ever written." Her face was inscrutable. "You can't lie in your music, can you?"

"No," he replied. "Of course not. Your music is your higher power, right?" She nodded, looking very serious. "How can that tell anything but the truth?"

"It can't," Shan admitted, then was quiet for a few moments. She seemed to be collecting her thoughts, formulating them into words, so he waited.

"In the song," she began, after a bit, "you're talking about how you need me, right? That's what I was hearing, I think."

"If that's what you heard, then that's what I meant. Like I said, the music doesn't lie."

"All this time," she continued, "I thought I was the one who needed you. A lot of the work I had to do in therapy was about that, how needy I am. It's what defines a junkie, you know. The need."

"Everyone has needs," he said. "It isn't a bad thing, necessarily."

"It is when you need something so much you can't live without it, especially when it's something toxic, like heroin."

"Or me?" he asked quietly.

She knit her fingers, twisting and clenching them together. "I thought so. It seemed so one sided, the way we were. I always felt like I'd die without you, but that you'd get along perfectly well without me."

"That was never true," he told her. "Never."

She nodded. "I'm beginning to understand that, because I heard it in your song. 'Rock Angel' is about how you've learned to need me and that's why you didn't like 'Puppy,' because that song is about me learning *not* to need you. I do need you, though, Q. I always have." She stopped wringing her hands, instead folding them in her lap.

When she did, Quinn noticed the green and gold ring circling her finger. It hadn't been there three hours earlier.

His knees seemed to give out and he sank down until he was kneeling at her feet. He reached out, touching the ring with one finger. "What does this mean?"

"It means I'm ready," she said softly. "Here I am, Q. I'm all yours. If you still want me."

Ten minutes later, Quinn collapsed with a groan.

Shan waited until her own breathing slowed to normal, then tried to move. It was difficult, as they were crammed on the floor between the couch and the coffee table, plus they were tangled in their clothes. She tried to move again, then winced.

Quinn opened his eyes. "What's wrong? I didn't hurt you, did I?"

"No," she said, "but my ass . . . *ow!*"

He twisted around to examine it. "Looks like a rug burn," he reported. "Sorry, babe." She sighed happily as he nuzzled her throat.

Then his mouth began to travel south. "I love you," he whispered and dropped a kiss against her breast. "I love you," he repeated, kissing the curve of her stomach. His long hair trailed over her skin like a caress as his head moved down her body. "I love you," he said again, this time kissing the inside of her thigh.

He kissed her all the way down to her toes, stopping every few inches to assure her that he loved her, then pressed his lips against the sole of her left foot.

"I love you," he said, and moved to the right foot.

She giggled as he began to work his way back up her body, still dappling her with kisses. "I know—you love me!" she exclaimed when he opened his mouth to speak again. "You've said that more times in the last four minutes than you did in four years."

"I know. I have a lot to make up for." He rested his head against her thigh to gaze up at her and she noticed, for the first time, an ineffable sadness in his eyes.

Her smile faded. "What's wrong?"

He turned his head to stipple kisses over her scars, then spread his hand over her leg, covering most of them. "You've been hurt so much, angel."

"It's okay. It was a long time ago," she added, because it would never be okay, really, what her father had done to her.

"Still. You've had to deal with more pain than anyone should ever have, inflicted by someone who was supposed to take care of you. Someone who was supposed to love you."

"It's *okay*," she said, more insistently, because she could see, suddenly, where he was going with this.

"All I wanted was to make you happy, but I hurt you, too," he continued, and the look in his eyes made her own chest hurt, "even though I was supposed to be the one loving you and taking care of you."

She touched his hair. "You made a mistake, Q. You're not perfect. Nobody is."

"But I broke your heart, sent you into a relapse. I still can't believe I did it. It wasn't just once, either," he said, the look on his face turning to disgust. "There were many, after we split up."

She winced. "That's over with, too. Let's just move forward, like you said before."

"Can we?" He pulled away and now he looked scared. "Will you ever trust me again?"

"I never did before, really. I always felt sure I'd lose you someday, that you couldn't possibly love me the way I love you."

"That was my fault, too, because I hardly ever told you," he insisted. "And after what I did . . . how *could* you trust me?"

She thought about it, then shrugged. "Okay. It was both our faults, but I'm ready to trust you now. It's not as scary as it used to be, because I know I won't break if you let me down. I can take care of myself." She felt a glow knowing, for the first time in her life, that those words were really true. "For real, now. I still need you, Q, but because I love you, not because I can't survive without you."

"You'll never have to, because I won't let you down, not ever again. I promise you that, angel."

"You're human, so you're going to make mistakes, just like I will, but we'll forgive each other and learn from them. No more frequent flyers, though," she added. "That's a deal breaker, Q."

"Of course not. Never again. I'll never hurt you and I'll take care of you, keep you safe, and Angie, too. I'll be everything you need me to be. I'll be perfect," he added, clearly missing the point.

She took a deep breath. He didn't get it. "I don't need you to be anything except what you are. It's not your job to take care of me or save me, either. I'm not a homeless little girl anymore or an orphaned puppy, some fragile thing that would wither away and die if it wasn't for you. And you don't have be perfect for me, Q. All you have to do is love me."

He regarded her soberly for long moment, then shook his head. "I do love you, but that isn't enough. I know what a dick I can be, how opinionated and arrogant and controlling." His eyes were taking on a glow, too, but it was a weird, fanatical one. "You're always telling me, you and everybody else, and I can change. I'll stop being such a dick. I promise I will." He crept closer to lay his head in her lap.

Uh-huh. Her eyes narrowed. "All right," she said. "I'll hold you to that, especially when we're writing. Speaking of which, there's some work we need to do now."

"Okay," he mumbled, burrowing farther. "Did you bring your new songs?"

"*My* songs are perfect," she said. "I'm talking about yours." As she watched, his shoulders stiffened. "'Rock Angel' is the song that needs work, Q."

"I thought you said it was amazing." There was an edge in his voice. "The best thing I've ever written."

"It could be. It has great potential, but the start of the second verse is a little dull," she said, watching his hands curl into fists. "A guitar fill would liven it up. I never heard a hook, either," she added. "I can fix that for you."

When he spoke, his voice was steady. Steady and measured, just like the song. "*You* don't need to fix *anything*. It's *my* song."

"Okay, but you should at least let Ty play with it," she said, zeroing in for the kill while she watched his jaw tighten, "because the bass line *sucks!*"

He lifted his head off her lap. His face was very red, she noted with satisfaction.

"I don't agree. I think the song is fine as it stands." His voice was deadly quiet. "For the record, though, I *do* agree that it's the best thing I've ever written."

"It's honest and it's pretty," Shan said, "but it could use some balls."

His eyebrows snapped together. "Then the last thing I need is a twat rocker telling me what to do with it!"

She felt a fit of giggling bubble up inside her. She slapped her hands over her mouth, but she couldn't hold it in and burst into peal after peal of laughter. He stared at her incredulously for a moment, then let forth a heavy sigh.

"Okay. You got me," he admitted. "It might be harder to change than I thought." She nodded, wiping the tears from the giggling fit from her eyes.

"You know I'm not an easy person to get along with," he warned. She nodded again, snickering now.

"It's not funny," he snapped. "I'm difficult."

She grinned. "Yup."

He frowned. "Demanding."

Her grin widened. "*Yup.*"

"I'm a dickhead, sometimes. I know that, but I don't know if I can help it." She covered her face as she began to giggle again and his frown morphed into a scowl. "Stop laughing, for Chrissake! I'm trying to be honest with you. Are you sure *this* is really what you want?"

"*Yup!*" She pulled her hands away from her face. "A difficult, demanding, arrogant dickhead. That's what I want. Because," she added as she felt the love welling up inside her, so much that it felt too big for her chest, "*that's my Q!*"

She flung her arms around him. He hugged her back, very tightly, and held her for a long time. Eventually she drew back to find him regarding her with a frown. "What now?"

"So what's wrong with the song?" he asked.

"Nothing," she said. "It's beautiful. The most beautiful song I've ever heard."

"But you said it needed work."

"*I didn't mean it!* I was just messing with you. It worked, too," she added, with an impish grin.

He continued to eye her dubiously. "I can't believe you don't have any critique at all. You always have *something* to say."

"Well . . ." she began, then hesitated. There was something, actually.

"Well what?" he pressed. "Come on, I can take it."

"I listened to it over and over. Then I started singing with it." Again she hesitated.

"And?"

"Well, what would you think about adding a vocal interlude between the verses? I'm thinking a female harmony," she explained. "Something that sounds like angels singing."

He looked thoughtful. She waited, but he didn't comment, and she sighed. "You think it would be schmaltzy, don't you?"

"No, angel," he replied. "I think it would be perfect." She ran her hand over the golden hair on the backs of his forearms, feeling the goose bumps rise beneath her fingertips.

Questions and Topics for Discussion

1. Addiction is a major theme in *Rock Angel,* the most obvious example being Shan's heroin dependency. What other addictions does she struggle with? What about Quinn and the other characters—what types of addictions do they exhibit? Can any of these dependencies be viewed in a positive light?

2. When Quinn finds out Shan's age, he is shocked. Were you? Why, or why not?

3. Twice in the book, Shan sings lines from David Bowie's "Putting Out Fire with Gasoline": *Feel my blood enraged / It's just the fear of losing you.* Could this be seen as her theme song? Why?

4. Shan missing her mother is a recurrent thread throughout the book. Quinn's issues with his mother come up over and over again, as well. What are the differences between the two mothers? Are they alike in any way? What kind of mother do you think Shan will make?

5. After Quinntessence hits big, Shan's gender receives enormous attention from the rock media. During an interview she states, "I'm sick of people acting like testicles are a requirement for playing a hot guitar lick. . . . It's about talent, not balls." What other performers have faced this challenge and how have they responded? How many female rock guitar players can you name?

6. What do you think of the term *twat rock*? Is it an accurate representation of the way women are viewed in the rock community?

7. When Shan goes into the abortion clinic, she sees grief in Quinn's eyes. What is he grieving? How does this influence Shan's decision not to terminate the pregnancy? Is this a good choice or a bad one?

8. When baby Angelica is born addicted to methadone, Shan holds herself responsible. She is treated badly by some of the nurses and social workers involved in their case. Does she deserve this? Should drug-addicted mothers be considered criminals?

9. Oda refers to arguing as the language of Shan and Quinn's relationship. Is this a good or bad thing? Why? What other unusual forms of communication do Shan and Quinn employ?

10. In her efforts to kick heroin, Shan attends twelve-step programs but struggles with the "higher power" tenet. Eventually she comes to accept music as her higher power. In what way is this true?

11. In the end, it is the music that brings Shan and Quinn together, just as it drew them together in the beginning. Did the music ever drive them apart? How?

12. Throughout the book, it is the music that heals Shan. Does it heal anyone else? What are some examples? Do you believe music to be a healing force? Why, or why not?

ADVANCE EXCERPT FROM

angel on high

BOOK TWO IN THE ROCK ANGEL SERIES

Join Shan, Quinn, and the rest of the band in Angel on High *as their star continues to rise. From the Grammy Awards to sold-out shows all over the world, Quinntessence's collective dreams are coming true. Soon enough, though, some of those dreams turn to nightmares. Caught in a spiraling vortex of excess amidst relentless media scrutiny, threats of blackmail, betrayal and the crush of rabid fans, Shan discovers that it's a long, long fall from the top of the world.*

Shan woke up with a profound sense of well-being, a knowledge that all was right in her world, and an absolute certainty that she was going to come.

The orgasm jolted her more fully awake. "Wow!" she gasped when it was over. "What did I do to deserve *that?*" She peered under the covers at the blond head between her legs.

Quinn rested his head against the inside of her thigh and grinned up at her. "Happy Valentine's Day, angel."

Valentine's Day? "When did you decide that was something worth celebrating?"

"It's a bullshit holiday," he admitted, squirming out from under the covers and pulling her into his arms. "Just something for the card and candy companies to capitalize on, but it's still an opportunity to show you how much I love you."

"You tell me all the time," she pointed out, snuggling against him.

And he did. Over and over, a dozen times a day. He said it so many time that it annoyed their band mates. "Please shut him up," Ty had begged her during the previous day's practice. "I feel like I'm drowning in mush."

She'd laughed and agreed, but knew she'd never get tired of hearing Quinn say those words. She had waited far too long to hear them.

Right now her mushy man was reaching over her, tugging open the drawer to his nightstand to remove a long velvet box which he handed to her.

"A present, too? Wow," she said again. "Who are you and what have you done with my husband?" When she opened it, she gasped. Within lay a delicate white gold chain encrusted with diamonds and three cascading strands of gemstones in various shades of blue.

"I thought it was about time you owned a piece of serious jewelry."

"I have one." She waved her left hand.

"That doesn't count. It's not jewelry, it's a fixture," he said, knowing that her engagement ring never left her finger. Not since they'd gotten back together, at any rate. "I had this custom made. There's room to expand it, too."

"Expand?" She held the necklace up. The stones sparkled in the sunlight. It was so beautiful, so elegant. It seemed too grown up for her.

"I thought you'd figure it out right away. Look," he pointed to the strands. "Sapphires, aquamarines, tanzanites. September, March . . ."

"December," she finished. "You, me, Angie. Our family!"

"And don't forget this," he said, indicating the small black stone that fashioned the clasp. "Onyx."

Suddenly she had a lump in her throat. "For Sugaree?" At the foot of the bed, Sugaree raised her head when she heard her name, tail thumping against the mattress.

"Yup. No family portrait is complete without her, right?" Shan swallowed hard as Quinn fastened the necklace around her neck. "If you cry, I'm going to take it back."

"I'm allowed to get choked up over an incredibly meaningful, romantic gift." She pushed the stray lock out of his eyes and smiled. "I love it and I love you, Q. I feel bad that I don't have anything for you, though."

"I can think of something you can give me." He grinned wickedly. Releasing her, he rolled over onto his back, flinging the covers aside. "Quick, before Angie wakes up."

"That old thing again?" Shan chuckled, but she was already nestling against him, nuzzling, beginning to work her way down the body she knew so well. She loved every inch of it, from the cowlick that caused a lock of his hair to keep slipping down over one eye to the tiny star-shaped freckle on his lower abdomen. She paused to kiss that spot before turning her attention to a more insistent body part, one that was not at all mushy.

She was still smiling a few hours later. She and Denise were at a fancy Rodeo Drive boutique, where Shan was being fitted for her first couture gown. It was a Valentino, a magnificent creation with vibrant colors in a retro floral pattern, which had been selected by Rachel, her stylist. "You'll like it," Rachel had assured her. "It's just your taste, Boho Chic, but very high end. It will articulate your artistic free spirit."

Shan didn't know about her free spirit, but she adored the dress. It was light and gauzy, its airy silhouette floating about her slim frame in a swirl of greens and yellows and blues. Its strapless bodice accentuated her small breasts, giving the illusion of some cleavage. "What do you think?" she asked Denise.

"Gorgeous." Denise looked gorgeous herself, in a sleek silver sheath that hugged her body like a glove. "You look an Indian princess, Shan."

She'd settle for looking like a rock star, a role that still felt strange even though she'd be attending the Grammy Awards in March. Quinntessence was nominated for three awards: Best New Artist, Best Rock Performance with Vocal, and Best Album, for *Quinntessence: Odyssey*.

"I feel like a princess, sort of," she admitted to Denise as they carefully removed their gowns, "but a fake one. It's all so Technicolor, like a Disney movie or something."

"Well, you deserve it and I'm glad for you," Denise said. "You've never looked happier."

"I am," Shan confessed. "I can't believe how great everything is going. I mean, Quinntessence is nominated for three Grammys! And at home . . ." she paused then shook her head, a little dazed. "It's like a dream. Life just couldn't be more perfect."

They confirmed their next appointment, then headed for the car. "I'm glad," Denise said, picking up their conversation right where they left off. "Enjoy it, because you know it won't last."

"Thanks," Shan said, shooting her an annoyed look. "I needed that, because I'm certainly not capable of killing my own buzz."

"It's just the truth." Denise shrugged. "These things cycle. I want to make one more stop before we go to lunch, okay?" she added, instructing Shan to drive to West Hollywood.

Shan complied, following Denise's direction to Santa Monica Boulevard. After they parked and got out of the Jeep, Shan looked up at the enormous red disco heart on the front of their destination. "The Pleasure Chest," Shan noted. "Really, Denise?"

"Really," Denise said, heading for the front door. "I'm giving my husband a Valentine's Day present he'll never forget."

Shan sighed, but followed Denise into the shop. It was the biggest sex toy emporium in LA, which was saying a lot since one could be found every few blocks. The vast space was crammed with cases displaying vibrators, massage oils, condoms, and other items Shan was less familiar with, like nipple clamps, handcuffs, and butt plugs. There were rows of videos and racks of racy lingerie, all dominated by an elaborate flower burst logo over the checkout desk. Shan glanced up at the logo, admiring its intricate design until she realized that what she was looking at was a stylized orgy.

She hurried after Denise, who was riffling through a collection of bustiers. "What do you think of this one?" Denise asked, pulling one off the rack. It was black leather, outfitted with studded boning and crosshatched with silver laces. The cups looked far too small for Denise's ample bosom and Shan surmised that they were shelf-style, the kind that presented the breasts like melons on a serving platter.

"Kind of slutty," she replied. "Is that really how you want to look to your husband on Valentine's Day?"

"Yes," Denise said firmly. "Dan is surrounded by sluts every time you go on tour. I want to keep that horn dog part of him satisfied, so he doesn't stray. Every man feels the urge to stray," she added, holding up a pair of crotchless leather panties.

This provided Shan with a mental picture she neither needed nor wanted. She murmured a vague sound of assent, then drifted away as Denise began rooting through an adjoining rack containing similar accoutrements for men.

Ick. Too much information, but perhaps she had a point. Shan sometimes worried that she was too vanilla for Quinn, even though he'd slept with enough kinky groupies to last most men ten lifetimes. During the six months they'd been separated the previous year, he'd immediately reverted back to that life. She experienced a familiar knifelike pain in her chest when she recalled how it felt to catch him in the act, with two groupies in his bed.

Why not spice things up a bit? She paused before a display of vibrators in various shapes, sizes, and colors. Orange eggs. Blue bullets. Purple triangles. Some looked big enough to fill a tuba bell. Others were more flute-sized, petite and almost dainty.

She selected a midsized one that was smooth and pink, very non-threatening. She turned the box over. It read "Ruff Rider Dog Dick."

She hastily put the box down, then picked up a neon pink device that looked like a more traditional vibrator. She pressed the button that brought it to life. It buzzed like a hive of angry bees. She tried to turn it off, but instead it switched to another, louder setting. Shan continued to click, assuming it would cycle through and turn off eventually, but the silicone phallus continued to buzz louder and louder.

"You have to hold the button down," somebody said and when Shan turned she discovered one of the sales clerks, a tall young man with a blonde buzz cut, several piercings, and a veritable mural of tattoos covering every exposed inch of skin on his body.

"What?"

"The button," he continued. "Hold it down to shut it off."

Shan complied. The vibrator stilled and she hurriedly set it back on the shelf.

"They all have their little quirks," the clerk continued, "but you'll get used to it. I sure did." He grinned. "Can I help you select something?"

"Oh . . . no. No, thanks," she added hastily, turning bright red and heading for the door. En route, a display of videocassettes caught her eye.

Porn. That seemed like something relatively okay, the kind of thing a free-thinking wife would surprise her husband with on Valentine's Day. Perhaps she could work her way up to more exotic toys, although she couldn't imagine herself ever getting excited over a dog dick.

She went over to the display rack and perused some of the titles. *Barely Legal.* She made a face. *Axis of Anal.* Ewww. *Fisting Freaks.* Good grief.

She made her way farther down the racks, which seemed to get less weird towards the front of the store. There was a special case trumpeting "New Arrivals" and she paused at one that bore the title *Quinntessential Quickie.*

Perfect! She was taking one of the videos off the rack as Denise joined her. "Did you find something?" Denise inquired.

Shan nodded. "I think so. This is . . ." She looked down at the videotape.

And froze.

The cover depicted a man up on his knees, head thrown back and fair hair cascading past his shoulders, while two buxom blondes attended to his erect penis. The picture was grainy and the member itself was obscured behind a black rectangle, but Shan knew what it looked like.

Particularly because she'd seen it up close, when she'd ministered to it so tenderly just that morning. "What the *fuck?*"

Denise looked at the photo, then gasped. "Oh no! It can't be him, Shan. It must be a lookalike."

It wasn't, though. The man on the video box was Quinn. Shan knew it.

She'd recognize that star-shaped freckle anywhere.

Acknowledgments

I suspect that this part of the book is a source of stress for most authors, the I-couldn't-have-done-it-without-you part. There's so much influence, so many voices that go into the making of a novel that it might be downright impossible to list them all. *Rock Angel* is a story about musicians and their music, written by a librarian whose only hands-on musical experience came from guitar lessons during which the instructor kindly suggested I acquire a metronome. I also sang in the South Junior High School chorus, where the voices of fifty other members drowned out my off-key efforts. But from it I gained a lifelong love and appreciation of music, largely thanks to David Huxtable, the hippest music teacher ever, who later gets a nod in this book. I couldn't be a musician because I don't have the talent, so I used the written word to make my music. Here it is.

First and foremost, I need to thank the real music makers who helped bring this book to life. Linda Worster, who crafted most of the songs that Shan and Quinn wrote together ("The Wedding Song," "Echo Flats," and "Wanderlust"). "Rev Tor" Krautter, who allowed me to borrow liberally from his original lyrics ("Fallen Angel," "Voluntary Exile," and "The Black Mile" began as Rev Tor songs). John Zarvis, guitar god and troubadour of "On the Roof," Matt Mervis, who graciously permitted me to lift his lyrics for "The Only Perfect One," and Elizabeth Thorne, lyricist of "Puppy." Thanks to all of you for helping me put the music into Quinntessence. And thanks to Joan Jett and Blackheart records. Thanks, too, to Valentine Miller, daughter of Henry, for use of his quote.

Thanks to all the people who helped me understand the technical stuff behind a rock band, how to run cord for a microphone, what a drummer sits on, how to pick a name for your guitar, and more: the aforementioned Linda, Tor, and John, Paul de Jong, Tistrya Houghtling, Allen Livermore, Dan Broad, Mike Basiliere, Jeff Martell, Rick Leab, Dave Lincoln, Aubrey Atwater, Bruce Clapper (who also earned a nod), Gina Coleman, Kali Baba McConnell, Jason Webster, Bernice Lewis, Bill Patriquin, Mike Dermody, David Grover, Robin O'Herin, and Jeff King. Thanks to you all. I really couldn't have done it without you.

Then there's Frank Kennedy, who deserves a paragraph all his own. Thanks for the technical advice, the music education, the long-suffering tolerance when I couldn't talk or think about anything but this story but, mostly, the love. This is his book almost as much as it is mine, which is why it's dedicated to him, my only perfect one.

Thanks and much love to my mother, Micki Bogino, for all the love, support, and encouragement. Thanks, too, for reading *Rock Angel* in all its stages, Mom, even though I know you skimmed the dirty parts. Thanks to my dad, Buster Kohlenberger, who loved me and believed in me, too. I wish he were here to see this book published. Thanks to Marion Boure, my gram, for her love, faith, and firm belief in my general awesomeness whether I deserved it or not. Thanks to Geordi and Juniper (aka Sugaree), the heartbeats at my feet, for the puppy love, wags, and long walks where most of the writing actually took place.

Thanks to Deb Francome, überfriend, ally, and chief cheerleader. She's been further into Shan and Quinn's world than anyone except for me. Also, she's the best person I know.

Thanks to the readers. Julie Angello, my first and foremost reader, the one who in so many ways made this book happen. Thanks to Margaret Holes, forever friend and first editor. Thanks to my aunts Betsy Emery and Berta Schreiber and my friends Ami Levine, Sue Hunter, Wendy Krom, and Marlene Ullmann for reading the manuscript in its earliest, thousand-page stage (that's dedication!). Thanks to Elizabeth Holleran Hess, Julia Pomeroy, Jeannine Tonetti, John Zarvis (again), Betsy Hess, Dr. Robert Taylor, Betsy and Max Gitter, Jane Feldman (who also shot my author photo), Danny and Clellie Lynch, and Dr. Robert Benner for much appreciated technical advice on everything from social workers to contracts to drug-addicted infants. Thanks to Bill Reichert, best English teacher ever, and Sonia Pilcer, my mentor, who both shaped me into the writer I am. Thanks to Tresca Weinstein, Amy Herring, Sandy Herkowitz, Chris Adams, Richard Matturro, and Alex Olchowski—every writer needs a group.

Special thanks to Marlene Adelstein, editor extraordinaire and my copilot on this literary journey, and Wendy Lipp, publisher, friend, and an angel in her own right. Thanks to Crystal Patriarche, Christine Marra, and super special thanks to Gina Coleman, my own personal angel, who has an uncanny knack for appearing at all the truly pivotal points of my life. I love you, sister.

And thanks to my "family" friends, the ones who keep me sane through hours and hours and days of the whole messy process of living and writing: Elizabeth Clough, Susan Brown, Michael Prescott, and Margaret Holes (again). Your music is in these pages, too.

About the Author

 By day, Jeanne Bogino is director of a small but busy library in rural New York. By night, she writes at her western Massachusetts homestead. She's published short horror, fantasy, romance, memoir, and gay fiction, and is a regular contributor at *Library Journal,* where she was named 2011's fiction reviewer of the year. An expert on zombie lit and horror films, Jeanne has published articles and appeared on panels devoted to these subjects. *Rock Angel* is her debut novel with Prashanti Press.

Prashanti Press LLC is an independent publishing house dedicated to producing and distributing various types of thoughtfully developed media. We are inspired by creativity, and seek to produce works that reflect our authors' and artists' experiences, interests, and personal truths. To learn more, please visit us at prashantipress.com.

SparkPress is an independent boutique publisher delivering high-quality, entertaining, and engaging content that enhances readers' lives, with a special focus on female-driven work. We are proud of our catalog of both fiction and non-fiction titles, featuring authors who represent a wide array of genres, as well as our established, industry-wide reputation for innovative, creative, results-driven success in working with authors. Spark Press, a BookSparks imprint, is a division of SparkPoint Studio, LLC. To learn more, visit us at www.sparkpointstudio.com.